I0760325

The Red Citadel & The Sorcerer's Power

Craig Halloran

The Red Citadel and the Sorcerer's Power

By Craig Halloran

Print Edition

TWO-TEN BOOK PRESS
P.O. Box 4215, Charleston, WV 25364

ISBN eBook: 978-1-946218-49-0
ISBN Paperback: 978-1-720503-81-1
ISBN Hardback: 978-1-946218-50-6

www.craighalloran.com

Publisher's Note

This book is a work of fiction. Names, characters, places, and incidents either are the product of the author's imagination or are used fictitiously, and any resemblance to actual persons, living or dead, events, or locales is entirely coincidental.

Table of Contents

Free River
Riftwood River
The High Peaks
Umpton
The Jade Citadel
Toozan
The Surge
The Seven Kingdoms
Herclon
Archmenis
The Violet Citadel
The Barrier
The Fringe
The Blackwood Sage
The Gallatan Sea
The Free River
Varland
The Black Tower
Marsh Lakes
Zarnai
Rayland
Zorgaz Mountains
The Green Basin
Mendes
The Red Citadel
N

The Sorcerer's Curse

Part 1

Chapter 1

Tarley's Tavern sat high on the hill, up and away from the small town of Marcen. The rickety building had stood, braced against the highland winds, for hundreds of years. Over the course of history, some of the realm's greatest heroes had passed through Tarley's. Some guzzled ale, many told tall tales, and others sat quietly, wanting nothing more than to be left alone. More recently, the life within the tavern was of a more common sort. Rough-skinned farmers, ornery tradesmen, merchants, and restless men and women went there seeking a little excitement to alleviate the quiet of the farm town.

The builders of the durable and weathered establishment were long gone, and new faces had taken their place over the years. Now, within the walls, the tavern's current owner, Tuberlous, threw another log on the fire. The embers crackled, and a warm glow permeated the room. Nobody noticed. Instead, the dwellers drank, gambled, and cursed. The barmaids posed on the laps of lavishly clad merchants. Pipe smoke and the smell of cherry tobacco made for a dreamy atmosphere. Within the haze, the discreet sulked in the corners while others went on without an ounce of shame about their business. Every once in a while, joking, jesting, and wild, victorious cheers rang out.

In the rear of the tavern, a lone spiral staircase led up to a balcony that overlooked the tavern floor. Stiff winds made the wooden rafters in the vaulted ceiling groan. The candlelit iron chandeliers quavered time and again. On that balcony, a man sat behind a small desk, pouring wine out of a clay carafe. He wore garish robes, with a large collar, that were long overdue for cleaning. The unique garb was laced with intricate patterns and lavish colors. His head was bald, face slender, gray-black eyebrows peaked. Every move he made was purposeful and fluid. His name was Finster. Long ago, he had been a magus of the highest order. Now, he drank. He drank a lot.

A farmer entered the tavern with his cloth hat clutched in his hand. A cold breeze followed him, causing some unpleasant mutterings from the dwellers. With effort, he pushed the door shut, turned, and looked up. He caught Finster's penetrating stare. Rolling his long fingers, Finster beckoned the man upward. Head down, the farmer shuffled through the crowd and slowly climbed up the stairs.

"Oh, hurry up, will you?" Finster said in the voice of an impatient schoolmaster. "I haven't got all night, commoner." He looked over the rail. "No, wait a moment."

The farmer stopped.

"Tuberlous!" Finster shouted down at the barkeeper. "Are you blind? I have a customer!"

Tuberlous slid out from behind the bar with his belly bouncing underneath his greasy smock. He faced the farmer with his hand out. "That'll be a copper, Varney."

The farmer handed the barkeep the coin and headed upstairs.

"My rent is paid today!" Finster shouted to the barkeep. "Let that take the grief from your puffy lips." The farmer walked along the balcony, glancing over the rail once before taking a seat on the wooden stool in front of Finster's desk. Finster leaned forward. "Varney, is it?"

The man nodded. His eyes attached to the bookshelf filled with many leather tomes, potions, vials, and other trinkets. His grubby hands wiped the sweat on his lip. "Hello."

"Aren't you the chatty one? Hmmm, let me try to figure out what it is you need." Closing his bright eyes, Finster touched the side of his oblong head. "Let's see. You need a special seed for your crops—ah, no, that's not it. Oh, wait, I see it now—you need a special seed for your wife." He opened his eyes. "Yes, your wife's crops need fertilization. You have no sons to help you with labor. Lucky for you, I have just the thing for that." He reached for his shelf.

"No, that's not it. I have sons. Many." The farmer's eyes slid to the people below them.

Finster slapped the table. "No one is listening to you! Out with it, then. What do you need? Your secrets are safe with me. What we speak of is fully anonymous." He hiccupped. "Excuse me. I have a strange illness." He took a swig of wine. "Ah, I'm cured. Now, where were we?"

"I need something to help me and, er, the wife, say, find the passion again?"

"So I was on course." Finster leaned forward with his elbow on the table. "Tell me, Varney, about this wife of yours. Is she ample?" He winked at the farmer. "You know, bosomy?"

"I don't see how that is helpful."

"It makes all the difference, farmer. Don't you come up here and insult me about how to go about my business. Is she ample or not? Come now. I need details."

"She's rather full chested."

Leaning back in his chair and toying with the hairs on his chin, Finster said, "Interesting. Very interesting, Varney, seeing how I know that your wife is as flat chested as a twelve-year-old boy. So you desire to fool around, eh? Well, it's not my business."

"You said you'd be discreet."

"And I will be. If anyone inquires, just say you wanted my advice about the harvest. That's what everyone says." He reached into his shelves and grabbed a glass vial. "Ground mandrake, but remember, 'Lust is blind but not your neighbors.'"

"What?"

"Nothing." He slid the small bottle over the table. "This is what you want. It'll be three silvers."

Varney's dirty fingers picked at the inside of a small pouch. He slid over three coins.

With his finger, Finster touched two of the three coins. They rose from the table. He stacked one coin on top of the other. "See? A little trick, for free, in case you doubted my powers as a wizard."

Varney tucked the vial in his sheepskin vest. "You'll be discreet, right?"

"And dare draw the wrath of a farmer like you? Of course I will."

Giving Finster a funny look, Varney got up and started to walk away.

"Do you see that strapping young fellow down there at the bar? Brawny, with sandy locks."

"Yes, why?"

"That's Plowboy Roy, just so you know. So don't be ashamed about your secret nuptials."

Varney shook his head. "What are you talking about?"

"Young Roy has been plowing your wife's fields for quite some time."

"You lie!"

"No, she's paid a visit to me as well. Perhaps it's time that the two of you have a long, open, honest, and pathetic conversation."

Clutching his cap and with anguish building in his voice, Varney said, "Why did you have to tell me that? I thought you were discreet."

"Oh, yes. I forgot to mention—that costs extra." He flicked a silver down toward the bar. It landed inside a glass with a clink. "Tuberlous! More wine! Lots of it."

Without warning, the front door of the tavern burst open. Many soldiers, well armed and dressed head to toe in leather armor, filed through the startled crowd. The hard eyes of the men scoured the room. One of them pointed up at Finster. He was a tall man in a dark leather tunic who stood out among the rest. Something sinister lurked in his dark eyes. He called up to Finster in a gravelly, authoritative voice, "You, sir, are a wanted man."

Chapter 2

Hands on the rail, serene in expression, Finster replied, "I beg your pardon, Commander, but I believe you are mistaken. I'm not guilty of any crime that I am aware of. I'm a lone sage, a mere novice of elixirs working toward the betterment of the community and myself. Eh, perhaps you are searching for those grave robbers that have been trolling about. We've seen strange folk heading west, two days gone by now."

"Is that so?" The commander nodded to a pair of soldiers, who moved to the bottom of the spiral stairwell. He took off his chainmail gauntlets, dropped them on the table, and unrolled a scroll. He tilted his head, eyes squinting. "I have a drawing that fits your description. I'm certain it is you."

"I have very keen eyes," Finster said, craning his neck. "May I see it?" The commander showed the picture. Finster's brow lifted. It was an exact image of himself, take away a decade or two. "I don't see the resemblance in the slightest. You've mistaken my identity."

"Is that so?" The commander showed the image to the barkeep. "What do you think, man?"

Tuberlous's crinkled brow burst into beads of sweat. His eyes flitted to Finster for a moment then back at the picture. He swallowed. "I can't say for certain."

"See, you're mistaken—common soldier—eh, what do you call yourself?"

"Crawley. Commander Crawley of Mendes, the ruling kingdom. Pursuer of villains, liars, murderers, and the like."

"It's so hard to tell one from another these days. As a matter of fact, many I've come across have borne a remarkable resemblance to you. Scruffy, rough-handed men that tend to spit a little too much when they talk." He rubbed his throat. "No offense. Tuberlous! I'm getting dry again. Tell you what, Crawley. Will you let me buy you a drink?"

Tuberlous poured a mug of ale from a keg tap. Crawley glared at him. The barkeep set the mug down, wiped his hands on the rag and said, "I think I smell something burning in the back." He vanished through a small door behind the bar.

"See what you've done, Crawfish, you've frightened the only bartender for leagues." Finster slammed his hands on the rails. "Outrageous. Don't you know how hard it is to train a man to pull a cork out of a bottle and not ruin the bouquet? But, I'll forgive, and believe me when I say, I am not who you think I am. You're mistaken."

"Lying is a crime," Crawley said. "Resisting arrest is an offence. Bribery, well, that makes me really nasty."

"A man of passion. Good for you. Crawfish, can you tell me the name of the man you are looking for? Perhaps I can offer some assistance." He tapped his chest and belched. "Pardon me. I see many new faces. I've a bit of a reputation. The other day, for example—"

"Shut up, you old doddering crone!"

One of the tavern dwellers tried to slip out. A soldier stuffed him back in his seat. Crawley unrolled another scroll with his meaty fingers. "You want a name? How does this sound? The Whistling Cauldron, Pine Bender, Master of the Inanimate, the Silver Snake,

Guardian of the Mystic Forge, Iron Keeper, the Secret Slayer, Rodent of Whispers…"

He lists many I've forgotten about. Those were the days. Young, powerful, deadly, and delightful. So amazing.

"… the Metal Scourge, and finally, Finster the Magus of the Ninth Order." Crawley rolled up the scroll. "Do you still deny that is you?"

"Those are just legends. Old stories and tall tales that women tell their whiny children to get them to sleep after a meal." He drummed his fingers on the railing. "Besides, I can't imagine a man such as yourself trifling with the man whose legend you just described. It extends beyond the borders of reason." Finster's brows knitted ever so slightly. "That would be suicide."

The soldiers eyed their commander. Sharp steel scraped out of sheaths. Men cranked the lines back on their light crossbows and took aim at Finster.

Without a blink, Crawley said, "Don't underestimate a man you know little to nothing about, old magus. It could be fatal."

Finster saw the iron resolve in the commander's eyes. Crawley wasn't a foolish youth, but a veteran, with marks to show for it—a true fighter skilled at slaying, judging by the heavy steel on his hips and rank on his arms.

Toying with his lips, the magus said, "I haven't been to Mendes in decades. Do you care to tell me what I'm allegedly charged with?"

"As of now, just treason."

"Treason? I stand accused in the low kingdom. Seems really thin. Treason can be fatal."

"There will be a trial."

"I'm well aware of how those trials go. They are death sentences ofttimes. I don't have any intention of turning myself in. I'd be better off committing suicide."

"I don't want you to do that. You're wanted alive. Come on down, Finster. Make it easy. You never know what will happen. After all, you might be innocent, heh-heh." Crawley stepped right beneath him. "I've been doing this a long time. Never failed to get the man, woman, or wizard I pursued. Don't test me."

Impudent, curly-headed brute! How dare he? I'm a master—well, former master—of the ninth order! Finster gave the men in the room further study. Greasy and durable, this entourage from Mendes, if that was where they were really from, wasn't your ordinary ilk. They were hunters, true killers who struck in the dark of the night. Cutthroats. *Oh, how I hate men that can only use brawn rather than brains to negotiate. Weak-minded fools. I'll turn their brains into pig food.* "Crawley, I'm sorry to say that you've given me no choice other than to defend myself and my place of business."

Tuberlous returned. He dabbed his forehead with a rag and started rubbing the bar.

"Look around, Finster. I've brought in my lot of wizards, lost some good men—well, some good, bad men—and trust me when I say I won't have any problem with you. You're washed up. Weak. Pathetic. Not even a reflection of the days of old. Don't be a fool. Come to Mendes, and see what the judge has to say."

He's lying. Why would Mendes want me? Crossing his arms over his chest, he looked at Crawley. "I can't abandon my arcane abode. I like it here."

"It was hard enough to find your little alchemy stand. I'm not going back empty-handed." Without taking his eyes off of Finster, he backed into the bar. With a tap of his hand, the barkeeper poured him an ale. He drank it then said, "You'd better come down here before I finish this."

"I suppose I can't bring any belongings."

"No, you'll be shackled, and we aren't carrying it." Crawley drank half the mug. He sneered at the contents. "I won't take any chances, but I'll take you to Mendes fed and safe. That's a generous offer."

Crawley couldn't have come at a better time. Finster was drunk.

Not only that, but he was far from the top of his game. For years, he'd hidden from those who'd sought him out. He'd just wanted to fade away. Now, his past had caught up with him. His judgment day had come. "Crawley, there's an old saying in Winkley. Perhaps you've heard it before."

"I've heard a lot of things, but nothing worth remembering from Winkley. Indulge me."

Finster cleared his throat. "Never wake Finster from his slumber."

Chapter 3

The crossbows took on a life of their own as, with a single thought, Finster reshaped the wood of the crossbow bolts. The tips pointed toward the gabled ceiling. The soldiers pulled the triggers, and the bolts shot out in loop de loops, sailed short of the mark, and clattered into the stairwell.

"Get up there!" Crawley ordered two soldiers who stood at the base of the spiral staircase. "His parlor tricks won't last forever."

The husky soldiers rushed up the steps with wary eyes.

Summoning more power from the mystic well that fed his blood, Finster focused on the stairwell. With his hand in an open grip, he twisted it in the air.

The stairwell groaned. The iron railing bent. The wooden steps cracked and popped. The heavy staircase livened like a snake, and the metal coiled around the soldiers, constricted, and crushed. The soldiers screamed.

Looking up at Finster, Crawley started for his sword, but his hand pulled back.

Finster winked at him. "Having second thoughts, Commander Crawley?"

"No, just changing strategy." He shouted out, "A dozen gold to the man who brings him down!"

The soldiers, just shy of a dozen, moved in an organized scramble. *Oh, dear. There are so many of them.* The Master of the Inanimate got to work. He reached deeper than he had in years. With a thrust of calculated thought, the chairs, stools, and tables on the floor took on a life of their own. The patrons, still in their chairs, screamed in horror as the wooden objects carried them and charged into the hard-eyed soldiers, bowling one of them over. Another soldier was knocked to the ground by a table. In a small world gone mad, a soldier with a large eye patch stabbed a patron through the chest.

"Easy on the people, Arly! It's only sticks you're fighting!" Crawley snatched up a walking stool and smashed it against the bar. "It's just firewood!"

A large rectangular table blindsided two more soldiers. They went down howling and chopping with their blades. The table legs jabbed into the men's bodies and limbs.

Seeing his ragtag army of furnishings getting chopped and smashed to bits, Finster executed another command. He caught Crawley looking away and made a twitch of his fingers. The floorboards beneath the commander curled back one by one and swallowed him whole. Dusting off his hands, Finster said, "Ah, that should buy me enough time." He went to his bookshelf, gathered a few choice items, and tucked them into a rustic leather travel bag. He slid one bookshelf over, slipped through the crack, and snuck down into the kitchen. A back door awaited him, half open, with green fields beyond it as far as the eye could see.

Eyeing the pots bubbling on the flames, he considered burning the entire place down. *It will be such a time-consuming pursuit if I don't. Besides, it would be the soldiers' fault, not mine. They started this. Then again, what about my supplies? Perhaps I can send for them.* The clatter and angry hollering in the tavern grew louder. *I hope I don't regret this.*

Without looking back, he walked right out the door. The fields of green were darkened on the left side and right with over fifty heavily armored soldiers. Finster froze. There was no way out of this. Even in his prime, he'd have had trouble with it. *I hate soldiers. They don't have enough brainpower, so they must rely on manpower. Every brute thinks he can fight, and they breed like rabbits. Abominable!*

He puffed, and his knees wobbled. He hadn't exerted himself like that in years. He was drained.

Crawley appeared from around the corner of the building. He dusted the dirt off and walked up to Finster. Looking down at him, he said, "That was a nice trick, Finster. You dropped me right into the cellar." He showed a bottle of wine held in his grip. "I found this down there. A good year."

"Consider it a gift. I'll put it on my tab."

"Why, thank you." Crawley swung the bottle into the side of Finster's head. The magus dropped to the ground. "Huh, look at that. The bottle didn't break. Seems it's more sturdy than you." With a scowl, he kicked Finster in the gut a few times. "How about a drink, Finster?"

Wheezing, he replied, "Sorry. I only drink with friends. You aren't a friend, but you had your chance."

"You should have come peacefully, Finster. I told you there was no way out." Crawley uncorked the bottle and drank. "Not bad for this pig pit." He tossed the bottle inside the kitchen door. "Sergeant. Make sure all of my men are out, kill anyone that's not one of us if they haven't had the sense to fall, then burn it to the ground. When the villagers wail, make sure they know that Finster did it. That's the price you pay when you resist men of authority."

Finster spat blood. "I knew you were bad. Anybody with a face like that has to be bad."

Crawley let out an evil chuckle. He gave a nod to his men. They dragged Finster away. Crawley took Finster's travel bag and threw it inside the door. Within a minute, the tavern caught fire. It burned like a huge pyre. Innocent men were put to the sword, including Tuberlous.

"There's a price for slaughtering the innocent," Finster managed to say.

"You should know," Crawley replied. "Strip him down, sergeant." The sergeant was a greasy brute with more beard than face. His fingers were like sausages. "We need to make sure he doesn't have any tricks up his sleeve. Search him. Search him good. Everything from his ears to his, well, you know."

After the search was over, the sergeant brought Finster to Crawley. The magus wore nothing, but held his robes in his hands. "Well done, sergeant. Now, time for step two." Crawley held up a black pouch and emptied it into his hand. A jade, beetle-shaped object filled half of his big hand.

Finster recoiled. The blood in his face drained.

"You know what this is, don't you, Silver Snake?"

Finster replied, "I swear, you'll get no trouble from me. Not *that* scarab. Please, don't put that thing on me!"

"I have orders. Besides, I'm curious to see what this little jewel does. I think you know. Perhaps you can tell me?"

"It will deprive me of my talent."

"Really? So it will make your tongue shrivel. No more smart-alecky comments. I like it. Perhaps I should get one for my wife. Heh-heh-heh." Crawley dangled the object in front of Finster's eyes. Its small insect legs popped out. Barbed feet spread out and wriggled.

"You're sweating again, Finster, and it hasn't even pricked your skin yet." He nodded at the sergeant. "Arly, spin him around."

With strong hands, Sergeant Arly whipped Finster around.

"Crawley, please, don't do this! I'm not worth it! That is a rare item. Not the scarab! Please, not that cursed scarab. Use it on one more worthy than me. I'm harmless."

"No, I've got orders. I follow them." Crawley slapped the hungry beetle between Finster's scrawny shoulder blades. "It's done."

The claws of the scarab bored into his flesh. Finster let out a bloodcurdling scream.

Chapter 4

Writhing on the ground with Crawley's and Arly's boots in his back, Finster shouted out every slur he knew. The jade beetle's barbed feet pierced his skin. They bored into his muscles. Burning needles, like hellfire, spread through his back. Arly giggled. Finster's eyes rolled up in his head. He arched, convulsed, and squirmed. His slender fingers clutched back and forth in knots. His blue veins, bursting under his skin, turned green.

"Let him be," Crawley said, removing his foot. Sergeant Arly stomped on Finster again. "Boy, that looks painful, but he's harmless now—trust me. Huh, this is like watching a worm caught between the cobblestones and sunrise. See, he shrivels up."

Finster heard the sting in the words. Crawley's condescending tone gave him a little fire. He stopped screaming even though the beetle's legs were still boring into him. On his hands and knees, trembling, he let the jade beetle do its excruciating work. Things were growing inside him. Sharp worms squirmed inside. The blinding pain came to an end, but the nagging had just begun. He opened his eyes. His sweat dripped to the ground in steady drops. His lip ached. He'd bitten through it. He found Crawley's face. "Now that you've ruined me, I don't suppose I could have a drink. After all, there's little else to live for."

"Maybe later."

With rope, Crawley's men bound Finster by the wrists. They tethered him to Arly's horse, and the long march to Mendes began. Finster only wore his sandals and robes. A few hours into the trek, his soft feet had blisters on them. The group camped that night, but he ate nothing and slept shivering in his robes. The wind biting his extremities was one thing, and the chronic nagging in his back was another. He ached. He survived, unwillingly.

"How about that drink?" he said to Crawley the next morning. Finster smacked his parched lips and rubbed his eyes. "Please."

"Give him some of my share, Arly, but don't overdo it. That booze is the only thing that will probably keep him going."

Drinking from a wine flask, Finster said, "As unlikely as it seems, I appreciate the mercy."

"If it were up to me, I'd just skin your hide and leave you in the cold." Crawley mounted his horse. "Lucky for you, that's not what I'm paid for… this time. But my patience has limits."

Finster focused on whatever he could learn. He counted soldiers and captured names. Any little bit of information could give him an avenue for escape. Parched, he lumbered along, tripping and stumbling in wagon ruts only to be dragged until Arly felt compelled to stop. Crawley was right: only those drinks throughout the day kept Finster going.

Three days into the journey, he and Crawley struck up another conversation along the muddy road.

"I have to say, I'm flattered that so many were sent on my account. Near three score soldiers coming after a washed-up magus. Why so many?"

High in the saddle, Crawley said, "Your reputation precedes you. I think you know that. When I was a buck, not even eighteen summers, I was at Caterwaul—what was that, thirty years ago? I saw what the likes of you did not to hundreds but to thousands."

Finster shrank in his robes. "I was rather young myself."

"Yes, but I was there. I saw you and many others gloating over the dead. Women and children. The wailing was indescribable. Did you know that nothing has thrived there ever since? They say the trees bleed red on wet days like this. The wind is filled with haunting moans and cries. The women can bear no children."

"A pity. I was following orders." Finster moved closer to the man riding in the saddle. "Many of my works, I must admit, were a travesty. But there are only two kinds of people in this world: conquerors and the conquered."

"Yes, I learned my lesson that day. Almost everyone I knew was wiped out." Crawley made his little laugh. "I was determined to fight for the winning side after that. Now, I command these men and many others."

"Tragedy shapes us all for good and bad. You seem to fit in quite well with the bad. Your destiny suits you." He cleared his throat. "Like a glove. There's nothing worse than seeing a man trying to be something that he is not. How about another sip?"

Crawley tossed over the wine skin. "Finster, you're almost likeable. Direct honesty gives a man a certain appeal. So many are scared to say the truth anymore. Even among my own men. I find your candor refreshing."

"I wish I could say the same, but I'd be lying." He sucked down the last gulp. "At least your men fear you enough not to share the truth. You'd probably kill them."

"It's happened."

Scanning the horizon, eyes squinted in slits, Finster said, "I've done my fair share of traveling, and this isn't the way to Mendes. We move east of it. So if we aren't going there, then where are we going?"

"Can't you tell? We're almost there."

With nothing but riders in front of him, Finster moved parallel to Arly, stretching out the rope as far as he could. The gentle plains made a straight line against the jagged hills. Tucked between bumps in the rocky terrain was a huge fortress made from red stones. Black banners, the size of specks, waved on the top of the citadel. Finster's heart sank. He knew the ominous facility. Carved from rocks and built up with the same stone, the castle city was the stronghold of a peculiar high-ranking official.

"You're taking me to the home of the Magus Supremeus?" He gaped. "What on earth would he want with me?"

"I don't ask questions. I just execute the orders. I'll tell you this, Finster: you aren't the first to make the visit."

Finster wandered back in line. He tracked through his past. For over a decade, he'd lain low, moving from town to town, not drawing any attention to himself. He'd made plenty of enemies all over the world, but there was none worse than a rival wizard. He'd abandoned the order. He had that right, sort of. There was a price to pay for leaving, but never one so grievous as having a jade beetle stuck to his back. As for the Magus Supremeus, he didn't even know for certain who it was, only who it used to be. He stared at Crawley. Chin up and eyes forward, the stone-faced man's expression offered no answers.

Finster's shoulders ached all the more. *The worst has worsened.*

Chapter 5

The Wizard Haven—also known as the Scarlet Citadel, home of the Magus Supremeus—was an imposing slab of stone squeezed between nature. There were no windows, only parapets on the high walls of the tall, rectangular building. It was always stark, day or night. Commander Crawley led them inside the dark mouth of the mountain home. There wasn't a courtyard or people within, only granite walls inside an unnaturally deep facility.

"I see they're still using the same decorator," Finster said to the sergeant. The water spilled over the inner walls in clear sheets, which made them shimmer, then emptied into a channel where huge goldfish swam. "Yes, nothing has changed in a thousand years, the way I understand it. Quite boorish for men and women renowned for their imaginations."

Arly dismounted. The rest of the soldiers moved on, disappearing through archways into the strange facilities beyond. He handed Crawley the rope binding Finster. With a nod, Arly led his own horse and Crawley's into the hallways beyond. The clomping of horse hooves echoed then faded the moment Arly disappeared behind the stone archway.

Looking around, Crawley said, "Is it good to be back, Finster?

Home of the wizards. The training ground. It all seems so impersonal to me. Not a potted plant in the entire place."

"We aren't known for our gardening. We have common folk, like you, to do those menial chores for us." He wiped his nose. "A splash of color wouldn't hurt, I suppose."

"It's your homecoming. Let's go. The Magus will be expecting you." Crawley gave Finster a shove.

Shuffling along, Finster said, "I hardly think I'm presentable for the high magus. There is a matter of decorum in his forum."

"No, the Magus was very specific. Besides, you aren't the first. I've brought in many others in far worse shape. Some of them dead. Others just disabled."

Finster didn't hide his sneer from Crawley. If he could, he'd have turned the man's skin inside out. He hated lugs like Crawley. His kind were entirely too cocky. *Buffoon! Ten years ago, I'd have made you eat that sword of yours whole.* He turned his attention ahead. His sandals flopped on the bottoms of his heels, making an uncomfortable echo in the grand chamber.

Above him, the vaulted ceilings were crisscrossed with beautiful archways. Gaudy murals were painted between the bricks. The images were depressing scenes that seemed to move the longer he stared at them. A chill hung in the stuffy air. Right and left, between the support columns, were statues carved from obsidian. Each was the image of a magus in his prime. Some carried staves and wands. Others wore strange hats and exquisite robes. The magi depicted were all dead, but each statue seemed alive in a special sort of way.

"I hear it's the highest honor for a magus," Crawley said. "I bet you hoped for that—an image of you for all eternity."

"Nothing lasts forever. But I'd be lying if I said it didn't matter to me once." He eyeballed the statue of a wizard with a horned toad on his shoulder. "That's Ellister the Marvel. He had his choice of familiars, from great cats to lizards, but preferred that toad. We had to learn all about each and every one of them. We studied the spells they created. I always had trouble with Ellister's intricacies. I just didn't care for animals, insects—particularly beetles—or anything that lived with a wee little mind in general. Like you, Crawley."

"You just can't control your sharp tongue, can you?"

"It's the only weapon I have left."

Crawley gave him a hard slap on the shoulder. "At the moment."

At the end of the corridor was a single door made from a solid slab of granite. Two stone cauldrons, with dragons carved into them, burned with a bright-orange fire on either side of the entrance. A stone staircase, wide as the hall, led up a full flight of stairs. Finster stood at the bottom. Another statue caught his eye. He gaped. "Magus Supremeus! Zuulan the Arcane! He was the last I knew. What treachery is this?" He looked at Crawley. "He cannot be dead. Stepped down, yes, but dead… no."

"Like you said, nothing—or in this case, no one—lasts forever." Crawley headed up the stairs, tugging Finster along by the rope.

The slab doorway had mystic images, ancient as the sea, carved all over the stone. There weren't any handholds or handles. No tremendous men or beasts were present to lift the door by way of chains or pulleys.

Crinkling his nose, he said to Crawley, "Are you going to knock?"

"Don't play games, Finster."

Finster rolled his shoulders. He took another glance back at Zuulan the Arcane. He'd liked Zuulan. *The man was an ass, but oh, so powerful. Armies could not defeat him. He turned the Genesis Magi Guild into bloody goop.* He gave the door a long look. Whoever was on the other side was formidable, but Finster couldn't imagine who that might be. Perhaps the Wizard's Citadel had fallen to some otherworldly power. He scratched his eyebrow, gave Crawley a glance, and stepped forward.

"At least your knees aren't quaking like the others'. I'm impressed. The statue of Zuulan seems to get to them." Crawley looked up.

A ball of dark-blue light snaked through the channels of the massive door. Winding its way down, it came to a stop a few feet above their heads, looking like a round spot of light. It slid open to show what looked like a great eye. The eyeball moved just like a real, flesh one. The creepy gaze made Finster's skin crawl. The eye was a vile monster, a guardian of the Magus Supremeus. Its lone stare froze men and women like ice.

Finster glared at it. He hated the eye. The eye did more than watch the door. It wandered everywhere, prying into everyone's business. "Oh, get on with it, you filthy little shade. I'm ready to meet my captor."

The eye narrowed on Finster for a long moment then closed, and the ball of light vanished. Slowly, the door began to rise. The majestic throne room of the Magus Supremeus was revealed. The throne was made of pure silver and iron. The metal was studded with jewels. The arms were made of curled dragon horn. The crimson cushion was empty, but the seat was guarded by dozens of soldiers—the citadel guardians. Each was a stalwart man wearing a burnished mask of hammered steel with rectangular eyelets. Their robes were brown, their sinewy arms bare, and each wore a sword belt and scabbard at the waist and held a spear with an iron tip pointing upward, its butt end on the floor.

"Welcome, Finster," a familiar voice said from the corner of the room.

He turned toward the source. *It can't be.*

Chapter 6

"The Sly Swan returns," Finster said under his breath. He felt Crawley's eyes boring a hole in his back. Crawley didn't faze him, but she did. He watched her glide from behind her soldiers, an amazing specimen of a woman with the dark robes of the high magus clinging to her modest curves. She was much younger than he, a platinum-haired lioness with ice-blue eyes. The loose sleeves of her robes draped over the arms of the chair when she sat. An easy smile formed on her lips. His knee began to bend toward the floor. *What am I doing?* He straightened. "Ingrid the Inverted. I thought you were gone… forever."

"Is that any way to greet your former prodigy, Gray Cat?" Her icy stare danced with the flickering power of a coming storm. She rested her gentle hands on the arms of the throne. She wore eight rings, one on each finger, each made from a unique precious metal and stone. They all sparkled with secrets and power. "You seem so very, very surprised. And you look like, well"—she crinkled her nose—"something that crawled out of a pig pit."

"You can thank your errand boy for that. He was quite merciless in his acquisition of me, but also very unrevealing as to the true nature of my kidnapping. I tried to dislodge it from his simple brain, but his stubborn nature failed to let me loose it from his crooked lips. Care to explain, Ingrid?" He pointed at his back. "Also, the jade beetle is quite… extreme."

"A precaution, old mentor. Consider it mercy. You've fared much better than several other members of the order."

"I'd be very interested to learn more about their demise and the purpose behind it. Perhaps we could talk over a drink." He licked his lips. "Much like old times?"

"What makes you think I brought you here for conversation?"

"Please…" Finster gave the soldiers and Crawley the once-over. "The citadel is all but abandoned. You must be starved for real conversation. These men are capable of little more than fighting and farting. I'd hate to imagine an actual conversation. Unless you are keeping them to satisfy your neurotic passions."

Ingrid waved a finger. "Be careful what you say to the Magus Supremeus, Finster. I'm not your protégé anymore, nor your friend."

"No, of course not. Friends don't treat friends like this—or threaten or kill them, for that matter."

A female servant dressed in thin layers of silk appeared from behind the soldiers. She approached the throne with a tray loaded with a bottle of wine and a single goblet. Ingrid took the cup in hand. "I'll be drinking alone today, as I often do."

Eyeing the goblet, Finster licked his lips. *Stifle your tongue, Finster. It's the best way out of this. Seek her mercy.* With a long shrug of his narrow shoulders, he said, "Please, Ingrid. Look at where you are. I played a part in this, didn't I? Was I not good to you?"

Her eyes smoldered for just a moment. "You have become a sot, Finster. I'd heard such things, but I had trouble believing it. You, of all the magi, took the greatest care of yourself. You were impeccable. Now you are soft and scrawny, and the natural charm that danced the skirts off many ladies is gone."

"Did I not tell you that magic takes a toll on you? Finally, I admit, it got the best of me." He made a feeble and helpless smile. "I'm master of little more than the bottle now."

"Is this true, Crawley?" She leaned back in her seat. "Was it a simple task to track down and capture this drunkard?"

"He posed as big a challenge as any. He made the tables, chairs, and stairwells dance," Crawley said. "He's got power—plenty of it."

"*Had* power," Finster corrected. "Ingrid, why this cursed scarab of all things? Why me? I'm not even part of the order now. I'm just one that wants to be left on his own." He held out the grubby palms of his hands. "I'm harmless."

"I know better, Finster. I'm certain that you remember telling me that a time comes in every wizard's life when he must make the choice. You told me you'd answer the call to good if pressed. Despite your own misgivings, you are still sworn to defend the order."

"What order? It appears you destroyed it. And those words? Why, those were that of a mentor trying to impress a pretty girl. I don't even recall it. Besides, you weren't so naïve. You knew what was going on. Every wizard in the citadel wanted you."

Her eyes smiled. Her crossed leg kicked.

Finster went on. "Did I not save you—an innocent girl—from a life in the brothels? That's why I took you from the place that you were born in. You had wisdom. A talent. I found it."

"Yes, you, oh so noble, found me in a brothel." She sipped her red wine. "It makes me angry."

"You've always been angry. That was your weakness. I thought you might have cooled off by now. As for the brothel, that was a mere coincidence. I was weak and had needs. I think it was destiny."

"Yet you sent me away."

"What are you talking about?"

"The missions. Those boorish trips between where the sun rises and falls, to help, grow, and learn. All it did was incite me!"

He wagged his finger at her. "You and I parted ways long before that happened, Ingrid the Unpleasant. I, on the other hand, moved on to face my own failures. Don't throw your problems on me. Look where you are now." He gazed at the splendor of the throne room. "You are the Magus Supremeus, and you complain?"

Her eyes narrowed.

Finster's finger popped out of joint. "Gah!" He dropped on his knees. Eyes watering, he said, "Why did you do that? Can't you see I'm impaired enough? Spare me a finger, please!"

Ingrid stood. "Don't talk to me like I'm your adept. I'm the Magus Supremeus."

"No, you are Ingrid the Inept!" he said, huddled over his finger. "Tell me, how did you steal this throne?" He leered at her sensuous legs. "Though I'm pretty sure I could guess."

In a gloating fashion, Ingrid held up her fingers. "These trinkets that you know so well, I earned in the battle of orders. In my fight to attain the tenth order, I bested many. The rings, among other things, are trophies. You've had your share. You boasted to me about that. I reached the level of the ninth order. My skills garnered the attention of Zuulan the Arcane. He was so fond of me that we married."

Finster rolled his eyes. *Zuulan, you fool. Why would you marry a fellow magus? And Ingrid of all people. She was too talented and dangerous. She brought nothing but chaos to the order.* Guilt stirred in his belly. Finster had been the one to discover Ingrid. He'd had high hopes, but she had a dark fire that couldn't be quenched.

"You are partially right, Finster." She crossed her legs. Running her fingers from her bare thighs to her knee, she said, "I used my ways on old Zuulan. As it turns out, the only thing he loved more than magic was flesh."

I could have told you that. Oh, his birthday celebrations. They made brothels look like cathedrals.

She continued. "It was easy to pull the wool over Zuulan's hungry eyes. I liked him and respected him. I kept him distracted with many things. At the same time, in the background, I began my own secret war on the members of the order. With the help of Crawley, I killed them all." She toyed with the rings on her fingers. "One by one." She touched one of the masked soldiers. The citadel guardian turned to water and spilled over the floor. She touched another man. The guardian's skin shriveled up into a husk. He hit the floor and collapsed to dust.

Finster saw the whites of the rest of the guardians' eyes behind the masks. Many Adam's apples rolled. Crawley's own finger moved over the pommel of his sword.

Invisible spiders crawled up Finster's spine. *This is bad. Oh, so bad.*

Chapter 7

"Impressive," Finster said, wiping his sweating palms on his robes. He popped his finger back into joint with a grunt. He'd seen the power of the Magus Supremeus before, but this display was different. Ingrid took the lives of the guardians as nonchalantly as a child stomping a worm underfoot. The guardians of the citadel were devotees of the order, the high magus's personal soldiers. They pledged their lives in the order's defense, but they weren't livestock. *Warriors—so brainless in their bravery. Always trying to prove something. Glorified farmers. Eventually, they have it coming.* "So I suppose you murdered Zuulan, then. I seem to recall rumors of Ingrid the Assassin."

"No." Ingrid drank from her goblet. She took a deep breath, expanding her enticing chest. Her eyes drifted for a moment. "I didn't need to murder him. Instead, I challenged him before he discovered what I was doing. You should have seen the shock in his face. His jowls hung to the floor. The betrayal. Hah, it weakened him. I think he held back. Actually, I was counting on that. You see, I'd learned enough to advance to the tenth order. But I'd learned something else he didn't know—how to use the power of all these rings as one. It gave me the edge I needed."

Finster's eyes watched the treasury on her fingers with hungry fascination.

"Yes, Finster, it is exhilarating. The amplification of power I hold in my hands, I must say, is intoxicating."

"All power is, and only a few can handle it."

She gently shook her head. "Poor Zuulan—he didn't have the fight in him. Pitiful. Whimpering, his eyes sank back into his head right before his bones turned to water. He was nothing more than a sack of sand made from flesh. I cremated him, literally. No sense in having a coffin funeral for a bag of flesh."

Finster held her eyes. "Now that you have the high seat, what do you intend to do with it?"

"The only thing that must be done: take over the kingdom. I grew so tired of all the folly I saw when I walked the world on the missions." She fought off a sneer. "These kings and queens are fools. The people would be better off without them. I'd be better off without them. I'll have vengeance on all of them."

"What would life be without vengeance? Ah, yes—peaceful." Sniffing, he rubbed his nose. "The order is about protecting the kingdoms, not running them. The magi are guides, the higher minds of reason. We offer advice and direction."

Ingrid's voice rose. "The magi have been pawns! They are the dirty fighters behind these endless wars and skirmishes. You know that as well as anyone, Secret Slayer."

"You are mad, Ingrid. The people like their kings and queens. So be it! You might take Mendes, but you'll never rule."

"Oh, but I will. You see, the King of Mendes, Rolem the Grand, is due another suitable queen as her ladyship recently died."

"Let me guess—her heart gave out."

"Exploded actually."

"I see... and you've sunk your claws into him. Relationships between the order and the royal lines are forbidden."

"King Rolem is an innovator. Open-minded. He believes in change."

Oh, not this again. Change my arse! It's just another word for control. "And pray tell, what is my role in all of this?"

"You don't have a role, Finster." She stepped away from the throne, came down the steps, and faced him. "I certainly have a fondness for the once-handsome magus that saved this young girl from living among the sordid people in the taverns, but I only need one thing from you."

"Obviously, it's not my advice."

"No, something more useful." Her lips brushed against his ear. "I want you to tell me the location of the *stone*."

"What stone?"

"The *stone*. Don't play games with me, Finster. I want it. I'll have it."

"Ingrid, the *stone* is a myth. At least I'm convinced of that. I merely told you about it to impress you."

"I know better, Guardian of the Mystic Forge."

"Are you daffy?" He started to tremble. "I'm a drunk. Always have been. I abandoned those dreams and delusions." From his knees, he begged her. "Please, let me be your servant. A simple servant. I'll do it for wine. I'll sleep in the stables. Ingrid, please!"

Teeth clenched, she hauled back to smack him.

Finster flinched.

"All I have to do is touch you, Finster!" She stuck her fist in his face. "You would be at an end. It's sickening what you've become. You were destined to be a tenth. A tenth! Maybe the high magus. But I promise you this: if you know the whereabouts of the *stone*, I will extract it from you. I know there is still a man in there. A man with secrets. I will have them!" She marched toward the throne. On her way, she touched another guardian. The man's neck snapped. "Crawley, you know where to take him."

"Please, Ingrid! Take this beetle from my back! Please!"

"Why, Finster, I thought you'd relish being attached to the mystic pet that you created. Aren't you enjoying my precious gift? The jade beetle has been a very effective tool in my conquests."

"Ingrid, please, I beg you. Let's have a drink. The trip has been long. Perhaps some concoctions will revive my addled mind. I'll tell you what I can remember."

Crawley grabbed hold of him by the nape of the neck.

Finster clawed the air. He showed Ingrid a gaping smile. "I'll be a wonderful servant! I learned to make excellent soups."

She shooed them away.

Crawley popped him in the back of the head. Finster's knees buckled. He climbed back to his feet with the help of Crawley, begging for mercy. Crawley shoved him out the door and down the steps. He led Finster on a long walk through the citadel's catacomb-like halls. They took steps that wound down into the subterranean level. The stones were slimy under Finster's feet. It stank and left a rancid taste in his mouth. A wet chill hung in the air. He buried his nose in his sleeve.

Two sentries opened the door to the main dungeon, a place Finster had been to several times before. The circumstances had been far more favorable then. They stopped in front of a cell.

Crawley shoved Finster's face between the metal bars of a cell. Inside, a brute of a man the likes of which Finster had never seen lay balled up and half naked. He didn't stir.

"A relative of yours, Crawley?"

"No… your cellmate."

Chapter 8

"Is this really necessary?" Finster was inside the cell, sitting with his back against the wall. With help from the guards, Crawley shackled Finster's ankle to the barbarian's ankle with a fair length of chain. "I'm inside a cell. I'm not some pickpocket that can break out. Please, Crawley. I deserve better than this. You know I don't get along with inbreeds, aside from yourself of course."

Crawley squatted down—eye to eye with Finster. "Funny, but I know better. Never trust a wizard. Besides, maybe your cozy new relationship will jar your memory. He's one of those northern barbarians. The hairless tribe. Odd for a northerner. Their skins are so thick that their bare feet don't freeze in the snow. They call them the Blue Toes. Heh-heh. They like to snuggle with each other on cold, damp nights." He tested the chain and stood up. "When he wakes up, there's no telling what he might do with the likes of you. But if he kills you, oh well. Nothing lost, nothing gained."

Finster eyeballed the brute form huddled on the floor like a passed-out drunkard. The savage knots of muscle in his back rippled with every breath. The barbarian was skinned up and scarred from head to toe. He looked like he'd run naked through a patch of heavy black thorns a dozen times. The only thing covering the bestial man up was a pair of goatskin trousers.

Crawley stepped outside of the cell and closed the door. "I wouldn't resist if he wants to curl up with you. You might be a warm little pig to him. A pet." He held his hands up. "But don't agitate him. We came across him by accident. He took offense to us crossing a stream where he was fishing. He killed five of my best men before their steel could snake out of their skins. Huh." He gave the barbarian a look of admiration. "Those barbarians are outstanding woodsmen. They just aren't so wise in the ways of warcraft."

"I'm surprised, Crawley. The barbarians are deft at evading capture. How ever did a man of your common education pull off such a feat?"

"Just so happened we had a really big net with us that day. And he's a young one, alone. We cornered him and took him down like a wild gazelle. I've never missed a mark."

"So why not kill him?"

Leaning his shoulder on the metal bars, Crawley said, "As it turns out, Ingrid took an interest. Given the marvelous constitution of these wild men, she thought we could breed a fantastic army of soldiers." Crawley let out his wicked chuckle. "A silly idea. An army of civilized barbarians wouldn't be very frightening, would it?"

"You're asking me? You're their descendant. That strong protruding jawline is a dead giveaway."

"Whenever you're ready to talk about that artifact, Finster, just give the guards a shout. In the meantime, enjoy your new tavern." Crawley and the guards departed. Their footsteps faded down the halls.

Finster raised his arms over his head, stretching his burning back. For the most part, he'd led a charmed life of mystic gifts and intelligence. Other than facing the wizard's trials, he never allowed himself to be in a situation that made him uncomfortable. He liked comfort. That had always been a benefit of the order. The intelligent were drawn to it. Now, for the first time, he was truly destitute.

He covered his nose and shuddered. *The stink alone should kill me.* His frail chest heaved in and out. His eyes drifted to the barbarian. *Please don't wake up. Ever.* He pulled his knees to his chest. The length of chain scraped over the stone floor. The barbarian stirred. *Easy, Finster. Easy.*

With heavy eyelids, Finster gathered his thoughts. *Ingrid is insane! Did my passions blind me so much I did not see it?* He'd come across Ingrid more than two decades earlier in a small tavern in a city called Shangley. She was a fetching girl, serving tables, who'd caught on to his magic. He hoped to do some good with the promising adept, but her upbringing had been too marred and jaded. She'd seen too much bad in the world. Hatred fed a dark fire she held within. It fueled her ambition. Finster could not change that. He liked her drive. She consumed everything he taught her. Finally, seeing his pupil blossom into a flower filled with venom, he broke away. Just like the father and mother she'd never come to know, he had abandoned her. *I can't be the sole one to blame, can I? On the brighter side of things, I breathe. That's more than most of my counterparts can say. Perhaps living a soldier's life is more desirable than making these world-changing decisions.*

Finster yawned. His lids closed. He tried to fight off the exhaustion overtaking his body, but couldn't. He leaned into the corner and slept.

Something jerked at his foot. His head dragged down the wall and smacked into the floor. Wide-eyed and drooling, he heard a tremendous sound. The barbarian—whom he was still chained to—rammed the dungeon door with his shoulders. Built with the shoulders of a bull, the monster of a man hit the door like a wild animal, and the effect was jarring.

The sound of flesh colliding with metal pounded Finster's ears.

He covered them. "What are you doing?" Finster shouted. He'd never seen a man so big before. No one living had ever frightened him so. "Please don't hurt me."

Chest heaving, the barbarian seemed to fill the entire cell. He stood over seven feet in height. His wild eyes, burning with intensity, looked right through Finster. He lowered his shoulder once more and rammed the door. The hinges groaned but held fast. The barbarian moved to the back end of the cell, dragging Finster by the ankle like a babe, and took a run at the door. He hit it at full speed with a resounding *wham*!

"Will you stop it?" Finster said, gathering his leg, trying to keep it from being jerked out of its hip socket. "You oversized idiot! You can't break down that door!"

The barbarian collided with the door at least twenty times. The man was as wild as a cornered animal. He pounded the door with ham-sized fists. He kicked the metal and bit the bars.

"Oh, please. I know stampeding cattle that are smarter than that!"

The barbarian head-butted the metal. Blood trickled down over the bridge of his nose.

Finster rubbed his aching head. "You're an embarrassment to your own kind! Stop it!"

Laboring for breath, the barbarian glowered down at Finster. The wild eyes turned sullen. He seemed to see Finster for the first time. Holding the chain, he lifted Finster off the ground by the ankle.

Hanging like a fish on the line, Finster said, "Oh dear."

Chapter 9

The barbarian gave Finster a couple of fierce shakes before finally setting him back down. His heavy stare landed on the wizard's face. The heavy brows of the semi-primordial man seemed to push Finster down at the shoulders. The barbarian was a creature from another time, long lost before shimmering cities grew from straw-topped huts into spires that yearned to kiss the clouds.

Hands up, Finster said, "I'm not your enemy. Do you understand me?"

The barbarian's chin dipped. His head tilted. The gray eyes probed Finster's. There was a spark of reason lurking behind that dead stare. At the same time, there was also the hunger of a prowling tiger. There were savages in the world—men who slaughtered and devoured their enemies. They ate the raw flesh of animals. Barbarians were little different from savages, but they had their own kind of civilization. As far as Finster knew, they drew the line at eating people. They were capable of a few other things, such as working metal in a forge, trapping, and farming. Finster wasn't certain whether there was a difference between this man and a savage.

Aside from the black brows knotted between his eyes, the barbarian didn't have a shred of hair. His skin was ruddy and smooth. The rest of his body, except for blood smears, dirt, and scars from many wounds, was clean of paint and strange tattoos. Grabbing the leg chain, the barbarian tried to pull the links apart. The barbarian's muscles bulged in his arms and neck. Sinew popped up along with blue veins that strained to burst from his skin. The metal groaned the slightest bit. After a long minute of struggle, the barbarian stopped. He dropped the chain and moved forward, staring through the cell's bars.

Finster leaned forward. His fingers toyed with the length of chain. "My, that was impressive. I swear, for a moment I thought that link would snap. That would be quite a feat. This chain is tempered, but you were oh, so close. Interesting. Even wild bulls can't snap it."

If the barbarian heard him, he didn't acknowledge it. The only reply was a loud groaning in his stomach.

Finster scooted back as far as the length of chain would allow. *He sounds like he could eat a herd of cattle.* He pushed up his sleeves. "I have little to offer in regards to nourishment. No, just skin and bones. Wizards, such as I, believe exercise profits very little. We focus on more divine things." He scratched his head. *I can't believe I'm talking to this illiterate imbecile. How desperate I've become—and starved for conversation. With a barbarian, no less.*

The barbarian's eyes searched every crack and crevice of the dungeon. Finster didn't bother looking. He'd noted every detail the moment he'd walked in. If he was going to get out, it would take cunning. *And perhaps a dash of brute force.*

Within the hour, the barbarian had slammed the cell door again. It happened all day long, on again and off again. It was like watching a ram butting a giant oak tree. Finster pleaded with the man. "Stop, you gigantic baboon! Save your energy!" He shouted himself hoarse. It went on for days, while Finster suffered painful withdrawal headaches and the scarab burning in his back.

The guards never came despite the annoying sounds, but late in the night, they brought scraps of food and placed them down at the edge of the cell along with a ladle in a bucket of water. As soon as they left, the barbarian's fingers stretched for the food. He scarfed all of it down, every last morsel. He slopped the water into his mouth.

Finster didn't care. He was accustomed to days without eating, but was not used to going without wine or ale. As the long days went on, he started to shake and shiver. He began to scream and yell absurdities. "Guards! Morons! Wine! Chinless bastards! Wine now! I must have it! I'll kill you all!" His head ached. He broke out in cold sweats. The madness between him and the barbarian went on for what felt like weeks. Finally, the withdrawal, added suffering, and fever died. With clarity, he sought the wooden bucket. Hands shaking, he grabbed the ladle and drank. "Oh, that's what water tastes like. I'd forgotten. Very bland."

He nibbled a few leftover scraps of food on the tray. The barbarian woke from his slumber. The time came for the hairless brute to try to tear down the gate again.

Finster locked his arms in the bars. "Listen to me! Stop this madness. If you want out of this, work with me."

The barbarian pried him away from the bars as easily as a monkey peeling a banana. The wild man charged the door again. When he stopped, Finster caught the man's eye. "Listen to me! You must—" Stopping short of his complete thought, he turned toward the back of the cell. The guardian eye from the doors of the Magus's throne room appeared on the dingy wall. "Please, Magus Supremeus, take me out of this cesspool. I'll help you find the artifact. Together, we'll seek out the stone."

The eye hung on the wall, watery and unblinking.

The barbarian caught sight of the strange eyeball orb. He charged, dragging Finster behind him. He punched the wall with his fists, making loud smacking sounds. The orb drifted along the wall, unharmed, and disappeared. The barbarian ran his hands over the rock with the gentleness of a physician.

"It's gone now, but it will be back, barbarian," Finster said. "If I'm going to have to continue these one-sided conversations, at least give me a name to address you with. Make a sound or something."

The barbarian scratched at the wall. A moth that would fit in the palm of Finster's hand flew into the cell. The barbarian's thick neck tilted. Without looking, he swiped the moth out of the air and ate it.

Finster made a sour face. "Ew. In all my travels, I've never seen moth fancied as a delicacy. Of course, I've never watched a man try to run through steel bars before either. Humph. Now, where were we? Oh, yes. A name." He watched the barbarian swallow. "I think I'll call you Moth. Any objections?" There was a short pause. "Good."

With greater clarity than normal for a mind that had been dulled by years of endless drinking, Finster reflected. Ingrid wielded eight rings, each with its own power, and she—with the help of her own training—had mastered them. She'd cleverly picked apart anyone who could challenge her. At least anyone that Finster knew of. He didn't doubt for a second that she could achieve what she'd set out to do. The effects would be catastrophic. The entire kingdom would be at war. Countless innocent people would die. He knew that because the same thing had happened in the histories he'd studied.

Long ago, the Magus Supremeus—called by a different name at the time—had tried to overtake the kingdoms. The devastating results could still be seen everywhere—mountains had been leveled and cities destroyed. In response, the Order of the Magus had been created to protect peace, at least enough that men would never fully destroy themselves. The new order swore never to interfere directly with the world of men again. They would be guides, sages, and seers. Peace was pursued, but not at all costs. After all, the magi were flesh and blood, like other humans, even though they wielded a convincing power. To maintain order in the world, they had to keep order among themselves. And even the magi, from their lofty perch, had problems. That was one of the reasons Finster had walked away—he'd tired of the problems. The magi wrought much good, but evil was never undone. Still, deep inside, he'd realized he had to do something, or the world as he knew it would perish.

"Moth, it's time to get out of here."

Chapter 10

Finster removed his robes. The draft bit his shoulders. Goose bumps popped up all over his body. He reached his long arm behind his back and touched the jade beetle. The cursed thing's tendrils clenched. He jerked his hand away. "Gah! I never would have thought I'd have created my own undoing!"

The jade beetle was a magical device of his own design used to thwart the powers of his opponents—other magic users in the world who didn't agree with the high order. The jade beetles, very difficult and expensive to make, would crawl into homes unseen and attach themselves to the order's unsuspecting adversaries. A beetle like the one on Finster's back had brought Harlock the Reaper down. "I almost feel pity for that mystical marauder of innocent flesh." Finster took a deep breath.

Removing an attached beetle that had burrowed into one's skin was fatal. Once implanted, it could never be removed. It was terminal. At least, that was what Finster had led everyone to believe. *Nothing done cannot be undone.* He'd created the beetle and knew it could be removed, but the risk was great. The pain would be unbearable. The risk of paralysis, blindness, senselessness, and even death was high. Finster had figured if a beetle was ever used on him, he might as well be dead anyway. *I can't believe I'm going to do this. For the kingdom!*

He reached up and snapped his fingers in the huge man's face. "Moth, listen to me," he said, turning and pointing to the beetle. "See this insect between my shoulder blades? I need you to pull it out." He gesticulated. "Pull it. No matter how loud I scream—and I'll scream like a thousand wailing inbred infants—*don't stop!* It has to come out." He faced Moth. "If you do this, I think we can get this door open. I hope I can. But we must be quick. It is this or neither one of us will get out of here alive."

Moth, neither handsome nor ugly but just naturally scary, stood like a statue, unblinking.

"Listen, barbarian, you have to do this! I know you understand. I see a flicker in those dim eyes. Now, pull this bug out of my back." He turned and faced the cell door. He locked his fingers around the bars and squeezed his eyes shut. "Go ahead, Moth. Do it!"

The dungeon fell quiet. The seconds were long.

This brainless barbarian is not going to do it!

Finster started to twist his neck over his shoulder. A rough hand touched his back. Fingers dug in around the beetle and pulled. "Yargh!" Finster screamed at the top of his lungs.

One-handed, Moth pulled at the beetle. Finster's grip was ripped from the bars. He stumbled back into Moth's chest. Bursting into a sweat, he said, "Mercy, that hurts!" He caught his breath. "Try it again!" Finster stuck his arms through the bars and hugged them tight. "Try again!"

Moth's hand, filled with the raw strength of a grizzly bear, latched onto the beetle once more. He pulled.

Finster shrieked, "Eeeee-yargh!" His arms strained to hold onto the metal bars. "I can't hold it!" His arms gave way. His fingers slipped. "It's going to be impossible to get that thing out of me—*urk*!"

Moth stuck one large foot in Finster's back and drove him into the door. He locked his free hand around the bar. With the other hand clutching the beetle, he renewed his efforts.

"Eeeeeee-yaaaaaah!" Finster screamed. Lightning flashed under his eyelids. His eyes pulled back into his head. Something was being ripped out of his body from the top of his fingers to the bottom of his toes. He continued to yell. "Aaaaaaaaaaah! You're killing me!"

A sickening sucking sound caught his ears. It felt like his entire back was being yanked out by a giant fishhook. Something unnatural stretched and squiggled. There was a high-pitched *skreeeyal* sound followed by a loud *pop* and *snap*.

Shaking, Finster slid down the sweat-slickened bars, drooling. He panted. He trembled. Somehow, he managed to turn his body toward Moth. The giant man held the beetle in his hand. Thin, long tendrils with tiny barbs dripped blood onto the floor. Slowly, the tendrils coiled back up into the beetle. Moth set the beetle down. He raised his heel over it.

"No," Finster sputtered. He crawled over and grabbed the beetle. The object was cold in his hand. The damp air became icy. The chills were painful. He gathered his robes and stuck the beetle in his pocket. Then he huddled in the corner and shook uncontrollably for hours. His vision came and went. *That unforgiving itch is gone, only to be replaced by an unbearable burning sensation.*

Meanwhile, Moth started banging into the bars again. His strength and determination defied reason.

Finster rocked in the folds of his robes. He could feel the warm blood on his back. He swore a hunk of his flesh was gone. Somehow, he lived. Not that he thought it was impossible, but the pain alone was more than enough to make any person's heart fail. He retched in the corner and wiped his mouth. "That's better."

With the jade beetle out of his back and his mind sober, Finster's strength slowly began to return. He was inside the belly of the Wizard's Citadel. The entire building was a conduit to the mystic realm, from which sorcerers drew their power. A little bit at a time, he drew more energy, gathering enough until he was able to stand.

He was just about to make his way up to his feet when the mystic eye appeared again.

Sitting against the wall, Moth stirred.

Finster didn't acknowledge the brute. He merely gazed back at the eye. "Please, Ingrid, let us speak and drink. I beg of you."

Moth pounced at the wall. The move jerked Finster underneath him. Moth pounded at the eye, chasing the strange orb all over the cell, dragging Finster along with him.

"Will you stop this madness?" Finster demanded.

The eye vanished.

Moth scanned the walls with his inflamed eyes. He clawed at spots with his hands.

"It's gone, Moth."

The bald brute continued his search.

Finally, Finster said, "I've got enough strength, I think, to get us out of here." Moth paid him no mind. Finster stepped into his path and pounded Moth's rock-hard chest. He pointed at the door. "Out! Escape! Freedom! Think of all the sheep waiting to be molested out there."

Foaming at the lips, Moth glowered down at him.

Hands up, Finster said, "The sheep part was only a jest. Please, pay attention." Grimacing, he edged toward the dungeon door. He tapped the locking mechanism. "Everything has a weakness. With doors, it's not the bars but the locks and the hinges. I can use my power to weaken them." He pointed at the lock. "But you must push right here. Do you understand?"

Stone-faced, Moth said nothing. He turned and sat down against the wall.

Chapter 11

"Now you want to take a rest from your mindless battering?" Finster marched over to Moth and kicked him in the thigh. "Ouch!" With the chain rattling behind him, he dragged himself back over to the door. He placed his hand on the lock. "Listen to me again, Moth. We can break the mechanism. Together. I have just enough energy for it. We must try."

Moth closed his eyes.

"Unbelievable!" Desperation began to set in. His stomach quavered. His limbs were weak. Even with the beetle out of him, the thing had taken a toll. He was fragile. Feverish. A raspy quality clung to his breath. "We aren't going to get many more chances at this. Time is fleeting."

Moth let out a sigh. It was the kind of sound an animal let out just before it died, when all of the vibrant strength in its limbs had failed. The taut muscles in the barbarian's body eased.

Head sagging, Finster shook his chin. "I suppose I can try it without you." His fingers dusted the metal on the locking mechanism. It was a stalwart lock made of heavy, unbreakable parts. The construction was of the finest craft. Everything in the Red Citadel was.

Finster closed his eyes. Summoning his sorcerous powers, he explored the inner workings on the other side of the metal plate. He tried to feel the tumbler within. He wanted to move it with his mind. The lock, however, had a special design. Unlike the common sort, it was designed to hold against wizards.

Perspiration built on his forehead. Gasping, he stepped away. "I… I can't do it. Nothing more aggravating than locks that a wizard's tools can't penetrate." He placed his hands on his knees. "Moth, you have to help. Even someone little smarter than cattle deserves to frolic among the manure again. If we can't get past this door, I can't get you out of this cursed citadel."

The barbarian's chin slipped to his chest.

Turning away, Finster took hold of the bars. They were solid steel, a full inch thick in diameter. *It wasn't so long ago I could bend this metal like a noodle. When I was at full strength, at least.* He tugged on the metal. The bars were vertical and horizontal, making one solid piece, more like a gate than a door. He touched the inside of one of the bars' angles. *Am I not the Master of the Inanimate? I can do this by myself.* He channeled his energy. He envisioned the metal coming to life, spreading apart. There was a discernible creak of metal. The bar in his grip bent the slightest bit.

Moth came alive. On his feet, the big barbarian stepped across the cell. He grabbed the bars with savage intensity. An animal-like *hurk* sound erupted from his lips.

Finster funneled more energy into the metal, spreading it out, attacking the angles. Veins popped up at his temples. His mind pulled at the bars.

The hardened metal began to bend. The barbarian's great efforts doubled. He let out a guttural cry. Freedom lay just beyond the threshold. The bars peeled back. The metal ripped open like webbing. Moth's arms and Finster's mind spread the steel wide open.

"We did it!" Finster said with a gasp. He dashed the sweat from his brow. The gap in the cell door looked like a mouth of busted metal teeth. Before he could say another word, Moth squeezed through it.

The sharp metal drew blood. Finster teetered through on wobbly knees. The jagged steel snagged and tore his robes. "Slow down. I need my breath, Moth. Most men don't have the endurance of a spawning salmon."

With the grace of a prowling cat, Moth slunk by the other cells toward the door that led outside the dungeon. It was thick, made of iron and wood. He gave the iron handle a fierce tug, and it came off.

Finster wedged himself between the door and the hairless man. "Listen to me. The guards will come. Then we strike." He smacked his fist into his hand. "Wait for it, Moth."

Moth pushed him aside.

A voice called out from one of the cells deeper within. "Is that you, Finster?" Moth turned along with Finster. "It is I, Gregory the Grand." Jutting out of a distant cell, an arm—without a hand—waved.

Finster knew the voice. He angled for a better look and saw Gregory's dopey face pressed to the bars. "Gregory, why wait to reveal yourself now? I can only assume you are a spy, Gregory the Guileful."

"I saw no reason to strike up a conversation with the damned. Har! But you, Finster, have fooled death again." He stuck the handless arm farther out. "She took my hands. I was loyal, and she took my hands and tossed me in this cell."

"Yes, well, as I recall, you weren't very good with your hands to begin with. Or anything else, for that matter. Perhaps it is a good thing."

"Finster! I was a fine member of the order. Let me help. I know things."

"I'm busy at the moment, Gregory. Please keep silent. I'm thinking. I don't need your useless thoughts clouding my serenity."

Moth swiveled toward the door. He bent at the knees. Footsteps and the jangle of metal could be heard on the other side of the entrance. The guards had come.

Chapter 12

Together, Moth and Finster stepped to the side of the hinges. The lock popped. The door swung open. Two soldiers, one carrying a tray of food and the other a spear, marched inside.

Moth pounced. The barbarian locked the men up in the crooks of his massive arms and lifted them off the ground. The food tray clattered on the stone floor. Eyes bulging and legs kicking, their necks gave two notable *cracks*. Moth dropped the broken guards like two bundles of rotting fruit.

Finster quickly huddled over them. He grabbed a ring of keys and fished through them one at a time. "Leg iron? No! Leg iron? No! Leg iron? No! Every key but the leg irons. I hate that Crawley."

Gregory's hollow laughter echoed. "You wouldn't have that problem if your feet were cut off like my hands."

"I'm busy, Gregory. Go and imagine you're a great wizard or some other absurd impossibility."

"You always were more arrogant than most," Gregory said.

"And that's why I'm out here and you're in there, idiot." He handed Moth the spear. "We must go."

Led by Moth, they hustled out of the door.

"No, barbarian, come with me! I know the way."

Moth was unrelenting in his path. Finster had no choice but to keep up with him. Shuffling as fast as he could, he said, "Moth, will you listen? I know the way out. The way you're going is certain doom."

Moth slid into the next hallway. They ran smack-dab into an unsuspecting guard, dressed in chain mail and studded leather, who caught the dungeon-door handle in his face. He crumpled beneath the blow. One-handed, Moth jabbed the man repeatedly with the spear. The guard died from blunt-force trauma.

Finster looked at the mangled man then at Moth. The blunt end of the spear was bloody. "You're supposed to use the pointed end of the spear, not the butt! Even I know that!" He pointed to the tip. "That end!"

The wizard citadel was a small city behind thick walls. Ancient in origin, it was a network of complicated alleys and halls, not to mention dimension doors that took a person from one place to the other. As a young man with a knack for exploration, Finster had sought out and found many of the citadel's secrets. He had used that knowledge to leave when he wasn't supposed to.

Scraping through the halls, half dragged by Moth, Finster dropped into a ball. "Listen to me, fool!"

Moth dragged him.

Finster yanked back. "You are going the wrong way. Up there, the guardians of the citadel will carve you to pieces."

Spear in hand, Moth stopped. He poked the spear tip in Finster's face.

"We are so close, Moth. So close." He pointed. "This way. I swear it. This way, and you'll breathe the fresh air of freedom."

Moth pulled the spear back.

Finster stood. "Good. You're smarter than you smell. Come along, Moth, you curious man with the brain of a child."

Ambling along at a ragged gait with a giant-barbarian shadow behind him, Finster traversed the mind-bending catacombs of the citadel. Typically, the students, soldiers, servants, and guardians roamed the main sanctum of the inner city above, leaving the stark hallways of the sublevels, damp in dew and moss, empty.

Finster slipped into a narrow pass Moth could barely squeeze his shoulders through. It emptied into a chamber, small and discreet. A damp woven carpet covered the floor. This was the study chamber named after Constance the Chameleon, a high-ranking teacher who had taken a shine to Finster.

Moth became uneasy. He paced back and forth in the cramped room.

"A moment." Finster muttered a quiet incantation. The stones that made up the wall, stacked up like tiles, shuffled, moved, and spread apart. A dark tunnel waited. "This way."

Finster appeared inside the mouth of a cave a few miles from the Red Citadel. Moth appeared uneasy. Finster wasn't going to spend the time explaining to him that they'd just transported themselves through time and space. "Moth, we need to get these shackles off. What we should use for that is not far from here. We need to take advantage of our head start. No doubt, Crawley and his band of illiterate misfits will be coming. No offense."

Down the hillside they went with the sun setting over the mountains. A small town at the base of the craggy hills greeted them warily. Doors and shutters were closed. Women and children scurried out of sight. Holding a length of chain in his hand, Finster walked into a barn where a strapping young man wearing a blacksmith's apron was shoeing a horse. He fell off his stool when he saw Moth.

"Listen, boy, would you be so kind as to bust these shackles from our ankles? I have a special affair to attend to, but it's exclusive. I need to rid myself of this hairless ape."

Stammering, the young man said, “You look like criminals. Did you escape from the citadel? To help you would be my death.”

“Pfft! Escape from the citadel? Really, farm boy. Have you ever known anyone to escape from the citadel?”

“Well, no.”

“Good. Now, bust these irons off.”

The young farmer gave the shackles a glance. “That’s no ordinary steel. I can’t break that.”

“I bet you can. I imagine this steel alone is worth years of your labor. You might be able to purchase the finest cows to show the local maidens.”

“I-I can’t.”

Moth snatched the hammer from the farm boy. He dragged Finster over to an anvil and straddled the chain with it. He pounded the metal with the hammer in thunderous blows. Sparks flew.

The metal heated in a chain reaction. Finster could feel it in his ankle.

With awesome force, Moth beat the link in the chain until it heated up red. “That’s it, Moth. Keep hitting!”

“He’s not going to break that,” the young man said. “I’ve never seen links so thick.”

Bang! Bang! Bang!

The weld in the chain link gave in to the force of muscle and hammer.

Finster poked the boy in the chest. “It’s a good thing you didn’t put a wager on that. Now, scrape me up something to eat. Quickly!”

The young farmer dashed away.

Finster studied the shackle on his leg. It was nagging, but he still had freedom. He locked eyes on the sullen-eyed barbarian. “Moth, go. Be free. Go and spawn with whatever two-legged heifer will have you. I’m sure the women will swoon at your return. Bring a new litter of savages into the realm. Just raise them far, far away. There won't be much left of this part of the world if I don't save it."

The horse the young man was shoeing whinnied.

"Hmm. I believe I do have a faster means of transportation," Finster said to himself. "Ah, the beast is saddled. Even better." He mounted the horse. "Good-bye, Moth. May the light of day never knit our shadows together again." He dug his sandals into the horse, rode out of the barn, and jumped a length of fence on the way out. "I may not be able to saddle them, but I can ride them."

Finster took a glance back at the barn. Moth was gone. *Founder's Stone, I'm coming.*

Chapter 13

Crawley entered the throne room. He took a knee at the bottom of the steps.

Sitting on the throne, Ingrid said, "Yes, Crawley."

"I have unpleasant news. Finster and the barbarian escaped. A handful of guards are dead."

"So soon," she said with a playful look in her eyes. "Impressive."

"You anticipated this?"

"It was a gamble, yes, but I felt Finster could pull off the feat. He's much more formidable than you think. Don't let his shabby appearance fool you. Though I'm curious to know how he pulled it off."

"Gregory reported that the barbarian ripped the scarab from his back. It restored his powers, or some of them." He stood up. "It won't take my riders long to catch them. Shall I bring them back?"

Ingrid rose from her seat. "No. We will follow them, but not too closely."

"We? You're coming? I beg your pardon, but why?"

"Because he will lead me to the artifact. The Founder's Stone. Not only do I want it—I need it."

"I thought you weren't certain that it existed?"

The servant girl draped a dark, fur-lined cloak over Ingrid's shoulders. "We'll know soon enough," Ingrid said.

"And if it does exist? Won't Finster use it?"

"If he could, I believe he would have. Either way, Finster dies." Ingrid strolled out of the room with the citadel guardians behind her. "It will be a joy killing him. Then, with the Founder's Stone, the kingdoms will be mine."

Chapter 14

Coughing and hacking, with a steady rain chilling him to the bone, Finster ambled through a village. He'd just talked a man out of a shovel by giving him advice on how to increase his crops. He mounted his horse and rode hunched over at a trot a few more miserable leagues. He stopped at a rocky area where the sun sank between two high sets of hills. "One can only hope it is still here."

He dismounted and, using the shovel for a cane, traversed the closest hill. Then he slipped, cracking his knee on stone. Dark spots blurred his vision. *What would life be without pain? Yes, delightful.* Nearing the top, he wandered around a bit. Several large stones were scattered over the soil. Tall grasses and daisies sprouted up between the rocks. The terrain was overgrown but natural. *It's hard to make it out with all of these plants.*

He pushed foliage aside. Stepping from one rock to another, he spied a rose bush with small purple blossoms beginning to bud. *Ah, the only plant I ever planted.* There, among the small green leaves and thorns, was a triangular stone. He beat the rose bush back with the shovel. The thorns scratched his hands and made them bleed. He labored through it, sickly and panting.

Years before, Finster had abandoned the order to go on a personal quest. He'd sought the Founder's Stone. He'd done an agonizing, harrowing search only to one day find the stone almost by accident. His venture had led him to a small keep where three streams met. The building was abandoned and overgrown. He crept into its walls, seeking shelter, and encountered a dangerous lich, which he battled to the point of death and won. The lich, a female, turned human and, in her last dying breath, thanked him. She pointed to a wall and said, "Fate."

Finster searched the wall and found a concealed chamber behind the stone. A small treasure lay within—a golden ring, like a crown for a child, with a gemstone in it. Also, a stone lay hidden in a simple traveler's pouch. It was smooth and opaque. It came to life with smoky energy the moment he touched it. He knew instantly what it was: the Founder's Stone.

All of the power he'd ever wanted was in his hands. But there was a problem. Despite Finster's efforts, he hadn't been able to tap into the stone's mystic forces. A lesson learned long ago from his teacher, Constance the Chameleon, had haunted his mind: *It takes power to control power.*

Finster wedged the shovel underneath the triangular rock, and with a grunt, he tried to pry it up. It didn't budge. Wheezing, he dug around the edges. *I've got a hole in my back and soon will have calluses on my fingers. Disgraceful. Before long, I'll probably start eating my nails.* He dug one small shovelful at a time, making little progress. He slung the shovel to the ground and sat. *So close. Now I'm too weak to move a bloody stone. I can't let her win like this. Perhaps I should let this be buried and run as long and far as I can. Let someone else stop her. Maybe I'll die of old age before she finds me.*

Shivering, he cradled his shoulders. The wind picked up. The rain stung his face. He needed time and shelter. There was neither to be found. Ingrid and Crawley would be coming right after him. By his assessment, he had maybe half a day on them at most. They'd come. They'd bring many. He'd need the stone in order to make one last stand. The scary thought was that he didn't have the power to control it, but Ingrid, now a tenth of the order and wielder of many rings of power, certainly would.

I can't let her have it. With my dying breath, I won't let her have it! The stone is mine! I'll have it!

Without looking, Finster reached for the shovel and found a huge bare foot. He lurched back. "Gaaaah!"

Moth stood like a statue. His heavy gaze searched Finster's face.

"What are you doing here?" Finster said, summoning his strength to stand. "Lords of Creeping! Did you run all this way? I don't see a horse."

Moth lifted his chin, eyes spying the landscape Finster had left behind. A trail of ant-like figures wended their way over the tops of the distant ridges.

"They are close, but taking their time." He grabbed the shovel and began digging again. "I'm not sure why you are here, but if you aren't going to help, then get out of the way."

Moth nudged Finster aside. He bent over, grabbed the rock, and ripped it out of the ground then sent the stone bouncing down the hill.

"I'm not paying you for that." Finster pulled a worm from the damp soil. "Well, you're welcome to this." He shoveled down another foot, slinging the soft dirt aside, and dug a silk pouch out of the grime. Then he slapped the grit from the sack. He could feel the stone inside. Finster opened the neck of the pouch. The stone fell out. It was a dull pearl in the fading light. "It doesn't look like much, but it is everything… I swear it."

Moth moved down the hillside. The spade he held looked like a child's toy. His eyes were fixed on the coming army. Over fifty riders were on their way.

With the stone locked in his palm, Finster's body began to warm.

His vitality returned. The magic in the stone flowed into him, but only a trickle of its omnipotent power. He squeezed it in his hand and tried to gather more power. *I suppose I should be thankful for what I have.*

He made his way alongside Moth. "Do you plan to fight them? Is there a grudge of some sort? You're going to need a bigger shovel, one that looks more like a sword."

With the ease of a great cat, Moth headed down the hill and stood by Finster's horse. The mount looked too small for him.

Finster climbed into the saddle. Without taking the reins, Moth led the horse away from the hill, toward the forest flush with thickets and briars. Finster had no idea why he let the barbarian lead, but he was fairly certain self-preservation had something to do with it. In the meantime, he cupped the stone in his hands and concentrated. Aside from the additional warmth and vitality, there was nothing. He spoke in every ancient language he'd learned, using commonly understood salutations. Nothing. *Gah!* He hauled back to throw the stone. *In these thickets, that would be stupid.*

Moth pointed at an overhang among the thickets. He gestured with his chin toward the opening.

"You want me to go in there? For what purpose?"

Moth slapped the horse on the flank. The beast reared up and tore through the thickets.

"Why did you do that?"

Shovel in hand, Moth vanished into the forest, leaving Finster all to himself.

"Never trust a barbarian."

Chapter 15

Crawley lined up his soldiers at the rim of the forest Finster and Moth had entered. "Get those torches lit," he said, leaning over the saddle horn. "It shouldn't be too difficult to fish him out of there, but be wary. If you see him, give a signal. He's a magus. Dangerous."

Finster's horse burst out of the thickets, startling the other horses. Crawley's horse remained still. One of his men led Finster's horse back to their group by the reins. The beast had briar gashes all over its body.

"Get the axes out, Arly. Go on foot. It's too dark and nasty in there for the beasts. Cut us a path wide enough to run a wagon through if need be." He pulled his leather gloves over his fingers. "Send our scouts in first. I don't see any reason why we can't sneak up on the old man."

A dozen soldiers silently slid into the forest. Another dozen began hacking through the brush.

Crawley looked behind him. Nestled with their backs to the hills a hundred yards away, Ingrid waited with the citadel guardians. *If she wants Finster so bad, she should send her own men in there.*

Under torchlight, the soldiers began chopping through the woodland thickets. Saplings went down by the dozens. The laboring men were an hour into it when the torchlight vanished among leaves. Silence fell over the forest. A large object smashed through the branches. It landed with a thud at Crawley's feet.

He leaned over his saddle and peered down. It was Arly's head. His face looked like it had been bashed in with a shovel. The neck was cut in a crude fashion. Another head crashed through the branches, followed by yet another. Crawley's men's eyes became bigger than saucers. Another head landed at their jumpy feet. It was mounted on the torch stick.

"Ryant!" Crawley called out. A burly man with wild hair and a beard, wearing a shirt of chain, stepped out of the ranks. "You've been promoted. Take a dozen men, stay close together, and get in there. If anything moves that's not one of us, swing."

Hunkered in the bush, Moth waited. A soldier crept among the trees. The man's eyes zeroed in on Moth's position. Sword in hand, the soldier hustled right toward him. Moth popped up. He jabbed the top of the shovel into the man's throat. The man dropped like a blood-slick stone. A quick second stroke severed the head. He carried the dripping head along with the shovel slung over his shoulder. His keen eyes picked up every unnatural sound.

The soldiers' breathing was loud. Their sweat gave them away. The soft scuffle of metal didn't help their mission. They weren't one with the land. They smelled of the vile city. Moth perched among the boulders, eyeballing a knot of men coming right at him as one. He greeted the first one by hurling the skull into the man's face.

In the darkness, the fighters didn't stand a chance against the savage giant. Moth smashed a scout in the head so hard the neck of the shovel snapped. His fist shattered a man's jaw. His foot crushed one man's chest. He snatched up one man and tossed him on top of two others. They chased, screamed, and stabbed. He filled his hands with their steel and killed, killed, and killed again. They fled with blood covering their frightened faces.

"It's a demon." Ryant carried a limping man with him. Only three of the twelve that had gone in came out again. The chopping of wood and brush had also fallen silent. "I swear it, Crawley! It strikes with the silence of a snake."

Crawley unsheathed his sword. It was a well-crafted and heavy thing. The edge appeared sharp enough to split a hair. "It's not a demon, Ryant. Those wounds come from mortal metal. Do you hear? Now, get over here!"

Ryant approached with his chin sunk into his chest.

Crawley split his skull. "The only thing in that forest is a man or two," he said to the rest of the soldiers. "You can face them, or you can face me!"

"Is there a problem, Commander Crawley?" Ingrid stood on the other side of where he was talking. Her icy stare was fixed on the dark entrance to the forest. She was flanked by two of her guards.

"No, the men are just spooked is all. I believe that savage is in there. It's not a problem, I assure you."

"That doesn't sound very reassuring." She stood in the wind and rain with the expression of an irritated goddess. She rolled her fingers. "He's in there. I can sense it. Not alone, either."

"It must be the barbarian, then. A strange alliance. We caught him once. We will catch him again, or kill him, even if I have to do it myself."

"Make it quick, Crawley. I'd hate to get my hands dirty over a simple matter like this."

"Certainly. Save your energy. I'll take care of it."

"I'm waiting," she said with a puckered brow.

Crawley dismounted. It was either go into the forest or piss off a woman who could turn him into dust. He grabbed a torch from a soldier. "Get those axes, and follow me." He led another large group of men down the path they'd cut out already. At the end, five men lay dead in their own blood and guts. "You two, get to work. I'll keep an eye on things." He peered into the blackness. There was little he could do with all of the chopping and the torches ruining his night vision. He waited for the barbarian to strike.

A large stone flew out of nowhere and crushed a man's skull. A second man was yanked back by a vine. His desperate gurgles ended in the blackness.

"Stand your ground!" Crawley ordered. "Keep chopping!" He ducked. A stone whistled over his head and clacked into a tree. "Aw, the hell with this." He made a sharp whistle and hollered back down the path. "Turn loose the wolves! Let them dine on barbarians tonight."

Huge, slavering dogs, five in all, flew down the channel. They were Crawley's special breed, part wolf and part bloodhound. The last thing he wanted to do was put them in harm's way, but in the end, that was what they were bred for. The wolfhounds flew right by him, barking and howling, and vanished into the forest. "Follow those dogs!"

Chapter 16

Finster sat up. The occasional rustle had caught his ear, but now he heard dogs. He rubbed the Founder's Stone between his thumb and finger. "I don't know what it takes to ignite you, but if you indeed have a purpose, now would be the time to reveal it."

Something frigid hung in the air. Ingrid was close. Her power alone disturbed the natural order. A magus could sense such things. *It's only a matter of time now. The end of my journey.* He considered burying the stone and lying about it, but by that point, she surely would have come across the area he'd retrieved it from. *She knows. She wouldn't be here if she didn't. I suspect she wanted me to escape all along. The clever witch bested me. Curse my lusty eyes.*

In the darkness, he searched for answers to how to use the stone. He'd spent years trying to master it with no luck. He was only given a taste of what the stone offered. It was Constance who'd mentioned the stone to him, and her mentor to her, and so on. Once, she'd said, "Extraordinary things work in unconventional ways. Even the cursed can aid you."

"I suppose I could swallow it. Perhaps it would eat me from the inside out. I'd hate to give Ingrid the satisfaction of getting it."

The barking grew louder.

Finster scooted farther into his nook. Something rubbed against his thigh. He reached into his robes and retrieved the jade scarab. *Why not?* He spewed out a fierce incantation. The beetle's wings unfolded, revealing a dark-green crystal within that was the power source of his insidious creation. He replaced the crystal with the Founder's Stone. The wings closed tight. The beetle pulsed in his hand. *For the kingdom, I suppose.* He attached the beetle to his back. Its claws dug in. Finster's back arched. His forehead creased. Unbridled pain coursed through him. He bit his tongue instead of screaming.

Moth brained the first two wolfhounds with a woodsman's axe. He drew a yelp from the third when he gave it a swift kick in the ribs. The other two ravenous dogs latched onto his forearms. The one he'd kicked jumped on his chest and bit his neck. Moth bear-hugged it. He bit the beast back. At the same time, he crushed the crying dog. Its neck snapped. Wild-eyed, he fought to shake the dogs off his arms. Their slavering jaws were locked. Moth butted skulls with the one on his axe arm until it fell away.

Crawley and his men emerged from the grim forest. Brow furrowed, Crawley said, "You killed my dogs! You animal! I'll make you pay!"

Moth managed to cock the hatchet back and release a clumsy swing.

Crawley's sharp steel sliced Moth's hand off at the middle of the forearm. Blood spewed from the sharp bone and meaty stump. "I ought to carve you to pieces myself! I'll let the dogs have their revenge first! They'll devour you bit by bit!"

The dogs forced Moth back into a tree.

Crawley inched forward. "I'm going to enjoy watching you bleed to death. You live like a savage, and you'll die like one too." He spit on Moth.

In a wink, Moth struck Crawley in the neck with the sharp bone protruding from his stump. The man's eyes popped. His mouth gurgled. Moth jabbed Crawley again and again. He gouged holes in the stunned man's neck and eyes. The commander hit his knees. Blood oozed down his face and neck. He teetered and died, pumping the last of his life's blood onto the forest floor.

Moth bashed the dog that was still on his arm into a tree until its skull cracked. He slung it off, grabbed the other wolf by the nape, and eyed it. The dog whimpered. It slunk off the moment he dropped it. He picked up the torch and stuck his stump in the flame. His jaws clenched. Flesh burned. The stump cauterized, and the blood flow stopped. Bathed in sweat, Moth swayed. He set his broad back against the tree. His bloody chest was heaving.

The soldiers who'd fled returned minutes later. They snaked through the brush. This time, they came with spears. Moth leaned down and scooped up Crawley's sword. Ten soldiers had him surrounded.

Then something clanked through the forest that caught everyone's attention. A manlike form waded into the ring of warriors. The figure had spears for legs and a spine. The head was a pair of axes. The arms were swords. It moved with unnatural bends but with a determined purpose. The animated warrior made from wood and steel attacked.

The soldiers, jabbing spears, hit the mark in glancing blows. The magic automaton mowed them down with devastating sword strokes. The blades pierced chests and gouged throats with uncanny precision. The axe-blade head of the metal stickman split a skull with a head butt. The blades twirled. Bowels were spilled. Limbs were lost. Necks were detached from shoulders. Droplets of blood kissed the leaves like rain. After minutes of battling side by side with Moth, every soldier who'd entered the willowwacks lay dead.

Finster strolled through the brush. The whites of his eyes had the glow of the moon. He eyed the handiwork of his creation. He said to Moth, "There is a reason they call me Master of the Inanimate." With a wave of his hand, the steel soldier collapsed.

Finster's eyes found Crawley. "Ah, a pity. I was so hoping to kill him myself. Well done, Moth. For a barbarian, that is." With a twist of his fingers, the shackles fell away from his and Moth's ankles.

Moth picked up his hand and walked away.

In a mystically enhanced voice, Finster said, "Ingrid, I'm coming for you." The birds scattered from the trees. He followed Moth. With every step he took, his toes barely touched the ground.

Chapter 17

Outside of the forest, many horses remained. What was left of Crawley's men had joined forces with the citadel guardians. Finster's eyes narrowed. Ingrid and her troops galloped away. "What a pity. I thought Ingrid would remain to offer me some congratulations." His eyes slid over to Moth. The barbarian was gashed up and bloody. The charred stump of an arm was ghastly. Finster's stomach churned a little. "You really must have a larger grudge against her than I do."

Moth stuck his hand in a saddlebag and his foot into the stirrup of a dapple-gray horse. One armed, he swung himself up into the saddle. The huge man was oversized for the beast.

"What? No more running today?" Finster mounted a horse. He sat tall in the saddle, shoulders back, like a proud general prepared to lead his troops into battle. He had control of the Founder's Stone. Its boundless energy surged through him. Every arcane practice he'd ever mastered was enhanced. *This must be how Ingrid feels. Invincible. I delight in it.*

He pondered his future. He had mastered the stone. That had been his dream. But even with the artifact in his possession, Ingrid still had power that rivaled his. The eight rings combined to make a powerful artifact. Even though Finster had the stone, she was certainly a match for him—perhaps more so. He didn't know. *Perhaps I should warn the King of Mendes of her treachery. Most likely, the buffoon will take her word over mine. Men are so easily seduced by the ladies. Hmmmm. Perhaps I should stay out of this altogether and just enjoy my abilities for now, but for the sake of the order, I must finish this. I hate my conscience.*

Moth urged his horse forward. Hooves splashed in the mud.

"Why don't you take these horses and return to your lands?" Finster asked. "For the life of me, I don't see what your stake in this is."

The barbarian rode on, silent, his broad shoulders slightly sagging forward. He looked like he'd been regurgitated from the jaws of a devourer. The bite marks alone were more than enough to kill a man. He bled, but slowly. The fire in his eyes seemed to keep him going.

The horses moved through the night at a steady walk. There was no need to chase after Ingrid. She wasn't going anywhere. She'd be waiting. Finster and Moth didn't stop until later the next day. The Red Citadel loomed in the distance. Plumes of smoke snaked out of the granite building's smokestacks. The smell of burning flesh hung in the air.

Finster's fingertips tingled.

"I don't know if you'll be open to it, but I plan to enter the same way I left. I just don't find it very likely that she'll let us through the front door. What do you say, half-dead? Oh, never mind. You'll probably have more to say in the grave. Looking forward to it."

They returned to the cave they'd departed from. Moth lumbered into the portal with a face devoid of expression. It led them right back to the study room of Constance the Chameleon. From there, they slunk into the empty hallways of the underground level and headed up the stairs. They made it into the great hallway that led to the throne room. The citadel guardians, spears in hand, waited. A score of them shielded the door. The metal-masked men gave cold, unresponsive looks.

Finster stepped out into the middle of the hallway. He approached a few dozen yards from the stairs that led up to the throne-room door. "Citadel guardians, move aside. I would have words with Ingrid."

The warriors lowered their spears.

Finster's chin dipped. Power flickered in his eyes. "Peril comes to those that don't heed nature's warning."

The guardians advanced down the steps.

Suddenly, the spears writhed in the guardians' hands. The wooden shafts coiled up, and the spearheads bent back like snakes. The animated weapons struck out at the guardians, piercing flesh and bone.

Moth crossed the distance between him and the guardians in gigantic strides. He met them on the steps. A full head taller and far thicker in sinew, he cut into the ranks. The first blow of his steel cut a man from the clavicle to the belly. The second strike sheared a masked head from its shoulders. The snake spears struck out at the men who held them. Chests were punctured.

Moth painted the stairs with guardian blood. The wild-eyed butcher split a metal mask right between the eyes. The heavy steel blade cut to the chin. He yanked it free and attacked again.

The guardians abandoned their spears. They whisked their swords out of their scabbards and circled Moth. In unison, they jabbed and cut at any piece of the wild-eyed barbarian they could find. Steel bit into the meat of Moth's thigh. Moth gored a guardian's chest.

Finster added another tactic. Fingers spread wide, he made a squeezing motion. The metal masks began crushing the skulls they protected. Finster's clawed fingers clenched harder. The citadel guardians dropped their swords. Steel clattered on stone. Hands tore at masks. The guardians screamed.

Like a butcher in a meat shop, Moth executed them one after the other. Within seconds, all of the citizen guardians were dead. Sticky blood oozed down the steps leading up to the door.

Finster pulled his tattered robes up above his ankles. He tiptoed up the stairs. His feet slipped on the blood. “I’m going to need some new sandals after this. These are ruined.” He stood directly in front of the door. The glowing eye waited at the top of the doors. He called up to it. “Did you see that, Ingrid? That was just a sample of my power. Child’s play. I suggest you surrender.” He tried the words that had once opened the doors. Nothing happened. “I see you changed the password. I probably would have done the same thing.”

The eye lowered. The pupil moved back and forth between Finster and Moth. It rose up to the top of the door and vanished. There was a long, awkward moment. The sound of dripping accompanied it.

“Humph. I don’t think she is going to let us in.” Finster rapped on the door. It made a hollow sound. “Ingrid, there is only one way in and one way out. How do you suppose you’ll marry Rolem the Grand if you’re hiding in there? Come out, or let me come in. Perhaps we can come to an arrangement.”

He looked at Moth. The man stared at the door, chin out, bleeding badly from many places. Pus festered from a bite mark on his shoulder.

“Those wounds don’t look so good. You might want to have that looked at once this is over. I used to make a wonderful concoction for it called—”

The sealed seam in the massive doors split. Silent as shadows, the doors swung inward.

Finster smiled. “How about that drink?”

Chapter 18

Ingrid the Insidious sat on her throne. She was alone, splendid as ever. "I see you brought a friend." Her eyes glanced over Moth. "He suits you."

"I honestly don't know why he's here, but clearly, he doesn't like you. Ingrid, let's be civilized about this. Plenty have died today. Look at the blood. You can't get those stains out of marble. Think of your guests. Be wise. Surrender."

With her elbows resting on the arms of the throne and ringed fingers locked together, she said, "Finster, stone or no stone, I don't fear you. I, unlike many others, never did. You can't kill me. You won't kill me. There is too much compassion in your heart. Mine is absent of that."

"Yes, you have a heart of coal that beats. What a shame." He arched his brow. "Besides, I never said I'd kill you. Perhaps I'll do the same to you that you did to me—probably worse. All I can say is that if you surrender, I'm willing to be merciful."

With Crawley's sword dripping in his hand, Moth started forward.

Ingrid's hand drew back. "Call your dog off before I send his bowels to the floor."

"I don't have any more control over him than you do," Finster replied. "Believe it or not, unlike your citadel guardians—who are all dead—he has a mind of his own. A small one, but still his." His heightened intuition stretched out. There was another presence in the room. He couldn't see it. To his surprise, Moth stayed his advance, nostrils flaring. "This isn't going to end well for one of us, Ingrid. But it is going to end… unless you surrender."

"Do you remember what you told me once, Finster? You said that artifacts of magic take a great deal of time to master. You've barely had the Founder's Stone for a day." She showed him her hands. Every ring twinkled with life. "I've been acquainted with these rings for quite some time. I like my chances against a washed-out wizard who was never able to control the power that he had to begin with."

Finster knitted his brow. His chin dipped. "I promise that I'll hold your youth and inexperience against you. One last chance, Ingrid. Hand over the rings. Surrender."

She laughed. "And give them to you? Finster the Rodent of Whispers. You would end up doing things worse than even I've imagined. In the order, you were known as the master of disorder. There were reasons they forced you out."

"I wasn't forced. It was mutual, very mutual."

"No, no, it wasn't. I came to know more of you later. Your experiments were quite abominable as I recall. The people of Reenik—remember them? Reenik is now the Sleepless City because of your atrocities."

"That's a misunderstanding, and it happened a very long time ago."

"Not so long ago. You've only been banished for the last ten years. The guilt shows on your face. That fragile frame of yours bears the burden." Her index finger toyed with the armrest. "You were so handsome and dominating back then. You could have had me. After all, I wanted you. Now look at you. A shadow of yourself. Your sagging jaw complements your potbelly."

"Really? I'm feeling quite spry at the moment. I think I'll exercise my regained vitality once I'm finished with you." He placed his hands together as if praying. "Time to get on with this. Good-bye, Ingrid. You had your chance."

The throne came to life. The arms of the chair coiled around Ingrid's wrists. As she struggled against the bonds, her chest heaved. She gripped the chair's arms. Her eyes became like fire. The grand chair—ancient and priceless—peeled away from her body. She stepped away from the mangled throne. "Pathetic attempt, Finster!"

The Founder's Stone sent a warning pulse through his back. A blur, coming right at him, blocked his view of Ingrid. He took a quick step back, hands up, fingers firing radiant power. His heel caught in his robes. He stumbled. Power erupted from his fingers, striking the ceiling. A blur pounced right at him.

Sharp metal sliced through the air.

Moth sank his sword into something invisible but tangible. Cartilage and skin ripped. An invisible citadel guardian appeared, gasping his last breath.

Unseen forces came at them in a rush of soft footfalls. Steel cut into flesh. Moth counterattacked with the striking speed of a cobra. The heavy blade driven by his powerful arm found its mark time and again. Blood sprayed. Bodies fell.

Out of nowhere, a small ball of green fire blasted into Finster's chest. The only thing keeping his ribs in place and his skin from catching fire was the protection of the Founder's Stone. He casually patted out the lingering flames eating his robes. "Admirable try, Ingrid, but I'm not all about animation." His hand filled with a glaring red fire. A stream of flames shot from his hand, arching over the floor and toward her.

The fires danced and sizzled off an icy orb that shielded her body. The flames were extinguished in a hissing cloud of steam. Ingrid's platinum hair clung to her face, damp and wet. "It's good to see that you can still dance, Finster, but for how long?"

Finster flicked his fingers out. The marble tiles in the floor rippled in waves. Ingrid stumbled. The tiles piled up on her by the hundreds. She was covered in ten feet of rubble. "How long doesn't matter, so long as I can dance better than you can."

Nearby, Moth struck out and hacked into another invisible body that had appeared the moment Ingrid was buried. Two more citadel guardians became visible. He charged them. A hand's breadth from the tips of their swinging swords, he leaped high and came down hard, driving a big-boned man to the ground. He smashed the metal face of the guardian into the floor several times.

Finster turned the last guardian's sword against him, bending it around the man's neck and choking him to death. Gazing at the pile of tiles that covered Ingrid, he said, "That should do it for the witch. Now, where's that servant girl? I could use some wine."

Behind him, a sweet voice said, "Here I am."

He turned. Ingrid punched him square in the chest with all eight of her shimmering fingers.

Chapter 19

Finster sailed through time and space. He could see Ingrid and Moth. His eternal soul had separated from his body. He hit the wall on the other side of the room hard. His essence hovered over his crumpled form. He was dead, yet he wasn't. He was cold like the bottom of the layer of ice between the water and the frozen lake.

Ingrid turned her attention to Moth. The barbarian was lifted off his feet by the unseen strings of a master puppeteer. The sorcerous eyes of the woman were stars of radiant purple. Moth slung the sword at her. The blade stopped inches from her face. She shook her head. The blade turned handle over end and shot across the room like an arrow. It impaled Moth's chest. He hung in the air, chin on his chest, bleeding.

Ingrid cracked her neck from side to side and moved toward Finster. He looked between her and his motionless body sprawled out cold on the floor. Ingrid lorded over him. She was speaking, gloating maybe, but he couldn't hear a word she said. He couldn't hear anything at all. *One more chance. I just need one more chance. I won't go like this.*

She pulled down his robes, revealing the beetle lodged in his back. She touched it and let out a scream, clutching her burning hand. Without warning, Finster's essence jumped back into his body. A wave of sound hit him first. It was Ingrid cursing. Fighting the numbing pain that coursed through his body, he swept his leg underneath hers, making her fall. He pounced on top of her. Filled with the breath of life that he'd never take for granted again, he said, "I will end you!"

"You live!" she yelled in his face. "You die!"

Hands locked together, he and Ingrid wrestled over the floor in a tangle of limbs. The rings on her fingers sent deadly energy coursing through his hand, and his skin sizzled and smoked. Minds entwined with the artifacts, locking them together, ancient, fathomless powers reared their ugly heads. The will of one magus was pitted against the other. Their bodies lifted from the floor. They soared back and forth, smacking into the walls.

Finster fought back with a surge of his own energy. Tapping the stone's awesome power, he shoved back against the rings and Ingrid's will. Their arms changed from fire to ice to stone. They locked eyes while spinning through the air.

"I hate you, Finster!" she said with breath as hot as coals.

"You shouldn't hate me, Ingrid." He pushed back against her limitless strength. His mind was burning. "I'm more than just your mentor. I'm your father."

Her raging eyes softened. "What?"

One with the Founder's Stone, he turned loose everything he had from his core. The might of him and the stone blasted her wrecked body away from the rings she'd been wearing. She hit the wall and fell to the ground. Her robes were smoldering. Yellow vapors rose.

Finster sailed across the room. His body, ravaged by magic powers, began to cool. He landed in front of her, holding the rings of power. "Surprise, Ingrid. I'm not your father, but I am an old fox." He took a breath. His knees quaked. His limbs ached. He wheezed again. The powers within him drained.

Her face showed it all. Failure grew with the creases in her face. Up on her knees, she swayed. "I should have known," she said, shivering. "If anyone could stop me, you could. Perhaps I wanted that. There is an old saying in Shangley."

"Oh, really?" Finster said, panting. Hands on his knees, he glanced away, looking for Moth. Then he looked back at Ingrid. "And what might that be?"

A dagger appeared in her hand. She stabbed him in the gut. The rings fell from his fingers. "Always hide your dagger inside your enemy's belly." She scooped up the rings, closed her fist, and slugged Finster in the jaw. He skidded over the blood-smeared floor.

Ingrid rose. The hot-eyed woman's battered, nubile figure radiated with power. She glared at Finster, marched right to him, and said, "Good-bye, Finster."

A massive man rose up from behind the broken tiles.

"Good-bye yourself," Finster replied.

A spear tip burst from her chest. The purple gleam in her eyes turned cold. The rings slipped from her scorched fingertips. They tinkled on the tiles. Her body flopped sideways on the ground. Moth stood with Crawley's sword still protruding from his body then sank down to his knees.

Clutching his belly and spitting blood, Finster laughed. "You know what, Moth? You make a fine barbarian, if there ever were such a thing." Life turned cold. His vision blurred and blackened. "Too bad you're not half the barbarian that I am a sorcerer. I just wish we had the time to share a drink. Cheers, Moth. Cheers."

Chapter 20

Eyes fixed on the rings, and clutching his bleeding gut, Finster scooted. Somehow, the Founder's Stone was keeping him together. His body was a wreck. Every breath was painful. Moments before, he'd felt his life slipping away toward the cold land of death. He hung on, striving for a few more moments.

Almost there.

Moth hadn't moved. Eyes closed, his head was bent down. Blood seeped around the sword in his chest. His only set of fingers rested on the ground, twitching.

Stretching out his fingers, Finster leaned over. His fragile limbs gave way, and he fell on his side. Lances of pain streaked through his eyes. His fingers still strained for the rings. Any one of them might aid his cause. Inches from one lone ring made of black iron and decorated with rubies, he scratched at it.

Oh, let me live. A little closer. Let me live.

The Founder's Stone magnified his powers. It protected him as well, but it wasn't an object that could heal. Matched with his own stubborn will, it gave him enough strength to press on.

I won't die like this.

His fingertip touched the ring. He made a toothy smile. "Heh-

heh-heh-heh," he muttered in a deranged manner. Trembling, he clutched the ring in his hands. There was warmth. A vibrant energy.

Lucky day.

A hand the size of two of his seized his wrist. Moth plucked the ring from his grasp. He eyed it, popped it in his mouth, and swallowed it.

"You gigantic eejit! Why would you do something as insane as that?" Finster's belly wound no longer burned. The gem-studded iron ring had closed his wound. He felt like his old self again. His eyes went to the other rings. He lunged.

Moth scooped all seven rings up with one hand and swallowed them whole.

Holding his face, Finster screamed, "Noooo!"

Moth pulled the sword free of his chest. Blood pumped out a little then stopped. The gaping wound closed. The gigantic man, smeared in blood and with new scars aplenty, appeared refreshed. Sword in hand, he stood, nodded at Finster, and exited the room.

"Come back here, Moth! You can't just leave." Finster summoned a charge of power. "Don't make me rip your stomach out of your back!"

Moth trod down the blood-damp stairs.

Finster levitated a foot above the floor. He drifted after the barbarian and down over the steps of carnage. *Oh, sometimes I long for the days when I wouldn't have hesitated to kill you—or anyone, for that matter.*

Moth made his way through the citadel and down the stairs with Finster close behind him. He squeezed into the alcove of Constance the Chameleon. Finster gave a quick nod to an image of the former magus made out of shards of broken glass. Finster had made it for her. *I think she might be proud of me, wherever she may be.*

The black portal in a nook in the room led the two men to the cave far outside of the Red Citadel. The horses were still there. Moth climbed up on his dapple-gray steed.

Finster mounted his horse. "You aren't going anywhere without me. Not with those rings in your gut. They'll come out eventually. Sadly, I'll be there, but I've done worse." He gave the citadel one last look. "I should stay, but the hell with the order. Let them figure it out for themselves."

Moth sheathed his sword in a scabbard that hung on the horse. He opened a saddlebag and fished out his severed hand. Its vibrant brown skin had grayed. The cut was clean, though. He matched it up with his stump.

"You can't possibly think that will happen," Finster said.

The barbarian butted the hand against the stub a few times. Then he held it firmly against the stump for a long minute.

"Feed the birds with it, I say, Moth. Don't waste your time."

But thin tendrils of sinew grew out of Moth's stump like worms. They fastened to the hand. The hand grafted to the stump with the sickening sound of muscle, bone, and skin coming together.

"The one thing I hate about magic is it's so unpredictable." Finster shook his head. He had all the power he ever wanted, but with the rings so close, he felt incomplete.

Moth urged his horse onward. Down into the plains he went.

Finster dug his heels into his horse. The beast lurched forward. "I don't know where you are going, Moth, but until I get those rings, I will be your constant companion. Your shadow. Only death will take me away." *Your death, that is.*

The Sorcerer's Power
Part 2

Chapter 21

"Finster, Finster, Finster." The dungeon cells of the Red Citadel were abandoned save for one. Gregory sat on a wooden bed, rocking back and forth with his handless arms around his knees. His dopey eyes were fixed on the wall. Around his knees, a bulging eye as big as a man's head hung like a mirror. Its stony lid blinked like a living thing. "Show it again," Gregory said.

The eye's pupil and sea-green iris vanished, replaced by the image of something else. The mystic eyeball revealed the throne room of the Magus Supremeus.

Gregory watched the final battle between Ingrid, Finster, and Moth. It had happened days ago. Finster and the savage triumphed over Ingrid's wickedness. They killed every guardian inside the citadel, leaving Gregory abandoned. His stomach groaned. He hadn't had a scrap of food since. He tried to rub his mouth with fingers that were no longer there. He sighed. *I'll never get used to feeling them, but not having them.* He kicked the wall.

"I cannot believe that arrogant fool, Finster, fell into this! Of all wizards, why him? He should have died. I would have had a small kingdom of my own if he had." With his stump, he brushed brown locks from his eyes. "When I get out of here, I'll get what's coming to me. Finster won't see it coming."

In truth, Finster wasn't a fool. If anything, he was wise not to trust Gregory. Accusing him of being a spy was accurate. Indeed, Ingrid did cut off Gregory's hands in exchange for his life and servitude. He didn't have the ability to use his magic, but he was connected to the citadel's guardian eye. He could see anything that occurred within the walls as well as anything coming a mile outside. Ingrid told him it was a gift. It had been one he took full advantage of.

He waved off the eye. "Go. I've no use for you until the King of Mendes arrives." He stomped his foot on the floor. "I'm starving! Lead him here when he comes." He stood up. Dizziness assailed him. Groaning, he lay back on his stomach. He'd finished off the last of the water in his bucket a day ago, and there was no one left to bring him any more. Typically, the Red Citadel had numerous servants. Ingrid sent them all away or, in most cases, scared them all away.

Fully confident in her triumph, Ingrid had made arrangements for King Rolem of Mendes to visit her at the Citadel. Typically, kings would never travel to such a place. They rarely left their kingdoms, aside from going hunting or perhaps going to war if they were needed.

"She must have promised him pleasures beyond his wildest imagination." He made a hollow whistle. "I suppose I would have fallen for her wiles, too. After all, I did let her cut off my hands, but only after promising to restore them. I just have to find Finster and that barbarian." He tapped his stumps together. "Slaying him won't be easy. Not with the power he now wields. I never would have believed there was a Founder's Stone if he hadn't shown up with it." He cleared his dry throat. "But how will I kill them?" His wicked machinations came to life in his mind. He found sleep with a crooked smile hiding his teeth.

A presence stirred Gregory from a deep, drooling slumber. He sat up on the edge of his bed. The eye had returned to the wall of his cell, and there was an image in the eye—men in brightly burnished plate armor swatting at flies that lingered over the dead citadel guardians lying on the steps to the throne room. The soldiers fought to pry open the doors to the throne room, but could not.

"Heh heh." Gregory cracked a smile. "They'll be here soon enough."

It was hours before the soldiers' search led them to the dungeons. They checked all of the empty cells before coming to a stop in front of Gregory's. The rugged soldier with long blond hair and peaked eyebrows said to him, "Stay back. Stay silent." To another soldier, he said, "Fetch the king."

Gregory sat with his arms and legs crossed. No one talked, but his stomach made loud gurgling noises.

Finally, a man stepped in front of the bars. The insignia of a king was emblazoned on his shoulder. Dressed in a fine traveling cloak, the king was a tall man, slight in build, with a beard of rich chestnut mixed with red. His light eyes were soft, but his voice carried strength. "Who are you, man?"

Gregory dropped to both knees and laid his stumps on the ground. "Your majesty! My savior! I am your humble servant."

"Yes, everyone in this kingdom is. Now, stop groveling, stand, and give me your name. I won't ask it again."

Gregory rose. Eyes downcast, he said, "I am Gregory, a former practitioner of the Seventh Order of the High Mages. Now, as you can see, a prisoner."

King Rolem arched an eyebrow. "You? A magus? You don't have any hands. And even if you had hands, you don't look the part of a wizard." He slapped the chest of the blond-headed knight. "What do you think, Buckner? Is this wizard without hands what he says he is?" His voice darkened. "Or is he a liar?"

Buckner rubbed his chin. He stepped forward, inspecting Gregory head to toe with his eyes. "My king, I'm certain you don't need to be reminded I am a man of the field, not accustomed to the actions of wizards. With that said and being a person of instinct, I believe this man is not what he says he is. Might you indulge me with an example?"

"Please do," the king said.

"Your majesty, if I didn't have any hands, would you assume I was a swordsman?"

"Ah." The king toyed with his chin whiskers. "I see where you are going with this, but I would dismiss you as a swordsman. Rather, I'd make the claim that you are a lousy swordsman."

The young knight blanched. "Er… well said, sire."

"Ha! It's a jest, Buckner! Laugh. All of you laugh."

Buckner began to laugh. The other soldiers in the room laughed, too.

"What are you laughing for?" King Rolem screamed. His face reddened. "The Red Citadel is a bloodbath, and my bride is missing! You find this amusing?" He snatched a crossbow from a soldier and shot the man in the chest, piercing his breastplate. The man crumpled to the floor. Rolem handed the crossbow to Buckner. "Reload it!"

Buckner found the dead soldier's quiver, locked back the string, and loaded another bolt. Shaking, he handed it to Rolem. "It's ready, your majesty."

"Excellent." Rolem pointed the crossbow at Gregory. "You have five seconds to convince me that you are a wizard. One…"

Chapter 22

Covering his face with his arms, Gregory said in a shrill voice, "I can get you inside the throne room. I swear it! I'm the only one that can get you in."

Putting pressure on the trigger, Rolem asked, "How did you know we were trying to get into the throne room?"

Gregory swallowed. Rolem was quick. He was forcing Gregory to reveal his hand, and he didn't want to do that just yet. He didn't want to die, either. Trembling, he said, "The guardian eye. I can see through it. Look for yourself."

"I don't see this preposterous eye you are talking… oh, now that's interesting."

Peeking through his arms, Gregory saw Rolem shoulder the crossbow. He was staring right at the eye that had appeared on the wall inside his cell.

"So this is the Eye of the Citadel. Ingrid mentioned it. Gregory, please explain to me how a prisoner such as yourself has the ability to control this… thing?"

"Your majesty, I had an arrangement with Ingrid. I am her spy. I sacrificed my very hands to serve her. To serve you, my lord."

Rolem tilted his head. "I'm supposed to believe that you willingly gave up your hands to serve her? Don't take me for a fool, groveler. Be honest." He lowered the crossbow again. "Your life depends on it."

"Sire, I'm a weak man. She caught me observing her in a moment of privacy. It angered her."

"Stop lying! Ingrid was as modest as a tavern whore, Gregory. Actually, less so, but keep that between us men, Buckner," he said, half joking, to the men. "Granted, she did have the body of a goddess, and I could hardly blame the man whose eyes defiled her. Still, your tale is a lie, and I'm losing patience. The truth, now, Gregory!"

"I stole from her."

"And what did you steal?"

"A ring. It had a charming power."

Rolem started laughing. He tossed the crossbow to Buckner. "Gregory the Guile. I would say I'm pleased to meet you, but given the circumstances, I'm not. Let him out."

Gregory's jaw hung open. Finally, with awe, he asked, "Forgive me, your majesty, but do my ears fool me? Ingrid spoke of me?"

"Yes. She was very open about many things, particularly the men in the Red Citadel. I wasn't comfortable with her being surrounded by the perverts rumored to run the tower. She gave me assurances. You were an example she shared. I almost would never have believed it if I hadn't seen it for myself. Come."

They headed out of the dungeons and up the stairs to the main courtyard that led to the throne room. Gregory's mind raced as he tried to put things together. He hadn't gotten the impression that Ingrid was so intimate with Rolem. She shared more than he would have expected. And the way Rolem spoke of her with fondness and admiration alluded to the two of them relating on a deeper level. He thought of the man that Rolem had impaled with the crossbow. That had been a coldhearted act. He ran the scene through his mind once more. Standing at the door, he shivered. *The maniacs were meant for each other.*

King Rolem gazed up at the huge door made from a single slab of granite. On each side, the fire in the cauldrons carved with stone dragons still burned. In the flickering light, the arcane symbols quavered as if they were alive. Rolem asked, "Tell me, Gregory, have you seen what is on the other side?"

"I have," he replied.

"Is she… dead?"

"Yes."

Rolem took a deep breath and let it out slowly. "Open it."

"As you wish, your majesty. It will be a grisly sight."

"I don't need a warning. I'm a king. I've seen what I've conquered. Not even the smell disturbs me."

Gregory spoke out the enchanted words. The massive granite door lifted, and the stench of death hit him in the face so hard he stepped back. The soldiers covered their noses.

King Rolem waltzed inside as if it were a sunny day filled with spring air. He made his way to the throne of the Magus Supremeus. The silver-and-iron throne was now stained with blood. The mangled chair arms were pulled outward. The gems that encrusted the throne, the ones not covered in the dried red grit of battle, still twinkled. He sat on it. "A marvelous piece of craftsmanship. Certainly once worthy of Ingrid." His eyes scanned the bodies. Flesh hung from muscles. Maggots wriggled in the flesh. "Ah, there is my fallen queen."

Gregory covered his nose with his forearm. He tried to ignore the buzzing flies that landed on his face, but it was impossible. He didn't have anything to swat at them with, either. *I used to kill two flies at once with my hands. Now I can't kill any.*

Rolem laid his cloak alongside Ingrid's deteriorating body and pulled the spear from her chest. Aside from the gaping wound, she was surprisingly well preserved. Rolem scooped her up with the tenderness of a lover and set her on the cloak. As he held her cold, dead hands, tears streamed down his face. He lifted his face to the cracked, vaulted ceiling, and screamed upward in a shattered voice, "Why? By the gods, why? Two great loves are gone!" He swayed. "Grant me vengeance, lords of the skies! I will avenge her! I will kill the dogs that murdered this sweet love of mine!" He covered her body in the cloak, picked her up, and laid her in the arms of the throne.

The soldiers cast nervous looks at one another.

Gregory's own heart was racing. *He's going to kill someone. I know it.* He shuffled a half step away from the nearest soldier.

Rolem rubbed his puffy eyes and took a breath. "Whew!" He regained his composure. "Buckner, get all the dead out of here. Quickly!"

Buckner saluted. "Yes, my king!" He scrambled the soldiers. In a few minutes, they had all the dead out of the room except for Ingrid.

Gregory found himself alone in the throne room with the king. The man's soft eyes blazed with a deep and dangerous inner fire. He'd seen that same fire in Ingrid.

"Now that we have a moment, Gregory, tell me who killed my ravishing bride-to-be."

"It was a magus named Finster."

Chapter 23

"Finster. I know this name," Rolem said. "Why does it sound so familiar to me? Ingrid never mentioned him."

Approaching the throne, Gregory said, "He is a notorious merchant of death, a renegade mage with a hunger for power. The order banished him decades ago, as his work was full of treachery. Do you recall Shangley, the city that never sleeps?"

"That's where Ingrid hails from. Those people walk like the dead now, I hear. This Finster is the monster behind that?"

"He was one of *those* mages. Yes, sire."

King Rolem looked askance. "I'm to believe that Finster, a powerful mage, gored her with a spear, then? That doesn't make sense to me."

"He is the animator. Common objects are his to command. He bends wood and metal to his will."

"I see. And how can you be certain it was him?"

"A fine question. The Eye of the Citadel revealed it to me. I watched in horror, helpless to do anything about it." Gregory's fingertips tingled even though they were no longer there. He wrestled with whether he should be fully forthcoming or not. He hoped he wouldn't have to reveal the power of the eye, but Rolem was clever. His hand was forced. Almost-full disclosure was the best option.

"Finster did not operate alone, either, your majesty. There was a savage. Ingrid had Finster defeated, but the savage, a northerner, proved to be her undoing."

"You reveal vivid details."

"I can barely sleep because of it."

Standing over the throne, Rolem stroked Ingrid's platinum hair. The flies did not buzz in her presence. Her soft skin was still supple. "I was curious about the bloody footprints. I found it difficult to believe that Finster had such large feet. The size of those prints is almost inhuman—though there is a servant in my castle, Eljoy, with feet bigger than paddles. He works the wine vats day and night. Do you like making wine, Gregory? Without your hands, you'd be well suited for it."

"I was never a drinker, but I am at your disposal always, your majesty." He watched as Rolem made his way around the throne room. He traversed the broken tiles and piles of rubble with wide-eyed fascination. It was clear that Rolem had a keen eye that took in every detail. Rolem's family line was renowned for knighthood and hunting. Their bloodline was thick and deep. "May I shed light on anything, your majesty?"

From a squatting position, Rolem removed his dagger from a scabbard that was fastened to his belt. He speared a severed hand with the point of his dagger. "This was quite a battle. This savage, describe him."

"He was a hairless brute, I'd say seven feet tall, with an arm span as great as an eagle's wings. He didn't speak. A mute, I believe. He was incarcerated with Finster. They escaped."

"Ah, that explains those bars in the dungeon that were torn asunder. That is most formidable. Gregory, I feel you still aren't being very forthcoming with me. I shouldn't have to remind you that I converse daily with nothing but the kingdom's finest liars and swindlers. I hang them routinely."

Gregory swallowed. He swept his forearm over his sweating brow. "Ingrid sought after an artifact called the Founder's Stone. She believed that Finster had it. As it turns out, Finster used to be her mentor, so she had him brought in. She was the Magus Supremeus. She wanted more power. She felt she needed it."

Rolem nodded. "Continue."

"I was placed in a cell near Finster, who shared a cell with the barbarian prisoner. I was supposed to spy on Finster, gain his trust and, hopefully, discover the location of the stone. But he wasn't fooled and knew me for a spy. Finster and the barbarian escaped. Ingrid allowed it, hoping he would lead her to the stone. She and Commander Crawley pursued them, taking the Citadel Guardians as their army. She returned with the Guardians. Commander Crawley didn't. Then Finster came. He and the barbarian defeated her. It didn't seem possible, but they did."

"Why would a barbarian aid a wizard? Perhaps Finster controlled the man."

"I suppose it's possible."

Rolem held Gregory's eyes with his own. "I noticed Ingrid's rings are missing."

Sweat dripped into Gregory's eyes. He didn't know why he was so forthcoming, but something compelled him to be truthful. Unable to bridle his tongue, he revealed more than he wanted. "That savage swallowed them."

"Swallowed them? Swallowed them with his mouth?"

"Absolutely. He and Finster departed after that, heading north." He wiped his brow again. The throne room became humid and hot. "Sire, I've not eaten or drunk in days. Perhaps I could refresh myself?"

"Certainly, Gregory. You have been a great help. Buckner!" he yelled. "Bring rations."

Buckner brought in a flask of water and some dried meat and

tried to hand them to Gregory. He gave Gregory's stumps a puzzled look.

King Rolem started laughing. "Oh, that's delightful. Well, you have children, Buckner. Feed him."

"I can manage, your majesty." To Buckner, Gregory said, "If you'll hand me the flask and just set the food at my feet." He clasped the flask in his stubby arms. Buckner departed. Gregory drank deeply and gasped. "Thank you, your majesty."

"Tell me, what do you think Finster's intentions are?"

"Perhaps he wishes to have a kingdom of his own. He's a drunkard and known for being unpredictable and power hungry. There is no telling what he might do."

"With such power, he is a true threat to the kingdom of Mendes. I can't allow that. And I cannot let the murderers of my fiancée get away with it. Finster and this barbarian must be captured and made examples of. Wouldn't you agree?"

"Certainly, your majesty."

"You've been very forthcoming, Gregory." Rolem gave him a firm slap on the shoulder. "You have shared with me, and now I will share with you. Since we are alone, I'd like to have a new ear to bend in something of a confession." He began removing his leather gauntlets. "Ingrid was special to me, very special. Both of us had the same passion and a zeal for gaining more power. Yes, she was using me, and I was using her. We realized we needed one another and came to an agreement. In exchange for killing my former wife, Carlotta, I would make Ingrid my bride. I imagine she told it to you differently, if she told you at all."

Gregory lost his breath. He was floored. Ingrid had given him the impression that she killed the queen to gain Rolem's favor, but it was the other way around. *The deceit runs even deeper. But why?*

With his hand on Gregory's shoulder, he started walking him

back toward the throne. "You see, Queen Carlotta hails from the kingdom of Rayland. You are familiar with Rayland, aren't you?"

"Yes. Rayland is known to have the richest soil in the realm."

"True. They are a neighbor to Mendes and a very rich kingdom. In the not-so-distant past, we warred with Rayland, but our marriage kept the peace for a time. With Carlotta gone, and with the help of a new queen, I had hoped to expand Mendes's territory quite significantly. I was counting on Ingrid and her command of the Red Citadel to help see things through, but it seems we've hit a stumbling block. I don't like stumbling blocks, Gregory. They often prove difficult to move."

"How can I be of assistance, your majesty? I'd be honored to offer my services to hunt down Finster."

"No, that won't be necessary. You've served your purpose by lending your ear to my confession. You see, the priests in Mendes can't be trusted, and I need to get my dark ambitions off my chest. Only you and I know about them."

"I'm honored."

"Good. You will have an honorable death." King Rolem rammed his dagger through Gregory's spine. The magus gulped for air and died in seconds. "Buckner!" the king hollered. He slid his dagger out of the man's back as Buckner rushed in. Wiping the blade free of blood on Gregory's clothing, he said, "Gather five hundred of your finest. The kingdom is in peril. A new hunt begins."

"Yes, my king!"

Buckner departed. Rolem caressed Ingrid's body. His gentle fingers found their way to her exposed abdomen. A gemstone that glowed with an internal fire sat inside her pierced belly button. "You will be avenged, my sweet." He kissed her stomach. "We shall be reunited, and the realm will be ours."

Chapter 24

Slouched over the saddle horn, Finster shivered. The northern winds kissing his face came with a nasty chill. His cold fingertips clung to a flask of wine he had acquired from merchants traveling the same road but in the opposite direction. He'd finished the first bottle an hour ago and was halfway into the second. "Barbarian, will you please tell me where we are going?" he asked, slurring his words. "It's been four days, and we haven't arrived anywhere."

Ten horse lengths ahead, Moth rode a dapple-gray steed into the bitter winds. He was shirtless, but there wasn't a chill bump on his body. His pale skin rippled with muscle.

Finster drank from the flask and hollered, "Moth, would you care for a drink? I'll only offer it once, and that's an honor. After all, I'm an all-powerful wizard, willing to let you put your lips to my flask. We shall share that drink. A man and an animal. No offense. Brr! It's cold out here. One would think, with all the power at my disposal, I could stay warm, but I cannot."

Swaying in the saddle, Finster began singing a song about field mice and fireflies. From time to time, he reached behind his back to scratch where the scarab with the Founder's Stone was embedded.

The beetle's feet still dug into him. The wine dulled some of the chronic painful effects.

"Moth, I have an idea. Tonight, we will build a fire. I'll sleep with the warmth to my back while you cuddle on a bed of varmints. I only say varmints—you know, raccoons and such—because I assume the bears are hibernating." He took a swig. "Moth, do you hear me? I made a jest. An insult. I accused you of sleeping with animals. The fact that you aren't outraged leads me to believe that I'm on to something." He sneezed. "Oh, that made my head rush."

The barbarian glanced over his shoulder. His protruding brows hung over his lazy eyes like the rocky mountain ledges. He turned his horse and vanished into the thickets.

Finster wagged his finger. "I saw that. You won't lose me." He lifted his voice. "I'm a magus. I'm a ranger!" He started laughing. "Oh-ho, that made my belly hurt." His horse pushed through the thick brush. They moved higher into the hillsides. "It's not very likely that we'll find tolerable company in this bitter wilderness, but if you are taking me to a land filled with ample-breasted barbarian women, I say let's have a go at it. So long as the journey does not extend too long. Perhaps I alone can breed the savagery from your kind yet."

The journey continued the entire day. Finster lost sight of Moth an hour before sunset. He'd finished off the second flask and dropped it to the ground. Blurry-eyed, he rocked in the saddle. Head rolling from side to side, he didn't see any sign of Moth. "Where did you go, barbarian? Huh? Are you hiding? Did you find a bear's cave to cuddle in? Moth! Where are you?"

Chapter 25

Finster woke up the next morning freezing cold and with a blistering headache. Coals of a fire, hours extinguished, were about six feet from his face. He didn't remember blacking out, but he did remember one more flask of wine. Pushing off the ground, he rubbed his head and eyes. "It seems sobriety diminished my inhuman tolerance. Never again."

His horse nickered. Its reins were hung up in a bush.

"You could have left, you know," he said, rising to his feet. The campfire was surrounded by small stones, sticks, and bushes ripped from the ground. They were all tangled and twisted together. It made a wall around him three feet high. Scratching his bald head, he said, "Humph. I suppose I must have done this. Interesting." Lifting his robes, he stepped over the wall. Boulders bigger than a man were piled up in a neatly organized mound. It was over ten feet high. "I don't suppose I'm going to remember why I did that either."

The horse whinnied when he approached. He snagged the reins out of the bushes. "There, there, beast. Let's feed you." He fed the horse from a meal bag he'd acquired from the merchants. It wasn't uncommon for him to travel and take whatever he thought he might need. He opened the last flask of wine, raised the bottle up to the rising sun, and said, "To the grand dawn that precedes the dreary day of despair."

A spasm sent shockwaves through his back muscles. His teeth clenched. "Gah!" The scarab seemed to shift deeper into his body from time to time. It always burned like a candle flame an inch from his back. "I don't suppose I'll get used to that, either." He stuck his shoe in the stirrup and climbed into the saddle. "Let's go find that barbarian."

Finster had a keen sense of where Moth was. The Founder's Stone gave him a sixth sense for magic. He could practically smell and taste the raw power emanating from the rings Moth had swallowed. The scent was strong. He hoped, at some point, Moth would crap out the rings. Finster had sifted through worse than barbarian slat for treasures worth far less.

Taking the cold air into his lungs, he sighed. "What to do? What to do? What is the most powerful magus to do?"

The horse trotted higher into the sparse woodland. Finster resumed talking to himself.

"On the one hand, I could leave the barbarian be. The rings would be lost forever, perhaps. After all, a savage would not know how to use such things. They don't trust magic. They will destroy it." He shifted in his saddle. "However, I can't let those rings fall into the wrong hands. These savages have witch doctors. No, I believe what is best for the realm is that the rings stay in my possession. Perhaps I'll redistribute them. I'll reorganize the order of the Red Citadel. Certainly, that would bring decades of peace that would last for generations to come."

He drank some wine.

"I would be the perfect Magus Supremeus, wouldn't I?"

The horse flapped its ears.

"Oh, what do you know?"

The horse snorted.

"Yes, I realize that I should be satisfied with the power that I have, but I am not. You don't understand. I'm protecting the realm. I'm doing it for them. Not for me. Besides, I just want to exercise a little with their power. That feeling you get when you place a magic ring on your finger… there is nothing like it. The finest wines, supple women scented with erotic perfumes—even they don't compare. Of course, you are a beast, and you don't understand such things. No offense."

He moved deeper into the hills. Snow dusted the tops of the pine trees that swayed in the wind. Near the top of the hill, the scarab pulsed. Grinding his teeth, Finster pulled his shoulders back. "We are close."

The hill crested at a bald landing with a steep overlook. Moth's horse stood alone. The barbarian was sitting on the ledge. He didn't move when Finster approached.

The magus dismounted. There was a valley of trees hundreds of feet below. Small huts were thatched together in the clearing. Finster sat beside Moth, letting his feet hang over the rim. The barbarian's broadsword, the one he'd taken from Crawley, rested in his lap.

Kicking his legs, Finster said, "I hope you came up here for the view of this savage land."

Moth sat mute, unblinking. It was as if his sullen eyes were frozen open.

"Either you've come this far to meditate or to jump. I suggest you jump. I don't think you'll survive the fall. I'll bet you a bottle of wine—no, a herd of sheep. You could feed your village or start a harem."

Moth's eyes remained fixed on the village below. There were dozens of small huts. People moved about, carrying tools and laboring in one plan or another. Their movements were very stiff and distinct, their limbs unnatural and rigid.

Goose bumps rose on Finster's arms. He squinted and noticed

white paint on the naked bodies of the men and women. Their eyes were black circles. "Those are Wargoth!" Finster said, exasperated. "You fool! Why would you lead us into their midst?" He stood up and backed away from the ledge. He slowly spun around. "If they sniff us out, they'll flay us, cook us, and eat us!"

Farther down the mountain, a dry branch snapped. The horses whinnied.

Moth jumped to his feet. Out of nowhere, a huge, hairy beast rushed out of the woods and attacked Finster's horse.

Chapter 26

A razor-backed grizzly bear, with a head bigger than two men, bit down on the neck of Finster's horse. The bear drove the horse to the ground.

"Do something, Moth!" Finster commanded. He moved forward, fingers flickering in the air as he summoned his power. He could control most anything that wasn't living. Nature was more of a weakness. Aside from being able to lift stones, there was little else he could do. Under his power, a rock the size of his fist lifted from the ground. Using his mind, he flicked it at the grizzly. The rock smacked hard into the bear's head. It rose up to its full eight feet in height and roared.

Finster gestured, lifting another stone, but Moth shoved his hands down and gave Finster a fierce look that would crack a lesser man's spirit. Finster let the stone fall. The bear dropped back onto all fours. Sinking its massive jaws into the dead horse, it dragged the animal over the hill.

"That was my horse! Not yours!" Finster said. He ran across the top of the hill and found a wine flask shattered on the ground. "And my last flask. Filthy maidens! From here on out, I'm riding your horse, and you are walking."

Moth's attention was back over the ledge.

Finster ran over and took a look. Wargoths scrambled up the hillside. It was a steep climb. It would take time, but the ghoulish men were undeterred. They were bred in the wild terrain. It would slow them little.

"I can only assume you have a vendetta against these fiends. Otherwise, why would you be here?" Finster asked. He started to pace. "Did they devour your herds? Steal your unruly children? It would be best to ride back down the hill and as far away from them as possible." He took another peek over the rim. "Kings of Pain! They move fast!" He looked to Moth. "You aren't going anywhere, are you?"

Moth thumbed the edge of his sword. The muscles in his tremendous body flexed like an animal's. His nostrils flared. The fire behind his dull eyes ignited.

"The Wargoth's touch paralyzes, I'm told. You don't have a stitch of armor on. They'll end you. They'll end me, too." He stepped in front of the barbarian. "Be reasonable. Ride out of here. Whatever your need is, we shall figure it out."

Moth peeked over the rim.

Finster climbed onto the dapple-gray horse. "It's not too late. We can ride south, find a tavern, be neck-deep in perfumed wenches by nightfall. Come now, Moth. Give me a chance to civilize you."

The towering barbarian stood his ground.

Finster sighed. *Why not let the man die? Perhaps I can come back and acquire the rings later.* Even with the Founder's Stone's boundless power, he had no desire to wage war against anything out of his comfort zone. The Wargoths were many. It created uncertainties. There was risk.

It would be different if he had the rings. They would grant him another level of power, both offensive and defensive. He clenched his fist. *Finster, why do you hold back? Just rip the rings from the savage's stomach. You'll be doing him a favor, just not as big a favor as you'll be doing yourself. As it should be.*

The horse stomped his hooves.

"They are getting closer." Fingers needling the air, Finster reached out for the rings in Moth's stomach. He'd been tempted to do it before, but there was an odd kinship with Moth that he couldn't explain, so he'd held back. But now it was for self-preservation. The scarab pulsed on his back. From the distance, he could feel his fingertips on the rings. Moth turned and looked at him with a deadpan stare. "Just close your eyes. This will be over with in a moment." The rings shifted away from his mystic touch. He closed his fist. "Horseflies! They evade me!"

Moth turned away. The first Wargoth climbed over the ledge. He was a bestial man with powerful shoulders. The white paint on his body was cracked, and his black eyes were sunken. He had long fingernails like a wild animal. His teeth were filed to points. Unarmed, he charged Moth.

Moth struck downward with his sword. The Wargoth dodged the sword and slipped behind Moth, locked his arms around his waist, picked him up, and slammed him to the ground.

Finster stiffened. The smaller man attacked the barbarian with the raw power of an animal. The Wargoth raked his sharp claws down Moth's skin. Without a word, Moth cracked the Wargoth in the skull with the pommel of his sword. On the second blow, the skull gave. Red blood oozed from the wound. *They bleed red! A good thing!*

Woozy, Moth dragged the Wargoth corpse to the ledge and pushed the man over the rim. He staggered. The rips in the flesh over his ribs bubbled. His bald brows knitted together. A Wargoth's head crested the ledge. Moth split the savage's face, but he still climbed. Moth wrenched the sword free and hit him again. The Wargoth's face and clawing hands slid back down the rim.

Five Wargoths appeared on the top of the hill. Finster heard more fast footsteps coming from the woods. A crude spear with a stone head sailed right past his nose. Suddenly, the painted men scurried out from all directions. He spun the horse around. *Where in the kingdoms did they come from?* He and Moth were surrounded.

Chapter 27

Finster tapped into the Founder's Stone's power. *Do something. Anything!* He hadn't spent as much time learning about the stone's abilities as he should have. He'd been more focused on the rings. Now it might cost him. His powers might be amplified tenfold, but he was still flesh and blood. As if from a burst of wind, he flung dust and natural debris into the faces of the savages.

Spitting the dust from their mouths, the Wargoths crept toward him. They clacked their sharp teeth. The sharpened nails on their fingers hung down at their knees, moving like the legs of spiders. An ancient evil lurked under their heavy brows, cold and compassionless. They weren't so different from Moth—smaller, but still hulking and primordial. Without a word, they all rushed Finster at once.

Finster clung to the saddle horn. The master of the inanimate, the horse, and the saddle lifted into the sky. The horse whinnied. The Wargoth let out a dry, husky howling. Finster had used his power to lift the horse into the air by his saddle. The saddle's buckles strained against the horse's weight.

Concentrate, Finster, or you'll have a dead horse on your hands. He lifted them about twenty feet above the ground. The horse kicked in the air. The savages' necks were stretched skyward, haunting eyes fastened on him. *Normal people would have fled in sheer terror by now. I miss normal people.*

A Wargoth cocked back his spear and hurled it at Finster.

Oh, none of that, now.

In midflight, Finster took control of the spear. The missile made a loop in the air. It came down and pierced the middle of the Wargoth's spine. His arms flailed, but the Wargoth did not scream. It grabbed the bloody spear and, with the help of another, pulled it out of himself hand over hand.

This will be a problem if they don't die. They're flesh and blood. They have to die. I'm going to have to see about not dying myself. Today will prove to be a good exercise for that.

The impaled Wargoth cocked back the same spear. Blood oozing from his backside and belly, he hurled the spear with all his might. The aim was true.

Finster stopped the spear in midair. *Time to teach these ghouls a lesson, if at all possible. If the results aren't favorable the first time, then make them even less favorable the second.* He turned the spear around. He shot it like an arrow from a bowstring into the Wargoth's face. The man landed on his back, arms outstretched, head pinned to the ground. *Let's see you throw it back at me now.*

The Wargoth's arms came to life. His hands grabbed the spear.

Finster's heart skipped. The horse dipped down in the air. *Impossible!*

The hands of the Wargoth slid down the spear until his fist touched his face. His body no longer moved.

Finster's shoulders slumped. *That's one down.* The hilltop was covered with dozens of the Wargoths now. They brandished hatchets, hammers, and spears made from stone and hurled everything they had at Finster. He deflected the weapons. Maintaining control of the others, he formed a wheel in the air. The stone weapons started to spin like a grinding wheel.

This would work much better with sharpened steel, but I'll give it a go.

"Savages, allow me to introduce myself. I am Finster, Master of the Inanimate. Feel my wrath, you wretched things!"

The wheel of stone spun into a wheel of death. It slammed into the Wargoths, tearing their painted flesh to shreds. Blood sprayed over the sparse field of stone and grass.

Finster laughed, but it was cut short when a hurled stone slipped through his defenses and cracked the back of his head. He fell from the saddle toward the hard ground and the savages awaiting him below.

Moth sank his sword hilt deep in the Wargoth's chest with one hand. He punched an enemy's eye out with the other. The Wargoths gathered around him in a mindless, flesh-rending flock bent on his destruction. They latched onto his legs, and sharp teeth bit into his calves and knees. With one hack after another, he hewed them down. The heavy blade shaved arms from shoulders. Necks were gored. Blood flowed freely into the ground.

The Wargoths bunched together. In a sea of silent rage, they surged against Moth. Bigger and stronger than average men, the Wargoths unleashed their savagery.

Towering against them, Moth killed three more. He was his own silent, savage assassin. The Wargoths latched onto his arms and fought to pry the sword from his fingers. Burning from their paralyzing fingernail slashes, Moth's raw strength began to wane. His vibrant limbs became sluggish. The Wargoths covered him like a great heavy tide and sent him crashing to the ground.

Chapter 28

Finster woke with a loud thumping in his head. One eye was swollen. His hands were stretched behind his back and tied around the trunk of a tree. His feet were strapped down at the ankle. He noticed the gray bark of the tree at his feet and glanced up. The leaves were green maple, rustling in the breeze. His body ached.

Why must life be so painful?

Adjacent to him, Moth was secured to a tree in a similar fashion. Cords of rope wound around his body. The barbarian's eyes were alert, and he wriggled against the restraints. The barbarian didn't look any worse for wear. His pale skin was unscathed. He looked as healthy as if he'd been born yesterday.

Pearls and gold bring rejuvenation. Pah, if I only had that ring myself.

It was a mystery to Finster that the rings could work without Moth knowing how to use them. But, somehow, the barbarian had tapped into them. Or perhaps the rings tapped into him. He didn't seem any the wiser for it, though.

Who would have ever dreamed that swallowing the rings would be effective? Forget about the rings, Finster. You need to get out of here.

Behind Moth were the huts made from stone, wood, and grasses woven together. Moth's horse lay on the ground, dead. A handful of the savages had begun to skin the beast. Finster's skin crawled when a Wargoth, up to his elbows in blood, came his way. The savage carried Moth's sword. Catching Finster's eye, the man walked right up to him. He pinched Finster's face in his bloody hand.

"Can I help you with something?" Finster asked, wrinkling his nose. "A suggestion, perhaps? Have you heard of bathing or chewing leaves? It freshens the body and the breath."

"He wants to cut off your face," a woman said, appearing from behind the Wargoth. She was painted the same as the men—white with wide, jagged black streaks all over her supple body. Her black hair was short and spiky. Long feathers, dyed in black, hung from her arms and legs. Her eyes, framed with crow's feet, were icy blue. She moved with grace.

"You speak the words of the kings," Finster said with relief.

"I speak many things," she said in a seductive manner. "What is your name, stranger?"

"Finster. And yours?"

"I am Ravenlock." She put her hand on his chest. "The Wargoths tell me you wield marvelous power." She closed her eyes and breathed deeply. Her chest swelled inside her feathered vest. "I sense it. I will have it."

"It is not mine to give. If anything, I am cursed with it, Ravenlock."

"No, no, no," she said, touching her black-dyed fingertips to his lips. "You will give it to me. I always get what I want, Finster." Her blue eyes glowed with a haunting aura. "Yield your power to me."

Seeing the hunger building in her eyes, Finster said, "You aren't a Wargoth."

"No, I am Ravenlock, their goddess. You are their sacrifice to me. They are such a faithful people. They give me everything I want." She ran her hands over his body. "I can feel what I want. So close."

"You are not a goddess, Ravenlock. You are a witch doctor."

"To you, maybe. To them, I am what I say I am. Can you speak Wargoth, Finster?"

He shook his head.

"I speak many languages. It is a gift. It amplifies my influence over them. That and my magic." She pressed against him. "Tell me, do I have to kill you in order to get what I want?"

"You sound like a reasonable woman. I think we can settle this without killing one another. Perhaps we can talk about this elsewhere?"

"No." She spoke to her men in a coarse and broken language. A Wargoth ambled over, holding a clay bowl in his hands. Steam and a weird stench came from it. Ravenlock dipped her finger in the bowl, and a red yolk-like goo clung to her fingers. "But I will feed you."

Finster knew plenty about the concoctions of the uncivilized. He'd dabbled in similar natural alchemy himself. The last thing he needed now was to let his mind be altered in any way by some stomach-wrenching swill. He shifted the conversation. "You seem too civilized to live among the Wargoth."

"I could say the same of you. You align yourself with this Blue Toe barbarian. It's very odd company to keep." She fingered the collar of his robes. "However, I should be grateful. You brought the last Blue Toe to me. To the Wargoth. They believe the total annihilation of their enemies enhances their power. Today is everything I envisioned."

"He is the last of the Blue Toes?"

"The last of his clan, more likely. This clan will believe what I say. I am their goddess. I give them destruction. They are lost without me. Now, eat."

"This isn't a Wargoth village, is it? It was the Blue Toes'."

"Very observant. The Wargoth reside in the home of their enemy until they have consumed them all." She nodded to a blackened fire pit in a clearing a couple dozen yards away. Scorched bones lay among the ashes. "The Blue Toes were tied up. Hot coals gathered from deep in the rock were heaped on their bodies, the same way civilized races roast a pig. They devoured the last remains of the Blue Toes a sunset ago. We were satisfied, ready to depart, when I sensed you coming." Her fingers grazed his bald head. "I am curious how you and that savage paired up."

"He molested the king's herd of sheep. Since he was proving to be evasive, I was hired to hunt him down. I was about to pounce when your brood interrupted my triumph."

Ravenlock sneered. "You're a very bad liar, Finster. No matter. I'll have the truth and more soon enough." She put the goo up to his lips. "See you in the next world."

Chapter 29

"Ravenlock," he pleaded, "I don't have the stomach for your porridge. I'd rather die with my wits. If you let me live, I'll tell you what you want. I have power, yes, but it is not my own. It is attached to me."

She drew back her fingers. "Where?"

He sighed. "Do you promise to let me live?"

"Certainly."

"That answer is a little vaguer than I hoped for. I should have been more specific. Oh well. On my back, there is a scarab. It is the source of my power. It is yours, but I don't think you will be able to take it. No offense."

"No tricks." Turning, she spoke in Wargoth. The man set down the bowl and untied Finster from the tree, leaving his hands and fingers bound. Several rough hands turned him around and shoved him face-first into the tree's trunk. They lifted Finster's robes, revealing his back.

Ravenlock's icy fingers touched Finster's skin, and he broke out in chill bumps. "Shades, woman! Are you living or dead?"

"My blood runs warm, but my touch is death." She traced her fingers around the scarab and sucked through her teeth. "Fascinating. Such power. What is it?"

"A curse. That's what it is. Can you not see my veins? They are green!"

"I like your green veins. It makes you unique." She tugged on the scarab.

"Gah! Don't do that. It digs in like a tick when you fool with it. Aside from cutting it out, I cannot remove it."

She spoke to the Wargoth. The one who had held the bowl pinned Finster to the ground. The Wargoth with the sword took a knee and drew a sharp knife made of stone. "Yes, I see your problem, Finster. And per your suggestion, I shall have it cut out."

"But you said you would let me live."

"And you will live… through the process. Maybe even longer. I'll have my Wargoth be gentle. I almost hate to do it. After all, I've enjoyed our conversation. I miss talking to people from my own lands."

"And where might that be?"

"The Kingdom of Rayland."

"I see. You're an affiliate of the Helene Principal, aren't you? I thought I smelled the taint of a novice study in the arts. It's common in your order. No offense."

"Ah, you must be one of those arrogant fools of the Red Citadel."

"Former member, mind you. We had a falling-out quite some time ago. I assume you had a falling-out as well."

"We aren't going to get cozy, Finster. Any member or former member is an enemy of mine. I'm going to enjoy ending you. It will certainly feed my power."

"No offense, Ravenlock, but that isn't going to happen." Like snakes, the ropes that once bound Finster slithered around Ravenlock's and the Wargoths' necks. The ropes constricted, and their tongues protruded. The bindings on Finster's hands slunk over the ground, up the enemies' bodies, and into their mouths. Coming to his feet and rubbing his wrists, Finster asked, "Did you say something, Ravenlock?"

With eyes as big as moons, gagging, she clawed at him with her fingers.

"Are you still speaking Wargoth? It's very garbled."

Ravenlock fell face-first into the dirt. Her body jerked, gave one violent shudder, and died beside the others.

The Wargoths in the village began to stir.

Still using the power of the stone, Finster tore Moth's ropes away and sent the broadsword flying over to the man. Moth snatched it out of the air. Finster said, "Avenge yourself, barbarian!" He looked at his fingernails. One was torn off. "You savages will pay for this atrocity!"

Moth descended on the Wargoths like a raging bull. He ran through the camp, cutting down enemies that swarmed into his path. His sword struck out with alarming speed. He cut clean through the waist of one man and gored another, hoisting him into the air like meat on a stick and flinging him into the others. Bone shattered, and blood gushed from the seething knot of bodies.

Moth disemboweled a man. The Wargoth held his guts in long enough to catch the broadsword's blade between the eyes. Moth ran. Moth chopped. Moth hacked. With two-handed overhand blows, he cut one Wargoth into many pieces. The soft grasses of the village grew slick with blood and sweat.

Finster strolled into the village. He turned the Wargoths' weapons against them. In twos and threes, unwilling to release the weapons that moved with a mind of their own, they assaulted themselves. A savage busted his own nose with the crude end of a hammer. One Wargoth's spear carried itself through another.

I'd enjoy this if I wasn't so angry.

Moth was a whirlwind of action. Every Wargoth that approached him fell. The barbarian's eyes blazed with the fires of a devil. He mutilated and killed. Every wound he suffered bled briefly then sealed itself up.

Finster turned the stone huts into weapons. A hail of rocks slammed into the Wargoths with crushing impact.

Finally, after long minutes of melee, no one in the village moved but Finster and Moth. All of the Wargoth warriors were dead.

The green veins in Finster's hands and arms pulsated. His back burned like fire. He took deep breaths, and his body began to cool.

Covered in gore, Moth disappeared into one of the huts. He came out carrying a dead baby swaddled in a blanket. He located a shovel and started digging a hole just outside of the village. Finster noticed goatskin trousers and other clothing of barbarians, not Wargoth, scattered throughout the village. Scalps and human skin hung from the branches of a dead tree. There were skulls and bones as well. It was a sickening sight. Moth buried the child.

"Sorry for your losses, Moth," Finster said. "Centuries of inbreeding gone to waste. A shame for your kind, but not so much for mankind." Moth cast his heavy eyes on him. "No offense. You've had your vengeance. Now what? Please, let me take you to the nearest town. You could use some new trousers. Soon enough, that goatskin and gore is going to reek."

Chapter 30

As Finster watched, Moth burned everything that would burn in his village, except for the dead barbarians. He buried the remains of his people. The northern winds fueled the fire, and his eyes reflected the flames for a long time. Then, after long hours laboring, Moth turned his back and started walking.

Finster followed with a restless mind. For all intents and purposes, he was lost. He didn't feel lost, however. Instead, he felt liberated. He now had power, true power, and he was learning to harness it. He had been undisciplined when he fought Ingrid. She beat him. He underestimated her, just as she'd underestimated the elemental will of the barbarian. With the power of the Founder's Stone, he wouldn't allow that to happen again.

Still, this scrimmage with Ravenlock could have killed me. I need to be more disciplined.

When he'd dealt with Ravenlock, Finster had learned all he could about her before he struck. He didn't underestimate her power. *She* underestimated *his*, and it was her undoing.

Be wise as a serpent, Finster. Keep it up, and you will go far.

Moth led them off the bitter hillside to where the lands flourished with tall grasses and white-tailed wildlife. He waded through the waist-deep grass toward a river valley.

Finster sighed, and the tightness in his back eased. *Civilization! Praise the impoverished that feed it!*

Without having any idea what the shirtless savage had in mind, Finster took the lead. "Moth, when we get there, let me do the talking. Not that you would say anything, but I suggest that you don't make a sound either. Small towns like this are full of fragile people, and your appearance will, most likely, be perceived as a threat. I will put their minds at ease. Then we will eat and drink until our bellies swell."

Moth's long strides surpassed Finster's. The mage had to trot to keep up with him. They walked until they came upon a split-rail fence. Moth swung his leg over the top, and Finster slipped between the top and bottom rails. In the field, cows started mooing.

"Ah, I see the ladies are welcoming you home. I'll continue on if you need some privacy. No offense."

It was late in the day when they arrived in the riverside town. It was a small establishment made up of about thirty log buildings, with a single road running down the middle. Children were jumping into the river from the boat docks that eased along the coast. The people they passed were friendly. Many of them made polite smiles and waved, hustling along as they went about their business.

These people are possessed. We look like we just crawled out of a hellhole. They should be running for their lives.

A heavyset man wearing a tavern apron flagged them down with his hairy arms. He had more hair in his moustache than on his head. "Blue Toe! Blue Toe! Come!"

Finster peered about. There was no one in the street but them. "Is he talking to you, Moth?"

The man pushed aside the tavern door, which consisted of nothing more than a dark wool curtain. Smiling, he said, "Welcome back, Blue Toe. We missed you!"

Moth ducked inside.

"Er, hello. I am Finster."

"I am Raul. I own, run, and clean this tavern. Welcome to Swift Rivers. Any friend of Blue Toe's is a friend of mine."

"You are Moth's friend?"

"Moth?" Raul's brow drew down in confusion. "Who is this Moth?"

"That is what I call Blue Toe."

"You call Blue Toe 'Moth'?" Raul burst out laughing so hard his belly jiggled. "We never knew his name. He does not speak. We just know him as Blue Toe." He gave Finster a hard slap on the back. "Bwah-ha-ha-ha-ha! Where did you come up with this name 'Moth'?"

"It seemed fitting at the time because he eats them."

Raul tossed his head back and laughed again. Meaty hands on his hips, he said, "Ha! He eats anything. I like it! Finster, come inside. I want to hear more about you and Moth. Tell me, do you like wine?"

Finster broke into a delighted smile. "All of it."

The toasty air inside the Swift River quickly warmed the chill that had settled in Finster's bones. Raul seated him at a small table near the stone fireplace. "I'll be right back," he said. Finster spied a couple of plump maids with big smiles on their faces, leading Moth by the arms toward the rear of the tavern. "Er, Raul, where are they taking Moth?"

"Oh." Raul waggled his brows a few times. "They are going to take Blue Toe—pardon me, Moth—to the waters and clean him up. Every time he comes in, he's very messy. He does not seem so bad this time."

"He spends time here? Not among the cattle and sheep?"

Raul held up a finger. "I'll be back. Would you like one of my daughters to warm your lap?"

Finster scanned the room. The women were little more appealing than the livestock. "Perhaps next winter." *Assuming it's a bitter-cold one.* "For now, the wine will do."

"Wine and soup. You will like Raul's soup." The tavern keeper hustled away, disappearing behind the bar and into the kitchen in the back.

The smoke in the tavern stung Finster's eyes. The longer he sat, the heavier his eyelids became. There were about fifteen people spread out between the bar and tables, eating and drinking. Light came in through skylights in the ceiling. None of the candles in the candelabra or wall sconces were lit.

This reminds me of Tarley's. Poor old Tarley. It's not been so long, but I miss those days already. Farm people. I'd have to feed myself without them.

Raul returned with a clear bottle of rose-colored wine in one hand and a baked-clay bowl of steaming soup in the other. He set the bottle in front of Finster and said, "Try this. It's come down the river on a ship to Mendes from Rayland." He winked. "I've got a connection that set me up with a case. Drink."

Finster pulled the cork from the bottle. He sniffed. "The bouquet is delightful." He'd sampled some of the finest wines known to man. Often, the scent spoiled the taste. He tilted the bottle to his lips and drank. In this case, it was excellent. "Delicious." Finster started chugging the wine. Raul's eyes grew to the size of saucers. When Finster had finished off the bottle, he rapped it on the table. "Excellent, Raul. I'll have another!"

Chapter 31

Drunk as a skunk, Finster floated around the room in a wooden chair. The patrons in the room either fled or hid beneath the tables. Raul was cowering behind the bar. He was waving a rag and pleading, "Finster! Finster! Please, you are frightening all of my customers. I will lose much money."

Finster glided around the room with a bottle of wine in his hand and a smile on his face. "It will be fine, Raul. Don't worry yourself. Pretend it's just an illusion. Someone, play some music. I like the strings."

A man wearing a brick-red scarf crawled beneath the tables on his knees and elbows. He was heading toward the exit. Suddenly, the table over him came to life. The legs of the table wrapped around his ankles and moved like a person, walking backward, dragging the man with it.

Finster's chair lowered, hovering inches from the floor in front of the man. He leaned forward and asked, "Can you play the lute?"

"No, no!" the man said. He shook like a leaf.

"Do you know anyone who does?"

"There's a woman who plays a lute with two necks. Please don't kill me! I have many children that need me."

Finster rolled his eyes. "I don't care, unless some of them can play the lute or the harp. Or perhaps the toot of an iron horn?" His voice rose. "Well, what are you waiting for? Find me this woman you are talking about. Quickly! And don't have any more children. You're ugly, and the world doesn't need any more ugly."

The man fought to free his legs.

Finster's power pulled the man up by the neck with his scarf. The man's legs were freed of the table, but his eyes were bulging. Tilting his head, Finster said, "I like this scarf. You don't mind if I borrow it, do you?"

The man shook his head.

"Good." The scarf unwound from the man's neck. It floated through the air and draped itself over Finster's scrawny shoulders. The fear-stricken patron dashed through the curtained front doorway. Scanning the room and rising higher in his chair, Finster asked, "Where did everyone go? And why have your faces paled? I'm providing amusement." He hiccupped. The chair dipped in the air. Flapping his hands, Finster rose up again. "I am a bird. Say, Raul, watch this."

A tray filled with metal dinnerware spilled out on the bar. Forks, spoons, and knives stood up on their ends. Piece by piece, they came together, forming two people a little over one foot tall. The fork heads made for hands and feet, fingers and toes. One had a spoon head, and the other had a fork head, the tines contorting and waving like womanly hair. Arm in arm, they walked across the bar right before Raul's enlarging eyes.

"Everyone clap, whistle, sing, or something!" Finster said. He drank with one hand and snapped his fingers in loud pops with the others. "Come now! When else will you get to see dancing metal people?"

The cowering patrons slunk toward the door.

Finster barred the exit with a stack of tables. "Don't be rude, commoners! You will draw my wrath!" He shook his head. The entire building trembled. One by one, chairs lined up in front of the bar where the metal figurines danced. Finster addressed the patrons with a glowering look. "Take your seats."

The people scrambled to the chairs and planted their butts in the seats. Their sweat-glistening faces turned toward the metal figurines. The chairs and stools that were free of occupancy came to life. They took on the shapes of skinny men and clapped their wooden arms together in a steady rhythm of wood knocking on wood. The candelabras, now lit, floated from the walls to hover over the metal dancers, creating a warm, illuminating light. Tensions began to ease as the figurines started to dance.

With the gentleness of a hospitable host, Finster said, "Enjoy the show, friends of the Swift River."

The metal figurines performed jigs and ballet. The audience oohed and aahed as smiles crossed their faces. They clapped and patted knees to the lively rhythm of the animated silverware. Raul's cheerful face bounced from side to side. There was childlike wonder in his eyes. Finster, drunk as a skunk and with questionable intentions, had won them over.

"Enjoy, enjoy," Finster slurred. His lids became heavy. His chair lowered to the top of a table. He smiled at the other patrons. The hard lines in their faces started to ease. "Yes, enjoy, lesser peoples."

A shadow crossed the skylight momentarily, blocking the light from Finster's face. He didn't notice. He yawned and snapped his fingers while hugging the wine bottle to his shoulder.

"Simple things for simple people."

The figurines finished a waltz and bowed. The patrons were clapping. A woman, one of Raul's daughters, wiped tears from her eyes. An early night of terror had turned into one of splendid delight.

Clapping his chubby hands together, Raul said in a voice that all could hear, "Thank you, Master Finster! Your gifts are most welcome here! Bravo!"

The patrons cheered Finster, whistling and applauding.

Finster nonchalantly flipped his hand at them. "Oh, please, I don't deserve it. On second thought, yes I do! More, I say! More!"

Shattering glass broke up the celebration. A black birdlike creature swooped into the room. With an earsplitting shriek, it bore down on Finster. It slammed into his body, knocking him from his chair, and driving him hard onto the floor. Hands like a bird's talons wrapped around his throat.

Finster's gaze fell on Ravenlock's face. She was more bird than woman now, with a crow-like beak for a nose.

She pecked him hard between the eyes and shrieked, "I'm going to kill you, Finster!"

Chapter 32

Drunk and defenseless, Finster's frail body couldn't withstand Ravenlock's viselike grip. She pecked at his face. He turned his head aside, fighting to summon his power, but her talons choked him.

I can't breathe!

Focus was one thing. Survival was another. His baser instinct kicked in. He wriggled on the floor like a worm.

"Does that hurt, Finster?" She pecked his noggin, peck-peck-peck.

He couldn't reply. His mind grasped at anything he could get ahold of. A table soared across the room and smashed into Ravenlock's back. She shrugged it off, laughing.

"I am at full strength, fool! Mortal objects cannot harm this immortal body! Die, Finster, die!" She slammed his head against the planks.

Finster started to black out.

No, I won't go like this! I won't be a meal for this harpy!

The tables and chairs in the room clustered into man shapes.

Ravenlock sneered. "No more of your tricks!" Still squeezing, she slammed his head hard into the planks. *Bam!*

Finster's body went limp. His concentration faded. The animated objects around him went still. With his own blood leaking in his eyes, his consciousness darkened like the night. His lungs burned like flames.

Covering his mouth, she said, "Goodbye, Finster. The Wargoth are now avenged."

The pupils in Ravenlock's bird eyes grew large. Her body was wrenched away from Finster. Coughing and rubbing his neck, he sat up.

Moth had Ravenlock in a bear hug. In her bird form, she was as big as he was. She shook the barbarian off with supernatural strength, and he landed on the other side of the bar. She turned her attention back to Finster. "Fools! You cannot kill me!" She stretched her winged arms out wide. Her clawed feet raked the floor. "I am a goddess!"

Moth sprang onto the top of the bar. Wild-eyed, he launched himself through the air onto the harpy. This time, he got his mighty arms wrapped around her neck. Ravenlock thrashed through the tables, trying to shake him off. He held fast, squeezing his forearm against her throat. She rammed her back into the walls, but the jarring impact didn't loosen his grip. The barbarian remained silent, muscles popping out over his body as he increased the pressure. Her spine snapped with a loud crack. Moth twisted her head around until it came clean from the shoulders. He tossed it into the fire.

The fire turned an angry green and blue. The burning face let out one final shriek that shook the tavern, then it exploded. Ravenlock's body deteriorated into a pile of black feathers.

Climbing into a chair, Finster said, "Goddess my arse. She was a harpy." Wheezing, he added, "I hate harpies."

Late the next morning, Finster dug a spoon into a steaming bowl of breakfast stew. "It will give you the vitality you need," Raul had said when he served it. Finster chewed. His jaw was sore for some reason. He didn't remember getting hit in the jaw. He ran his fingers over the scabs on his face. Ravenlock must have pecked him a dozen times. *I hope it doesn't scar. I have enough scars. I prefer them inside as opposed to out.*

At the back of the tavern, Raul had piled up the wreckage Finster had made of the tables and chairs. He considered bending them back together, but he didn't feel like it. It hurt just to think. His back ached as much as ever. He didn't want to admit it, but using the scarab seemed to take a toll on him.

Raul crossed his path. His eyes were puffy. He leaned forward on his broom and asked, "Are you leaving soon, Master Finster?"

"I take it that I've overstayed my welcome."

"Well, this isn't the first time my furnishings have been destroyed. It's just that you make me, my daughters, and my patrons uncomfortable." Raul started sweeping. "I hope you understand."

Finster cast his heavy stare in Moth's direction. The barbarian sat at a table with a pile of food in front of him. The women that had bathed him were now feeding him. The pale-skinned brute was all cleaned up. His bloodstained trousers had been replaced with new ones with heavy leather stitching on the side, and he wore a vest made from sheepskin dyed dark red. Expressionless, he ate by the mouthful. There was a restlessness in Moth's eyes, like he would spring at any moment.

"And my stone-faced comrade? He's welcome to stay?"

"Blue Toe comes and goes. We are used to him, but not used to you."

"Are you saying 'Blue Toe' or 'Bluto'?"

"Bluto."

Finster eyed the man. "Are you making reference to the blue toes on his feet?"

"He is Bluto. I don't know how else to say it. His toes are not blue." Raul craned his neck in Moth's direction. "Even though I cannot see his feet at the moment, I don't remember his toes being blue. Perhaps on a very cold day." He reached down to take Finster's food away. "I wish you well in your travels, Master Finster."

Finster froze the bowl in place with his mind. Raul tried to pull it away, but it wouldn't budge. "I'm enjoying this, Raul. I suggest that you remove your fingers before I do it for you."

Raul's jaw hung open. "Er, eat heartily. You'll need your strength for your journey, wherever that might be." He slipped behind the bar, keeping his head down, and started polishing it.

Finster finished the stew one slow spoonful at a time. Across the room, Moth ate with vigor while the women giggled at his side. He hadn't said a word, but the women were pawing all over the brute, whose rugged exterior was anything but handsome. Finster couldn't figure it out. *That man is as scary as any I've ever met. Yet they adore him. It must be the muscles. It could only be. It certainly wouldn't be his mind. That's what Isaac the Elemental would say. He hates muscles.* He pushed the bowl aside.

Raul moved in like the wind and scooped the bowl up in his hand. "No charge, Master Finster." He hustled over to the door and pulled the curtain back. "Enjoy your journey."

Finster ground his teeth. He felt insulted. Hurt. Moth was welcome, but he was not. It didn't seem natural. Of course, given the history of recent events, he remembered he was dealing with primitive people. Turning loose his powers must have terrified them.

My powers are not something they can wrap their feeble intellects around. Perhaps, if I was inferior, I would feel the same. He pushed back from the table, got up, and headed for the door. Without a word, he passed beneath the blanket into the face of the bright, shining sun. He turned back to ask Raul about the ships that ran along the river, but the curtain was closed.

Chapter 33

King Rolem's chief commander, Buckner, had surveyed many things in his life. He'd seen firsthand the bloody wounds of war. He'd smelled the reek of death. He'd watched men die right before his eyes. That was war. It took a toll, but he enjoyed the spoils as well. Now he was leading five hundred experienced riders after two men. The journey was unique.

He picked up an empty flask of wine he found tossed in the grass. Not too far away was a camp where boulders were stacked up neatly, almost a dozen feet tall. Staring at it, he brushed his flowing blond hair back out of his eyes. Something snaked up his spine that wasn't caused by the wind. He spoke to the man riding next to him. "What do you make of this, Satrap Chen?"

Satrap Chen was an elegant man, clean-shaven, with a proud look in his slanted eyes. His garments were spotted like a bright leopard, colorful and garish, completely out of place with the soldiers who rode in full plate armor. His entire face twitched when he spoke. "What do I make of what?"

"The stones? They are stacked up like a child's building blocks, and these hills aren't known for giants. I certainly don't think the wind caused it."

"It could have." Chen sneered when he said it.

Buckner, gripping his reins with white knuckles, said under his breath, "I hate that man." The satrap was highly regarded by King Rolem. He was a court wizard, trained in the black arts, known for his strange and sorcerous ways. He had been one of the king's top advisors until Ingrid came along. Now the satrap was back on top, making the journey even more miserable.

Buckner gave the signal. "Onward."

For the next few miles, they rode in silence, with only the wind whistling through their armor for company. The farther they rode, the more rigid the winds became. There was something stark in the cloudy hills that always lingered. It made Buckner itch. Still, he rode in the lead, spying the terrain, carefully following two sets of horse tracks.

"How much farther?" the satrap asked.

"Ah, he speaks, only to ask a trivial question. I can't answer because I don't know how far our prey has traveled," Buckner said.

"You would know if you were a wizard."

"You're the wizard. You tell me, Chen."

"Don't be insolent, Buckner. I was not brought here to do your duty. But it is your duty to honor me. I have more favor with the king than you. Don't think your knighthood and battlefield bravado is greater than that. This, I warn you."

Buckner laughed. "What in the Seven Kingdoms are you talking about? This is a manhunt, nothing more or less. You are here to help assess the strength of our enemy. Your talents, matched with mine, should help us apprehend them. Or kill them, for that matter."

"Your weapons will be useless against the ones we face."

Buckner stopped his horse and turned it aside, blocking Satrap Chen's path. "You are more than welcome to apprehend the murderers without our assistance."

"Don't be foolish, warrior." Chen let out a lengthy sigh. "Your skills will be needed. Your shiny weapons and armor make for a marvelous distraction. That's what pawns are good for—protecting the king and his higher subjects, like me."

"You overvalue yourself."

"Compared to you, a man with the wit of a tree stump? Your brawn might win some battles, but it's minds like mine that win the wars."

"Have you ever been in a war, Chen?" He eyed him up and down. "Not a *war-drobe* but an actual war? Not something you play on the game boards in your lofty towers."

"It is in those towers that we forge the destinies of men."

"Really? And all this time, I thought that was where you perverts took silly captive women under the cover of darkness."

"You have a sharp tongue for such a young man."

"I'm not young by any means. I attribute my excellent exterior conditioning to the good loving I receive when I return home from conquered cities. The wife gives me my vitality. My mistress gives me everything else."

"Your criteria are as soiled as mine."

"Good. At least now we have something in common."

Chen chuckled, but his musings didn't last long. They rode to the top of the hill. "Powerful forces were at work here," he said.

Buckner noted the bloodstains on the terrain. A smoky smell lingered in the air. He led his horse to the edge of the hillside overlook. Fires still smoldered below. "Sergeant, you and a hundred men will ride down there with me. Be wary."

They traversed the long path to the bottom of the hill. Men painted in white were lined up across the ground, facedown. Their bodies were butchered. Flesh fell from their bones. Buckner dismounted. Holding a finger to his nose, he fanned the buzzing flies away as he rolled one body, mostly intact, over. Dark circles were painted around the man's eyes.

"Wargoths. These savages are fiercer than any man I've ever

known. They've been in and out of the butcher shop more than once, I would say." He coughed. "These are sword wounds, most of them. What do you say, wizard?"

Chen spoke with his eyes closed. His nostrils flared as he inhaled deeply. "We are close. Very, very close. Be wary."

Chapter 34

Standing on the docks, Finster couldn't get anyone to speak to him about the ships. They were awfully big for such a small town. Every time he approached someone, they put their head down and hurried away. "Oh great," he said with his hands on his hips. "Now I'm suddenly the all-powerful, outcast leper. And I don't even have leprosy." He started scratching his arms fiercely in front of a wide-eyed woman who was passing. Her jaw dropped with horror. Scratching hard, he said, "Perhaps I do!"

She ran away.

"Pah! This is outlandish. The savage is welcome, and I am not. I feel deplorable." He rubbed his nose. "Not that there is anything wrong with that."

Sailors in striped shirts and black hats with wide brims were loading cargo onto the ships. The river was wide, spanning at least a quarter mile from one side to the other. There were three ships docked, each one the same as the other. They were brigantines, medium-sized vessels with two masts, capable of carrying a crew of thirty men. A sailor climbed into the crow's nest. Large barrels were rolled up the planks, and small barrels were carried on shoulders. Burlap sacks filled with grain and wheat were hustled up the loading ramps. Every man at work was in a lather.

Finster studied the ships with interest. The Free River ran along and through the edges and boundaries of all Seven Kingdoms. He had sailed it from one end to the other more than once in his lifetime. The Kingdom of Mendes hugged the western coast of the Gallatan Sea. The Free River emptied into the Bay of Kings. There was always something going on along the river. It was full of secrets and dead men's tales.

They seem to be in an awful hurry. Interesting.

The Mendes flag—a canary-yellow cross on a field of deep sky blue—flew from the back of the ships. Below the main deck, a portal door flipped open, and a sailor popped his head out. Finster caught a glimpse of more men inside wearing chainmail armor. It wasn't uncommon for the supply ships to arm themselves with paid protection, but it seemed extreme for a routine run up and down the river.

How odd. The ships are moving away from the ocean, against the river. What is the kingdom of Mendes up to now? Oh well. It isn't my concern.

A burly mariner marched up the loading ramp. He was carrying two small black barrels on his shoulders. Another sailor followed behind him. They disappeared into the hold.

Interesting times indeed. Something in the air tickled Finster's nose, and he sneezed. "Achooo!"

The brigantine vessel sank two feet into the water and popped right back up. A surge of waves beat against the docks. All of the sailors froze as the boat rocked side to side. Their eyes were as big as plates.

With his nose in his sleeve, Finster wasn't fully clear about what had happened himself. He fought back another sneeze, thinking, *Did I do that?*

Once the sailors got back to work, Finster moved on. He found a bench at the end of the docks, away from all of the action, and sat down. He didn't have any idea what Moth had in mind, but he didn't want to part company with the barbarian, either.

I need those rings.

The fight with Ravenlock had given him a scare. He almost died despite his newfound power. The Founder's Stone was everything he'd dreamed of, but there were limitations. One of them was his mortal body. He looked at the green veins in his hands. They weren't as prevalent now as they had been. There was strength and vitality in his limbs that he didn't have before. Nothing extraordinary, but the stone fueled him. It gave him awareness. Confidence.

Perhaps I need to take some time and reacquaint myself with some former practices.

When he was a magus, he'd spent countless hours studying the arts and mastering new spells. There were mind-control spells, potions, and scrolls written for deadly intents and purposes. It was all very time-consuming. As a magus, he had a unique practice for which he was gifted. He could animate objects, so long as they weren't alive. It worked primarily on stones, dead wood, and metals. At least, that was what came in the handiest. He had always been able to bend inch-thick steel bars with his mind, but now, he could do much more than that.

I moved those boulders in the hills. Perhaps I can move even more.

A shadow fell over him, and he looked over his shoulder. Moth was blocking the sunlight. "Well, if it isn't the master of popularity. What's the matter? Did Raul's daughters lose interest in your company? Or did you lose interest in theirs? Did you hear the call of the lonely sheep?"

Moth's heavy gaze flickered.

"I suppose that's getting old. You've proven yourself to be more man than animal, for the time being." Finster crossed his legs and looked the other way. "I have to admit you are more human than you appear. Those lumpy women took a shine to you. But of course they did. They melted like butter, I'm certain, when you swallowed them in your arms."

Moth sat beside him. He took up most of the bench.

Finster, almost child sized by comparison, scooted away. "Do you mind? I was having a moment. Why are you here, anyway? I figured you were done with the likes of me."

Moth didn't say a word.

"We make for an odd pair, don't we, Moth?" He laughed. "Perhaps we are on a star-crossed path. But why?"

Chapter 35

A path ran along the Free River. Ferns, richly colored in green and red, basked in the sun. Finster followed behind Moth. The barbarian moved in a long, easy stride with his arms swinging slightly. His sword and scabbard were bound to his hip, and he had a sack slung over his shoulder. Raul's daughters had brought it out to him before he and Finster departed.

Hustling to catch up, Finster said, "I'm not sure what your ambition is, Moth. I do wish you would tell me. Even so, I do know the river leads to all kingdoms. Is that your plan? To conquer the kingdoms?"

Moth pushed away an overhang of branches that dipped into the river.

Finster hustled past it. His robes snagged on some briars, and he tore them away. "Honestly, man, I feel like a fool for following you. Or are you following me?" He blocked the path. "Just stop!"

Moth did.

Finster held his fingers out and spread them wide. "Inside you are eight rings. I can sense them, and let me be frank—I want them. Moth, if you will part with them, I will depart from you. You can be free to go about your life, hunting in the wild, slaying the various goths, fathering mute children. You understand me?"

Moth's eyes were dull. He eased by Finster with the grace of a cat and continued up the path.

"Moth, you don't need those rings. I do." Finster sped up. "Listen to me. There is an order that must be maintained in the world of men. Magi like me see to that. We try to keep the peace. But in order to keep the peace, you must have power. And if that power falls into the wrong hands, you have chaos, death, and endless suffering." He scurried in front of Moth again. He wouldn't move out of the man's way until he came to a stop. "Just give me a sign that you understand me."

Moth gave the slightest nod.

"I'll take that as a yes. I have, too. Listen, Moth. Your kind does not care for the arcane arts. It's a curse, a demon. You don't want those rings to possess you. They will torment your spirit. Believe me, I know."

Moth's bald brow furrowed. His hand touched his stomach.

"Yes, the magic will eat you from the inside out. Look." He pushed his sleeve up past his elbow. Green veins spidered up and down his skinny arms. "Certainly, you can see this is not normal. It's a curse. The scarab lodged in my back is uncomfortable, to say the least. I can only imagine there is an unwelcoming fire in your belly."

Moth's throat rumbled.

"Ah-ha!" Finster hoisted his finger in the air. "He speaks. Now we are getting somewhere. Listen to me, Moth. You want to be free of this burden. Let me liberate you from these chains. Work with me."

The barbarian brushed him aside with a forearm that was thicker than Finster's thigh.

"Don't fall in love with your strange powers, Moth," he called after the brute. "It will take its toll. Trust me. No one knows this better than me."

Finster continued on the path, still following in Moth's wake. In his mind, he could see the rings that once decorated Ingrid's fingers.

They were beautiful things, rich in sorcerous glory. He'd witnessed her destroy men with a single touch. Recalling it sent shivers down his spine.

"How about this, Moth? Just part with some of the rings. I'll take some, and you can keep the others."

The barbarian kept walking.

The Ring of Rejuvenation was the one Finster desired most. He had touched it in his battle with Ingrid. He was on his last dying breath when it healed him enough to keep his blood in place. Without it, he would be dead. Now, somehow, Moth had tapped into its power. His wounds, aside from the scars, were healed.

Following the barbarian for hours on end, he reflected on the Rings of Power. Each of them had been possessed by a high-ranking magus, at least an eighth ranking in the order. The fact that Ingrid had acquired them was quite impressive. She defeated or murdered all of the possessors, one by one. Somehow, she hid her victories from Zuulan, and when the time was right, she struck. With all of the rings in her possession, she was practically invincible.

Or so she thought. Finster laughed to himself. He had duped her when he said he was her father. She let her guard down just enough that he managed to remove the rings by seizing them with his reanimation power. *If I could have just held them a moment longer! Lifelong victory snatched from my grasp by a savage.*

Ahead, Moth moved with an easy grace. His lengthy strides were one with nature. If there were any side effects from the rings, they didn't show. His head turned. The three brigantine ships that had been docked at Swift Water were now sailing up the river. They glided over the water. All of a sudden, Moth darted into the brush.

"What is he doing now?" Finster climbed up the bank. He didn't stop until he was on the dusty road that led to the next city. Horses and riders were coming from Swift Water at a brisk trot. Hundreds of soldiers in full armor carried the banner of Mendes. Finster crept back into the woods between the road and the trail. There wasn't much land between them. *I don't like the sound of those hooves.*

The horses thundered by, agitating the dust on the road that led into the woods.

Finster started coughing. He backed down to the trail along the riverbank. There, he got a surprise. A blond knight on horseback approached. A man in wizard's robes rode at his side with a frown deep as the river. There was an endless line of soldiers behind him. Finster heard a splash. He turned to see Moth swim across the river and vanish below the surface. The wizard pointed at Finster and said in a harsh tone, "That's him. That's Finster."

Chapter 36

"I beg your pardon," said Finster, squinting at the oriental wizard in the saddle, "but do I know you?" He shifted his gaze to the blond-headed knight. "Or you, for the matter? I am but a weary traveler looking for a fishing spot." His eyes drifted over the river water. There was no sign of Moth. "If I am in the way, I'll gladly let you pass."

"I am Buckner, Knight of Mendes."

Finster gave him a bow. "A pleasure to meet you. And who is this little adept you've brought along?"

"Don't pretend you don't know me, Finster," Chen said with a sneer. "Your memory isn't that dull, no matter how big of a drunk you are."

"I'm sorry, but I don't recognize you at all. One would think I'd remember those audacious robes. They are blinding. But you have one of those flat faces that all look the same to me."

Chen stiffened. His lips wriggled. "The magi from the Red Citadel are filled to the neck with arrogance. They are nothing more than wine-soaked sots."

"Have I offended you in some way, little man?" Finster asked with a gloating expression.

"Enough, Chen," Buckner said. He walked his horse forward. "Finster, I can make your life easy, or I can make it miserable."

"I'm always amenable to easy. Just ask anyone who knows me. But not that Chen fellow. He doesn't know me like he says."

"You spew manure, Finster!" Chen said.

Finster shifted out of Chen's line of sight, putting Buckner and the horse between them. "Buckner, might I ask what this is all about?"

"The murder of the Magus Supremeus, Ingrid."

Finster played up the shock. "The Magus Supremeus has been killed! How alarming!" He buried his face in his hand. "She was such a delight. The realm won't be the same without her. Oh my, oh my! Whoever will King Rolem fornicate with at night? There's a tremendous shortage of powerfully insane women in the realm."

"Don't besmirch the king," Buckner warned.

"Besmirch! Ha! I did the king a favor, even though that was not my intent. I didn't have any choice in the matter." He reflected on the moment he could have abandoned Ingrid to her whims and moved on. "Actually, I suppose I did, but she would have hounded me one way or the other."

Chen moved into view. "So you admit it?"

"Adept Chen, I merely defended myself and the kingdom from certain disaster."

"I am no adept!"

"Certainly you are. Where did you learn to cast magic? In that lovely lavender tower?"

"It's not lavender!"

"Purple, then."

"The Violet Citadel is known for superior magic!"

"Yes, at children's celebrations. Please, Chen, don't get in a huff. There are major towers and minor ones, and the lilac tower you hail from ranks near the bottom."

"Violet!"

"Should I be under the impression that you brought Chen to apprehend me?" Finster asked Buckner.

"Chen and five hundred soldiers," Buckner said. "It was the king's orders, and as always, I will see them through. You seem reasonable, Finster. Can I assume that you will come along willingly?"

"Oh, no. You should never assume that. After all, I've been accused of a crime of which I am not guilty. It was self-defense."

Buckner showed a handsome smile. "The king is a reasonable man. You'll get your day in court."

"Oh, yes. The judges and jurors are such honest people. Let me make you this guarantee: I'll never be judged in that court of fools." The riverbank had filled from one end to the other with soldiers on horseback. A squad of them waded into the river, cutting off the last avenue of escape. He warned Buckner, "I'll die first."

"Lucky for you, the king wants you alive, Finster," Buckner said. "Once you're found guilty, he aims to make an example of you. If I were you, I'd surrender and enjoy the sunny ride back to Mendes."

Finster didn't reply.

Chen spoke up. "We need the barbarian, too. Call him back, Finster."

"What barbarian?"

"That tree with limbs that dove into the river. He'll have his trial, too."

"Is that so? So we are both accused of killing the same woman? I can testify right now that he did it. There, problem solved."

"We know what happened, Finster," Chen said, tucking his hand up in his droopy sleeves. "Your fellow magus, Gregory, shared what the Eye of the Citadel revealed to him. Even though, according to King Rolem's account, the scene fully explained itself. We know about the Founder's Stone, Finster, and the rings. We intend to have them."

"We? Or the king?"

Chen shrugged. "I am the king's viceroy of magic now. I am entrusted with these treasures to be sure they are well cared for."

"The items of which you speak are well beyond your command, Chen."

"I could say the same for you," Chen said, looking at Finster's hands and face. "It's clear the stone is taking a toll on you."

"If you are talking about the holes in my face, those were caused by one of yours turned harpy. Her name was Ravenlock. Sound familiar?"

Chen stiffened. "Where is she?"

"Dead. She was the stench in the Swift River tavern. I'm sure you passed through there. Am I going to be accused by the King of Rayland of her murder, too?"

"She was a renegade and no longer associated with our order. I'll be sure to pass along her loss." Chen leaned back in the saddle. "So, what is it going to be, Finster? Will you come quietly or not?"

Buckner's hand eased over his sword. He gave a quick nod to his men. Steel snaked out of sheaths.

Finster replied, "Not."

Chapter 37

Finster tapped the scarab's power. The air shimmered, and the horses jumped. Buckner fought to keep his horse beneath him. He looked at Chen. "What was that?"

"Power," Chen said. His face was drawn tight, and his eyes narrowed into slits.

"Chen, you know my power from before. Now imagine it tenfold, if not more," Finster warned. "I don't think you want to play this game with me."

He turned his attention to Buckner. "Do you not know what I can do with metal and wood? You haven't brought yourself an army. Instead, you've brought me one." Finster winked. Behind Buckner, two soldiers in chainmail were ripped out of their saddles. They soared high above the ground, startling the others, then fell as if dropped into the deep river. "It's not easy to swim in chainmail. I'll drown them. I'll drown you all."

Buckner's jaws clenched. "The more you murder, the more will come, Finster. I know Rolem. There will be no end to this."

"Rolem will lose his finest forces."

"And tenfold more will come, magus." Buckner leaned forward. "This will not end. These men will fight to their deaths. You aren't so powerful that you can stop them all. No one is."

Finster laughed. "My kind has leveled entire cities! Decimated populations! And you think your hundreds of men are a match for me? You need to reassess." He held out his hand, fingers splayed wide. Every soldier in a saddle was propelled into the air as if hit with a giant mallet. The only people still in place were Buckner and Chen.

"Do something, wizard," Buckner said to Chen. "This is what you were brought for!"

"I am." Chen's eyes came to life with a glowing fire. His hands appeared from inside his sleeves, covered in a mystic violet fire. "Try your powers now, Finster!"

Finster summoned the magic, and nothing happened. His powers stretched out into empty air. He was in a field of negative energy created by Chen. "Clever!"

"Not clever. I was ready." Chen tipped his chin to Buckner. "He is harmless for the moment, but hurry."

Buckner launched his horse forward. He leaned over the saddle and punched Finster hard in the face. There was a loud *smack* of gauntlet metal on flesh. Finster's knees buckled. He started to fall. Buckner seized him by the collar and pulled him onto the saddle of his horse.

Blood dripped down Finster's eye. *I think I'm bleeding again. I never used to bleed. What happened to me?* The air around him was empty of power. He was as helpless as a baby.

"The Silver Snake is captured," Chen said. "Now, let's find the other."

Look at that. Tight-Face is grinning. I'll not be bested by the likes of him. Bloody satrap, sycophant, fledgling, weakling! Finster made a pitiful slash through the air, aiming to get ahold of Chen's hands in a vain attempt to wrestle the power from him.

Chen laughed. "It's not my hands. It's the Amulet of Isander." In front of Finster's eyes, Chen dangled a prism of cut stones held together in a medallion of pewter. "A creation of the Violet Tower you spoke so ill of. Buckner, his eyes are open. Now, close them."

Finster felt the pommel of Buckner's sword rise over his head. He winced before the blow was struck. *Fine, knock me out, but please don't let it hurt.*

Moth erupted out of the water along the riverbank. He slashed Buckner's horse's legs out from under it. The beast fell over on its side.

Finster rolled across the ground and into the river. He ducked under the water and swam as far as he could, increasing the distance between him and Chen. He held his breath until his lungs burned. Finally, the power of the Founder's Stone and the scarab flowed back into him. He resurfaced, gasping for air.

On the riverbank, a vicious fight unfolded. Sword in hand, Moth attacked the soldiers like a ravenous wolf gone mad. He smashed one knight's sword into his face. Another blade snapped against Moth's raw power. He yanked a man from the stirrup, and wild-faced, he head-butted a horse. The soldiers scurried out of the path of silent doom whenever Moth came near.

"Mendes!" Buckner shouted. He'd climbed onto someone else's horse. Sword high, he charged at Moth. "For Mendes, brothers!" The steed galloped, intending to trample Moth beneath its thundering hooves.

Moth turned his shoulders into the horse's path. With a face full of rage, he caught the horse head on. Buckner, Moth, and the horse all went down in a crashing of hooves and limbs.

Finster heard Chen screaming. The oriental wizard stood on the bank, waving his hands and a Mendes flag at the passing ships. "Capture him! He's a fugitive of Mendes!"

The last ship angled into Finster's path. One of the sailors reached out with a pole that had a hooked metal end made for capturing lost cargo. He snagged Finster's robes. With help from another seaman, they hauled him into the boat.

Catching his breath, Finster tried to speak. Swimming and treading water were exhausting. His robes felt like they weighed a ton. "Thank you. Thank you, kind sailors."

The sailors locked his arms and stood him up. One of them punched him in the belly.

"Ooof!" Finster sagged.

"Those are knights of Mendes over there," a commanding man with a full brown beard said to the sailors. He was dressed in all black and wore a sabre on his hip. "I don't know who this scoundrel is, but he must be trouble. I don't want any bad omens. Bind him up, lower a rowboat, and get his skinny arse off my ship. Let those knights deal with it."

Chapter 38

Finster had reached his boiling point. For over a decade, he was a revered magus that no mortal with any knowledge of him would cross. Now, with ten times the power—perhaps more—he was being rough handed by little more than goons.

One of the sailors drew back to sock him again. The man had silver rings on his finger. Finster turned the action around, and the man punched himself in the face, knocking him out cold. The bewildered crew shuffled back. The ship's captain stared at Finster with his mouth wide open.

"Captain," Finster said, looking at him with eyes that could burn a hole in the man's face. "I'm taking your ship. Step aside or die."

The threat of taking the ship snapped the captain out of his daze. "Don't be foolish. I've cut men's throats for less than that."

"I'll start with your anchor."

The ship's anchor and chain moved to hang over the men like a cloud. Every eyeball on deck watched the object as the anchor whipped downward like a club. *Smack!* Bone caved upon contact with the metal. It sent the captain and a handful of his seamen headlong into the waters.

Finster seethed, and his chest heaved. The scarab sent an angry force through him. The entire brigantine lurched up and down in the water. Hot with rage, Finster said, "Get off of my ship!"

Some of the sailors dove into the river. Others cowered. A force of soldiers in chain-mail armor rushed up the steps from the hold.

"Fools!" Finster yelled in a gust of hot breath. The entirety of the ship rose up out of the water. It sailed higher into the air. "Get off of my ship!" He turned his wrist.

The entire ship tilted to the starboard side. Men clung to whatever they could get ahold of. It was that or sink like a stone in the river that raced beneath them forty feet below. Finster stood as if suspended in the air, one hand hanging fast to the ropes of the mast. He felt light as a feather and stronger than a sea storm. He shook his hand. The ship shook with it. The men lost their grip, and screaming for their lives, they plunged into the cold waters.

Enraptured by his surging abilities, Finster righted the ship in midair and moved it toward the riverbank.

Chen's face looked like it was about to break into a hundred pieces. He backed up the bank, lost his footing, fell, and bounced back up. "Finster, let's talk!"

Finster was too far away from the Amulet of Isander for it to have any effect on him. "I warned you, fool from the inferior tower."

The Amulet of Isander tore from Chen's neck and sailed into Finster's waiting hand. He tucked it in his pocket. "I'm a fair man. I shall exchange you one amulet for another. Or rather, one amulet for one anchor."

The anchor flew across the waters and crushed Chen beneath it with the sickening sound of metal conquering man. Chen's body was buried in the soft riverbank. Only his arms and legs were showing.

By this time, Finster had the full attention of the knights from Mendes. Some were firing crossbows at him from bended knee or from horseback. The missiles were turned aside, streaking far right and left. Finster let out a gusty laugh and waved his hand.

Seemingly from out of nowhere, the second of the three brigantine ships had come out of the waters like it was shot from a catapult. It crashed like a wave of wood into the soldiers. The planks popped and cracked like the sound of thunder. The main mast snapped over wriggling bodies. Men were busted up, broken, bleeding, and screaming for help in the wreckage.

Drunk with power, Finster laughed. "You brutes! You fools! If you wanted to avoid death, you should have kept plowing the fields! This is war! It's miserable, especially when you are on the losing end of things! Ha-ha-ha-ha-ha!"

Moth had one man by the neck. He ran a second man through the chest with his sword. One man, with hair the color of sunshine, slipped away. His horse didn't make it.

Soldiers were running full speed away from Moth. Many sought refuge by swimming across the river. He killed a few more, showing no mercy. Wet blood dripped from his sword. When the haze cleared, there was no one left but him and the boat in the sky. Finster stood on the deck with his eyes glazed over. Moth noticed one boat was shattered against the riverbank. Farther up the river, the lead boat of the three had capsized.

Right before his very eyes, Finster made a set of steps out of wood from the broken ship. The steps floated on air, but appeared solid as a rock. Finster walked down the steps one by one and then approached Moth. His power-glazed eyes cleared as he surveyed all of the carnage. The dead were piled up in heaps everywhere. He looked at Moth. "I think the two of us are officially at war with the entire kingdom of Mendes."

Chapter 39

Finster and Moth commandeered a rowboat salvaged from a brigantine. The boat was sizable, built for a dozen men. The oars, with life of their own, dipped into the waters in perfect harmony, pushing them up the river. Finster sat at the stern of the boat, letting the steady breeze kiss his face. Moth rode at the bow, gazing out over the waters. The craft moved up the river for two days straight without stopping.

Yawning, Finster stretched his arms above his head. "Normally, I wouldn't row the boat myself. I could just fly it, but I don't want to draw any attention." He waved his fingers at some men on the bank at a hard bend in the river.

The fishermen scratched their heads. The children ran waist-deep into the waters, eager for a closer look at the craft that was rowing itself.

"I find it strange that a barbarian such as yourself is so comfortable with my company. Surely you have some ambitions of your own, aye, Moth?"

The barbarian didn't reply. Instead, he hung both legs over the bow, dipping his toes in the water. He didn't seem to have a care in the world.

Finster found himself wrestling with the notion that his fate was entwined with that of the disproportionate man. The brute had saved him, and he'd saved the brute, so he thought. Then there were the Rings of Power. Finster had lifted an entire ship out of the river. Certainly, he had enough power. What more could he want? He kept talking, assuming Moth understood what he said. It was easier that way.

"They'll keep after us until we are dead. I think we can find refuge in Rayland for a time. Then perhaps we can move to the next kingdom. Perhaps it would be best if we wooed some queens and wed them? We could be kings, or at least princes. And what queen wouldn't want men of our renown with such endurance? This new stamina we have would be very fitting for satisfying a harem."

He talked about many things. Moth didn't show the slightest sign of interest. Late in the day, they passed the final bend in the river, where the trees on the riverbank reached high into the sky. Finster stood. "There it is. Rayland. It's quite a view from here. It's been a time since I've seen it."

Piers and docks ran along the riverbank for miles. Boats and ships of all sizes were docked at the marina. Beyond the wharfs and levees, the city began. Buildings and roads were built into the countryside's gentle slopes. Thousands of people moved along the storefronts and docks. There were hundreds of thousands more in the kingdom. Miles away, at the highest point on the hill, was the kingdom of Rayland's castle. It was rumored to be built at a high point in the land superior to the elevation of Mendes.

Finster rowed the boat to the docks where the crowd was thinnest. A handful of people cast wary eyes their way. Moth tossed a rope up to a wide-eyed black boy.

The boy tied it off on the dock and asked, "Where did you get a ship that rows itself, huh? Do you have ghost rowers?"

"No," Finster replied as he crawled up onto the dock, "but I do have a boat for sale. A quality deal. Will you find me a man that is interested?"

The boy rubbed his chin. "How much are you asking for this ghost ship, huh?"

"I'll tell that to the person who is buying it, child. Now, fetch me a river pirate or a merchant with feathers in his cap. Quickly now, or I'll sic the ghosts on you."

The boy ran off.

Moth pulled the oars inside the boat and scanned the countless buildings that filled the hillside. Made from stone, brick, and mortar, the city was divided into different levels, each one higher than the other.

"Rayland has plenty of places to hide, even for a man as big as you. We'll get you a hat, one of those nice round ones made from bamboo. I've seen them sizeable enough for your head. Just stay close." Stationed along the docks were soldiers in leather armor, carrying spears. They were preoccupied with the bigger ships and thicker crowds. "If we cross any soldiers, let me do the talking. I've a feeling if you spoke, you might stir them. No offense."

A robust black man sauntered down the dock with the boy hopping up and down at his side. Bullnecked and bald, his yellow eyes scoured Finster and Moth. He eased closer to Finster but kept his eyes on Moth. "I am Carl. I understand you have a ghost ship for sale?" He eyeballed the craft. "Fifteen gold."

"Don't insult me, man. It's worth seventy-five, but I'll take forty-five and nothing less."

Carl rubbed his chin. "It is stolen from Mendes, I know. I'm very familiar with their craftsmanship."

"I earned it fairly, captain. How else could I have acquired a ship from Mendes? But if it makes you uncomfortable, I'll take my business elsewhere. I wouldn't want you to make a deal that might haunt you at night."

"I'll give you forty."

"Fair enough."

Carl emptied his purse and counted out the gold talents. He handed them to Finster. "You should take your slave to the competitions. You can triple this money there." He nodded. "Good day."

"Moth, I think he wants me to sell you. That wasn't very kind, was it?"

Moth held out his hand.

Taken aback, Finster asked, "What?"

Moth eyed his fist full of coins.

"You want money? What are you going to do—swallow it, or spend it?"

Chapter 40

King Rolem the Grand stood on the battlement of his castle that overlooked the bay of the Gallatan Sea. His kingly robes rustled in the sea winds, and the sun warmed his face as he watched the boats, fishermen's ships, brigantines, and galleons working their way in and out of the bay. He enjoyed watching the ships, and even sailing, for that matter, but not today.

"How many men, Buckner?" he asked. Slowly, he spun on his heel and rested his backside against the battlement wall.

Buckner was down on one knee, his face downcast. He was covered in grit, blood, and sweat. "One hundred and thirty-eight soldiers were lost, your majesty."

"Including Chen?"

"No, that would make one hundred and thirty-nine. I wasn't counting him. He's not one of my soldiers."

Rolem sighed. His handsome face seemed to sag. Frustration was in his tone and eyes. "I gave you five hundred men to bring back two. You had three hundred and sixty-two soldiers left at your disposal, excluding Chen, of course." He crossed his arms. His fingers drummed on his elbows. "I don't understand why you didn't use all of the men at your disposal, Buckner. It's a complete waste of my resources. It would have been better if you hadn't come back at all."

Pleading, Buckner explained. "Your majesty, the magus, Finster, threw an entire ship on top of us. He dropped an anchor on Chen." His body trembled. He'd been on one knee for over an hour. This was his third time explaining it. "Only a hurricane could have wrought more damage so quickly."

Rolem's brows knitted together. He kicked Buckner in the jaw, and the man collapsed. "Get back up on your knees, Buckner!" His hands clenched together. He seethed. "It's hard enough to swallow the loss of my soldiers for two men, but the reminder that I lost three ships loaded with my cargo adds even more sting to the blow. What are the odds?"

Buckner gathered himself and made it to one knee. Both lips were split. He pulled his shoulders back and kept his chin level.

"I said, what are the odds, Buckner?"

"I don't know, sire."

"Knights fleeing from battle," Rolem scoffed. "Knights of Mendes, at that, fleeing from two people. All of the kingdoms in the realm will be laughing." He cupped his ear. "I can hear the town criers now. 'Rolem's knights flee like rabbits!' 'Mendes's finest dogs run with their tails between their legs!' It's preposterous that one man scared you so. You, Buckner, my bravest knight! Have I not told you that no man's power is unlimited?"

"I did what I believed to be best at the time, sire. I would have fought to the death, but you needed a fair assessment of your enemy."

"I would have gathered that myself when I came upon five hundred corpses and three sunken ships. It would not have required my cowardly knights reporting back." Rolem rested his hand on Buckner's head. "Now, tell me about this barbarian."

"He was a hairless Neanderthal of a man, spit out of the snow caps of hell. He suffered scores of wounds but kept fighting like a tiger. He tackled my horse, and it threw me to the ground. My very sword bit deep into his back. Deep. The wound opened and then closed fast. Your soldiers were less effective than children against him. They were being slaughtered." Buckner swallowed. "It wasn't natural, I tell you, my king. My hairs stand on end just thinking about it."

"You have failed, Buckner," Rolem said. He turned his back, put his hands on the grand stone battlement, and faced the sea. "I hate failure."

"Sire, I would rather die by your hands than those of a filthy savage. I returned, willing to pay the price for my cowardice."

Roland tapped his fists on the battlement. "No, Buckner, I'm not going to kill you. I like you too much. Your service to me has been nothing but exemplary. If not for that, I assure you that you would be dead. However, I am disappointed."

He faced Buckner. "I've fought many battles myself. I'm one of the few kings in the realm who have tasted blood and steel, perhaps the only one. I stand here and ask myself, if I had been there, what would I have done? I presume I would have led the men in a coordinated effort to capture this barbarian. I could have used the advantage of a lance or spear and gored the man from a distance. I can't imagine this man being fully effective with shafts of ash wood run through him." He shook his head. "There would have been so many ways to subdue him. But I've dealt with supernatural elements before. There was a man that lurked in the Caverns of Zarnath. He was more boar than man, a terror in our hills. No mortal weapons could harm his skin. Do you know what I did?"

"No, sire."

"I, with only a little aid from my men, threw a net over him. We weighted it down and dropped him in the bottom of the bay. He's never been seen or heard from since. He is still out there"—he pointed to the bay—"dead perhaps. But if he's still alive somehow, I sleep well knowing that he is suffering."

"Your majesty, I beg for your forgiveness. I panicked. Give me the opportunity to capture these men one last time. With your wisdom, I know that I can do it."

The soft-eyed king smiled. He leaned over and put his hands on Buckner's shoulders. "No, Buckner, you've served me well enough. I realize I'll need a different kind of net to capture this pair. You are dismissed." He looked up, over Buckner's shoulder, and nodded.

A dagger tip burst from Buckner's chest. Stunned, eyes fading from light to dark, he gasped. "You said you wouldn't kill me, my king."

"I didn't kill you. She did."

Buckner turned. A woman shimmered out of thin air and quavered in his sight. His last dying word was "Assassin."

The woman's robes were made of rich fabric that seemed to move with a life of its own. Her face was pleasant, her eyes cold, and her disposition deadly.

"Did you hear all you need to know, Alexandria?" the king asked.

Her voice was a whisper. "More than enough. The Circle will handle this."

The Sorcerer's Command
Part 3

Chapter 41

Sitting on a small terrace in the kingdom of Rayland, the middle-aged Finster sipped on a goblet of chilled wine. It was late morning, the sun shone on the Free River, and boats were moving up and down the river, docking and pulling out. A girl with yellow hair and a rich brown tan fanned Finster with a large wooden fan shaped like a leaf.

"A little faster, child," Finster said, wiping the sweat that ran down from his temple with the sleeve of his robes. "The humidity is stifling."

The little girl's speed didn't change. She just waved the leaf, up and down, with her eyes fixed on Moth.

Agitated, Finster snapped his fingers in front of the little girl's face. "I said speed it up, urchin." The little girl put more of her shoulders in it. "No, you're waving harder, not faster. I want faster." Seeing the confusion in the girl's eyes, he shook his head and said, "Oh, never mind. I'm not in the mood to deal with any more stupid." His eyes slid to Moth. "Or mutes for that matter."

Moth sat on the terrace wall with one leg dangling over the side. His eyes were cast on the waters. Finster had purchased new clothing for the both of them. He'd tossed away sorcerous robes for something more common. His robes were beige, but with some golden flair woven along the hem. Moth wore a linen pullover and a pair of sandals. His muscular bare arms were still exposed, but he looked more human than savage for a change. Almost casual. As always, he hadn't said a word, but remained a huge shadow at Finster's side.

"Lord Finster," a woman said, stepping out onto the terrace from within the apartment where they were staying. She was very pretty, with the same golden hair and deep tan skin as the little girl. She wore silks that clung well to her curves. A wooden tray with food was clutched in her hands. "Are you ready to eat? I've prepared a fine meal. Meat, baked flatbreads, and hen eggs. It will hold you through the day."

"A little later, Dizon," Finster said, rubbing his temples with his fingers. "I just want to enjoy the morning with few interruptions. Eh, is it possible that you can find another young imbecile more proficient using a leaf? This one is lacking."

Taken aback, Dizon said, "Lord Finster, my daughter is no imbecile. She's just shy. What is it you wish?"

"A breeze, that is what I wish," he said, letting out a long sigh. "For the sake of the Red Citadel, where is the breeze? We are on the river. There should be a breeze."

Dizon set the tray down on a small table near Moth. The barbarian turned his head toward it. "Eat, oversized one. Enjoy. As for you, Lord Finster, you are thinking of the sea. The wind doesn't always blow on the river. Now is the time of the ebbs. It will pass." She slipped behind Finster, put her fingers on his head, and started to massage him. "Just relax."

The tight muscles in Finster's neck eased. "Your fingers are magic, Dizon."

"I know," she said.

The scarab in Finster's back, containing the Founder's Stone, throbbed. The chronic pulsations were so intense that he hardly ever got any sleep. He couldn't even recollect sleeping for a solid hour in the past several days. Things had happened fast since he acquired the stone and harnessed its power. He battled Ingrid to the death and fought off a small army of the king's men. It was a lot to deal with. So, he drank, heartily and heavily, dulling his senses, trying to put himself in a comatose slumber. That proved to be dangerous as his mind, body, and magic took on a personality of their own. Now, he was trying to avoid it.

Finster sipped his morning wine. It didn't have the same burn in his throat that most wines did. Rather, it was more fruit juice. It was sweet, like raspberries and honey. He put the purple liquid away from his lips and scowled down at it. "Nothing beats the real thing. All grapes should be fermented."

Dizon's hands moved down to his neck and shoulders.

Moth picked up a plate of food and began shoving it into his mouth.

Finster's shoulders tensed. He'd just as well be done with the savage, but he wanted the rings of power. All eight of them. Unfortunately, Moth had swallowed them all, giving the barbarian bizarre and unpredictable powers.

A soft, perfumed hand covered Finster's eyes. Dizon's lips brushed against his ear as she softly said, "Close your eyes, and forget about everything."

"That's impossible," he replied quietly, "but I'll try." Meditation was a big part of the sorcerer's practice, but it didn't come easily now. His will wrestled against the artifact imbedded in his body. It wasn't just something that he could turn on and off when he needed it. It had a life of its own. It dug, probed, and burned, taking a little bit of Finster at a time. He knew there were consequences in dealing with ancient magic, but he never imagined it would be a struggle like this.

And with great powers come great troubles.

By now, Rolem the Grand would have a bounty on Finster's head so high the collector could purchase a kingdom. Finster and Moth had destroyed three ships and killed over a hundred knights. No doubt, another army would be coming. Perhaps.

The king of Mendes was no fool. He didn't become the ruler of the most dominant land of the Seven Kingdoms by proxy. He earned it. Rolem was a king of ambition. He wouldn't have aligned himself with Ingrid if he hadn't been. She acquired the rings and came after Finster to get the Founder's Stone. With such omnipotent possessions in a king's grip, he would perhaps have enough power to rule the Seven Kingdoms of the Gallatan Sea.

"Are you feeling any relief, Lord Finster?" Dizon said.

"No, but keep trying."

On and off, Finster contemplated moving far away with the stone. He'd managed a low profile for years, but Ingrid the Insane found him. He came to the conclusion that he'd have the same result when dealing with Rolem. A king like that wouldn't stop. Ambition fueled itself. The king would use Ingrid's death as his motivation. He'd stop at nothing to find Finster or Moth. Finster considered moving far north, beyond the northernmost kingdom of Umpton, and into the wilderness beyond. But that wasn't Finster's way.

I have enough power to live my life the way I want now, and more than enough power to preserve it. The fingers in his veiny hands clutched in and out. The boats in the docks bounced up and down on the waters. Cries and alarms came up from the people jumping away from the riverboats that had suddenly come to life on their own. *If you want my stone, Rolem, you're just going to have to take it from my corpse. But you'll have to kill me first, and frankly I don't think that can be done, not by you, not by anybody. I am almighty.*

Chapter 42

Finster remained seated until the sunset came. Dizon and her daughter, after making their rounds, came to the apartment to check on him and Moth. He had dismissed the girl, whose little arms fanned him until she could fan no more, by saying, "If I knew you were going to be so bad at this, I would have just done it myself." Needless to say, the leaf-shaped fan floated in the air, waving side to side, creating a brisk wind. Finster controlled it without hardly thinking. His mind toyed with other things he could do.

"Dizon, who is the king of Rayland these days? Tell me it's not still Geoffrey. He was such a weakling and had too much of a fondness for pies and cakes. The last time I saw him, he couldn't walk. He just sat there, sinking into a bed of satin pillows." His head and neck gave a little tremor. "Eek."

Dizon came out on the terrace, running a comb through her hair. Her eyes shone like the sun. "No, Geoffrey is long dead. His heart failed him. But his son continues to thrive behind the walls of the castle. I used to be a part of his harem."

Finster turned his head toward her. His expression soured. "Is he like his father?"

"No, I'd say he's more like one of the River Knights. He's dark-headed and strapping. No one believes he's the true son of Geoffrey, but it doesn't matter what we think. Only what his mother thinks, and she thinks the young king is a god."

"Oh, don't they all. So, what is this king's name then?"

"King Alrick. He's very peculiar," she said, setting her comb down and sitting on Finster's lap. She stroked his bald head, running her fingers down to the sharp beard on his chin. "Not as peculiar as you, but I like peculiar. Is there anything I can do for you, Lord Finster?"

Her touch made his mouth water. His throat tightened. He ran his fingers down her slender waist, over her hip, and stopped on the top of her rear. He gave a gentle squeeze. "I paid for your privacy and discretion, Dizon. Perhaps I'll sample your wares another time, but now all of my time requires meditation."

"You suffer. You cannot meditate in misery," she said.

"No, this is what I wanted. It's a delight, just uncomfortable at times. It's very complicated being a wizard." He took her hands and kissed them both on the knuckles. She giggled. He was certain it was an act. She was a seductress, a temptress, a lady of the night who took pay and gave pleasure. Her beautiful eyes sucked him in. His heart sped up. "Oh, why not!" He smiled. "I can't even remember how long it's been. Oh, yes I do." His mouth twisted. "That was embarrassing."

Dizon let out a delightful squeal when he picked her up. "Finster, you surprise me!"

"You shouldn't be. You are as light as a feather." He started into the apartment. Moth sat in a chair, leaning over the terrace wall, watching the people go by. "Moth, don't go anywhere."

The huge hairless savage didn't say a word. No shrug, no grunt, no nothing.

"Does he ever speak?" Dizon asked.

"Not yet." Finster carried her inside. They spent the next hour laboring between the sheets in the throes of passion. Drenched in sweat, Finster put his robes back on. Dizon lay on her back, sleeping.

"I still have it." The sex did him some good. His back didn't burn so much between his shoulders. He felt loose. "She did things for me that wine couldn't. I need to remember that."

Finster made his way back onto the terrace. Moth was gone. "Bloody noses!" Finster said. He looked over the terrace wall. The apartment was on the top level of the buildings, with several levels of apartments below them. People moved up and down the streets that ran from one level to another. He searched as far as his eyes could see. There was no sign of Moth.

The girl walked out onto the terrace and stood by Finster. She looked up at him.

"Little dumb one, I don't suppose you know where the big man went?"

"My name is Rinny, and I don't think I would tell you if I did," she said, words rolling off her tongue like water.

"She speaks. How annoying. And here I made the mistake of thinking that I might be around another mute." He leaned toward her. "You draw my ire. Don't you know that you should be more respectful of your elders when those thin little lips of yours speak?"

The girl shrugged. "Will you do magic for me?"

"Are you bargaining with me, child?"

She shrugged again.

"Listen, you fatherless little cur, tell me where my, er, barbarian went, and I won't throttle the brains inside your skull." He poked her in the forehead. "My touch is death."

"I know who my father is," she said.

"I don't care. Where did Moth go?"

The girl climbed up on the terrace wall and made her way up the partition steps onto the roof. She pointed to Castle Rayland, which rested a few miles back on the highest point of the hill. Its golden banners on each and every spire top flapped in the wind.

With his back to the terrace wall, Finster said with his arms folded over his chest, "Am I to understand that Moth went to see the king?"

"No, that's where my father lives. He is the king."

Finster's chin dipped. Shaking his head, he said, "Listen, little nuisance, whether your father is the king or not is of no concern to me. Did you see where Moth went?"

She nodded.

Pulling at his chin hairs, he said, "Well?"

"Show me magic first. Like the fan. But better."

Pushing up his sleeves, he said, "Oh, I'm going to show you some magic you will never forget, little goat. Now, come down here and sit in this chair." One of the patio chairs slid over the deck into the middle of the terrace.

Eyes wide, Rinny hurried down from the roof and plopped her butt in the chair.

"Hold onto the arms… tightly," he said.

The girl's knuckles went white on the chair's arms. A big smile crossed her face.

The chair lifted from the ground. Slowly, it spun in midair, getting faster.

"Do you like that, little pest?"

"It's a delight! It's a delight!" Her hair covered her eyes. She brushed it away. "Faster, faster!"

"Tell me where Moth went?"

"To the stadium! He followed the crowd to the stadium! Wheeeee!"

With a twist of his finger, the girl spun so fast she flew out of her seat. Finster caught her in midair with his mind.

Holding her stomach, she said, "Let's do that again."

Finster patted her on the head. "When your mother wakes up, tell her where I went. I have to find an enormous idiot."

Chapter 43

"Of all the times to wander, he decides to wander now," Finster muttered to himself. He hurried down Rayland's busy roadways. A sea of people bottled up as they headed toward the stadium. "Please tell me he didn't go in there. Please." He caught a pair of women looking at him like he was crazy. Sticking his neck out and popping his eyes, he said to them, "Yes, I talk to myself. Is that a crime?"

Wringing his hands as the hem of his robes dusted over the stone-paved streets, he pushed his way up the road. He'd explicitly explained to Moth on more than one occasion the need for discretion. They needed to lay low and get some idea of what Rolem would throw at them next. That's why he'd hired Dizon. She had her ear low to the ground and would be able to tell him about any unexpected arrivals. Of course, Rolem might just send another tremendous force of knights after him, making his efforts obvious. As for Moth, he could never tell if the barbarian heard him or not. The savage was an enigma.

I need to just kill him. It would save me additional head pains.

Crossing the street, he stepped on a man's toe.

"Ow!" The thick-necked man glared at Finster. He wore a patch over his eye. His greasy hair was tied back in a ponytail, and a swashbuckler's sword and dagger were on his hips. Tattoos covered his chest and meaty arms. He grabbed Finster's wrist and jerked it. "Watch out, twig neck!"

"Excuse you," Finster said, giving the man a look of disdain.

"What?" The man pulled Finster closer. "I've killed men for less." He pushed Finster into the alley. Two other sailors followed.

"I don't care, river rat. Now, unhand me before I make a fool out of you."

The man shook him. "I hear a little jingle under those robes." With his free hand, he patted Finster down. "Your purse for your life."

Finster's eyes narrowed. "You really don't want to do this. And stealing is a crime in Rayland. You'll force me to call the authorities on you."

"Heh, we are the authorities. Now hand over your coins."

"If you insist." Finster fished out the purse from a pocket in his robes. The little leather bag was still mostly full with the gold he sold the rowboat for. Using his power, he dangled it in the air in front of the thug's eyes.

"What in the..." The man blinked. All three men's eyes were fixed on the bag. The little sack floated higher. "Bring that back down here, trickster."

"If you insist." Finster flipped his hand down. The sack of coin streaked downward, smacking the brute in the forehead with hammer-like force. *Whap!*

Blood ran freely from the man's face as he stumbled backward. His fingers fumbled for the handle of his sword. On wobbly legs, he yanked the weapon free. "You'll die for that."

"No, I won't." Finster bent the man's sword with his mind. The other two men closed in. With a single thought, Finster ripped the weapons free from the men's hands and held them to their own throats. The whites of their eyes showed brightly in the darkness of the alley. “Are we finished here, or must I finish all of you?” He bent his ear. “I don’t hear anything.”

“Aye,” both men said. The leader with the bent sword gaped at his sword blade. With blood running into his eyes, he nodded. “Aye, sorcerer. Apologies.”

The purse of coins flew into Finster’s awaiting hand. He didn’t like the evil glint in the biggest man’s eyes. Something about the man stirred him. Pointing with his pinky, he said to the man, “You better never cross me again. I’ll turn you inside out next time.” He put his purse away, backed into the street, and joined the crowd on their way to the stadium.

Aside from Mendes, Finster knew Rayland better than any other city. He was a man of the south, born and raised. Mendes was the largest of the Seven Kingdoms, whose census boasted over a million citizens. It had the largest army as well. The other Seven Kingdoms, all of which Finster had visited in his travels, numbered from the smallest of over one hundred thousand in Toozaan, to perhaps just a couple hundred thousand shy of a million in Umpton. All cities offered something different, but Rayland was a mix of all of them. The locals typically had tanned skin and lighter hair, whereas Varland, the kingdom on the rocky steppes, was ruled by the Orientals. That’s where Satrap Chen of the Violet Tower was from. Archmenis, residing on the bottom of the Surge, was the kingdom of the stone-face blacks renowned for hunting and working their iron mines that they treated like gold. All of the kingdoms feuded with one another from time to time, mostly over trade and business disagreements, but they were living at peace, for now.

Finster stepped in line to the stadium. The building was crafted from huge blocks of stone, accented in black and white marble. The perfect square stood four stories tall. Golden banners with black serpents entwined around a ship mast, the symbol of Rayland, hung from the outer rims. Entertainment of all sorts occurred in the stadium—music concerts, contests of strength and skill, even tradeshows. Finster couldn't have cared less. Stroking the hair on his beard, he shuffled forward, thinking about the kingdoms.

Peace. You can't have peace without the Red Citadel.

The Magus Supremeus of the Red Citadel was dead. Finster killed her, and she killed the one before her. The Red Citadel was little more than a tomb now that its greatest wizards and sorcerers had been dispatched by Ingrid the Insane. Ingrid took the rings of power from the mages she defeated and killed them all. That created a void. The magi of the citadel were the advisors and peacekeepers of the kingdoms. They kept the kings and queens from being at each other's throats. Now, the magi were gone, and without their wisdom, the kingdoms would begin warring with each other soon enough. That was what Rolem wanted, and Ingrid too. Rolem would turn his adversaries against one another, whittle down their forces, and strike when the time was right. That was Finster's theory anyway.

He paid his entrance fee and made his way inside. The vendors' concourse that ran inside of the stadium smelled of savory cooked food. Partakers bought large tankards of wine and ale as they headed to their seats. Finster made his way around the concourse first, searching for a man who towered over the others. There was no sign of such a man. Finster figured Moth would be going after food if anything. Even the roasted hen on sticks looked good to Finster.

I never should have given him coin.

Bumping his way through the excited crowd, he headed to his seat. He took the steps up and stopped where he had a good gaze at the open stadium floor. The stands were filling fast. People pointed and talked with vigor at the contraptions on the stadium floor. Finster's brow arched.

No wonder this place is packed with fools. They're running the Gauntlet.

His eyes found Moth on the main floor among the other contestants.

"Damn!"

Chapter 44

The Gauntlet was a time-honored tradition that dated back four centuries. Men and women from all over the realm came to pit their skills against the bone-busting challenges that always resulted in severe injury or death. The Gauntlet was built on scaffolding made from beams of iron and banks of bloodstained cedar. It spanned the full length of the arena in all directions, reaching over thirty feet high at the highest obstacle at the top.

A vendor carried a box filled with small green glass-blown bottles. Wine filled them to the rim. Up and down the stairs he called out, "Spirits! Get your spirits!"

Finster didn't notice the young wine-slinging lad at first, but his growing backache and the youth's high-pitched voice caught his attention. He'd gone a full two days without a strong drink. He hadn't made any promises but to himself. He needed his wits sharp. He needed control or the scarab's power could control him. He raised his arm and held up two fingers.

The young vendor caught Finster's movement immediately. He handed over two bottles, took the coins, and said, "Thank you, sir!"

Finster chugged down the first bottle. "Ah, that's better." He found a frumpily dressed woman with a nest of wavy hair looking back at him. "Don't judge me, cow-face. I don't judge you when you graze." He started into the next bottle as he watched Moth. The brute wasn't as out of place as the rest of the freaks who were dressed for their run. Men and women from everywhere wore costumes with their own personal flair. There were hats, feathers, body paint, and animal bones decorating many. They chatted among themselves as they did stretches and calisthenics. Moth's protruding brows faced the Gauntlet. A woman with a helmet of auburn hair spoke to the savage. He didn't even give her a glance. She kept talking.

"What in the Seven Kingdoms has driven him out here today?" Finster's knee bounced. He wanted to go down on the main floor and haul Moth back to the apartment, but it wouldn't do him any good. Moth didn't listen to him, or anyone. He just did what he did. "I think I'd have been better off if I hadn't chased him at all." Dizon slid into the bench seat beside him. He glanced her direction. "You made it here quick."

"My daughter's vomiting woke me up," she said.

"Don't you mean, the king's daughter?"

"Same one," she replied, eyeing his bottle. "I thought you were avoiding the drink."

"This is the stadium. Look around. At this festival, it's tradition. Even I'm not one to break with traditions. It can bring bad fortune."

"Fair enough. I see your comrade is making new friends. That could be fatal." Dizon put her hand on Finster's thigh. "No one has beat the Gauntlet in over one hundred years. They keep lifting the value of the prize as well. Every contestant enters by paying an entrance fee with their own gold. The prize is over ten thousand gold jacks. There is also the chalice encrusted in gems. Another fortune. I've heard the king's treasury is not so flush. So, nobody wins."

"Of course not. The king needs money for his harem." Finster chuckled when Dizon's fingernails dug into his thighs. "I hope you aren't getting too attached to me, Dizon. I'm a dangerous man to care about."

She looked at him with her painted eyes and long lashes. "It's too late. I love you dearly. I'll follow you to hell and back."

"Now you're being ridiculous. Do you have clients that fall for that phrase?"

"Usually, it's the other way around," she said with a smile.

"That I can believe. As for your footsteps walking alongside mine, I'm willing to entertain it, so long as the bastard born isn't involved. Not that I have anything against children. Even I was a child once, briefly. No offense."

"I'll just sell her. No worries, Lord Finster."

Under a compulsion that didn't seem to be his own, he put his arm around her waist. "You have a wonderful way with words. Your wine-red lips bring forth nothing but honey. How did King Alrick ever let you out of his sight?"

"All of the harem are dismissed when they are thirty. Many before that."

"Why, that couldn't have been more than a week ago."

"Now it is your lips that spew forth honey. I like it." She crossed her leg over his. "Very much."

Finster's blood stirred. Dizon was more than what she appeared to be. Born in the right place she would have been a queen. Instead, she was a commoner, born in the streets, probably to an unknown father, whose beauty was discovered by dubious slavers at a young age. Still, he liked her, whether she was the biggest flatterer or not. She almost seemed like a part of him. The wife he'd once longed for.

Don't even dream it, Finster. Remember what happened with Ingrid. All women are crazy in one way or another. Give her time, she'll prove me right. They always do.

The trumpeters standing on the lower level of the stadium sounded off their horns. They belted out a ceremonial series of notes customary before an important event. The men and women on the ground rose to their feet. On the other side of the stadium, a bare section was outlined with soldiers dressed in ring mail and carrying spears. They wore tunics over the armor with the colors and signs of Rayland on them.

The thousands of people in the crowd started to chant. "The king! The king!" They lifted their fists in the air and pumped them wildly. "The king! The king! Hail King Alrick!"

"The king is coming to this event? Doesn't he have better things to do?" Finster said. He couldn't have asked for a worse scenario. The last thing he needed to happen was for Moth to draw any further notice. Especially from the king himself.

"King Alrick, unlike his father, has always come, every year since he took the crown. He's very fond of the Gauntlet. It excites him." She shouted and started waving. "Hail, King Alrick!"

"I don't think he can see or hear you."

King Alrick entered, and the stadium erupted in deafening cheers. The king stood tall with a small gold crown on his head and wore an ivory-white suit with brass buttons. A wave of chestnut-colored hair almost covered his eyes. He was young, no more than thirty, and showed a gracious smile.

"It seems the people are very enchanted with him," Finster commented. "I admit, he is an improvement over his father. Will his mother be present?"

"She adores the festival, but not the games. The queen runs the castle when he is gone."

"I see."

King Alrick sat on a chair that looked like a small throne. The rest of the crowd sat down. The king leaned over and whispered in his head servant's ear. The man gave a quick nod, moved to the front of the stands, cupped his hands over his mouth, and shouted, "Let the Gauntlet games begin!"

Chapter 45

Sitting, Finster said, "This Gauntlet is much different than that last one I saw. Granted, I've only witnessed this once before. I seem to recall a Toozaan-born warrior falling to his doom in a vat of acid."

"The configurations are changed every year. And the engineers rotate from kingdom to kingdom, trying to outwit one another," Dizon said. Her fingers spread over his thigh, firmly massaging it. "Herclon created this year's Gauntlet. Mendes fashioned the Gauntlet before that."

"If anyone knows how to create traps it would be the descendants of the pirate king. It astounds me that that kingdom of black-eyed rogues stands a kingdom to this day." Herclon was the fifth kingdom north of Mendes. "Its people are nothing but a bunch of hairy-armed sea raiders. Even the women."

"They are a burly bunch, but you have to respect their creativity." She pointed her lips at a sheer wall, thirty feet high, with steel spikes sticking out of it. Spread out on the wall were small wooden finger- and footholds. At the bottom of the wall was a pit that was covered in a black canvas. Dizon tossed her hair with a swing of her neck. "The final obstacle. Though, I don't think any will make it that far."

"I could," Finster said.

"I know you could, shipwrecker."

Finster gave a thin smile. "Ah, so you heard about that."

"I hear everything. I pride myself on it. And such exciting news travels fast. There aren't many tales in the bars that can top a lone man capsizing an entire fleet."

Bare-chested men in dyed blue woolen trousers manned the different stations of the Gauntlet. Gold flecks of paint were sprinkled on their bodies, and black snakes were tattooed on their backs. There were levers and pulleys that operated some of the obstacles. Finster studied the contraption. The last thing he wanted was for Moth to finish the course. If anything, that would get him an audience with the king, and he didn't want that. He wasn't sure Moth wanted it either.

"Here goes the first scrapper," Dizon said with a hungry gleam in her eyes. Everyone in the crowd sat on the edges of their benches. Above, dark clouds passed over the open ceiling of the stadium. The facility was lit up by the glow of torches and hundreds of oil lanterns. Each and every obstacle could be clearly seen. "They call them scrappers because they are desperate for a fortune."

"Or just greedy. Greed will get them killed. But who am I to judge? Whatever will be will be."

The first scrapper climbed up onto the ten-foot-high platform. She saluted ten thousand screaming people. She was a wiry gal, just over five feet tall, with her hair braided on the top of her head. All she had on was a cotton shirt and cut-off trousers. Her feet were bare.

"She's a Herclon," Finster said. "I can see her hairy legs from here."

The first obstacle was a twenty-foot-long narrow beam of wood. Below it was a rectangular metal basin of oil that ran the length of the plank. The basin sat on a bed of burning coals.

"That looks simple enough," Finster said.

An official-looking man in seafoam-green robes with onyx stones sewn on the sleeves stood on the same platform. He gave the female scrapper a nod.

The Herclon woman spread her arms out as she stepped onto the beam. Slowly, she began to cross. She did a flip on the beam, landed with the ease of a cat, and bowed.

The crowd broke out in rousing applause as the scrapper did a little dance on the beam with the delicate feet of a ballerina. She executed another perfect front flip. The beam shifted forty-five degrees.

"Here goes," Finster said.

The scrapper's feet hit the edge of the beam. Her legs split open. She landed hard on her crotch. Agony filled her face.

The audience erupted in laughter as did all of the other scrappers. King Alrick slapped his knees. His head thrust back from laughter.

Finster spied one of the burly assistants in the shadows turning a crank at floor level, rotating the beam.

The grimacing scrapper scooted along the beam, pain etched on her face. She was halfway across, but the beam turned faster. She flipped over, using her arms and legs to hang on from underneath. She shimmied as fast as she could. Her fingers slipped. She hung upside down with her feet locked at the ankles.

The crowd gasped.

Dizon's fingers dug into Finster's leg. "Ouch," he said, calmly peeling her fingers away.

Hanging upside down, the scrapper tried to swing herself back up to the beam. Finally, she managed to bear-hug the beam with her arms and legs. The beam continued to spin, over and over, turning the woman like a roasted pig on a spit. Shouts echoed through the crowd, a few encouraging her, but not all.

"Drop, dirty Herclon. Drop!"

The words became a chant among many. "Drop! Drop! Drop! Drop! Drop!"

Neck straining, the scrapper shouted something that couldn't be heard over the crowd. Her arms and legs failed. She dropped with a splash into the vat of boiling oil.

There was a unified "Ewwwww..." followed by a chorus of "Yays!"

Without warning, the scrapper from Herclon burst out of the vat. Her boiled skin had bubbled up, was crispy, cracked, and peeling. With a monumental effort, she crawled out at an agonizing pace and fell over the scorching rim of the metal basin. She managed to stand once more before a gaping and silenced crowd. She lifted her charred and rigid arm, saluted, and died.

"That was awful," Dizon said with her fingers covering her open mouth.

Finster nodded. "Cocky will get you killed. Don't fool around with the Gauntlet."

Chapter 46

The next scrapper raced over the beam, not leaving it time to turn. He was a muscular black, shorter than most, with the agility of an acrobat. He patted his chest over the heart and let out a triumphant scream. Finally, a door opened to the next obstacle. The scrapper hopped through the door and onto the next higher platform. A row of huge axe blades, bigger than a man, dangled in the path to the next level. With help from the assistants who turned a hand crank, they started to swing as if hung from a pendulum.

The scrapper saluted. He cast his eyes downward. Beneath him was a long pit. His face bunched up.

Many in the audience rose up in their seats, straining their necks to see what was inside.

"What lies below the slicing blades?" an onlooker said. "I cannot see a thing."

There was some murmuring coming from the puzzled crowd. One man suggested it was snakes while another's thoughts were of hornets.

"What do you think it is, Finster?" Dizon asked.

"Wine, perhaps," he said, draining his second bottle. He'd ordered two more since the first event. "Have you ever bathed in wine before, Dizon? It's elating."

"No, but I've had my share of milk baths. I find them more refreshing."

The scrapper cupped his hands together and called out to the crowd. The people at the bottom level heard his words and quickly spread that what the man saw was a mirror.

"Interesting," Finster commented. "He'll see himself fall to his death. I like it. If only there were a way to get a painting of it to share with his family."

The scrapper rubbed his hands together and started forward. There were five swinging axe blades in all with barely a body length between them. The plank was wider than the beam on obstacle one, but footing would be difficult, given the short distance between the swinging blades. The scrapper could only advance so far between them. As the first axe blade swished by the man's toes, he shuffle-skipped forward. The blade came within inches of his hindquarters in the back and toes in the front. Standing between blades one and two, he watched number two. It slid by his toes. He moved forward. The crowd cheered the man on as sweat glistened on his body. The scrapper made a quick wave and slid between blades three, four, and five. He wiped the sweat from his face. Blade five swung left and right in perfect cadence. The scrapper jumped at the next opening. He landed safely on the end of the platform. The blades behind him came to a stop. The crowd broke out into applause as the scrapper went through an open door that led to the third and higher platform.

"That seemed easy enough," Finster remarked.

The third platform was a thirty-foot-long walkway that made a bridge from platform three to number four. It was suspended by chains with wooden planks on the links. The scrapper couldn't take the walkway from the top. It had to be taken from the bottom by using wooden finger- and footholds mounted on the bottom. If he fell, he'd land twenty feet down on a hot bed of coals.

Watching the scrapper rub his hands together, Dizon said, "He's going to have to cross that like some sort of spider."

"Yes, it's a formidable expanse. He'll climb like an insect and probably die like one too."

"The Archmenian is doing well, if you ask me."

"Yes, but I didn't, did I, Dizon?" he said, patting her knee.

The Archmenian scrapper secured his fingers underneath the walkway. He stretched out far enough to fasten the toes of his feet on the blocks. He turned and looked at the coals below him. Sweat dripped from his body and sizzled on the coals below. With the audience hanging with bated breath, he started to climb. He moved at a brisk pace, strong fingers locked tight on the hand- and footholds. His toes kept their purchase on the blocks. He hung and moved like a squirrel. He crossed the halfway point. The crowd shouted out words of encouragement.

"He's going to do it!" Dizon exclaimed.

A few of the assistants made their way on the top side of the walkway. They jumped up and down on the planks. Up and down they went, jostling the entire bridge. The bridge swayed and buckled. The scrapper froze in place, his eyes wide as he cast looks from side to side.

"He's not going to make it," Finster said.

The scrapper advanced a few more feet on shaky arms and legs. The toes on his right foot slipped from the blocks. He couldn't get his foot back up again. His sweaty feet slipped from the block. All at once, he plummeted into the hot coals. Landing feet first, he collapsed. The coals jumped up all around him. Ankle deep in the bed of fire, he screamed as he waded out. With blistered skin, he walked out of the arena, hunched over but waving his hand. The audience applauded.

A man sitting behind Finster cursed. "There goes my coin. That Archmenian was supposed to be the prize of the lot, and he didn't even make it to the pit at platform four. I would have made money if he'd made it that far."

The crowd started booing when the assistants left the bridge. They screamed, "Cheats!" and "Deceivers!"

King Alrick talked with his council. It was clear they were laughing and joking over the entire thing.

"Never bet against the king," Finster said in Dizon's ear. "The wealthy and powerful always have the advantage."

"Yes, and the engineers are well paid too. They don't get paid if someone makes it through, that's why it's nearly impossible."

He shook his head. "There are at least fifty scrappers who still remain. Do they still call on them at random?"

"Yes, but don't worry. I've seen at least ten drop out. See, look." She pointed at the men and women who broke from the contending scrappers. They took a seat on a bench with their heads down. "Seeing the Archmenian fail broke their spirits."

"If they were desperate enough to try the Gauntlet, I'd say their spirits were already broken."

"I think they like the challenge," she replied.

"If that were the case, they would go on."

She nodded.

"Of course, I could help out a poor sap or two and make it truly entertaining," he said with a wink.

"You wouldn't."

"Oh, I would. Are you a betting woman, Dizon?"

Again, she nodded.

"Then let's make you a lot more money."

Chapter 47

DIZON WENT TO POST THE bets while Finster observed. The games continued with one scrapper after the other traversing the Gauntlet to a devastating end. The plank at platform one turned more frequently. The square board would shift ninety degrees and stop. A man from Umpton with a long, lean build hopped up as the beam shifted beneath him. He made it across in three long, swift hops between the shifting of the beam. At platform two, the Slicer, he advanced. He crept forward too far, and the blades chopped off his front toes. Arms flailing, he clutched at the blades. He lost his fingers and fell. He crashed through the mirror into a massive bin full of broken glass. He was carried out, bleeding all over.

One after another, contestant after contestant failed. They fell in the boiling oil and died on two more occasions. The slicing axes killed a Toozan man instantly on an ill-timed first step. A gal with a long ponytail, thin as a mop handle, dropped from the bottom of the bridge. Her back snapped when she hit the coals. She caught fire, let out an earsplitting scream, and burned to death.

The crowd, lathered up in sweat and filled with profanities, egged the scrappers on and on. A cloud of smoke hung in the air. Wine and mead tankards slammed together. Fights broke out. A herd of wild pigs scurried through the stadium. Shepherds draped in sackcloth robes yelled as they ran by with their staffs raised.

Finster worked on his fifth small bottle of wine. His cheeks warmed. *One more won't hurt. I feel outstanding.* He'd tuned himself to every lever, handle, and pulley of the Gauntlet. He could feel them move right before they did. He controlled the Gauntlet.

Dizon returned. "I made the wagers."

"Good." He tapped his chest and burped. "Show me the scrappers."

She pointed to three men. They had wild hair, coarse brown beards, and branded chests. They were built like bears. They head-butted each other and snarled. "They're brothers. Wild Goths. True savages from the Fringe. Only a fool would bet on them, and I don't care if they die. I have two of them going to the third and one through the fourth."

"You didn't see them through to the fifth?"

"They don't deserve the prize. I hear they eat their own children. Let them die on the fourth, I say. I just want to see it."

Finster shrugged. "As you will."

The night went on. The deaths and injuries piled up. Less than ten scrappers were left, and only three more men made it to the bridge. The first Wild Goth scrapper was called to the plank platform. He stomped his feet and beat his chest like a drum. He let out a furious howl as if he were a roaring bear. The assistant signaled with a one-handed flick of his fingers.

The Wild Goth pushed the assistant off the podium. The masses heaved with laughter.

"Here we go," Finster said. He held the plank in place. The assistant tried to turn the crank, but it wouldn't budge. The scrapper ran across the plank, not stopping until he reached the other side. He hopped up and down, kicking his knees into his chest, and burst through the door to the Slicer. "Did I make it look too easy?"

Dizon shrugged.

Finster didn't even slow the axe blades of the Slicer. The Wild Goth traversed the trap with ease. At the bridge, the Wild Goth fastened his fingers to the wood underneath the bridge. He started the climb from one side to the other at a steady pace. The crowd was on their feet, hollering at the top of their lungs. The assistants received a rowdy chorus of boos as they climbed onto the bridge. They jumped up and down.

With a thought, Finster made the chain bridge's links galvanize like beams of steel. It didn't shake or tremble under the weight of the man. Seconds later, the scrapper crossed over to the other side.

King Alrick sat on the edge of his chair. His fingers drummed on the armrests. He cursed at his counselors.

"Hah," Finster laughed. "It seems the king is a betting man too. It will be a delight to see him squirm."

The fourth obstacle was a series of large metal hoops that were suspended from above. The scrapper had to be able to jump from the platform to the first ring. From there he or she would use swinging momentum to go from ring to ring that descended toward the bottom of the fifth obstacle, the Wall. Finster counted ten rings. All of them would be needed to make the trip. Below the rings was a bed full of spikes. One might survive the fall, but the injuries would be catastrophic. There was a small platform at the base of the wall that rose fifty feet high. It sparkled with glass and spikes that were among the small hand- and footholds. Nearing the top, it bent over at an inverted angle, dangling the climber right over the spikes.

Dizon gave Finster a hug. The smile on her face said it all. "He made it to the fourth. I made a lot of money. I thank you, Finster. You are a true man of your word. When we return, I'm going to prepare you something very delicious to eat."

"I look forward to it."

The crowd chanted slowly, "Goth! Goth! Goth! Goth!"

On a signal from the assistant, the Goth backed up to the edge of the platform. He eyed the nearest ring, fist-thumped his chest, let out a wild cry, and sprinted across the platform. He leapt high, propelling himself perfectly toward the awaiting ring. His outstretched fingers were only a foot from the ring. The ring yanked up out of reach. The Wild Goth swam in the air for a long second. He splatted face-first in the spikes.

The crowd let out a unified, "Ooooooh!"

The assistants ripped the Goth's body up from the spikes. Using a wheelbarrow, one of them carted him off.

Finster started chuckling. It turned into a full outburst of laughter. The commotion he caused drew a lot of odd stares.

"Lord Finster, compose yourself," Dizon said, trying not to laugh herself. "Please." She unleashed a quick chuckle. "It's not right to laugh at death so. It's a bad omen."

"I can't help it." He tossed his head back and cackled. He belly laughed so hard he almost couldn't sit in his seat. "I'm sorry, but that was one of the funniest things I've seen in a long time." He wiped the tears from his eyes. "Woo-who-who! Oh, my gut aches."

"Finster, you need to gather yourself. Moth stands on the platform. His turn has come!"

Chapter 48

Moth fixed his heavy stare on Finster. So much so, even at this distance the mage felt it.

"He's looking right at you," Dizon said. "How did he even know you were here?"

"The barbarian has a knack for sensing things, I suppose," he said.

"What does he want?"

"It's not what he wants. It's what he doesn't want. He's a big stubborn fool." Finster nodded at Moth and resumed his drinking. "I won't aid him, regardless of the peril."

"He could die."

"Yes, well, I'd like to hope so."

"But you could win the gold, the chalice, all of it." Dizon was on her toes, trying to see past the man who stood in front of her. "You should take it."

"No. Gold is of little necessity to me. I have power. That's all I need."

Dizon pushed the man in front of her into his seat. "Sit down!" The drunken man turned toward her. He pulled back his fist. In a flash, she pushed a small dagger against his throat. His glazy eyes popped open. "Sit or death?"

The man swallowed and sat down quietly.

"You know they'll all be on their feet again soon enough," Finster said, shaking his bottle.

She tucked her dagger back in her clothing. "Not this one."

Moth removed his robes. The scarred-up youth's corded muscles flexed with his slightest movement. He towered over even the burly assistants, standing like a giant among them. The look of a savage predator from the wild lurked in his eyes as he turned his stare to the gold-tattooed assistant on the platform. The man stepped back. He pointed his fingers and gave a nod. The first obstacle, the plank, began to turn quickly.

The course was made for smaller, lighter men and women with strapping builds. Bigger men often fell to their doom, unable to control the weight of their massive frames. But like a gorilla, Moth controlled his size with the same savage strength bred in the wild.

"The beam turns too fast. No one can cross that. Stop it, Finster," Dizon suggested.

"Whatever will be will be," he said as he scooted to the edge of his chair. "No offense."

Moth glowered at the turning plank. It went on and on without stopping. The delay drew the ire of the crowd. They shouted vulgar insults and profanities.

"Go, stupid savage! Go!"

"Jump, pig lover!"

"Die, bald abomination! Die!"

The diatribe went on.

"I'm going to have to remember some of these," Finster said. "I'm keen on the vomitus pisswiller. That's an otherworldly insult."

Standing before the beam, Moth squatted down, knuckles on the platform, like a white ape. In a burst of motion, he jumped. His legs and arms fully extended, propelling him forward, sending him sailing across the twenty-foot expanse.

The awed crowd gasped.

Moth landed safely on the other side with the ease of a jungle cat.

The king came to his feet. He applauded with hearty claps. The crowd rose to their feet, going wild. No man had ever seen a man so big jump so far before.

Dizon's ample chest heaved as her fingers toyed with the necklace of gems and pearls dangling from her neck. "I never would have imagined."

"Yes, well, don't go anywhere," Finster said, acting bored. "The barbarian is full of surprises. If you are into that sort of thing."

The assistant at the second obstacle, the Slicer, gave Moth the go-ahead. The assistants that worked the speed of the blades cranked their levers as fast as they could. Moth's eyes followed the brisk movements of the blades. In ten quick steps, he weaved through the blades like a snake slithering through a maze. Not a single sharp edge nicked his skin. He stood waiting on the third platform.

Down on the main floor, the engineers from Herclon argued with one another. One of them, with braids from the top of his head down to his chest, had a scroll crushed in his hand. He shouted at the assistants. The stout assistants scrambled to the top side of the bridge.

On the assistant's signal, Moth slipped under the bridge. His fingers latched onto the blocks. With a grip of iron, he fastened himself onto the bridge. Arms and feet went to work, and he crossed the bridge at a steady pace. The assistants, a dozen in all, jumped up and down on the chain bridge with all of their might. Steady as a caterpillar, Moth moved on, being swayed, bumped, and jangled.

The crowd howled in a titillating frenzy.

The assistants stomped harder. The engineers shouted up at their men. The blistering-hot coals made a hungry glow, waiting to sear fresh meat.

Moth passed the halfway point still going strong. The men above him jerked at the chains, swaying and buckling the bridge. It would have been easier to shake a tick. The brute moved on, crossing to the other side unfettered. Slowly, he slipped out from under the bridge and looked at the men on top, whose jaws were hanging. Moth bared his teeth at them, turned, and climbed up to the fourth platform.

The people jumped up and down, shaking the stadium seats. Their sour chants from earlier turned complimentary. Someone with knowledge of otherworldly men beyond the kingdoms let out a fierce chant calling out for the Blue Toe barbarian. But it sounded like "Bluto! Bluto! Bluto! Bluto!"

King Alrick engaged in a heated conversation with his counselors. The king's own excitement from earlier seemed to have been quelled by the possibility that Moth might complete the Gauntlet.

The fourth obstacle, the rings, was ready. The assistant on the platform gave Moth the signal. Moth eyed the first ring. The huge hoop of steel dangled too far from his grasp. It bounced up and down in the air, teasing him, but going higher than before.

"The cheats! Finster, they raise the ring!" Dizon's fingers dug into her palms. "Put a stop to it."

"No, he started it, he'll have to finish it. He's a big barbarian. He knows what he's in for."

Moth looked down over the edge of the platform. A bed of long spikes awaited him like a mouth of teeth. He backed up, took off in a sprint, and leapt. The moment his feet left the platform, the first ring was yanked up far. Moth's fingers weren't even close to the metal.

Chapter 49

Moth's fingers missed the ring by over a foot. His tremendous body continued to sail through the air toward the second-nearest ring. The ring was lower in level than the first ring and another ten feet away. The barbarian's trajectory arched up before bending down on a clear path to the second ring. His big paw of a hand stretched out to the fullest length. The fingers on his right hand latched onto the second ring. He held fast, dangling over the spikes like fish bait, defying death once again.

"Impossible!" many in the audience shouted. They stomped their feet, jumped up and down, and screamed cheers at the death-defying barbarian.

Finster's own heart pounded in his chest. He was up on his feet absentmindedly clapping. Dizon's golden locks bounced up and down as she hopped on her toes. "I can't believe it!"

"He's a wily savage, that one," he replied. Finster had no way of knowing if the rings of power aided the barbarian or not. Every move Moth made seemed natural, bordering on superhuman. It wouldn't be the first time a savage pulled off an outstanding physical feat that defied reason. In battle, they were known to fight for days on end without food and water. They blotted out pain and shrugged off wounds like a dog sheds water. "Crossing wits with the kingdom's finest. Amusing."

Moth swung his left hand up onto the ring. He pulled himself up, muscles bulging and knotting in his back like gnarled tree roots. He climbed up onto the top of the ring and began swinging as if from a vine. His wary eyes watched the eight rings that were left. The assistants tugged on ropes from the bottom, jerking the remaining rings up and down.

The king stood up, looking onward with his hands on the railing.

Engineers now manned the ropes and pulleys that operated the rings. The event was designed for the scrapper to descend to the platform at the bottom of the wall. Hence, the rings were lower the further on they went, shortening the fall. Now, they hoisted the rings up higher, leaving thirty feet below all of the rings.

With a heave, Moth swung back and forth. He jumped from ring two to ring three. Ring four to ring six. Ring six to ring eight. He made the obstacle look easy. The crowd roared with approval. Standing on the ring, he swung back and forth and leapt. Still using the ropes, he swung outward and aimed for the dangling ring. His strong appendages coiled around the ring like snakes. His fingers slipped.

The audience gasped.

"Something's amiss!" Finster uncharacteristically shouted. That's when his keen eyes noticed a filmy hue on the last ring. It was greased with oil.

Moth's hands alternated on the ring like a cat clawing at the air. He kicked out, trying to propel himself toward the wall. His fingers slipped. He plummeted downward, twisting in the air, hurtling toward the bed of spikes beneath him. Somehow, he stretched his long arm out and caught the edge of the last platform with the tips of his fingers. He hung on, suspended for a long moment, gazing at the sharp daggers between his toes.

"Hang on, Moth!" Dizon shouted. She latched onto Finster, half burying her face in his chest. "I can't look."

"Don't stop now. You don't want to miss this."

Every muscle in the barbarian's back and arms bulged as he pulled himself up by his fingers. He swung his other arm up to the platform edge and hauled himself up. As the crowd cheered on, he wiped his slippery fingers on the side of his trousers and approached the wall.

Two assistants barred his path. He picked up one of the smaller muscle-bound men and pushed the man over his head, tossing him into the spikes.

The crowd shouted, "Hooray!"

The second assistant abandoned the last platform.

The wall was ten feet wide, filled with handholds made from wooden pegs and coated with broken glass, as well as filled with metal spikes and razors. Halfway to the top, it inverted at a forty-five-degree angle. One had to climb all the way to the top and hoist themselves over the wall to the last stand, where the Chalice of Champions awaited. No one could climb it without bleeding… a lot.

Moth latched on and started his ascent. His chest, forearms, and legs scraped against the metal shards and glass.

"Oh my. He's bleeding." Dizon winced. "He still goes. Doesn't that hurt?"

"Of course it does," Finster replied, "but he's too stupid to know it. Either that or pain is like a salve to him. I hate to think it's the latter."

The muscle-laden barbarian ascended halfway up to where the wall began to bend. There were only another twenty-five feet left to go. He began the inverted climb with blood dripping from his limbs.

Finster was curious as to why. He'd seen the barbarian heal from mortal wounds. Now he bled. *Are the rings with him or not?*

As Moth shimmied up the wall at a brisk pace, it inverted even farther. Like a drawbridge, the top half of the wall began lowering.

The obstacle-altering move worked the crowd into a frenzy.

The king smiled and applauded.

Moth's ascent came to a halt. The bloody finger- and toeholds he used were smaller than the ones under the bridge, not to mention designed to be painful. He reached for another handhold. The wall dropped a hard notch down. His grip failed. He plummeted toward the spikes with nothing to break his fall.

Magus Supremeus. He's doomed. Though, that could be a good thing.

The barbarian fell over thirty feet, landing feet first on the spikes. The sharp rods of metal pierced him through the feet and legs. Anguish filled his face, but he did not scream. The crowd screamed for him. Suddenly, his fierce expression darkened, and his anguish turned to rage.

Chapter 50

With a gut-wrenching yank, Moth pulled his foot free of the spike. A second spike impaled clean through his calf. Brows knitted together, he lifted his leg.

Dizon looked away, holding her stomach. "I think I'm going to be sick."

The king leaned over the railing, gaping.

Blood ran freely between the bed of spikes. There was enough room between them for Moth to pass on bloody footsteps. The silenced crowd's eyes hung on the brawny wild man as he treaded back to the platform. He reached down and snapped two spikes out of the floor. He jumped on the platform, punched his spikes into the wall, and started to climb. His powerful arms did most of the work while his bleeding toes scraped against the glass and sharp metal. Once again, he ascended the wall. Up he went, ten feet, twenty feet. The wall inverted. Thirty feet. Forty feet.

The stunned crowd's energy resurged.

"Bluto! Bluto! Bluto! Bluto! Bluto!"

Hanging at a full forty-five-degree angle, the scraped-up savage stopped at the very top. He grabbed hold of the upper wall's rim. There, he hung by two hands. He pulled himself up and stood at the very top. A ladder led to the champions' platform where the chalice waited above all things on a white marble pedestal. As the crowd chanted and cheered, Moth made the final climb. He stood by the oversized golden chalice. Its outer rim was encrusted in rubies, diamonds, and emeralds. It was worth a fortune.

Finster seized Dizon by the wrist. "Come on."

"What? Why?" she said, hurrying along.

"Because, he's going to do something stupid."

"Like what?"

Pushing them through the crowd toward the king's side of the stadium, Finster kept his eyes on Moth. The savage had scooped up the chalice in his blood-smeared hands. His head tilted side to side as he stared at it. His fingers brushed over the twinkling gems. With an arm that looked remarkably long for a man, he lifted it high over top of his head. The frenzied crowd called out to him. The cheers were deafening. No one had beaten the wall in over a hundred years.

Looking at his comrade, Finster saw a glint in Moth's eye and said, "Oh no."

From the raised platform, Moth spiked the Chalice of Champions on the platform. The gold rim dented. A few precious gems popped off and fell to the floor. Many in the crowd swarmed out of the stands, trampling the assistants and one another. Many died on the spikes where the small gemstones lay.

Outraged, King Alrick called out at the top of his voice, "What is he doing? Seize him!"

Soldiers in ring mail and metal helmets marched up the platform, surrounding Moth. Their eyes were wide and their expressions nervous. There was nowhere for the barbarian to go.

"Bring him before the king," Alrick said.

Moth took the catwalk that led to the lower level of the stadium, where he was led before the king. One of the counselors, wearing a set of golden robes with sky-blue trim, said, "Kneel before the king, savage!"

Sullen-eyed, Moth stood like a statue looking down on the king.

"Kneel or die," the counselor said again. He gave a quick nod to the soldiers. The men advanced with their halberds. The tips dangled less than a foot from Moth's skin.

King Alrick studied Moth from head to toe. "Can you speak, barbarian?"

Moth flipped over his palm. His fingers were caked with blood. Most of the skin was torn open.

"Ghastly," the king said with fascination. "You are like a wounded animal that does not know when to die. And you're dripping all over my stadium. Put your hand away."

Moth did not comply.

"Counselor Trenner," the king said, as he twisted the pointed hairs on the tip of his beard. "I am of the impression that this savage wants to be paid."

"Sire," Trenner, a long-faced older man, said, "this scrapper was ineligible the moment he fell from the fourth obstacle. Also, he demolished the chalice, creating a spectacle. There can only be prison time for him. A lifetime, I'd recommend."

King Alrick took his eyes from Moth and surveyed the crowd. Most of the crowd's gaze still hung on the king. They'd begun chanting "Bluto" again. "I'd hate to disappoint my subjects. Who finalizes the rules on the Gauntlet, Trenner?"

"You have the final word, sire, but I highly recommend an example is made of this one. It's clear he cheated. No man could have survived that fall."

"Yes, he's dangerous. A spy perhaps. Yet, intriguing. Barbarian, speak for yourself. Perhaps you can persuade me to not send you to the black mines of Hovel."

Moth did not speak. He didn't pull back his hand either.

The king waved him off. "Take him away then. Counselor Trenner, I'll let you feed the people a sufficient explanation."

"King Alrick! King Alrick! It is I, Dizon! Your majesty, please, turn."

"Eh," the king said, casting his eyes over his shoulder. A smile broke out over his face. "Dizon! Is that you?"

Standing with Finster, she eagerly nodded. She pointed at Moth. "He is a mute. And this is his interpreter." She pulled Finster forward. "Please let us clear up the confusion."

Trenner said to the king, "I don't recommend this, sire. Dizon is of a notorious background, and I can only suspect the same of this man she cavorts with. Best we move on."

"No, I want to hear what she has to say," the king said. "Guards, let them into my presence."

Dizon hustled to the king and dropped to her knees, kissing the rings on his fingers. Finster, behind her, took a knee and bowed.

Lifting her to her feet, King Alrick said, "Tell me, Dizon, what do you know of this man who just conquered the Gauntlet and embarrassed the Herclons as well?"

"I cannot speak for the blue toe, but this man, Finster, knows him quite well."

"This savage is your slave, then?" the king said to Finster. "And you entered him in the contest?"

"The barbarian has his own free will, but we are linked by fate. I cannot control what he does, but I assure you, he means no harm to the crown." Finster rose. "You see, this savage has the mind of a child, and I can only assume the Gauntlet tempted him. I apologize that he made such a spectacle of things, your majesty. But we are willing to forfeit half of our winnings, if it pleases the crown."

The king erupted in laughter. Composing himself, he said, "Oh, there will be no winnings, but I will render this savage one thing. Trenner, bring me the chalice or whatever is left of it."

The guards passed the Chalice of Champions up to Trenner. It had a huge dent in the rim, but many of the precious stones were still intact. Frowning, he handed it over to the king.

"I was always fond of you, Dizon. You had discernment." King Alrick took her by the hand and led her to Moth. He looked up at the barbarian. "This is all you'll get. Don't damage it again." He handed it to Moth.

Moth took the chalice. The king grasped him by the arm, and together they held it up.

The audience's cheering shook the stadium. As the king waved at them, he addressed Dizon and Finster. "All of you are coming with me."

CHAPTER 51

LATER THAT NIGHT, IN THE confines of a dark alley, the roughnecks who tried to rob Finster earlier lay dead in pools of their own blood. All three men's throats had been cut open. Their eyes were frozen stares transfixed toward the moon. Their slayers cleaned the blood on their blades on the dead men's clothing.

A man entered the alley. He lowered a hood, which hid his face. "Alexandria," the man said in a soft voice. "The targets have made much commotion. They have very brazen ways. They are in the king's castle. We should have struck earlier, in the midst of the crowd. It would have been easier."

"Nothing will be easy about killing these two," she said to the man. She wore a nondescript cloak similar to the other assassins in the alley. The members of the Circle were amazing at blending in. If one were to pass them, they wouldn't think them any different than any other traveler in the city. Alexandria, slender-faced with hard, penetrating eyes, gave a nod. The small group of assassins closed in on the man who was speaking. Their daggers pierced his body. Gasping, he sank to the ground.

"Don't ever question my decision-making," she said to the dying man. "There is a reason I am the guild master of the Circle. I've never failed. Sink them in the river."

Alexandria departed. She walked the streets, getting a feel for things. For two decades, she'd killed from one kingdom to another, never missing the mark. She was good, very good, and she took her time about things. Now, she spent time gathering information about Finster and Moth.

She slid into a bar, took a seat, and ordered wine. The patrons couldn't stop talking about what transpired in the Gauntlet. Though some of the stories were as bloated as their bellies, it became clear that the savage had powers beyond comprehension. Either that or the sorcerer was aiding him. As for Finster, she'd been sizing him up by pumping information out of the thugs he crossed earlier. She needed to understand as much about him and his powers as she could.

"Master of the inanimate," she said, sipping her wine. The heavyset barkeeper glanced her way. "Is there something I can help you with?"

"No," he said, rubbing his rag inside of a mug. "I didn't see you talking with anyone and thought you were talking to me, shipman."

"I assure you, I wasn't," she said in an amiable man's voice. "Just recollecting my crossings." She pushed the sleeves up over her arms and wiped her nose. The robes she wore disguised her as a sailor—average age, height, and build. The deception blended in with the rest of the patrons just fine.

"Just let me know if you want me to keep them coming. I've got plenty of that Herclon wine I need to unload. The Herclons are mad that their Gauntlet lost. I wish I'd seen it." The barkeeper chuckled. "Herclons pouting. Never thought I'd see the day." He moved on, taking other patrons' orders.

In the comfort of her disguise, Alexandria tuned in to all she heard and recollected all that she knew. It angered her that she'd missed an opportunity to see Moth and Finster in action at the stadium. She'd taken it out on her own henchmen after the fact. If she'd just made her way into Rayland a few hours earlier, she could have caught the troublesome duo in the act. Now, she contemplated what she knew.

Ingrid acquired eight rings of power from the magi of the Red Citadel. The now-dead Magus Supremeus allied herself with King Rolem. Together they were going to take control of the kingdoms with soldiers backed by magic. Ingrid went after Finster to find the Founder's Stone. They battled, and Ingrid lost. She lay dead in a tomb. Finster, Alexandria and Rolem both agreed, was in possession of the Founder's Stone. As for the rings, based off what had been witnessed, there weren't any signs of them. The rings didn't adorn Finster's fingers or the savage's, but she was confident one of the two had them.

She drank a little more, letting the cheap wine burn on the way down, recalling that it was a tavern such as this where she made her first kill.

Finster could animate objects. Whether or not it was silverware or ships, his power was awesome. He turned arrows aside and bent sword blades with his mind. His awareness, she was certain, was uncanny. But he had a flaw. He drank, reveled, and became unpredictable. That could be dangerous. He didn't seem to have control over flesh and bone, or anything living for the matter. Perhaps it was the edge she needed.

As for the barbarian, it seemed he could be stabbed, but his wounds would heal. Nothing broke him. That was the confusing part. Alexandria didn't comprehend where the power came from, unless Finster was the one keeping the man together. Based off what she knew of the rings, the one made with black iron and rubies could regenerate, but there was no sign of it. She'd come to understand most all of their powers, so much so that she wanted them for herself. Yet they evaded her. And it was difficult to kill someone who could regenerate. She'd killed a man once, stabbing him clean through the heart, only to see him rise at nightfall. He was a lycan, part wolf and part man. She finally finished him off with blades made from silver. Her fingers ran over her belly. Thick scars puckered the skin where the wolfman had nearly disemboweled her.

She left two silver jacks on the table and departed the tavern. She walked the roadway that led to the castle. The night winds from the river tore at her cloak. The locks of her dark hair fell over her shoulders, and she had the appearance of a woman again. She walked the hill in long strides, coming to a stop about halfway from the castle's main gates. Her slender fingers tapped on the pommels of the daggers that hung on her hips.

Perhaps it's time that I get a closer look at this pair for myself.

Chapter 52

Finster, Moth, and Dizon were seated in the king's dining hall. Every decoration from the ceiling to the floor was exquisite. Scenic murals of meadows were painted in the archways above their heads. The walls were made from an off-white marble filled with flecks of gold. Long scarlet drapes accented the windows. The floors were square white marble tiles with gold accents between them. The grand table seated twenty and was covered in crystal glassware, plates that shone like pearls, and silver flatware with gold handles. Platters of steaming food were set on the table by servants wearing gold aprons with royal-blue clothing underneath.

"Dive in, everyone," the king said with a ravishing smile. A small golden crown rested on his head with an emblem of a lion on a medallion in the middle. His curly dark-brown hair hung just over his eyebrows. "I'm famished after this evening's events, and typically I dine much earlier, but tonight is a special occasion. It's very odd company we have in our midst." He lifted a wineglass.

"Odd indeed," Counselor Trenner said. His hands were down on his lap as he watched the servants fill his plate with steaming fish, rice, and vegetables.

"It's an honor," Finster said, hoisting his glass. He and his companions sat across from Alrick and Trenner. It was only the five of them at the table, but one more plate was being loaded with food, and the wine glass had been filled. "Not to be impolite, but I'd hate to start if you are expecting someone else."

"Well, the queen, my mother, may or may not come. She always has an invite, and we keep a place for her." He placed his napkin on his lap. "She becomes a savage herself if we don't include her… in everything."

Twelve men covered in full suits of plate armor from head to toe stood with their backs to the wall. The armor was a brilliant steel accented with gold plating on the edges. The River Knights were the king's personal guard, composed of the most resilient, loyal, and tested soldiers. It was said one knight alone could handle any five well-armed men. They stood so still they didn't seem real unless you got a close look at the eyes that shone whitely behind the eyelets in the helm.

Moth had been cleaned up and dressed the moment he entered the castle. The maidens hauled him off and bathed him before dressing him in a set of robes that was at least one size too small. He ate with his fingers and grunted a little. He drank from the chalice, which was filled to the brim with wine.

The king studied Moth. Not hiding his fascination, he said, "His wounds closed up. How is that possible?"

"I can't really say for certain," Finster said, which was true. He could only guess that the rings of power caused regeneration. "Moth is a bit of an anomaly."

"You make for a strange pair, you and the brute." The king sawed into his fish and took a bite. "Tell me, how did this come to be?"

Finster took a long drink. "Sorry for indulging myself, your majesty, but this is the finest wine that I've had in years. Is it from your vineyard?"

"No, its grapes were drained in the vineyards of Varland. Now, don't stall with me, necromancer. You wouldn't want to draw my ire.

I've been patient enough." King Alrick turned to Dizon. "I thought you vouched for this one. I hope you weren't misleading me, Dizon. I don't like disappointment."

She shook her head. "Never, your majesty."

"I'm sorry, King Alrick, but I do enjoy the wine. As for me and Moth, well, I freed him from prison. He's clung to my side ever since."

Counselor Trenner broke into the conversation. Brows knitted together, he said, "Is the king supposed to guess why you let him free? Hmm… Finster? You are being impolite. Difficult! You should be whipped."

"Easy, Trenner. Let the man speak. I'm certain that wasn't his intent. Please, Finster, out with it now." The king set down his fork and hung his gaze on Finster. "What compelled you to free this man? And where did you free him from? What you've said is very intriguing."

Regardless of his lack of fear of the men in the room, Finster still didn't want to make an enemy of the king. "I was a prisoner too, taken against my will to the Red Citadel. It was from there that Moth and I made our escape."

The king pushed back in his seat. "So, you are a fugitive." He looked at Trenner. "Am I harboring a fugitive, counselor?"

"You are harboring a former arch magus, my king. This is Finster, also known as the Shadow Keeper, Master of the Inanimate, the Gray Force, Guardian of the Mystic Forge. His reputation precedes him." Trenner leaned on his elbows. His hawklike gaze locked on Finster. "It is rumored that he slew King Rolem's queen-to-be. That he capsized Mendes galleons. Is this not true, Rodent of Whispers?"

Finster held up a finger. The River Knights' swords snaked from their scabbards, and they advanced a full step. Dizon jumped from her seat. Moth chewed his food with a dull expression on his face, but his eyes swept the room. Finally, Finster said, "Your majesty, may I speak?"

The king nodded.

"I am who your counselor says, but I have no desire to harm you or anyone in your kingdom. If anything, our paths have crossed as a result of destiny."

The king pushed back in his chair. "Oh, now that is an interesting take on things."

"It's preposterous," Trenner blurted out. "These men are murderers in the king's court, no less."

Finster rolled his eyes. "Counselor Trenner, your flair for the dramatic is overtaking your senses. If I wanted to kill the king, I could have killed him the instant I saw him. And that includes you as well."

"My king! My king!" Trenner said, jumping out of his chair. "He just threatened the very crown itself. River Knights, seize them!"

Chapter 53

The River Knights stood in place. Yet, there were scufflings inside of their armor. Behind their eyelets their eyeballs glanced nervously in all directions. Finster yawned. "Your precious Knights of the Water won't be going anywhere, oh king. Please, while I have the stage, can I at least offer an explanation? One crown pursues me, and I certainly don't desire another. *Hic*!"

Red-faced, Trenner shouted at the knights, "What are you standing there for? Take this monster down!"

Finster looked at the king, whose expression had paled. "I don't think he understands what is going on here." With a wink, he slid Trenner's chair into the back of the man's legs, knocking him into the seat. "With your majesty's permission, may I continue to explain? I promise that I won't take up much of your time."

King Alrick glanced at Dizon.

"Your majesty, I've known many men, and this one is honorable. Please, hear him out."

The king sat up in his chair and swallowed. "Counselor Trenner, mind your tongue or be dismissed from the chamber."

"King Alrick, this sorcerer is dangerous."

The king hit his fist on the table. The tableware jumped. "It is your tongue that brings the danger, Trenner! Keep chattering and I'll have it cut out."

Trenner sank in his chair.

"River Knights, at rest! Finster, will you loosen your control on my knights now? No harm will come your way, though I think you knew that the moment you came in here. You have me at a loss."

"My pleasure, your majesty." The knights' armor rattled as they moved in place before going still again. "May I continue?"

"The table is yours," the king replied. With his hand to his chest, he took a breath. "Proceed."

Finster refilled his goblet. As he did so, the double doors to the room opened. Two soldiers escorted a woman into the room. The king and the counselor stood. Finster and Dizon did the same. The River Knights snapped their heels to attention.

"Mother," King Alrick said with a bow. "What a pleasure it is to have you join us."

Queen Annlee was a lovely and refined woman in her fifties. She wore a purple evening gown made from a soft linen that was a little too snug and revealing. Her hair was neatly combed back in a plume with a wave of gray in the middle. "It's very late for an invitation for dinner, Alrick. I thought I raised you better." She allowed her son to kiss both of her cheeks. She stared at the king's guests. "My, what sort of strangers are you consorting with now? And why is the harlot here? She was banished. And why isn't that monstrous man-thing standing?" Her eyes slid to Finster. "This sot sways."

"Mother, the savage is a mute called Moth, and he is the champion of the Gauntlet. These are his keepers, so to speak, Finster and Dizon." The king took his mother by the arm and helped her toward her chair, seated next to him but across from Moth. She jerked her arm away.

"Unhand me. I can sit myself." She plopped her fanny down in the chair across from Moth.

The barbarian grabbed two fluffy white rolls in his fingers and stuffed them in his mouth. He washed them down using the goblet.

"Disgusting," she said.

"Mother, you sound a little hoarse. Are you well?"

"Well enough, but not hungry." She made a stiff shake of her head and sighed. "Continue with your sordid business. I'm more than curious to know what it is all about. Seeing how it is so late, I can only imagine you didn't think I was coming. So here I am. All ears. Go on."

"Yes, Finster, go on." The king shifted in his seat. "You were telling me about King Rolem."

"King Rolem?" the queen said, straightening up in her seat. "This should prove interesting. What is he demanding this time? The entire Free River? The black mines? All of the fish in the sea?"

"Something to that effect, your highness," Finster said. "King Rolem conspired with the Magus Supremeus, Ingrid the Insane. They were to be wed, but I foiled their plans when I killed her. Prior to her death, Ingrid revealed to me that she killed several of the top magi from the Red Citadel, including the Magus Supremeus himself, Zuulan. It was a well-crafted plan that would have worked had she not involved me. When she tried to kill me and the barbarian, we ended up killing her instead."

"How can this be if she wielded so many rings of power?" King Alrick asked.

"Ingrid wanted me to lead her to the Founder's Stone, a rumored artifact of great power. She suspected that I knew its whereabouts. She was correct. I did know its whereabouts, and having been pushed to my limits, I was able to take command of its powers. It gave me, or us, rather, just enough of an edge to defeat her." He pushed back his sleeve, revealing the thick green veins pulsating through his arms. "The stone's power courses through my veins now, giving me significant power."

Queen Annlee's eyes widened. "If you are so powerful, then you are indeed as much a threat to the crown as this Ingrid was. Perhaps more so. Where are the rings?"

"They are not in my possession," Finster said, opening his hands. "Their whereabouts are more of a mystery than anything else." He wet his lips on the wine. "But let me assure you, I'm only here by circumstance, and since I'm here, I am warning you that King Rolem conspired to take over the kingdoms. That is what he wanted the stone and the rings for. But, being a member of the Red Citadel, a sorcerer of the ninth order, I have vowed to protect the kingdoms. The magi are the peacekeepers of the land, or at least they are supposed to be. I'll do what I can to keep that intact."

The people at the table grew silent. Alrick, Annlee, and Trenner appeared to be deep in thought. The only thing he heard was Moth chewing and Dizon patting his leg.

Finally, Counselor Trenner broke the silence. "May I speak?"

The king nodded.

"Though I find our guest contemptible, assuming what he says is true, it seems that King Rolem is not a threat to any kingdom without these rings or the stone. Certainly, he won't make an aggressive move without these items in his possession. And now, we are alerted to his attempts. This is a good thing. The only bad thing is, can we trust this sorcerer?"

"I'm a servant of the goodwill of the kingdoms. Nothing more and nothing less," Finster commented. "As for King Rolem, well, *hiccup*. Excuse me. As I was saying, this fight is between me and him as he blames me for the death of his insane bride-to-be. So, I am a fugitive who will defend himself, but hopes to avoid any more unnecessary casualties along the way. The last thing I need is another enemy or another kingdom angered at me."

"Given your predicament, I don't think that will be possible," the queen said, picking up her utensils. Her eyes narrowed on her food.

Suddenly, she swooned in her chair. "Get out of my mind, Finster! Get out of my head!" she yelled. "He's possessing me!"

"No, I'm not," Finster said with a perplexed look. "I can't possess anybody."

The queen convulsed in her chair.

"Finster, what have you done? Stop this now," the king demanded. Alrick lunged for the queen. She jabbed him in the gut with a steak knife. Alrick groaned. "Why?"

"I'm sorry, son, he made me do it," the deranged queen said. She stabbed him again. "I can't control it."

Chapter 54

Finster's blood ran to his toes. His jaw hung. The king's hands clutched at the knife in his belly. Counselor Trenner screamed and pointed at Finster. The words of the counselor didn't clearly register, but assassin, traitor, and murderer were among them. Finster's eyes landed on the queen. Her eyes were on him. A dark intent lurked in the queen's eyes. She winked at Finster.

Finster's wine-sluggish mind sped up. The queen was no queen. A darker façade took the queen's place. Finster looked deep into the imposter's cold, hard gaze. He'd seen the eyes of such killers before in his younger days.

Assassin!

He summoned his powers. The pommel of a River Knight sword cracked against his head. The world he knew started to turn black.

No, Finster, you can't black out. Not now! Nooooooo…

Chapter 55

Moth jumped aside as a River Knight chopped at his head. The blade bit through the back of the high-backed chair. Moth punched the knight in the face, knocking the man backward. He wrenched the sword free of the chair.

Without hesitation, the knights closed in on Moth, their mirror-like blades held in front of them. Moth jumped backward onto the table. He kicked the food from the plates. In an instant, he took in his surroundings. The king sagged to his knees, doubled over, with his hands on his gut. The queen moved away from the table. Her body shimmered as she made her way toward Finster. Finster lay on the ground with his lips almost kissing the marble floor. Dizon kneeled at his side.

A knight sliced at Moth's feet. He jumped high, striking as he came down. The longsword in his hand split through the metal of the man's helmet into the bone of the skull. Blood spit out. One knight was down. Eleven more to go. The knights weren't the enemy. The queen's imposter was. He raced down the table. His feet slapped on the wood. The flatware and plates bounced from the table.

The assassin had another dagger in her hand, a wet substance shining on the curved edge. She paid no mind to the savage trying to cut her off. She targeted Finster. She moved swiftly, rounding the end of the table. Her dagger was poised to strike at the prone Finster.

Moth pounced. His body collided with her just as she started to kneel. He crushed her underneath his weight, grappled with her, and squeezed. Her body shifted from the image of the queen into someone else—a younger, harder woman wearing a cloak that felt like skin.

Trenner gasped.

The dagger blade pricked Moth's skin. A stinging poison raced through his body. His limbs seized. The woman underneath him squeezed out from under his body, pushing out from under his rock-hard frame with a loud groan. A sword stabbed into Moth's side. Another blade jammed into his back.

The River Knights attacked the female assassin. She dodged and ducked. She slipped left and right, evading their steel. Her body shimmered. She scowled at Moth and vanished.

With his veins on fire, Moth tried to push himself off the floor. His muscles strained and rippled. All of his body trembled. The poison ate him up from the inside out.

Counselor Trenner took command. "River Knights. Kill them." He pointed to Moth and Finster. "Kill them both!"

Huddled over Finster's body, Dizon said, "No! They are not responsible! You saw the assassin the same as the rest of us. These men are not responsible!"

"You are a fool, whore! With the king dead, the people will demand justice. They will want their king avenged," Trenner said. "And I heard what I heard. The queen said Finster took her mind. I saw it myself. He will have the blame."

"That's madness!" Dizon said.

"That's how kingdoms are run. Besides, ridding ourselves of these two admitted murderers will win us great favor with King Rolem. A good witness from you could avail much for you too, harlot. What will it be?"

"I know what I saw, and I'll stand by it," she said.

"You are only complicating things for yourself, Dizon. Work with me and be a part of my small harem. Wouldn't living in the castle again, for a lifetime, but worth your while?"

"Not with you."

"I see. River Knights," Counselor Trenner ordered, "turn them into pieces. But leave the heads. We need to show the people their heads."

"Halt that order," King Alrick said. The agonized king managed to crawl into his chair. Panting through his nose and grimacing, he said, "I'm not dead yet, Trenner. I'm still the king. I'm still in charge. Knights, stay your blades. And you, Trenner, get me some aid, damn you!"

Face paling, Trenner said, "Er, yes, your majesty!" He bowed. "Immediately." He hustled to the door. The two soldiers who had escorted the queen opened them. He hollered down the hall, "Physicians! You, servant, summon the king's physicians, now!" Holding the hem of his garments up, he hurried back to the king. "Your majesty, they'll be here soon. Be strong."

King Alrick sat up in his chair. His hand was on his belly, and his face was ashen. His eyes made a frozen stare at the window across the room.

"Your majesty," Trenner said as he approached. He waved his hand in front of the king's eyes. "Oh, gods, he has died. I've lost him twice. Guards, summon the queen, immediately."

Another counselor entered the room wearing garb similar to Trenner's. He was much older, bald, and wrinkly, and didn't move too well. His expression was filled with worry. "The queen is dead," he said, casting his glance at the king. "We just found her in her room." His hands trembled. "Oh my, tell me the king is not dead too?"

"I'm afraid he is, Counselor Mather." Trenner took a long breath. There was a flicker in his eyes. The wheels of his destiny quickly turned. "It was the work of these two assassins. Guards, depart, close the doors behind you. River Knights, stay."

"So, these men on the floor are the assassins?" Counselor Mather asked.

"In a matter of speaking, yes," Trenner said.

"No, he's lying! How could they have murdered the queen when they've been here the entire time?" Dizon said. Tears streamed down her cheeks. "We saw the assassin. She escaped. Finster and Moth are innocent. All of these knights are witnesses to that."

"Dizon, dear Dizon, you understand how the crown works. The loss of a king and queen in a single day. The tragedy will break our kingdom." Trenner took the king's crown and placed it on his head. "Unless we have leadership. Strong leadership that is swift to act, capture, and kill the assassins. And since King Alrick never married, or sired any proper children, that leader will be me. Don't you agree, Counselor Mather?"

Rubbing his chin, Mather said, "Yes, it would be best for the crown. But there are formalities. There's the ceremony. The coronation. Oh, and the funeral. My, that will be lengthy."

"Yes, yes, Mather, I'm well aware. With that said, River Knights, as your king by proxy, kill all three of these assassin invaders. For the crown!"

"Aye," Mather said. "For the crown."

Chapter 56

The fire coursing through Moth's blood turned to icy water. The strength in his limbs returned. He sprang to his feet and hit the knight nearest to him. The knight's armor disintegrated. Without understanding, he attacked. From his punches came fire that cracked like thunder. A sword thrust slid into his ribs. He head-butted the metal face of the knight, sending him to the ground.

"To arms!" one knight yelled. "To arms!" The battle-hardened group of soldiers attacked as one. Skilled swordsmen, one and all, they swung at Moth with deadly precision. The blades bit into Moth's wrists and thighs. Blood flowed. "He bleeds! He dies!"

Fighting like a tiger, Moth flung himself into the men. He punched a soldier, knocking the helmet from his head. A hard blow of his foot busted another's groin. Biting a soldier on the sword hand, he wrenched a sword free. Strange powers channeled through his body. A blow from his sword turned a man to ash. Another knight drove his sword through Moth's back. Like a bucking bull, Moth flung the man to the ground.

"Those eyes!" a knight said. "They are of a demon!"

Every armored knight came at Moth with everything he had. Points of steel sank into Moth's body. They gored him, stabbed him, sliced him, chopped him. He bled, but his flesh mended. Moth made them pay. He rammed a knife under one man's chin. He chopped the leg off another. He slipped away from a decapitating blow, but the razor edge of the steel cut open his neck. His legs wobbled.

"We've got him, knights! Have at him!" The knights chopped in a frenzy.

Moth swung wildly. His body lost hunks, bits, and pieces. The backs of his legs were clipped. A spear thrust impaled his chest from one side to the other. He grabbed a knight's wrist and chopped off his arm. A dozen blows entered his body.

A knight knocked Moth's sword from his hand. Another chop to the backs of his legs dropped him on his knees. A death blow arced down on his skull. Inches from his face, it froze in space and time.

"That will be enough of that," Finster said. He stood at the edge of the table with a haggard look on his face. The specks in his eyes glowed green. Dizon stood by his side. She'd managed to awaken him. He thrust his hand forward. All of the knights lifted into the air and flew into the wall. There were only four of them left. Eyeing Moth, he said, "I should have let them gore you. You're a glutton for punishment. You know that, don't you?"

The sinew, bone, and cartilage started to mend all over Moth's body. The gaping wound in his neck sealed. He pulled the sword out of his back and a spear out of his belly. He dropped them on the floor, sneering at the knights as he did so.

"Counselor Trenner," Finster said. "We've had an excellent evening with you and the king, but now we will be leaving." His eyes casually swept the blood-splattered room. "I would suggest that you leave us alone too. There is a true assassin out there, and I aim to find them. Don't," he said, making the entire dinner table quake, "get in my way. Do I have your word on it?"

Counselors Trenner and Mather, flecks of blood on their faces and clothing, nodded. "Of course. Of course."

"I don't know how you are going to spin this with the people, but I suggest that you put the blame where it belongs, with King Rolem. If you put it on us, I'm liable to come back, and it won't be pretty." He took Dizon by the hand. "It's a shame about the king and his mother. They served good wine and seemed to be nice people. Very uncommon with the crown. Try not to ruin all they have striven to achieve."

Two chairs scooted out from behind the table. Finster sat on one of them and put Dizon on his lap. "Moth, take a seat."

Moth grabbed his chalice and sat down.

Powered by thought, Finster lifted them into the air. The large rectangular double-hung windows leading outside flew open. He looked at Trenner. "Oh, I'll be borrowing these chairs but won't be returning them." They departed from the castle, flying on the chairs with the wind in their hair, faces set against the warm breeze.

With her arms around Finster's neck, Dizon said, "Do you think Counselor Trenner will keep his word?"

"Of course not. The criers will be calling for the head of Finster the Kingdom Wrecker in the wee hours of the morning. Do you like the sound of that?" he said.

"No, it sounds awful."

"Yes, but I meant Finster the Kingdom Wrecker. I just came up with that. Don't you think it has a nice ring to it?"

She nodded. "I suppose. But, Finster, what are we going to do?"

"I'm thinking." At fifty feet high, they sailed through the air, making their way toward the city. The clouds were thick in the heavens, leaving them as nothing more than black dots in the sky. He sped forward, turned, and faced Moth. "Do you have any thoughts on this?"

The savage faced ahead, expressionless.

"Thanks to you, Moth, a good king and queen are dead all on account of your foolishness. Was I not clear when I said we need to maintain a high level of discretion?" Finster unleashed his disdain. "And all of this because you wanted to play at the Gauntlet! Now, you've wrecked a kingdom. A kingdom that could have been our ally."

"He could not have known about this assassin," Dizon said. "Could he?"

"There is no telling what he knows. Perhaps he planned all of this all along. Either way, at least I know what Rolem the Grand is up to." Finster rubbed his fingers into his temple. "He's sent an assassin after me and Moth. A very clever one at that."

"Do you think it was the Circle?" she asked.

"I can't think of anyone else better to hire if I were to try to kill me."

"Moth saved you, or else your throat would have been as open as a cleric's book. I couldn't have defended you from the likes of her, or him." Dizon kissed his cheek. "She can turn from one person to another, and vanish."

"Yes. The Circle. They have special powers and abilities. We saw that firsthand, didn't we? Bloody assassin almost pulled it off too. It worries me. With this power, I shouldn't have to worry. I'll have to rectify that." Finster turned his chair in the face of the wind. "Anybody could be anyone trying to kill me. I can't let that happen." *But, if I had the rings of power, I wouldn't have to worry about it, now would I?*

Chapter 57

Wincing, Alexandria stood alongside the King's Road that led to the palace. A small group of her assassins were with her. Together, they had watched Finster and the barbarian sail right over their heads, sitting in chairs, heading toward the city. As best as she could see, they were all alive and well. It was a testament to their power. She'd almost had one of them. Finster.

So close.

"Are our eyes in place?" she asked the assassin standing at her side. He was a man, little bigger than her, dressed in a comparable weather-beaten hood and cloak.

"Yes, our eyes are everywhere, as always, High Executioner."

"Let's go then. It will be interesting to see what Finster's next move is."

King Rolem's orders weren't entirely explicit. She was to kill Finster and Moth and retrieve the rings and the stone. She never would have guessed her journey would have led her to the king of Rayland's castle. It presented an interesting opportunity to learn more about Finster and the barbarian. It wasn't her intent to kill Finster, so much as to feel him out and find a weakness. The same for the barbarian. But when she realized the drunk had exposed himself, she took a chance.

Alexandria killed the queen and stabbed the king. Why not? Rolem needed this kingdom weakened anyway. At the same time, she got a crack at Finster, thanks to his dulled senses, letting a knight give him a whack in the back of the skull. She was just one second too late to deliver the fatal blow. That's when the savage pounced on her. If she hadn't gotten her poisoned blade through his skin, he would have crushed her to death. She'd felt three ribs crack from Moth's efforts. She'd fled. It had been a long time since she'd been so close to her own death. Still, it was almost a perfect night.

There was another caveat too. Her eyes weren't the only ones in the room. When she was disguised as the queen, the guards who'd escorted her into the dinner chamber were her assassins. They saw a full display of the savage's bizarre powers. There was water, fire, and lightning shooting from his body, they reported. It worked, then stopped. The savage pulled weapons from his body like they were acupuncture needles. Alexandria's poison didn't stop the savage, and it was the most lethal in the kingdom. Steel didn't end the brute either.

She rubbed her sore jaw. Her face got smashed when she wound up underneath the savage who pounced on her. She tasted blood on her lip. She'd failed once; she wouldn't fail again.

Moving forward, she pondered. What linked the savage and the sorcerer together? One thing was clear. In order to take down one or the other, they would need to be separated first. Based off current history, that shouldn't be a problem.

The game is set. We'll see.

Chapter 58

Hours after the incident in King Alrick's dining hall, the counselors and remaining knights were still there. The physicians who responded were sent away. They kept the doors closed and were staging what had happened. "Not that I question your wisdom, High Counselor Trenner," Counselor Mather said, "but contacting King Rolem might be premature at this junction."

The crown was tilted a bit on the short white hairs of Trenner's head. He paced on the other side of the room, away from the spilt blood, with his hands behind his back. "Did you not see what just happened here? The savage murdered our finest knights. The sorcerer, this Finster, flung the rest of them away like a child tossing his toys. We cannot have power like that wandering the kingdoms unchecked. They are a threat. A danger."

"But Finster said that he was on our side. It was King Rolem whom he warned us about." Mather's old, wrinkled hands shook as he spoke. "I think he was honest. I believe things just went… awry."

Trenner spun on his heel and faced Mather. "Awry? You call the king's dining hall, sticky with blood and reeking of the dead, awry? The king and queen are dead, and we can't put a face on it. Don't be foolish, Mather. We need all the help we can get. What servant am I if I cannot protect our people? No, we will send an emissary now."

"I've seen many things in my decades, and I've never seen it work out when one makes a hasty ally out of a potential enemy." Mather coughed into his fist. "I just want to have that on the record."

"I didn't ask you to render me your opinion, now, did I?"

"I am a counselor."

Trenner's fists balled up. His long face seemed to extend even further and redden. At the top of his lungs he shouted, "And when I am crowned I'm going to take your head off!" His chest heaved. He caught his breath and took a seat at the cleaner end of the table. "I'm sorry, old friend. It's been a hectic evening. If I'm going to be king, I suppose I should have better control over myself."

"It's quite understandable." Mather patted Trenner's shoulder. "The weight of the world rests on the shoulders of a king. And you need your health. After all, if something happened to you, the next in line is me, and I'm too old to handle all of this."

Trenner let out a chuckle. "Yes, yes, that would be preposterous. Why, the land barons and merchant seamen would run you over."

"Yes, if I were a younger and more able man, I'd be tempted to swipe the throne myself. I'd be lying if I said I hadn't dreamed of it." Mather wheezed and coughed into a handkerchief. "Did I ever tell you what I did before I came to serve the crown?"

"No, not that I'm really curious, but please humor me."

Mather leaned over and whispered in his ear. "I was an assassin." With a smooth swipe of a claw-shaped dagger, he slit open Trenner's throat.

A River Knight advanced on Mather.

Mather coolly wiped the blood on his handkerchief. Straightening from his slouch, he said, "Who would you rather be in charge, me or him?"

The captain of the River Knights, possessing the lone seabird on the crown of his helmet, said, "You, Counselor Mather." All four knights took a knee.

"Good." He shoved Trenner's dead body out of the chair. "Now, make him look like the savage did it." He rolled his arms and stretched his back. "It took me almost fifty years, but the perfect moment finally presented itself. One is never too old to be prepared. As for Trenner's plans, well, I couldn't have agreed more precisely with him. It's good to be the counselor, but even better to be the king."

Chapter 59

Finster literally dropped down from the sky with Dizon on his lap, landing softly on the terrace. It was there that Dizon pleaded to come with him and Moth. "It is too dangerous to stay," she argued. "You know they will come for me and kill me."

Finster wouldn't have been so reluctant to take Dizon if it wasn't for the little girl, Rinny. "I'm not bringing a child along. She brings no value to my ambitions whatsoever. To put it in layman's terms, she's useless," he said. "Most children are for that matter, unless they are rowing your boat or stitching clothing together. As you can see, I have no need for either." He held Dizon's hands. "I won't lie. I'm fond of you. Just move away from Rayland. A woman as savvy as you will do as well elsewhere as you do here."

Stroking his cheek, she said, "It's not about that, Finster. I want to be with you. You give me life. I enjoy it."

"Being in my presence for an extended time will only bring death. You saw what happened in the castle. I travel a roadway of nothing but trouble."

Suddenly, Rinny let out an excited "Wheeeeee!"

Moth scooped up the girl in his hands and placed her on his shoulders. She seemed like a tiny doll sitting on top of his massive frame. He still sat in the chair he'd flown in.

Finster's eye twitched. "Don't try to force my hand, Moth. The woman and the girl stay. That's final."

Moth looked at Finster with his deadpan stare. His chin shook a little left and back to the right.

"Did you just communicate with me? Was that a head shake or a no?"

Rinny crossed her arms over her chest and gave Finster a smirk. "Looks like we're going with you, Lord Finster. Come now, I'm ready to fly."

"It looks like you are attached to us for the moment, Lord Finster." Dizon kissed him on the cheek. "Give me a moment. I'll gather my things."

Two days had passed since the night of the massacre at Castle Rayland. They flew northeast through the sky for as long as Finster could hold them. They landed leagues from Rayland, ditched the chairs in the woodland, and walked to a small town where they paid for rations and a pair of sturdy horses. Now, they rode with their faces to the sun while bristling winds tore at their faces. They avoided the roads that led from Rayland to Varland. They moved beyond those caravan trails toward the lakes, where the wilderness overtook the roads.

Dizon rode in the saddle behind Finster. Rinny rode behind Moth. The girl couldn't even get her arms around the broad man's waist. Her fingers clung to the goatskin trousers at the side. The horses worked their way through the forest, thick in brush, elm, poplar, and oak trees.

"Lord Finster, can we stop in a tavern to eat?" Rinny said. Her face was pressed against Moth's back. The shine in her eyes had dulled. "I'm hungry."

"No. If you wanted to eat, you shouldn't have come. I made no promises to feed you." He pushed back into Dizon. "Either of you."

"We'll eat later, Rinny. Control yourself," Dizon warned her daughter.

"I don't want to eat any more dried meat and hard cheese. I'd rather eat bark."

"That can be arranged." Finster gestured to their surroundings. "There is a veritable buffet all around."

Rinny frowned. "That's not what I meant." She turned her head aside.

Finster sighed. He hadn't drunk in two days. Without wine to dull his senses, numbing the chronic burning sensation in his back that the scarab brought, it felt like a hot coal was between his shoulders. He shifted in the saddle. One of Dizon's hands massaged his neck and back muscles. "You are a comfort, Dizon, that much I must admit. But why you would follow me on this journey perplexes me."

"It should be obvious by now. If it's not, you are as blind as you are bald."

"Well, I'm not entirely bald."

"Then I hope you aren't entirely blind either." She hugged him from behind. "Relax, Finster. Don't take it all on yourself. Share what is on your mind."

The succulent blonde's soothing voice convinced him. "You know of the Circle, I suppose?"

"Yes, they are the assassins' guild of the Seven Kingdoms."

"So, you know what they say?"

"There is no mark they cannot find. There is no person they cannot kill." She nuzzled her cheek in his back just below the scarab. "Do you believe this?"

"What I believe is that they only conduct business in the kingdoms. Their eyes are everywhere in the seven cities. For the time being, I hope to avoid the seven. There will be no refuge there until this is all over."

"That could take a lifetime."

"No, it's not going to take a lifetime. It's just going to take lives. Thousands of them so long as King Rolem is behind it."

"Why don't you just kill him?"

The horse started up a ledge of rocks, jostling them hard in the saddle. Finster gripped the reins tightly. "Whoa! Whoa! Bloody beast has a mind of his own. Go around the rocks, not through them. Where were we, oh, yes, assassinate King Rolem. Well, that's not what a sorcerer of the high order does. If we did, the kingdoms would war all of the time like they did centuries ago. No, men have to learn to resolve their own problems. We are just here to guide them."

"But these are bad men. You should kill them."

"Only in a fair fight."

"Pisshaw! These kings do not fight fair. If they did, they wouldn't have sent assassins after you. I say, use your power. It's your destiny, Finster. I can feel it."

Unable to hide his smile, he replied, "You are not good for my conscience. Don't you know that magi have the most bloated egos in the realms? I have enough of a dilemma controlling the stone. Either I control it, or it controls me."

"How powerful do you think you are?" she practically whispered in his ear.

"I'm not sure I want to find out." He reached behind him and squeezed her leg. "Well, that's a lie."

"I know."

They rode for two more days with Finster weighing all of his options. Finally, he led them to where the wilderness turned into a marsh rich in willow trees with leaves that tickled the waters. In the middle of the overgrown, rancid-smelling, uninhabitable marsh was a small lake, rich in toads on lily pads and thick with mosquitos. On the other side of the lake stood a stone tower ten stories tall that rivaled the great maple trees surrounding it. Vines, moss, and ivy covered the tower from top to bottom. It stood eerily in the mist that hid its doors, leaning slightly to the right.

"What in the kingdoms is that place?" Rinny said.

"It's called the Black Tower."

The Sorcerer's Trick

Part 4

Chapter 60

The Black Tower stood defiantly against the ravages of time. Standing more than one hundred feet high, the great cylinder of stone covered in vines, moss, and floral overgrowth stood as haunting as a gargantuan tombstone. Critters and bugs crawled along the massive vines that seemed to constrict the sorcerous structure in an effort to swallow up the invader that had arrived long ago. If there were portal windows or a doorway to enter, the foliage had covered them.

"I don't see a door," Rinny said. The pretty girl, with her rich-brown tan and sun-lightened blond hair, seemed tiny compared to the brute whose shoulders she sat upon. Moth, skin as pale as the moon, was a stark contrast to her. The somber savage's muscular arms were bigger than Rinny's waist. "Are we going inside? It looks dangerous."

Finster swatted at a mosquito that could fill both of his hands. Sweat had soaked his robes thanks to the muggy swamp they were trudging through. He didn't care for the wilderness, let alone swamps and the additional natural dangers such as mudholes and crocodiles bigger than horses. He smashed the mosquito against his neck. Blood from the insect seeped between his fingers. "Nature is so disgusting." He eyed Rinny. "As for danger, well yes, there is danger, as I mentioned before you decided to come along on this journey. That's why I am going to let you go in first, child."

Rinny's eyes grew big. "Me? Mother?"

Dizon, Rinny's mother, sat in the saddle behind Finster. Despite the long journey, she appeared as attractive as ever, with wavy locks of blond hair flowing over her shoulders. She had her soft hands on Finster's waist. She beamed an easy smile at her daughter. "You must do as Finster says," she said. "He is our lord now."

"But," Rinny said, not hiding a growing frown. Seeing the serious look on her mother's face, she started to climb out of the saddle.

Finster felt like laughing at the simple act of obedience. He would have laughed if the scarab implanted in his back hadn't felt as if it had bored a hole through to his chest. "Be still, child. Your mother was jesting with you." He pushed back against the firm breasts of the woman behind him. He liked Dizon too much for his own good. She was the only thing that brought him comfort, considering there weren't any jugs of wine present. "There are few women worth bringing the whelp along for."

"And there is no other man like you," Dizon said in his ear. "But whatever you wish, I will do it. My daughter will do it."

"You certainly know how to stroke a man's ego. And to think the king released you from his harem. Pshaw." He fanned another mosquito away as he studied the height of the tower. "You could do a better job keeping these mosquitos away." Out of the corner of his eye, he watched Moth's spade-sized hand swipe a large fuzzy butterfly out of the air. The savage ate it. "I'm in too much pain to gag."

"What?" Dizon asked as she swatted at the bugs.

"Nothing," he replied.

"I'm glad we are in clothing suited for travel," she said of her long-sleeved cotton blouse and riding trousers. Her boots were made of soft leather. "But they are soaked, and my rear end is sore from riding. Are we going to dismount and go within, or is this some stranger sorcerous visit? What is this Black Tower, Finster?"

"Refuge. Sanctuary, I hope," Finster said. "Death… possibly. Centuries ago, before the other towers and citadels of the Magus Supremeus were built throughout the kingdom, magic was practiced in towers such as this. Wizards and workers of magic were despised then, but as time passed, alliances were made with the kingdoms, and brilliant people like me took up residence near the heart of the kingdoms to keep a closer eye on things. They left these towers, of which there are only a few, to return to the natural world that bred them." Where the stones weren't covered, he could see runes of warning and protection dating from an ancient age. "For the time being, it should be as good a place to hide as any. I don't think anyone will search us out here."

"Why is that?" Dizon asked.

"Because they are forgotten. I only know about them because I learned the history of the Black Tower through the former Magus Supremeus, Zuulan the Arcane." Finster's eyes scoured the lower wall. The door he had used the last time he was here was covered in twenty feet of new overgrowth. "Zuulan bragged a bit. He'd state how primitive the early magic users were that came from the outlying towers like this. He believed the powers magic users controlled now were so much better. Certainly, the citadels have more brick and mortar, but that has more to do with worldly success than magic. I wanted to understand, so in my own travels, I sought the Black Tower out and the other ones, all of which have fallen. This one, as you can see, still stands. For a reason, I believe."

"I imagine it was grand at one time," Dizon said. "Did you learn anything?"

"Yes, I learned to be prepared for anything inside the Black Tower."

"So, it's dangerous," she said.

He shrugged. "It's been a long time since I was here. There is no telling what lies within aside from invading varmints and insects." He held out his hands and began summoning his magic. Spreading his fingers, he used his powers over the inanimate to feel the lower walls of the tower with telekinetic fingers. Finster, the Secret Slayer, Guardian of the Mystic Forge, and Master of the Inanimate, had expanded powers now, thanks to the Founder's Stone residing inside the scarab in his back. He used them to find a doorway. "Ah, there it is." Sweat dripped down his temple and cheek.

The rough vines bulged outward around the egg-shaped doorway.

"You're opening it," Dizon said.

"No, I'm not," he replied. The horses let out wild whinnies. Hooves stomped into the soft ground. "Something else is moving the vine!"

A reptilian head burst out of the foliage. A creature with a head bigger than a horse pushed through the snapping vines. Jaws wide, it came right at them with thousands of tiny razor-sharp teeth.

Chapter 61

The horse underneath Finster and Dizon reared up, hurling them both to the swamp's soft ground. Finster twisted around just in time to see the lizard's great jaws close on the spooked horse's body. The horse bucked twice before its body went limp. The crushing jaws of the lizard clamped down, and bones cracked. With a whip of its neck, the lizard slung the horse's carcass aside. It squeezed its body out of the wide stone doorway that led into its den. Pushing through on short, stubby, powerful legs, claws sinking in the mud, the massive, twenty-foot-long swamp lizard set its eyes on Rinny.

Rinny screamed at the top of her lungs. The horse bucked beneath her and Moth, tossing them from the saddle. Now she was stuck, knee-deep in the muck and mire, waving her scrawny arms like battalion banners.

The lizard came at them, head low, eyes filled with hunger, dragging its hulking belly over the ground. Moth rushed into its path. Broadsword in hand, the brawny, bare-chested savage stood his ground in the path of the beast. It was one primordial creature versus another. Moth charged. He thrust the sword up under the lizard's jaw. The blade jutted up through the inside of the monster's mouth. The lizard pushed overtop of Moth, crushing the brute beneath its body and burying the man in the muck.

"Oh my!" Finster was on his hands and knees, gathering his thoughts. The violent act caught him off guard. Acting on instinct, he found the quiver of arrows and sent them sailing from his bowstring into the monster. The lizard let out a roar. Some arrows stuck in the thick hide of the beast, and others bounced from its hard flesh. "A mosquito would fare better." Gathering his senses, he sought a more formidable weapon. His eyes swept his environs, but surrounded by nature, he was weak. The monster fastened its eyes on the girl.

"Rinny!" Dizon sprinted for her daughter.

"No!" Finster yelled. With no more than thirty feet between them and the lizard, he watched the monster charge after the woman. The insides of Finster's eyes flared green. His veins pulsed with mystic fire. He stretched out his senses, finding a boulder half-buried in the earth. With his mind, he ripped the stone from the soppy ground and sent it hurling into the skull of the advancing creature. The monster's head whipped to one side, halting its rapid advance, then sprang back to center again. This time, it locked its eyes on Finster. Black tongues licked out of its mouth. It let out a sonic roar that sent Finster sprawling backward into the willow trees. His head smacked hard into the trunk, and he sagged into the surrounding murk. Shaking his head, the rickety-limbed sorcerer slung the mud from his fingers and thumbed the grit from his eyes. "That hurt."

Moth emerged from a muddy grave. Sword still in hand, he flung himself into the lizard. The broad blade chopped into the core of the lizard's body. Using both hands, Moth whacked into the scaly tissue in huge, arcing, flesh-rending slices. By the time the lizard let out a painful hiss, a hunk the size of a man had been cut out of its body. With a flip of its meaty tail, it smacked Moth, lifting the savage off his feet. The rangy seven-footer flipped head over heels before splatting shoulder first in the mud.

Finster got to his feet and ran toward the monstrous enemy, fingers spread wide. *Should I let the lizard win?* The stone he'd once hurled now, by his power, hovered over the ground. *Lizard wins, the rings can be mine.*

Sitting up, Moth chopped like a wild man into the lizard's snout at a fierce pace, chipping its teeth. Dark blood sprayed from the wounds, coating Moth in gore. Nose first, the lizard plowed into Moth once more. The monster remained in place this time, smothering the man underneath its tons of girth.

"Finster!" Dizon called out as she pulled Rinny out of the mud. "Do something!"

"I am!" he shouted back. With a moment of hesitation, he sent the boulder sailing into the lizard's head. The hard crack of stone against scale sent the lizard's jaw askew. Eyes searching for its enemy, it turned out of its spot.

Moth erupted from the mud, sucking air in huge gulps. Coated in the swampy murk, he struck out, cutting off the front foot of the monster. In a giant leap, he avoided the tail swinging at him. He landed by the back leg of the lizard. With a two-handed chop, he severed the limb from the body. Without breaking stride, he attacked the beast's rear, cutting off its tail in three hard and heavy chops.

The lizard squirmed. Its sonic roar boomed, but it wasn't going anywhere. It wriggled, bled, and sank deeper into the dingy ground.

Moth attacked with berserk fury and blood-maddened eyes. With tremendous swings, he turned the lizard into swamp food. Finally, the lizard let out one final death spasm and moved no more. The savage was coated in guts, scales, and blood.

Finster lumbered alongside the savage. He eyed the long, powerful, mutilated length of the lizard. "A bit overzealous, aren't we?"

Moth snorted lungfuls of air into his expanding chest. His battle-glazed eyes regained their dull, somber look. He helped Dizon and Rinny out of the mudhole then looked past Finster to the gap in the tower.

Rubbing his head, Finster said, "Let's go in, shall we?"

Chapter 62

The broad-shouldered Moth, gory sword in hand, led the way inside the Black Tower. The overhanging vines had been snapped through by the lizard, opening a dark gap to the doorway. Finster followed, with Dizon trailing behind him, holding Rinny's hand. With the aid of the daylight peeking through, they could see the dirt floor. The air was stale and musty. Once they had all crossed inside, Rinny sneezed.

"As if we haven't made enough commotion," Finster said as he covered his own nose. Ahead, Moth vanished into the darkness. His big feet made no sound. "And he's wandered off as always." He shook his head.

"What do we do now?" Dizon asked, keeping her voice low as her pretty eyes darted around.

"This isn't my first visit. It's not as bad as it seems." He stretched out his senses, feeling along the walls until he came across a torch in a bracket. He rubbed his fingers together like a man preparing a campfire. A flame ignited. The soft orange glow illuminated half of the fifty-foot-wide room. He spied more torches, and one by one, he lit them all. Insects, nestled in the nooks and cracks of the corners and stone archways, scurried into the darkness. "Light sends away that which thrives in the darkness."

There was no sign of Moth, and Dizon said, "Our friend is gone. This architecture is not what I expected." She ran her hand over the stones where the archway started up the wall and crossed over the ceiling. The ceiling was twenty feet high. There were six archways in all, holding up a solid grid of stonework above them. "It is fabulous."

"The sorcerers of the time were very practical. What they built was well thought out and built to last." Finster put his hands to the black stone wall. Upon closer inspection, he could see that the chiseled rock was rich in bits of mineral and ore that glinted dully in the light. A gentle jolt of energy passed through his fingers the moment he touched it. He withdrew his hand. "Huh."

"What is it?" Dizon asked.

"Nothing." He took her hand. "Come. Let's get out of the stink of mud and lizard excrement." He eyed a stone stairwell that hugged the walls and led upward to the next floor. "That's probably where the brute went, to eat more bugs or something worse."

Rinny sneezed again. It echoed loudly through the chamber.

"Please don't do that again. It annoys me," Finster said.

"I can't help it," Rinny replied. "My nose tickles."

"You're probably having a reaction to a fatal element that could quite possibly kill you. Maybe it would be best if you waited outside so that you don't die," Finster said. Using his power, he lifted two torches from their brackets and let them hover in front of him as he took the stairs up. "I imagine your issue will be worse the higher we go."

"Mother, what does he mean?" Rinny asked.

"Nothing. Just cover your mouth with your sleeve," Dizon said.

"But my clothes are muddy."

Finster rolled his eyes. He had enough irritation in his life: a burning scarab burrowed in his back, armies that wanted to kill him, assassins hunting him down, and now a girl who screamed and sneezed. *If I could eliminate one of the four, I'm certain it would be the girl.*

The second floor was laid out the same as the first, except the floor was made from large stone tiles. There were four spade-shaped portal windows, equally distanced apart, covered by the vines that had crept in through the outside. The torches were in the brackets on the walls, and an iron candelabrum, empty of candles or another source of flame, hung from chains above them. There were no other furnishings. The hot, muggy air remained suffocating.

Finster lit all the torches, found the stairwell to the next floor, and went up. The third floor was the same as the second, as were the fourth and the fifth. He lit up every level, and on the fifth floor, they met up with Moth again. The savage stood in the center of the room, sword down at his side, squinting as he turned in a slow circle. "I think we are safe for the moment," Finster said. His voice echoed when he spoke. "The higher up the better. We do have a loose horse on the run with supplies that we need. Perhaps you and the girl can retrieve it."

Without a look, Moth moved toward the door. He extended his arm. Rinny climbed onto his shoulders. With a smile, she looked at Finster. "Can I have a torch?"

Finster floated one over to her.

Together, Moth and Rinny headed back down the stairs.

"Be safe, Rinny," Dizon said as she sat down beside Finster.

"I'm always safe with Moth. He's invincible." Moth and Rinny vanished.

With a sigh, Dizon lay down on the floor and put her head in Finster's lap.

Stroking her hair gingerly with his fingers, Finster said, "Are you having any regrets?"

"No," she said. "As my daughter feels about Moth, I feel the same way about you."

He arched an eyebrow. "You think me invincible?"

"You are at least the closest thing to it," she said. "Finster, are we going to live here?"

"We are going to live here while I think," he said.

"Will that take long?"

"Perhaps. Are you that uncomfortable already?"

She shrugged. "This tower is well preserved but so barren. I don't think the few blankets we carry will make it that much more comfortable."

"I don't think this tower was made for comfort. And the sorcerers in those days did not maintain many possessions." His eyes grazed over the fine stonework in the ceiling. "They considered material items to be distractions and only lived off what they needed. It was here that they would train and practice magic. My guess is that they probably slept without blankets."

"What would they eat? There is no food aside from swamp rats and tree bark in this wretched terrain."

"True, but the landscape was probably different when they were here. And I'm certain they worked with merchants and tradesmen, the same as many others."

"Speaking of which, our own rations are limited. What will we eat if they run out?"

Twisting her hair around his fingers, he replied, "Whatever Moth hunts and kills for us, I suppose. And some fresh lizard and horse is still available."

Chapter 63

Back in the Kingdom of Mendes, King Rolem strolled along the castle walls that looked out over the sea. With his knights, in glistening suits of platemail armor, standing on watch nearby, he walked with the assassin, Alexandria. The handsome king's brow was furrowed as he read a letter that had arrived from the kingdom of Rayland.

"Who is this Counselor Mather? I've never heard of him." Rolem slapped his hand against the parchment. "I know Counselor Trenner, but this man, I don't know. Yet he makes a very interesting proposal in his plea to form an alliance. What do you know of him?"

Alexandria, tall, slender, and athletically built, with dusky eyes, walked as quietly as a cat beside him. Wearing the traveling cloak that augmented her unique powers, she said, "Mather was the queen's hand, an older, wizened fellow, who cut open Trenner's throat the moment King Alrick died. I've since learned that he was a member of the Circle long ago. It seems he retired, only to strike at the perfect time." She put her hand on the king's shoulder. "We don't need him to take down Finster. I can handle this mission."

"You might be the High Executioner, but you failed to execute your target." King Rolem rolled up the scroll. He stopped, put his foot up on the wall, and looked out to the sea. The harbors bustled with galleons and fishing boats. Men and women labored along the docks. "I want more. I have the funding, but I need the power to bring all of the seashore kingdoms under my control."

Without letting him see, Alexandria rolled her eyes. Her ambitions were simple. She only wanted to be the greatest assassin that ever lived. The king, however, wanted power that no man could possibly control. He wanted power over unpredictable people. Even she knew that was impossible. She massaged his shoulder and, with a reassuring smile, said, "You will have all that you want. I'm certain of it. As for Finster, I know his weakness. It won't take long to find him and kill him. No one can hide from the Circle in this world. Our eyes are everywhere."

"So you've told me." He pushed her hand away. "And if that is the case, where is our omnipotent sorcerer now?"

"He will resurface. The barbarian he travels with has a knack for foolishness. He would be hard to miss, Your Majesty."

"No, I don't suppose a man who indiscreetly jumps into the Gauntlet will be able to avoid another such temptation." Rolem swept his wavy locks of brown hair behind his ear. "They say this barbarian is an inhuman beast that bested the walls after spikes were driven through his legs. Is this true?"

"I did not see it with my own eyes, and the stories certainly stretch the imagination." She sat on the overlook wall and faced him. "However, that is what many witnesses say. I too saw this savage firsthand. He's quiet and shows no pain but has an intensity in his eyes like cauldrons of fire. What aids him I do not know—unless it's a power of Finster's. Perhaps this man was summoned from another world."

"No." The king shook his head. "The blue-toe tribes are real. Or were real. I can't keep up with all of them. Wargoths, Gorgoths, and Wild Goths are the only ones I've dealt with personally. Then there are all of the other outlying factions." He scratched at the side of his mustache. A warm breeze tousled his wavy hair. "Perhaps we can send them after this Moth."

"Your Majesty, I would make a plea that you trust me to take out this man."

"Oh really? And why is that? Do you think you are that much smarter than me? The king?"

"Certainly not." She took his hand and kissed his many rings. "I have deep respect for your authority, but would you risk such power, the Founder's Stone, and the location of these rings falling into another kingdom's hands? It is so much to risk."

He tilted his head toward the stone-faced woman cradling his hand in hers. "Perhaps you seek these items for yourself."

"No, I don't have that desire. I want to be the assassin that takes them for the crown. The assassin behind the ruler of the world."

"Perhaps you desire a chair right beside my own."

"I would be lying if I said I hadn't fantasized about it," she said with a sultry look. "As well as many other things that involve the king."

The king's palms became sweaty. He swallowed and breathed a shallow breath. "I understand the members of the Circle are masters of seduction."

As she massaged his hand, she said, "We are masters of all things that make another comfortable. I can make you very comfortable, my king. It would be an honor."

He cast a quick look at his knights then turned his attention back to her. "You are a ravishing sight for such a cold-hearted woman. You do realize that I can't take any chances when you enter my chambers. You'll have to be fully disarmed."

"I wouldn't have it any other way," she said. King Rolem was a desirable man, well-built and strong, but he doubted her. She needed to do what she could to turn the tide back in her favor. That would take time and more effort. She wanted Finster and Moth all to herself. "My body is yours."

King Rolem lifted her to her feet and said with a smirk, "Come with me then. My dungeon awaits."

Chapter 64

Finster sat in the center of the Black Tower's third level with his legs crossed and his eyes closed. For days, he'd spent hours in deep meditation, fighting to control the painful scarab in his back. If he could fully control the Founder's Stone's power, then he should be able to control the pain. It hadn't worked that way. The more he tried, the more he hurt. It felt like someone ripping out a second heart through his back.

"Guh!" he gasped as his narrow chest heaved. He opened his eyes. He patted his face dry with the towel folded at his side. "Oh, lords of zephyr, I need some wine. Anything to dull this throbbing pain." He tossed the small towel away and lay flat on his back. The cool stones offered little relief, but it was something. With his hoop sleeves falling down past his elbows, he looked at his skinny, vascular arms. Noticeable green veins spidered through his limbs, showing from his elbows clear to his fingers. "That looks awful. What am I, some sort of monster?"

Finster had all of the power he'd ever desired, but a curse came with it. He longed for the days when he had sat on the balcony of Tarley's Tavern in the town of Marcen, duping the pie-faced farmers. Now the greatest trick had been played on him, the scarab's trick that gave him power but, day by day, drained his life as well.

"Am I destined to be a lich, such as the one I crossed when I discovered the stone? Is that the fate for me?" With his hands on his chest, fingers interlocked, he rolled his thumbs. "Hmmm… the undead feel no pain. It's an option. But would the wine have any flavor at all?"

As he lay, he contemplated Dizon's earnest suggestions to just kill King Rolem. She seemed determined to convince Finster that was the only way to go about it. No doubt, she was smart and astute in the ways of the world, but she didn't understand the larger picture as well as Finster did. He was the last of the sorcerers from the Red Citadel. Ingrid had killed all of the others and taken the rings of power. It would be up to him to restore the order to the Red Citadel and find another Magus Supremeus. The mages were the guardians of the realm, and without them, the Seven Kingdoms would be in chaos. The idea was to find suitable workers of magic and endow them with the rings of power. It would maintain balance. There were many wizards from other citadels and towers, such as Satrap Chen, who came from the Violet Citadel of his orient people of Varland. Finster chuckled. *I killed him quite easily, didn't I? Fool. I could have done it even without the Founder's Stone in hand, or in my back, rather.*

Either way, there was going to be a fight. He considered a parlay with King Rolem to make peace, but considering that Finster had slain Ingrid, it didn't seem possible. At the same time, Finster didn't want to relinquish the power of the Founder's Stone. He wasn't sure that the stone would leave him either. They had become one, with it urging him into an action that he didn't understand. It was a presence, almost a mind of its own, yearning for something.

Getting to his feet, Finster ambled over to the portal window while rubbing his lower back. The vines had been cut away, giving him a full view of the back end of the tower. There was a semblance of a grassy courtyard that somehow remained untouched. There, Moth, Dizon, and Rinny worked together. They'd butchered the horse and begun cooking the meat. Moth had skinned the scales from the lizard and wrapped the meat in bundles, preserving it. Everything Moth did, Rinny imitated, except being silent.

Dizon, with her hands on her hips, boiled water over a fire in a pot they'd brought along. Meat cooked over the coals on a spit. As if she knew his thoughts, she looked up at him and waved. Finster flipped up two fingers. They were surviving the bug-infested mire. In theory, they could hold out for a long time, but in truth, Finster knew that he couldn't. His arm twitched against his control. It was becoming harder to control his own actions. His eyes slid over to Moth.

Somehow, the savage tapped into the rings of power, yet there was no evidence of him suffering. He went about his chores as effortlessly as the wind stirring the leaves. Finster's jaw clenched. His gut stirred.

If I had the rings, just one of them, I know I could control this pain.

Finster knew enough about the eight rings and their powers. There was no doubt that they could aid him. He could see them clearly as they had adorned Ingrid the Insane's fingers when she had sat on the Magus Supremeus's throne. Each was fine metal matched with a precious stone. He ran through what he knew of them by singing a little ditty in his head.

Ruby and black iron regenerate. Diamond and brass make fire. Sapphire with steel form ice and water. Dust and disintegration come from onyx and copper, while the garnet with silver yields telekinetic powers. Pearls and gold for shield and protection… oh, what are the other two? Peridot and platinum, topaz and bronze, I think. But what do they do? Think, Finster, think.

If any one ring would truly aid him, it would be the black-iron ring of regeneration. Moth survived the most vicious wounds, only to be sewn up again by the ring's power. Finster stared at the hulking savage who now stood in front of the fire, eating a hunk of cooked meat on a stick. Beside him, Rinny did the same. Squinting, with his magic-enhanced vision, he noticed something on Moth's hands. The brute's fingers bulged around the knuckles, lumpy underneath the skin. His heart leapt. He dashed for the stairs.

The rings!

Chapter 65

Practically drooling, his fingers clawing at the air, Finster eyeballed Moth's hands. "Look at that. Will you look at that? The rings are working themselves out."

Dizon stood beside him. "I didn't notice that earlier. It must have just happened. This is a very good thing?"

"A very great thing," Finster said as he eased in for a closer look. There was no denying that the rings had begun to appear underneath the savage's dirty skin. The rings bulged bigger than the existing knuckles. With wide eyes, Finster said, "Fascinating. How they worked their way through the body I'll probably never comprehend, but they have latent abilities all their own." He reached out a finger toward Moth's hand. Moth continued to eat, not paying Finster any mind. Finster withdrew his hand. "That might not be a good idea."

"What wouldn't be a good idea?" Rinny asked. "And why does Moth have an extra set of knuckles?"

Finster moved away, rubbing the scruff on his face. He found delight in the confirmation that all eight rings had revealed themselves.

Perhaps, in time, they will show fully over the skin. Then I can possess what should be mine. And the mute shouldn't have desire for them, now, should he?

"Does this change things, Finster?" Dizon asked.

"In what regard?"

"We know that Moth has the rings. Perhaps it is time for action rather than sitting here, waiting among the wet weeds." She got face-to-face with him. "I still say finish Rolem before he finishes you. Do it now, while you have the power to do so."

In truth, it wouldn't be that difficult for Finster. If he could see Rolem, it would take next to nothing to hurl a deadly projectile at him. But people would know that the Master of the Inanimate was behind it. No, he needed to restore order to the Red Citadel, and he'd need the rings to do it. The question was, who else in this world could he trust besides the loose company that he was with?

He had once had friends in many kingdoms. Many would have status and power now. But the moment he set foot inside their borders, he had little doubt the Circle would see him. By any means possible, they would try to strike him down. It wouldn't surprise him one bit if they had started to send armies after him already. He couldn't stay at the Black Tower forever. They would starve to death. And the Founder's Stone was sucking the life out of him already. He had to make a move. What would that move be?

Chapter 66

Alexandria departed from Mendes with her claws digging into her palms. King Rolem, despite their frolicking between the satin sheets, had sent out another bounty on Finster and Moth. He had tried to do it discreetly, but when the High Executioner commanded the power of a cloak that disguised and made one invisible, there weren't many things that slipped by her. Now, with a small host of her men, three in all, she rode toward the kingdom of Varland.

Riding at a trot, she unrolled a hand-drawn picture of Finster and Moth. It was only mildly accurate, but there were words on the parchment that gave an ample description. King Rolem had had them drawn up and sent out to his finest hands in the Seven Kingdoms—to men and women loyal to him, all of whom had sworn allegiance to the crown.

With a disgusted look on her face, she spat the dust of the dry road from her mouth.

I should not have missed Finster when I had the chance. I should have acted more quickly.

Not one for regret, she found herself put to task. It would now be a race to find and kill Finster. There would be mercenaries and wayward knights in deadly pursuit. The finest trackers in the land would be sent after the men. There was a warning on the letter's parchment too: "Extremely powerful. Extremely dangerous." In regard to Finster and Moth, that was an understatement. She'd stabbed Moth with her most potent poison, yet he had lived. The brute sent shivers through her.

Can I kill a man that can't be killed? Everything dies, doesn't it?

With the stiff winds of the plains beating against her creaseless face, she ran through her checklist. The kingdom of Rayland had already blamed the death of King Alrick and his mother, the queen, on Moth and Finster. The River Knights of Rayland had been dispatched. There was another inevitable problem brewing as well. Word had quickly spread throughout the world of wizards about the slaughter at the Red Citadel. The Violet and Jade Citadels would certainly be involved—not only investigating but finding suitable replacements for the men and women who had led in the Red Citadel. No doubt they would hunger for the Founder's Stone and the rings of power. If they acquired them first, it would weaken King Rolem's position. The Circle had been hired to strengthen it. That was what Alexandria had set out to do.

She'd dealt with the sorcerous benders of magic several times. They all had a weakness—primarily, overconfidence and a zeal for erotic pleasures. Many had died by the cut of her blade, completely oblivious to the danger the shapely woman posed. But the magi, the wizards, the sorcerers had strength and powers that she did not comprehend. Combined with wicked imaginations, their onslaught of power was life rending. She'd seen minds turned to mush from a sorcerer's heated stare, leaving men drooling, crying, and running for their lives from unseen terrors that sent them hurtling from high ledges and cliffs. The sages and sorcerers were supposed to be the protectors of the kingdoms, the peacekeepers, advisors, but in truth, they were only puppeteers with their own ambitions. To Alexandria, the assassin's guild was what truly kept the peace.

Perhaps we should start our own kingdom one day.

On a long stretch of road between Rayland and Varland, kingdoms hundreds of miles apart, Alexandria and her assassins entered a town called Rickle. It was a small, thriving livestock community, with straw-roof cottages all over the area and stony buildings no bigger than two stories tall. The air was rich with the smell of manure and hay. They hitched the horses to posts outside the only tavern late in the night. The door creaked open, and they entered a smoky pub half-full of drunken men and women with glazed-over eyes. With cackling in the background, they sat at the bar and ordered wine.

A woman rose from a corner table and approached. She sat down beside Alexandria as a mildly obese bartender with clammy hands filled her goblet. The woman was one of the Circle's eyes. She was older, with wispy brown hair and two front teeth missing. The moment the bartender moved out of earshot, the woman said, "It's been a long time, Alexandria. A pleasure to bear witness for you."

"Out with it, Carlyn," she said, taking her first sip.

"The man who served you, his son fitted the Raylander woman, Dizon, with horses and gear." Carlyn licked her cracked lips while she eyeballed the wine glass. "Eh, that's the good news. The bad news is, other interested parties have been informed. They pay well for information that my budget could not stifle."

Without looking at the woman, Alexandria pushed her wine glass to Carlyn. "Who else pursues the king's business?"

The older woman drank. "The River Knights of Rayland. Twenty stalwart men." She drank down half the glass and wiped her mouth against her moth-eaten sleeve. "Not to mention a few other strangers who passed through on thundering hooves. The roads are very busy with pursuit for Moth and this Finster."

"You are certain of their passage through here?" Alexandria asked in her callous tone.

"Aye, the barkeep's son, enchanted by the woman, Dizon, took tail after her. He saw her and the men you seek. The boy's a talker. She tried to use discretion on her departure, but the captivated boy's passion sent him into a deeper pursuit and took after her. The boy said they moved toward Varland, but he gave up the journey quickly. Said he got too far and got hungry. He's a homer." Carlyn scratched a fuzzy patch under her chin. "I, however, managed to make speed before the knights pursued. Heh-heh. I claimed witness and pointed them west, back toward the Free River."

"You think Finster went toward Varland?"

"That I cannot say for sure without seeing myself, but that is what the boy says. I just sent the knights in the direction I thought would be most unlikely," Carlyn said.

Alexandria nodded. "You've served well."

"I serve the Circle. Always." Carlyn finished the goblet of wine. "My life is yours to give or take."

Alexandria pressed a small purse of jacks into the woman's palm. "You gave. You will have reward." Her eyes fell on the barkeep. "The father and son. We can't have them talking to anyone else. You know what to do."

Carlyn sniggered. "Yes. What they know will die with them."

Chapter 67

Finster slept with Dizon in his arms on the fifth floor of the Black Tower. Rinny slept in the arms of her mother. One lone torch in the circular room still burned. A steady breeze made a low howling through the portal window, just enough to freshen the stifling, muggy air with a hint of honeysuckle. Still, it was a restless sleep. No matter how hard Finster tried, there was no comfortable position. The scarab saw to that. It probed into him, nudging him into a direction that he did not want to go—the direction desired by the stone and not him. The stone wanted Finster's body as a vessel to serve its own dark ambitions. It was anxious and hungry now that it was free. Its will wrestled against Finster's. He tossed from side to side, fingers flexing. Relief was nowhere to be found.

The Founder's Stone was every bit the powerful relic that he'd imagined it to be. It enhanced the powers of the user tenfold, if not twenty or more. But there were other powers within the stone, ancient, dark, and wondrous. It wanted to exercise that power with devastating effect. It wasn't a bauble created to protect mankind, it was a weapon created to destroy the host's enemies or any threats to it. Finster pushed back against it, but he wanted to give in. It was him against the will of it. He couldn't give in to his own desires. The stone would turn him into a weapon.

I swear to protect the weak, the wealthy, and the living of our kind, through the fires, the trials, and creeping ice of times. I am a magus. This is my sworn creed.

Decades ago, he'd made that pledge, but every man and woman that made it broke it at one time or another. Now he felt that he might be the only man in the world likely to save the order. Zuulan the Arcane was all-powerful but had been a total fool to be seduced by the witchy sorcerous Ingrid, who Finster, of all people, had trained.

I suppose I feel guilty. I should have known better than to trust that wretched, power-hungry girl.

Dizon's soothing fingers reached down and massaged his calf with a caressing touch. She was softly snoring when she did so. The woman had not asked him for one single thing. She cared nothing about his craft; she earnestly wanted to be with him. Which made him suspicious.

I came upon her by chance, did I not? Or was she waiting on me? Was I lured in? Sleep, Finster, sleep. Please, lords of the sea, let me have one good night of sleep.

He lay there for long minutes, eyes shut tight, then finally decided after the hundredth consideration. *With the Founder's Stone, I don't need any sleep.*

He slipped his arms away from Dizon. *Perhaps I'll go and see what the savage is up to. He's probably mating with a willow tree or one of those giant snapping turtles.*

In the shadows behind him, he caught a stirring in the window out of the corner of his eye. A mannish figure crawled silently through the window. At first, he thought it was Moth, but the silhouette of the figure had a leaner, muscular build. A second man eased through the same portal, moving like a spider. Finster's neck hairs rose. With a flick of his finger, he sent the torch sailing in the strange invaders' direction.

Arms raised, they cowered from the light. Long arm hair hung from the men's naked arms. Long strands of bone-white hair hung down past their shoulders. Their eye sockets were big and hollow, but small white pupils shone like diamonds deep inside them. They stretched their webbed fingers out, revealing sharp claws like hooks made to tear through flesh. They bared teeth like an animal. Humanity was far removed from them. They were the savages of the swamp called the bog men.

The bog men coiled low on their legs. Oversized knuckles rested on the ground. They swayed side to side, looking past the torch, fixing their eyes on Finster. Murder lurked in their gaze.

It seems we might have overstayed our welcome in the swamp. The question is, where is Moth?

Perhaps Finster had taken it for granted that Moth prowled the swamp like a watchdog. Over the last few days, that had seemed to be the case. Frankly, Finster hadn't thought anything would slip by the savage barbarian. Now his absence posed another concern. *What if Moth is in danger?*

All the while, Finster sent a coil of rope slithering like a snake behind the bog men. At the same time, he moved the torch side to side, blocking their view of him. The bog men's heads swayed as they dodged the light. Ignoring the torch, they crept forward, stretching forth their long, sharp fingernails.

Dizon rolled over onto her side. Looking up at Finster, she said, "What are you doing?" Her expression turned into a look of horror as her eyes followed Finster's to the bog men. She let out a sharp gasp.

The bog men launched themselves right at Finster.

With a twist of his fingers, Finster commanded both ends of the rope. It coiled around the bog men's sinewy necks and instantly constricted. At the same time, the rope lifted the bog men off their feet. The swamp dwellers clawed at the line, their legs kicking wildly.

Finster used his power to strangle the life out of their flailing limbs. The bog men's tongues stuck out of their mouths. They tugged at the rope and kicked out a few more times. Their faces turned beet red and purple. Both of them spasmed violently one more time and quietly died.

With his heart pounding in his ears, Finster took a quick breath through his nostrils. "I have a feeling there will be more. There are always more. Always."

Dizon was on her knees. She cradled a half-sleeping Rinny in her arms. With a shaky voice, she asked, "What do we do?"

Finster held a finger up. He heard the sound of soft footfalls coming up the stairs. He made out the shadows of men moving toward them. The torches that were still lit in the fourth level below them cast light against the movement. He positioned himself between the women and the stairwell. "Stay behind me and ready the quiver."

As more scuffling sounds slunk up the stairs, Dizon grabbed a nearby quiver that lay among their supplies. Finster had had her purchase a few other items that he could use for weaponry. Among them were scrap pieces of metal and arrows. She removed the arrows from the quiver and tossed them into the air.

Finster snatched the arrows with his thoughts, and like the rope, the arrows hovered with a life of their own at shoulder height beside him.

A bog man slunk to the top of the stairs. His hollow eyes landed on Finster. He made a lip-smacking sound that seemed to be a signal to the others.

With a flick of Finster's finger, an arrow jetted across the small expanse, burying itself deep in the bog man's heart. Clutching its bleeding chest, the bog man stumbled backward and fell down the steps.

A wild, angry howl swelled up from the horde of swamp dwellers below. It grew louder. Feet slapping against the stone, they came up in a rush.

"Lords of the Black Island!" Finster exclaimed. "There must be dozens of them."

Chapter 68

"Finster! The windows!" Dizon cried out.

More bog men squirmed through the spade-shaped window portals.

With perfect timing, the fully awake Rinny let out an earsplitting shriek.

Cringing, Finster said, "Must she do that?" Without the slightest movement of his fingers, Finster, using the power of the Founder's Stone, willed all portals in the room shut. The stone blocks closed like a mouthful of giant's teeth, crushing the bones of the bog men caught between them.

Savage, pain-filled howls echoed through the barren chamber. The bog men pouring up the step surged. They came at Finster in a furious knot of muscular, primordial swamp men.

"Back up! Back up! Back up!" Finster ordered Dizon. As she backpedaled away from the stairs, Finster pointed his fingers at the oncoming bog men. The arrows shot forth. The feathery shafts blasted through the savages as if shot from a close-range longbow. Arrows passed through bone and body and punched into the next bog man behind them. The ones that didn't die kept coming, shafts protruding through their bodies. In a matter of seconds, Finster, backing away, had used all ten of his arrows. "I need more arrows!"

"That was all of them!" Dizon yelled back.

With the wild white-haired savages screaming for blood less than thirty feet away, Finster had to think fast. With his mind the only weapon that he had left, he pulled the stones from the floor in front of him with the power of the Founder's Stone. Blocks, squares, rectangles, octagons, and many other shapes ripped out of the floor. The gap stretched from one side of the room to the other. He sent the loose, suspended stones hurling into the bog men's bodies. The blocks hit with ramming force, cracking bones and crushing skulls. The first wave of rock wiped out half of the bog men. The second wave he flung hit them like an aerial avalanche. He piled the stones up, sweeping the dead along with them, filling in the stairwell with tons of mangled flesh and rocks.

At the moment, they were safe.

Wiping the sweat from his eyes, Finster said, "I really hated to tamper with outstanding architecture. I suppose I can put it back. It will just be messy." He peered down to the fourth level, where there was a twenty-foot drop between the floors. Dozens of bog men still gathered below. Growling and howling, they jumped high in the air, raking their claws at Finster but never coming close. "They won't stop until they have us. There might be hundreds more out there."

Dizon stood beside him, looking over the edge. "They are a vile people."

"Primitive and evil, I'd guess. People that time forgot who somehow migrated here. My guess is they are relatives to Moth," he said. "Speaking of which, I wonder where he might be."

"Perhaps he is hiding," she said.

Rinny held tight to her mother's waist. "Moth does not hide." She took a look over the edge at the group of salivating men. "What are they doing?"

The bog men started piling up atop one another, creating a tower from their bodies. In seconds, they would reach the ledge.

Dizon looked at Finster. "Primitive, huh?"

"Just because one's kind is primitive does not mean that they can't think for themselves." Using his power, Finster pulled another stone from his floor loose and sent it flying into the face of the bog man anchoring the tower. The bog men above him tumbled. Some landed on their feet, while the others landed hard. Finster rubbed his chin. "They won't stop until I find a way to dissuade them. You might want to look away."

"Why?" Rinny asked.

"Because I'm going to brutally kill them all."

The girl shrugged.

Dizon covered Rinny's eyes and backed away from the ledge. "Do what you must do, Finster. I don't want to see it."

Finster used the same stone he had used before to bust up the men, with devastating effect. It was them or him, and the blood-coated rock plowed through them. Chasing the scuttling wild savages around with a bloody hunk of stone became tedious and tiresome. Using the stone empowered him. It grew stronger the more he used it. He flew the stone—something he could never lift under his own natural power—as easily as if it were an apple.

Just how powerful am I?

As he spread his fingers out wide over the gap, the green veins underneath his skin glowed and pulsated. His brilliant mind accounted for the carefully laid-out stones on the fourth level, and he dropped the entire bottom out from underneath the bog men. He didn't stop there. As the men tumbled through the air, he dropped the floors of the third and second levels. All of the savages, howling for their suddenly fleeting lives, met their deaths at the bottom level.

"Hmph," Finster commented with a degree of satisfaction. "That wasn't nearly as difficult as I thought it might be."

Rinny broke out of her mother's arms. "I want to see." She almost went off the ledge. Her mother caught her by the back of the pants. Rinny stared into the eighty-foot-deep gaping hole that was illuminated by the still-burning torches. "Whoa," she said with awe.

All of the bog men that had fallen were dead. A few of the ones from outside crept in, looked up, turned, and ran.

"I don't think they are going to bother us anymore," he said. With a wave of his hands, he put each and every stone back in place. "I'm getting used to this. I like it."

"What about Moth?" Rinny asked, tugging on Finster's robes. "Where is he? We have to find him."

Chin up, Finster said, "And we will once I finish reveling in my own glory."

Chapter 69

Finster waited until morning before he ventured out of the Black Tower. There weren't any signs of the bog men. He wanted to think with certainty that they wouldn't be back, but with wild men, there was no telling for sure. So he created two stone golems from the surrounding rubble and the many stones he had pulled loose from the tower. They were crudely made men, like something a child would make from building blocks of wood, with only a head, body, legs, arms, hands, and feet. Standing tall and foreboding, they moved quietly, as their mystically bound joints did not allow the stones to rub together. Wherever Finster walked, they remained close behind him.

With the help of Dizon and Rinny, they searched the tower's perimeter, looking for any sign of Moth. Since none of them were trackers of any sort, they didn't notice any signs of Moth's oversized feet. But what they did find were some of the tracks showing where the bog men had come from and where they had fled.

"Finster, what do you think we should do?" Dizon asked. Black bags clung beneath her tired eyes. The luster of her fair skin had begun to fade thanks to the lack of sleep and harsh, bug-ridden elements. "I know the barbarian is prone to roam, but I don't think he would abandon us."

"No, I don't either," Finster said, "but I don't have any desire to go deeper into this marsh. I think it would be best to wait him out for a few days."

"Moth is in danger. I can feel it," Rinny said. "We have to go after him. Something is wrong. I know it."

"You couldn't possibly know that," Finster said to the girl.

Rinny shook her fist at him. "You only say that because you don't care about him."

"While that is true, that is not why I am saying that." He looked to Dizon. "Can you not bridle her tongue? She was so quiet when we first met, and now her lips buzz like a hummingbird's wings."

"Rinny, be silent. Lord Finster knows what is best." Dizon put her arm around her daughter and added, "We can always look together. And we will. But for the time being, let's be patient. Moth will most likely return."

With her bottom lip stuck out and arms crossed over her chest, Rinny said, "Moth is in danger." She slipped out of her mother's grasp and walked away.

Watching her daughter go, Dizon said to Finster, "I believe her." She rubbed her upper arms. "I feel something haunting about this swamp. A watcher of some sort."

"Perhaps the bog men," he said.

"No. Moth would not have let the bog men attack unless he was indisposed elsewhere."

Finster couldn't agree more. Even he'd come to know Moth well enough to realize that he wouldn't let them be endangered. The savage might not care for Finster, but he was fond of the girl at least. Finster looked at the tower. At first, he thought he might have accidentally buried Moth. He put every stone back in place, fastening them by the magic that enchanted them from within. In doing so, he learned that the tower had been enchanted long ago. This made his efforts easier, though he did not understand its purpose. He looked away. Still, there were no signs of the savage northerner who had been raised on the icy steppes.

I have the power to shatter temples, but I can't find one lost man. He lifted a brow. *Or can I?*

"Dizon, do you mind? I want to try something," he said. One of his stone golems dropped to its hands and knees, forming a bench. Finster sat down.

"What do you want me to do?"

"The scarab is nagging. Just let your magic fingers do some walking, if you will. I need to concentrate and recall a spell that I haven't used in quite some time." He placed his hands on his knees and stared out into the forest. "It usually requires other materials, but with the Founder's Stone, it might be possible."

"As you will, Lord Finster." Dizon's strong fingers went to work massaging the tight, irritated muscles between his shoulder blades. "Is that helping?"

"No offense, but please, let me have silence." Manipulating inanimate objects had always been Finster's strongest talent. He was, however, very good at many nuances of the craft. He would not have ever become a magus of the higher orders if he had not been. In deep concentration, eyebrows knitting together, he inwardly recalled a magic protection spell that he practiced very often. When he was younger, he had often searched strange places for magic trinkets. As he matured, he practiced finding sources of magic that came from the earth. With those sources, he built up his practice in the town of Marcen, giving the local people aid in Tarley's Tavern. He did it with nuts, herbs, grasses, weeds, all ground up and mixed for one purpose or another. Now he used the spell he'd used countless times before to seek out the rings of power. They would leave a strong mystic trail. All he needed to do was get a sense of it. He envisioned Moth and a possible path the brute might be on.

Finster blocked out everything: the burning in his back, the sound of the wind rustling through the branches, Dizon's soft breath on his skin. There was just his mind, snaking through the swampy jungles, with mental tentacles stretching out to taste a mystical scent. Through the slimy varmint-infested bogs, he searched far, deep, and wide until, finally, he came upon a trace of magic that lingered in the air, hanging on the petals of a swamp lily. Finster mentally latched on to the magic scent. With invisible hands, he grabbed onto the mystic trail as if it were a rope and gave it a tug. His fingers tingled.

Finster opened his eyes and said with a wry smile, "I have it."

Dizon broke off her massage. "You found Moth?"

Rolling his neck side to side, Finster replied with new brightness in his eyes. "Assuming the rings are still attached to him, yes, I can find a trail to him." The spell had worked, and this was even better news for Finster. Now that he'd locked onto the rings, he should always be able to find them. Hence, Moth could never slip away from him again.

Why didn't I do this all along? It would have saved me a great deal of trouble. Perhaps the scarab in my back distracted me. Oh well. Onward.

Chapter 70

Standing on a stone, Finster glided over the murky water of the swamp. To his left and right, Dizon and Rinny were separately carried by the stone golems that floated along with him. The strong magic scent of the rings of power led him quickly out of the swamp to the edge of the lakes that fed the murk. The shoreline of the lake was rich in green algae and foamy water that brushed up against the reeds on the bank. The winds from the plains sent ripples over the water. The green water was still blanketed by the late morning mist. There was no sign of Moth—not a footprint or anything that Finster could detect.

With growing concern in her voice, Dizon asked, "Have you lost him, Lord Finster?"

"No. I can still sense the rings. I'm just wondering what in the world brought him out here." His gaze swept over the water. Small islands were scattered all over the massive lakes of the marsh. "I fear that a more sinister element is at work here."

"What does that mean?" Rinny asked.

"Hush," Dizon said.

Finster could see the faintest aura of the trail that the rings' passing had left. It was like a faded rainbow. His fingertips still itched as he kneaded them against his palm. "I am close. I can feel it." He gave Dizon a glance. "You'll be safe here. Wait until I come back."

"Finster, no, don't leave us on the edge of this abysmal lake all alone," she said.

"Do not fear. The stone golem will protect you, but I'm taking the other one with me." Still standing on the block, he sailed over the lake. The breeze kissed the thickening whiskers on his face. He looked down to see the water bubble up in different places. The marsh lakes were known for great fish that swallowed smaller fishing boats whole. With the golem in tow, he floated up higher. As for Dizon and Rinny, they were on their own. He had no way of seeing any danger that might threaten them. He had only told them the golem would protect them to give them a sense of security. Hence, he had lied, but with his skin crawling, he knew they were safer away from him than with him.

He was a mile away from the shoreline when he came upon an island that stood on a long bluff of stones above the water's wake. Goosebumps rose on his arms. A chill trickled down his spine.

Moth is here, but something else is as well. Something dark and hungry.

For the first time, Finster believed that Moth, indeed, could be in danger. In theory, with the rings appearing under the skin of the savage's fingers, it was possible that the random power the barbarian tapped no longer worked the way it did before. Moth would have no idea how to actually use the rings' powers, but they should still protect the man to some degree.

Time to take a closer look.

The misty island was half-covered in dead trees with gnarled branches and limbs that seemed to climb out of the ground. The surface was otherwise livable, with hard-packed dirt and wild moss and grasses. Judging by the tiny gray-black birds that darted from limb to limb, the inhospitable place was plenty big enough for a village of wild people, bog men, or hermits to live on. Finster moved along the outer bluff, quickly sailing along at a mile over the perimeter if not more. There were no canoes or skiffs or a dock of any sort along the rocky bluff. Of course, if the bog men were behind Moth's disappearance, they would have no need for a boat, as they were born with webbed fingers.

How did the savage get himself captured? Blue-toe savages are hard enough to trap as it is.

With the mystery lingering in his thoughts, Finster did his best not to assume anything. On the one hand, the bog men would have a leader, but on the other hand, were they smart enough to capture a man like Moth? He had to expect something else. From his rock, he moved deeper into the island's woodland, following the aura of the rings. More than one hundred yards in, he heard an eerie yet comforting call pulling at his sensibilities and luring him deeper within.

The call reminded him of the stories of the sirens that wrecked the ships and minds of sailors at sea. The beckoning harmony plucked at his mind and cradled his pounding heart. He floated closer and closer to the source of the sound.

Don't be a fool, Finster. You will not be taken down like this.

Strong, unseen hands grabbed ahold of his body, reeling him into the soft warmth promising a better today and an even better tomorrow. He glided onward, slow and steady, weaving through the trees, whose branches brushed across his elbows. He didn't resist the soothing sound of the welcoming chant. Instead, he let the words take him right to it. He floated lazily into a massive grove that was surrounded by a ring of towering pine trees. The floor of the grove was a bed of mushrooms, many of which were bigger than him. Large slabs of stone from a structure that had fallen ages ago were half-covered in moss. Transfixed by the music, Finster found himself coming to a stop less than fifty feet away from the prone form of Moth.

The savage was covered in snails with fuzzy mustard-brown and forest-green shells. Long, slimy antenna-like tentacles fanned out of the little monsters' heads and burrowed into Moth's clammy skin. The tentacles pulsated with a strange illumination.

Finster's stomach recoiled. His heart shot into his throat. He couldn't tear his eyes away from the disturbing scene. Finally, with effort, he turned his head, averting his gaze from Moth as new movement caught his eye. A few yards behind Moth, a snail shell the size of an elephant sat in the bed of mushrooms. The pinwheel shell was partially coated in fuzzy green-brown moss that would camouflage it with nature. The harmonious humming that Finster heard emanated from its body. The shell moved. Its front end tipped upward. A slimy, bulbous body started to emerge.

The stone Finster rode on lowered toward the ground. Snails from the grove, tentacles waving, began the slow crawl his way. The stone golem wobbled loosely in the air as Finster fought to maintain control of it. The stones that made up the animated golem dropped to the loamy ground, crushing the mushroom spores beneath them and sending up a yellow dust cloud. He coughed.

From underneath the giant shell, a humanish figure emerged. It appeared as a man coated in a wet and shiny slime. Antennas adorned the snail man's head. His features were that of the bog men—human—with long muscular arms and slender, glossy fingers that spread out like fans. The snail man's haunting eyes, green as the shrubbery on the banks, fastened on Finster's. He came forward, hard chest outward, hands extended.

Finster's limbs seized. Sweat dripped into his eyes. The field of snails crept dangerously closer.

Finally, the huge half man, half snail spoke with an open mouth full of gooey saliva. In a voice that bubbled, he said, "Welcome, feast. Inslay hungers."

Chapter 71

Dizon stared out over the lake with her hands cradling her elbows. By her side, sitting down on a rock, Rinny shared her view. The former member of King Alrick's harem had felt empty the moment Finster vanished from sight. When she was in his presence, she felt secure. The sorcerer, unlike most men she'd been with, had an inner warmth to him. It made her comfortable no matter the setting. She was uncertain what drew her to him. He had a handsome yet bookish demeanor. His physique lacked the vibrant firmness she preferred, yet here she was, ready to follow him to the end of the world. Hardly a moment had passed, and her heart ached.

Rinny tossed a stick into the lake. "They aren't coming back, are they?"

"Of course they are," Dizon said. "Why would you say that?"

The girl shrugged. "Men always part company with us. They are due."

Rinny gave Dizon a stark lesson of what life must have been like for her. Men came in and out of Dizon's home, wealthy men, mostly. Many made promises, but not one of them was kept. They came on the ships, and some stayed for days, pretended to be family, only to return to their true homes later. Rinny had liked them at first, but over time, she had seen through the veil and gained a better understanding of what her mother was. Moth and Finster were the closest thing to a family that they had had in a long time. Perhaps the relationship had run its course.

Dizon sat down. She cradled the girl in her lap. "Rinny, nothing in life lasts forever. What you love, enjoy it while you have it."

"You won't be with me forever either?" the girl asked.

"Of course I will be, so long as I last." She kissed the girl on the cheek. "Don't ever forget that."

"I miss Moth. I didn't think he would leave me."

"Men like Moth are hard to love. As you grow older, you'd be better off loving one that is more settled."

"Well, I just wanted to be friends with the savage. I didn't want to marry him."

Dizon's loud laughter carried across the water. Ducks skimming the lake scattered. She gave her daughter a fierce hug. "I needed that."

The sound of stone landing on stone made both woman and girl jump. The stone golem had fallen into a pile.

"Oh no," Rinny said. Her chin trembled. "They are dead."

In her heart, Dizon wouldn't believe it. "Don't think that. Not for a moment, don't think that at all. Remember, Moth is invincible."

"I hope that's true. Maybe only Finster is dead then."

Dizon took her daughter by the hand. "Let's try not to think about it. Finster is probably too far away, but he'll be back. I'm certain of it. Let's walk and keep our minds off it." She turned back toward the lake and gasped. A host of bog men had crept up on them and stood ankle-deep in the lake. All Dizon could say was, "Run, Rinny! Run!"

Chapter 72

Inslay, the giant-sized half snail, half man, stopped a few yards short of Finster. Though he was imposing in size, his head was little bigger than that of a normal bog man's. The tentacles on the top of his head swayed left and right. His fingers slowly crawled in the air. Bog men emerged from the sagging woodland by the dozens. His voice froze Finster's blood when he said, "I am the god of this isle. This lake. And beyond. You slew my bog men. Many, many children. For that, you will die slowly and painfully. I will drain the magic that you hold, same as the savage, and make it all mine."

The scarab burrowed in Finster's back pulsated, sending the constant signal of pain right through him. That reminder was the only thing that kept Finster's mind from being lulled into a deeper sleep. "You think you know pain," he said to Inslay. "Come, take it from me. I dare you."

Inslay's jaw tightened. The fatty ridges on the top of his back rippled. "You speak? You dare? My snails will nibble on your tongue for days."

Seizing control of his own powers, Finster cast a stone into a row of snails, crushing them all with a notable crunch. "Were you talking about those snails or the others? And should I address you as Inslay or the snail god?"

Inslay's voice rose. "You dare toy with me? At the height of my power?" He stretched farther out of his shell, coming face-to-face with Finster. "Perhaps I should kill you instantly. Or better yet, human defiler, perhaps I should kill the woman and the child."

Finster let out a startled "What?"

Bog men marched into the grove, carrying Dizon and Rinny in their arms. His friends' heads dangled, and their long, wet hair dragged on the ground. They were tossed onto the ground like discarded sacks of grain and lay limp.

"Please, human, harm another shell or bog man and watch my bog men peel the skin right off their bones."

"Perhaps you and I can make a bargain," Finster suggested.

Inslay recoiled and laughed out loud. "You are in no position to bargain. I will have what you have and suck the marrow from your bones."

Finster lifted a finger. "Yet, god of slime and saliva—no offense—you hesitate." He looked Inslay dead in the eye. "I sense you need to understand the powers that you draw upon."

Inslay's fists balled up. The muscles in his arms clenched. "I will drain the answers I seek out of you."

"It would be easier if I just told you." Finster lazily scanned his surroundings, searching for anything that might be helpful. He was borrowing time as Inslay's music continued to take a toll on him. Though mentally strong, he still battled for consciousness. He reserved what he could, waiting to strike when the time was right. He tried honesty. "How about I tell you about the power in the savage and the magic residing inside of me? After all, it was you that sent your bog men to rob me. What did you expect? That I wouldn't defend myself?"

"You are a trespasser," Inslay said.

"I am a magus of the Black Tower, and I have a feeling that you were once a magus too. How else could you have become so abominable?

Did your pursuit for eternal life go awry, Inslay?" Finster's statement was a guess, but he caught a flicker in the snail man's eyes. He noticed something else too. Moth's broadsword, the one he had taken from Crawley, stuck in a knee-high mushroom. "Tell me."

Inslay came closer. The tentacles on his head seized the magus's skull. "No! You tell me!"

Finster wailed like a banshee. His eyes rolled up into his head. A new burning fire coursed through his limbs, not feeding him but draining him. In stammering speech beyond his control, words gushed forth about the Founder's Stone and the rings of power. He held back what he could before going limp and falling to the ground, twitching and exhausted.

Inslay loomed over him, bright glowing fingers tapping together. "Interesting. All I have to do is rip that scarab out of your back and cut those rings from the savage's hands." He smirked. "That won't be a problem." He looked toward his bog men and gave them a nod.

The hairy-armed bog men hurried over to Finster. They lifted him by the arms and legs, leaving his head hanging toward the ground.

Finster lifted his head. "You don't want to do this."

"Yes, I do," Inslay replied. His tentacles latched onto Finster's face again. "Cut him open."

Chapter 73

Inslay's tentacles, latched onto Finster's face, didn't hurt this time. Instead, the eerie sound of music pulsated through them, sending Finster into a pure stage of serenity. The euphoric sensation had drool falling from his open mouth. His eyelids became heavy. His body, seized by rough hands, seemed to float in the air. He mumbled, "Whatever you are doing, don't stop."

The beautiful harmony brought relief as the tentacles massaged his temples. He envisioned Dizon, a glorious siren, covered only by her honey-blond hair, singing to him. She sat on the rocks along the banks, where a gentle tide splashed over her lower body. Her eyes, her lips, her voice captivated him. The pain of the scarab had vanished.

This can't be happening. It's not possible that I live without my curse. Is it? Is this life? Is this liberation?

Whatever arcane power Inslay had used to soothe Finster's chronic aggravations was working. Finster wanted to embrace the power and not resist the temptation. Yet the parts of him that had not stopped fighting continued to churn, pushing back against the warming mind massage. His body trembled. The illusion of Dizon sang, "Do not resist… sweet Finster, do not resist, do not resist, but embrace the illumination of your mind."

The knots the scarab had caused in his back yielded. His focus on reality fled. Finster was with Dizon, singing at her side like a bird. Together, they sang in perfect harmony, "It will all be over soon. It will all be over soon, sweet Finster."

A prick of a razor-sharp edge cut into the skin in his back. He felt every bit of the blade, yet there was no pain. Through a strange out-of-body experience, he had a vision of himself as he hovered in the air above his limp form. In the middle of his back, between the shoulder blades, was a scarred clump of skin the size of a fist. Below the thickness of the mass glowed the scarab, lighting up the cobweb of green veins in his back. It would have been a repulsive sight if he had not been in a state of elation. Using a sharp dagger, a lone bog man, incomprehensibly instructed by Inslay, began cutting off the massive callus on his back. Deep underneath his skin, like a massive tick, the emerald scarab pulsated like a beating heart. Its black legs had burrowed so deep that he could not see them. Finster thought to himself, "Take it out."

The bog man cut through the surrounding flesh with the dagger. The scarab's legs clenched. Finster's head snapped backward. He let out an inhuman scream. On instinct, his mind grabbed ahold of the rock he rode upon. He sent it hurtling into Inslay's shell. It hit with a resounding crack. The eerie music stopped. Finster's dreams turned into a nightmare of pain. Dizon and Rinny stirred. The girl saw the snail man. Eyes widening, she let out a bloodcurdling shriek.

Inslay's big hands clamped over Finster's face. His own face filling with rage, he shouted, "Cut that scarab out now! Kill him!"

Moth slumbered. The siren-like music covered him, and he felt as if he rested in a down-filled bed covered in soft fox-fur blankets. The world he knew was gone. The savagery was lost. Only serenity remained. All in the world was well until Rinny screamed.

His eyelids snapped open. The comforting sounds were replaced by a horrifying, frightening sound. With snails latched onto his body, he rose. Reality came back to him. He pulled them away in handfuls. The last thing he remembered was that he had been scouting the forest when the music came. Everything else had been a blank. He ripped more snails from his flesh. Like leeches, they left ugly blood marks all over his body. The snails, ugly green, yellow, and fuzzy, had mouths and tiny teeth. He crushed the shells in his hands and flung them away.

The sullen-eyed savage scanned the grove. A man sticking out of a massive snail shell had seized hold of Finster. Bog men stood about with their backsides to him. Rinny's screaming came from somewhere on the other side of the shell. The strange music resumed. He fiercely shook his head. Moth's eyes fell upon his sword, stuck hilt deep in a giant mushroom. He snatched it up and charged the part man, part snail. Plowing through the bog men, he swung hard into the massive shell. The blade skipped across the rigid shell. Chopping with vigor, he hacked into it again with the same poor result. Over a dozen wild bog men piled on top of him and dragged him to the ground.

"Kill him!" It was those words that snapped Finster's senses into place. The Founder's Stone inside the scarab had reacted on its own earlier. Finster wasn't sure if it was protecting him or itself, but it wasn't going anywhere. In the meantime, the bog men stretched him out by the feet and hands, pulling at his limbs like the corners of a blanket.

The bog man with the dagger lifted it high. With two hands, he plunged it downward. Halfway down, the dagger froze in midair. The bog man put all of his weight behind the dagger, pressing it downward, but it did not move.

"Foolish bog man, what are you doing?" the enraged Inslay demanded. "Just stab him!"

Though Finster fully desired that the knife not penetrate his weakened flesh, it was not him that had halted the dagger. The scarab had taken command, for he could barely lift a finger. Inslay's probing had left him woozy minded. He looked at Inslay and said with a smirk, "I told you not to try this."

Inslay backhanded him across the face. "Be silent, trespasser!"

The muscles bulged in the arms of the bog man wielding the dagger. He couldn't move it down an inch. Then suddenly, the dagger gave, and the bog man plunged it deep into his own belly. "Urk!" The frightened ghoul of the marsh let go, frantically backing away. The dagger pursued him, stabbing him over and over. The bog men dropped Finster to the ground. More of the surrounding bog men jumped up and down. They beat their chests and howled wildly. The dagger took after them, sending them scurrying away.

The eerie music coming from Inslay's shell continued to play. Inslay, in a foreign tongue or some sort of bog-man language, shouted orders. The bog men chased the dagger. Jumping and diving, they tried in vain to corral the menacing blade. The dagger twisted out of their grips. It slit throats and cut off fingers. Many of the primitive bog men, bleeding from mortal wounds, fled into the recesses of the island.

Surrounded by the chaotic carnage, Inslay glowered at Finster with burning eyes. "Stop this!"

Finster lay on the ground now in a half-fetal position. With a wobbly voice, he said, "I'm not doing it, though I wish I were. I think you are about to experience some dire regret… slug man."

With a mouth full of gooey saliva, Inslay fired back, "It is not I that will regret but you who will watch your women die." With a wave of his long hands, Dizon and Rinny were scooped off the ground by an invisible hand. The slug lord squeezed his hands into fists. The woman's and girl's eyes bulged. Their faces reddened. "Them first. You next," he said.

Chapter 74

Dressed in common traveling cloaks, three assassins followed Alexandria, the High Executioner, east to the outer territories often called the Fringe. Unlike the seven main cities of the kingdoms, the lands beyond their borders offered harsher and more rugged terrain. The rich farmlands fed by the rivers that spilled into the Gallatan Sea were replaced by small creeks and streams. The plains were sparse and rocky, offering little sanctuary from the glaring sun. They rode all day until they came to the trade city known as Portgul.

Portgul was an old city made from stone and wood and weathered by centuries of time. Half of the roads were paved with gray bricks. It still thrived because of the surrounding coal and copper mines. Hauling their tools in wheelbarrows and carts, hard-faced men and women wandered home from a hard day of work. Many called the rugged Portgul the last stop between man and civilization. Barbaric tribes thrived in the surrounding hills and were often troublesome and unpredictable. Soldiers in ringmail underneath unkempt uniform tunics with a black raven on the chest patrolled the streets, carrying spears. They didn't give the assassins a glance. No one did.

Hosting well over ten thousand residents, Portgul wasn't without its own charm. It was a place where rogues, fugitives, embezzlers, and shady merchants gathered. The great taverns that resided within the heart of the town stood three and four stories tall. All of them had large covered porches, where men and women sat on wooden benches and rockers, cackling, drinking, and smoking.

Alexandria dismounted at the largest tavern she came across. The tavern sign read "Lowport." Eyes from the porches below and above passed over her and the others. Her top assassin, Holger, cleared his throat. She followed his gaze. A row of fine stallions was hitched to the posts on the other side of the tavern's front entrance. They had the River Knights' sword-over-water insignia stamped in the leather of their saddles.

"Damn," she said.

Holger, sandy haired and dark eyed, standing shorter than Alexandria and the other two assassins, said, "It seems Carlyn's deception did not stay the course. The River Knights were not fooled." He dropped his reins over the hitching post. "I have a feeling they're going to be a pain in our bollocks."

"Let's find out." Trailed by her men, she walked up to the porch and passed a swaying oaf of a man with a black eye who held a tankard in his hand. He winked at her. She entered Lowport tavern. The big tavern could hold five hundred revelers easily, but the tables were only half-full. The smell of incense intermingled with smoky vapors. The scents of kitchen grease, charred meat, and roasted onions lingered in the air. A handful of barmaids in long skirts, smiling excitedly, hustled back and forth, serving the dozen or so River Knights who filled the tables. They whispered and giggled to one another while adjusting their hair and revealing their blouses. Alexandria slid over to the barstools and took a seat. Holger and the other men joined her.

"I like this place," Holger said with a crooked smile. "It has my kind of sordid element. Barbarians, knights, miners, and wenches. Could prove to be interesting."

The barkeep was a tight-faced older woman with black hair tied back in braids. She sponged down the bar top. "What will it be?"

"A row of ale will do," Alexandria said.

The barkeep gave her a wink and held up four fingers to the fellow who was manning the keg taps. Making light conversation, she said, "We don't get many knights in these parts. My girls have never been so excited. Aside from some of the Goth traders, they've never seen strapping men like this."

"What brings them through?" Alexandria asked.

"The same thing that has been bringing newcomers in like a wave: the bounty on this divine sorcerer, Finster, who kills kings and turns ships into planks." The barkeep blinked a lot as she spoke. "I imagine you are hunting the bounty too? Heh, I can tell."

Alexandria leaned forward on her elbows. "What makes you so sure?"

"I've seen the faces of murderers, wizards, merchants, and savages. I know when someone is looking for trouble." The barkeep rubbed her fingertips together. "I can feel it. And what I don't, I hear. Those River Knights, they are a gusty lot. Bold and brazen. They make a lot of high talk about killing this wild barbarian who conquered the Gauntlet with swords sticking out of his legs. He's a blue-toe. The dying breed. Just so you know, I haven't seen him or the magus, not that I would tell you if I did."

Holger turned toward the barkeep and, with an elbow on the table, said, "Why wouldn't you tell us? We are nice and curious people. And there might be something in it for you."

"Something better than the River Knights offer?" The barkeep laughed. "Hah. They practically promised the crown. The truth is, they can shove the crown where the moon won't shine, because we don't care about the kings and queens of the Seven Kingdoms. Rebels such as the savage and the sorcerer would be more than welcome here. But I haven't seen them."

The male barkeep set four tankards on the bar. The lady shoved them in front of the assassins. "That will be three silver jacks."

"Expensive," Alexandria replied. She put the coins on the table.

"My conversation makes it worth it. Do you need anything else?"

"No. Ale will do."

The blinking woman gave her a long wink. "Just holler if you do." She hustled to the opposite end of the bar. Two brawny savages covered in furs were banging their tankards on the bar. She waved her hands at them. "Settle down, you bloody Goths! More ale's coming!"

Alexandria turned toward the knights and leaned against the bar. Her frown deepened. If word about Finster's exploits had reached Portgul, she could only assume the rest of the Seven Kingdoms knew as well. It infuriated her. King Rolem and King Mather were fools to send more men on the hunt and not trust in the Circle. There was no telling who else might have been hired to begin the pursuit. But clearly, trackers had made it this far out and had begun asking questions. It was a problem. A big one.

Holger said, "So, what do you think?"

"It appears that this hunt is no longer a matter of discretion. It's going to be a matter of who finds the terrible twosome first," she said. With full view of the knights, who had begun to fill their laps with the barmaids, she noticed some other intriguing men among the group. Deep in the corner, shielded behind several knights, were three men. They wore long checkered robes in red, blue, and gold. They appeared smallish among the formidable knights. Alexandria knew better. Her nostrils widened. "Just what we need, more wizards."

"Huh, I hardly noticed them," Holger said, squinting. "Were they sitting there before?"

"I don't think they were."

Chapter 75

Underneath the pile of bog men, Moth cocked his powerful arm and stabbed. He buried the broadsword into chest after chest. A fighting tiger, he hacked into limbs, cutting a hole through the bog men. He bounded back to his feet and unleashed fury. Webbed hands flew through the air, making a spray of blood. Torsos were hacked in two. A bog man's leg came off. Still, they came.

The long claws of the bog men were sharp as fishhooks. Their claws peeled Moth's skin away. One after the other, they jumped onto his body. The blood-soaked Moth gored them. He stabbed one in the chest and lifted it overhead like meat on a stick. He slung it off to the side then spun a counterswing that took off the head of another.

The unfettered bog men came at him from all directions. Hanging on for their lives, they locked their bodies around his legs and grabbed his arms. The savage's raw vitality quavered against the numbers. A bog man bit down on Moth's wrist. The teeth sank deep. With a bog man hanging on his other arm, Moth drove a thumb into the biter's eyeball, pushing it in fully. The bog man's jaw released.

With his arm free, Moth hacked downward, cutting open the hairy brutes that fought like a pack of wild animals. There was blood all over. His blood. Their blood. Gore and guts. He had no understanding of what held him together. He did not care. The only thing that mattered was to slay and survive.

The net of bog men finally wrestled him back down to the ground. They pinned his arms in the soft dirt. Rocks smote Moth in the face, busting his nose. Claws sank into his abdomen, tearing his flesh open. He kicked in vain. His own great strength finally caved to the horde. Claws bared, they went for his throat.

Chapter 76

Fighting for his life, Moth's grasping fingers caught ahold of a bog man's elbows. The hairy arms of the fiendish swamp dweller caught fire. A rousing stink of black smoke started as the fire spread all over the bog man. The bog man let out a wild cry. He released Moth and jumped away, trying to pat out the flames. The fire consumed the swamp-born savage.

With big eyes, the bog men stared at Moth's now-free hand. The fist was consumed with flame.

Moth punched the closest one in the face, setting his hair on fire. With a flaming fist, he punched one after the other. The slightest touch of his hand turned the hairy bog men into burning scarecrows. In their panic, more flames spread from one to another as they fought to pat each other out. The ignorant swamp dwellers spread doom amongst themselves. They burned. They writhed. A black, stinking smoke filled the air. The smarter bog men ran for the water.

Back on his feet, Moth looked at his flaming hand and fingers. He tilted his head to one side then to the other. Sword still in his other hand, he turned to face the man inside the shell that loomed over Finster. As he gripped his sword in both hands, it caught flame. Using it like a spear, he rammed it into the giant shell.

Dizon and Rinny hung suspended in the air, fighting for their last dying breaths. Finster could see invisible fingers needling their necks. The mother's and daughter's faces turned deep red and purple. "Stop!" he shouted at Inslay. "Stop!" Inslay's gloating stare remained transfixed on the women. He chuckled with weird, bubbly laughter. Anger stirred inside Finster. He came up to his knees, concentrating on getting control of his powers. The scarab still throbbed like a burning coal inside his body. He had no command over it.

I must do something!

Forgetting about the scarab, he summoned his own powers, which still lingered inside the blood of his weakening frame. Catching sight of the dagger that had chased down and killed the bog men, he summoned his powers over the inanimate.

Obey me, steel! I command it!

He wrestled against the force of the Founder's Stone and wrapped his will around it. The mystic presence resisted at first before finding familiarity with an old friend. The dagger pulled free of a bog man's belly.

Finster set his narrowed eyes on Inslay. "Now I have you!" As one, he and the stone sent the dagger hurtling into the snail lord's chest.

Inslay's mouth gaped.

Dizon and Rinny fell hard to the ground.

With one hand, Inslay pulled the dagger from his body. "It will take more than steel to hurt me. I am a god! I am not simple flesh! I am… eh?" The snail lord stretched farther out of his shell and peered around his broad side. "What are you doing? Get away from me, insect!"

Finster, on wobbly legs, traipsed in the same direction. Moth hacked and stabbed into the shell of the snail lord with a sword consumed by flame. He splintered chunks of the shell like a lumberjack taking an axe to wood. Enclosed in a veil of dark-gray smoke, the barbarian worked with relentless fury, taking the monstrous snail body down hunks at a time.

The music coming from the shell stopped.

Slowly, with growing agony on his face, Inslay tried to turn. "Stop it, fool! Invader, get away from my nest!"

Moth waded into a doorway-sized hole he'd made in the shell. He cut away slimy globs of Inslay's flesh.

"Nooooooo!" Inslay screamed. He extended his hands, stretching the tentacles on his head at the same time. The probing tentacles opened at the tips like tiny mouths. They spit out black needles that buried themselves in Moth's arms and shoulders.

The savage's Herculean efforts slowed. He staggered one step back before leaning forward and swinging again.

Inslay's tentacles shot out more darts.

With the eerie music gone, Finster's concentration cleared. Full control of the scarab and stone returned to his sharp mind. Mentally, he picked up two stone blocks from the ground. "Snail lord, I would have a word with you!"

Inslay curled his body toward Finster. Looming over the sorcerer with his chest heavy, the snail lord said, "What, flea?"

"Goodbye." Finster used the blocks like a pair of cymbals to crush Inslay's skull. He did it over and over, crushing the bone and flesh, turning it all to soppy goo.

Inslay's misshapen head became unrecognizable. His dying body retreated halfway into the shell.

Moth took more heavy whacks at the body with sluggish limbs. The flame on the sword had extinguished. The savage, with long black needles turning his arms black and purple, chopped on until he emerged through the other side. There, he made his way to Dizon and Rinny where they sat on the ground, shaking but safe. The gore-coated Moth jumped in front of them, brandishing the sword and shielding them from any further attacks.

There was no sign of a single living bog man. All the snails had curled up into their shells.

Finster looked at Inslay's massive shell, which Moth had turned into a tunnel. "You could have just walked around it, mute." He swayed. "Dizon, if you have it in you, could you take a look at my back? I'm not certain, but I think it's missing."

The disheveled woman hustled over, stood behind him, lifted up his robes, and gasped.

"That bad, is it?" Finster asked.

"It's mortal. I don't see how you can stand." She wrapped her arm around his waist and guided him to a place in the grove where he could sit. "I'm so sorry, Finster. So sorry." She sobbed. "I don't know what to do about this."

"If it's any consolation, I feel quite alive, on account of the great deal of pain." He took a sharp breath. "It's not that much worse than it's always been."

"You don't deserve to suffer so much," she replied.

"No, I'm pretty sure that I do. I'm guilty of many treacherous things." He gave Moth a glance. The bare-chested savage squatted. With the help of Rinny, they were pulling needles from his arms, shoulders, and chest. The purple-black marks that had spread all over his body were clearing. "Never in my life would I have thought that I would envy a savage."

Chapter 77

Settling into Portgul's Lowport tavern, Alexandria and Holger took a seat at a small table near the knights and ordered dinner. Holger cast an occasional glance her way. She'd used the magic within her cloak to subtly alter her appearance. Lowering the buttons on her shirt, she noticeably increased her bust size. Her hair, which she kept straight and short, had more fullness and curls to it. Adding some gloss to her lips made her smile all the more alluring. She knew what men liked and what they wanted. It hadn't taken long for the knights to confidently strike up a conversation. Two of them now sat at their table.

A black-haired athlete with hawkish good looks introduced himself as Osgald. He had a neatly trimmed beard and wore a star embroidered on his River Knight tunic that identified him as the River Knight commander. He was older and spoke with curiosity but had a wanton eye. The other knight, stout, with half-inch short hair, was rugged and well-built and called himself Chet. He smiled and nodded at everything Osgald said.

Holger sat across from Alexandria, engaged but quietly eating his steak and potatoes.

With his arm stretched out, Osgald said, "Do you remember that, Chet?"

Chet nodded.

"I'd never seen such butchery before," Osgald said as he continued the story. "I am talking about the finest knights of Mendes piled up in heaps." He looked up at the cast-iron chandeliers. "Uh, the word I want to use escapes me. I was never one to be poetic, but they looked like plows had run over them." He looked at Alexandria with a long frown. "I'm sorry. I shouldn't be talking about such dreadful things in the presence of a beautiful lady." He took her hand, still sheathed in her soft leather glove. "Apologies."

Alexandria leaned closer to Osgald. "I don't mind. I've told you, I've seen my share of bloodshed. After all, I am a sword for hire."

Osgald reached over and grabbed her upper arm. Looking deep into her eyes, he said, "You are firm as iron. I believe you can fight. I see the steel behind your eyes." He glanced down her shirt. "But it's not your eyes that captivate me. I find you so ample and fascinating."

"I am both," she said. The knights had been drinking nonstop since they had arrived. Many of them were slurring their speech, and a few had taken barmaids to their rooms. Osgald's eyes were half-glazed from strong drink and lust, but he still seemed to have his wits about him. Aside from him, she noticed that not all of the knights were drinking. Still, she was curious why the knights seemed to be so loose about their business. It didn't seem right for men known to maintain a very high standard. "I hope you don't think me gruesome for asking, but tell me more about this battle at the Free River."

Osgald leaned back. His chair groaned under the weight of his platemail armor. "I'd be happy to, but only if you give me a little kiss." He turned a cheek. "I just have to feel the touch of those soft lips."

"I'm not some tavern wench that is easily wooed by the length of your sword," she replied adamantly. "I'm a fighter."

Osgald lifted his hands in surrender. "Apologies. Apologies. I will tell you. By the time we arrived, the crows were feasting. The rank smell would have made a Wargoth vomit. Isn't that right, Chet?"

The knight sitting across from him with a permanent grin on his face nodded.

"What struck me was the bloody galleon smashed along the bank of the river. It looked as if a sea titan had scooped it up and dashed it against the rocks." Osgald shook his head. "I'm telling you, it sent a shiver through me, and nothing shakes a River Knight."

"So, is that what brings you here?" she asked. "You are going to kill this savage and sorcerer?"

"Why, that is the king's business." Osgald lifted his tankard to his lips, drank, set it down, and smiled. "And a knight never tells."

Alexandria touched his hand. "Oh really. Well, there is something that I would like to tell you. My men and I are pursuing this savage and sorcerer, so it is ideal that you won't be in our way."

Osgald pulled his hand away. His tone lost its friendly edge. "Lady, let me warn you, it is best that you do not interfere with the king's business. I've crossed my share of sellswords and brigands, and no matter how formidable your skills may be, the men you would pursue can only be taken by otherworldly means." He looked over his shoulder at the wizards sitting at the table. They were quietly sipping their wine and talking among themselves. "The only thing you will find is death if you cross the savage and sorcerer's path."

Holger leaned on the back two legs of his chair.

Chet rested his elbows on the table, still grinning.

"You don't sound afraid to face them," Alexandria said. "Why should I be?"

"Face them? Hah," the knight commander said. "I have no intention of facing them at all. You see, you didn't let me finish my tale. I have seen this pair at work firsthand. They made the veins in my arms writhe like snakes." He took a long drink. "Believe me when I say that you don't want any part of them. Isn't that right, Chet?"

Using a cloth napkin, Chet wiped his face and nodded.

"Chet was present when the blue-toe, Moth, overtook the obstacles at the Gauntlet. It granted them the King of Rayland's chalice." Oswald gave her a knowing look. "And I personally saw the magus, Finster, sail away in a chair girded in metal. You should abandon your ambitions, Alex. That is all that I will say about the king's business." He wagged his finger at her. "And I'm beginning to suspect that you are probing."

"Me?" she asked, acting coy and a little offended. She quickly realized that Osgald, and possibly some of the other knights, had been guarding the king's dining hall the day she killed King Alrick. The River Knights in the room wore full helmets that covered their faces completely. They didn't speak either. Osgald must have witnessed the entire slaughter at the feast. *My, what interesting company I keep. I need to work this to my advantage.* "Osgald, perhaps I can be of greater service to you. I love the hunt. Perhaps, if I offered my services for free, we could cover more ground together. I've never been in the company of a knight before, and I would seek the king's favor."

Osgald drummed his fingers on the table. "What are you offering?"

"There is much ground to cover. My men and I are excellent trackers and information gatherers. With leagues to cover, we could aid you." She placed her hand over his, stopping his fingers from drumming. She pulled her shoulder back and leaned closer to him. "It would be a partnership, so to speak."

With hungry eyes, he swallowed and said, "Let's discuss the details in my quarters."

Chapter 78

Back at the Black Tower, Dizon cleaned Finster's back wound with a clean cloth she had boiled over the campfire using lake water. Stripped down to his pantaloons, he sat on a stone with his hands on his knees. Two days had passed since they had killed Inslay. Finster, though in pain, had full use of his powers once again. He had flown them all back using the stones from the golem. Both of the golems were once again standing beside them, faceless, unmoving statues.

Feeling the pressure of the warm rag on his back, he winced. "How does it look?"

"Awful… but the skin seems to be mending well on its own. I don't know how, but you are not infected." Her gentle fingers traced a circle in his back around the spot where the scarab had burrowed within. "How do you live with this?"

"If not for that enchanting relic, I surely would have died, and Ingrid the Insane would be ruling the world. I suppose it's the price for peace." He smirked. "Someone had to pay it."

Dizon moved in front of him. She put her soft lips on his forehead. "You don't have a fever."

He took her hands gently in his and kissed them. "Yet I burn for you."

A smile spread over her face. "Even in a dark time like this, you still want me."

"I'm a man. We never stop thinking about what we want." He moved his hands to her rear end and pulled her in closer. "And I want you, always."

"Obviously." She sat down on his lap and stroked his head. "And I'm always yours. But we can't hide forever in this swamp. We've come to the Black Tower and gained nothing."

"Perhaps from your perspective, but I've gained a great deal. I've learned more about the Founder's Stone, and as haunting as it is, I'm glad of it." The mystic sound that Inslay had produced had severed their connection somehow. The snail lord's abilities had not been strong enough to hold, thanks to several distractions, but it had been enough for Finster to learn that the Founder's Stone was possibly sentient. It seemed to have a will of its own, and if it did, he surmised it would only get stronger with time. The question was, was the magic in the stone truly sentient? Or was it just a manifestation of his own desires? Could Finster control it, or would it eventually control him? At some point, he feared he would have to make a choice whether to embrace the powers or not, but in the meantime, he had to keep the Founder's Stone and the rings of power out of the wrong hands. "I need to find someone I can trust."

"You can trust me," she said.

"I truly believe that." He reeled her in for a kiss. "King Rolem's plans need to be outed, but I'm not so sure that any of the other kings would believe me. Possibly Toozan or Archmenis. They are the most independent of the other sea-hugging kingdoms. They've never cared for the puffery of Mendes."

"I still think—"

"Yes, I know, kill King Rolem the Grand. My, you are a bloodthirsty wench, aren't you?"

"I'd never harm a fly if I didn't have to. The king's ambitions will only get more people killed. I say end it. In the end, it will be him or you. It better be you."

"I can't."

She looked him hard in the eye. "You can. From a great distance. No one would know it. Make it look like an accident. Drop a loose stone on him or something. Crush him like you did that snail."

"Heh-heh, you really are something. Regardless, someone will always come after me and Moth. The magi from all over will not rest knowing that the rings and the stone are about. Speaking of which." He looked left and right. There were no signs of Rinny and Moth. "Huh, it certainly is serene without them. I could get used to this. Just the two of us, living happily in a bug-infested swamp. We could be the new king and queen of the bog men."

"I think we both deserve better," she said.

"You don't have your eye on a crown in Mendes, do you?"

"Never. It's the simple life for me."

"Uh-huh, I see." He caught movement from the corner of his eye and turned toward it.

Moth and Rinny, on horseback, appeared from around the backside of the tower. The girl seemed like an infant compared to the massive savage who sat beside her. The lake water had rinsed the muck from the barbarian, giving his strapping frame a clean look. The sullen-eyed man held the reins. His dead stare hung on Finster.

"I think we are leaving," Rinny said.

"Is that so? And why do you say that?" Finster replied.

"Moth and I packed all of the gear up. Can't you see? The horse is loaded down."

Finster's eyes swept over the horse. Indeed, aside from the pot over the fire and a few other items, they were ready to go.

Dizon moved out of Finster's lap. "Rinny, I think Lord Finster will decide when it is time to leave and not time to leave." Dizon didn't hide her irritation. "Mind yourself."

"But Moth and I want to go," Rinny whined.

"You and Moth will have to wait!" Dizon replied.

Finster approached the horse and riders. "Little nuisance, does Moth communicate with you in some bizarre but unseen way?"

With her chin up, Rinny proudly said, "I just know what he wants."

"If that is the case, where does he want to go?"

Rinny looked about and after several seconds pointed south of their position. "That way."

Finster turned to Dizon. "Your daughter has no idea what she is talking about, does she?"

"No," Dizon replied.

Finster stole a look at Moth's fingers. The rings underneath the skin still looked like extra knuckles. He rubbed his mouth. *So close. I can feel them. What will it take to get them?* It didn't matter where Moth went now. Thanks to the detection spell Finster had cast, he could always find the savage or the rings. Now all he had to do was figure out what it would take to separate one from the other. And if he could detect them, other mages would be using their resources to detect them too. In the meantime, he had the feeling that Moth was content to stay wherever he was. *What to do, what to do, Finster?*

Dizon laid a hand on his shoulder. "Where you go, we follow. I think I speak for all of us, even the mute."

He turned his chin over his shoulder. "So, my back is not spread with infection?"

"No, the skin is growing callused again. But those green veins are spreading like ivy."

Finster looked at his bare arms. Dizon was right. The green veins that journeyed beneath his skin looked like a bizarre plant growing within. He knew he couldn't live like this forever. At least not without the rings of power. "How can you even bear to look upon me like this?"

She handed him his robes. "These help."

"Yes, but he's still gross," Rinny said.

Dizon shot her daughter a perturbed look then said, "It is your heart that matters to me." She helped Finster put his robes on.

The scarab tensed inside his skin. Finster's back muscles knotted between his shoulders. He twitched. Dizon's firm hand steadied him. "I'm fine. Just another glaring side effect." He glanced at the horse. "We can't all ride the same horse, now can we?"

"You can ride the rocks," Rinny suggested.

"No, I think we are going to use another mode of transportation." He backed away from the tower. "Move back." He stretched out his fingers and closed his eyes. Using the Founder's Stone's mystic abilities, he closed titanic hands around the tower. The blocks in the tower, though stone, were rich in ore that made them easy to manipulate. It was all part of a greater sorcerous design that he had not detected at first but had discovered recently. The ground trembled beneath the tower. With huge, invisible hands, Finster pulled the Black Tower out of the ground. Dizon and Rinny gasped. The horse whinnied. He opened his eyes. The tower, foundation and all, hovered ten feet above the ground. A stairway of rocks led inside. He made a wry smile. "Today, we don't need rocks or horses for transport. We're riding the Black Tower. Get in."

The Sorcerer's War

Part 5

Chapter 79

Alexandria, the High Executioner, found herself searching for the arch mage Finster with a much larger group than she normally traveled with. Back in the trading town of Portgul, she'd made an alliance with the River Knights from the kingdom of Rayland. Now, on horseback, on another hot and muggy day, they rode east with the host of knights, licking the road dust from their mouths. The knights' leader was a seasoned and charming man named Osgald. After she had slept with him, he'd become a fountain of information.

Being the leader of the assassin's guild called the Circle, whose vast network spanned the Seven Kingdoms, Alexandria was the sole beneficiary of the Assassin's Shroud. It was an ordinary traveling cloak in appearance, made from chestnut-brown and dark-green cotton fibers tightly woven together. The enchanted cloak gave Alexandria the ability to disguise herself in the image of any person she imagined. It could cloak her with invisibility too. It made killing easy, perhaps too easy. Though she'd never part with it, she tried her best not to rely on it too much. Even though it enhanced many of her natural gifts, at the same time, it could take away the edge that made her what she was—the greatest assassin in the world.

Now, riding with three of her finest killers, a score of the world's finest knights, and three mages the likes of which she'd never seen before, she found herself in new territory in two regards. On one hand, she'd never been so far away from the Seven Kingdoms, where the eyes and ears of the Circle's networks kept her safe and informed. On the other hand, she had to play along with Osgald the River Knight in an attempt to locate the notorious sorcerer, Finster. The large group made the hunt messy, but it was imperative that she use the kingdom's resources to advance her own agenda. It was up to her to recover the Founder's Stone and locate the rings of power. That was what Rolem the Grand, the King of Mendes, had hired the Circle for in his quest to rule the Seven Kingdoms of the land—that and to avenge the murder of his love, Ingrid, the former Magus Supremeus, whom Finster and the blue-toe savage called Moth had killed.

Riding through the heat, on foreign soil, along cracked and dusty steppes, she contemplated her plans. The River Knights of Rayland, according to Osgald, were content to help the mages find the savage and the sorcerer. As for the mages, how they would handle a conflict with Finster would be a different matter. King Rolem and King Mather of Rayland, it seemed, had an agreement to bring down Finster together. King Rolem had made this agreement behind Alexandria's back, not fully trusting her abilities. Even though she had tried to dissuade him from using others, she couldn't blame him. She'd failed once to kill Finster in Rayland.

Now, posing with her assassins as common mercenaries who'd joined in the hunt for the notorious Finster and Moth, she'd cozied up to Osgald well enough to tag along. If they found Finster, she would be there, and she would be ready.

The group of riders came to a stop at the top of a slope that overlooked a valley in which the brown terrain turned green. Alexandria licked the dust from her teeth. Beside her, Holger, her chief assassin, drank from a water skin. His sweat-drenched tawny hair was plastered to his forehead.

Holger held out the water skin to her. "Drink?"

"No." Alexandria's eyes were intent on Osgald. Sitting tall in the saddle, the hawkish man approached from the group of knights who rode ahead of them. He had a stern look on his face. He stopped his horse just ahead of hers. "It seems that the magi wanted to stop."

"Are their backsides sore from half a day of riding?" she asked in her stony voice.

Osgald wiped his face with a cotton handkerchief he kept tucked in his gear. "This platemail feels like it just came out of the furnace. It's probably the only thing that I don't like about being a knight—all of the encumbrances that come with it. I admit, on days like this, I envy sellswords like you."

She stretched her arms outward, showing off her sinewy muscles and flexibility. "I would too."

With a half smile, Osgald studied her fine frame and nodded. "Eh, well, the magic-wielding weasels require a bit of space as they prepare to engage in some spellcasting."

Her horse nickered and snorted. It shifted underneath her. She leaned over her saddle horn. "What sort of spellcasting?"

Wiping down his eyebrows with the towel, Osgald said, "It's something to aid us in finding this Finster. Our trail has gone cold since we left Portgul, and aside from riding about in the Fringe like wayward children, I don't have a better idea at this time. Do you?"

She shrugged. "No. I say we see what these sandbags who call themselves magi can do. So far, all they've been are decorations in the saddle."

"Heh!" Osgald laughed as he cast a stare over his shoulder toward the magi. "Yes, those showy robes are glaring."

She moved her horse forward, passing Osgald. "Yes, almost as garish as your shining armor."

He patted his chest plate over his heart and, half laughing, said, "You wound me."

The three magi had dismounted and formed a large triangle among themselves. Each of them wore a set of well-kept checkered robes. Slight in height and build, each wore a different color—red, blue, and gold, accented with white tiles. They fished out handfuls of crimson sand from leather pouches, sprinkled it onto the ground, and together made a circle. When the circle was complete, they spread out equidistant from one another to form a triangle, closed their eyes, and started to chant.

A brisk wind came from the south, cooling Alexandria's neck. She knew little about the magi who accompanied Osgald, and he had said that he knew little about them, other than that they were from the Violet Citadel. With the Red Citadel without leadership, another guild of peacekeepers had to step forward. These sorcerers had volunteered for it.

The wind picked up. The horse snorted, stamped, and whinnied. Hundreds of birds, black as crows and the size of robins, with beady red eyes and hooked beaks, appeared from what had been a clear sky moments earlier. They were carrion ravens, sometimes found in the cities, picking the streets like pigeons. Though small, they devoured flesh like vultures. They landed in the circle by the dozens, to the awe of the gaping knights.

Alexandria's arm hair stood on end.

The birds gathered by the dozens then the hundreds before increasing into thousands. They filled the circle, one piling on top of the other, making unsettling squawking sounds.

The sorcerers' weird chanting increased in volume. Fingers and hands gesticulated wildly in the air. The red sand they had poured became a ring of glowing fire that spread through the eyes and wings of each and every carrion bird. As quickly as the birds had come, they took flight again in a cloud of floating black and dispersed in all directions before vanishing into the sky.

Patting the sweat from his ashen face, Osgald said, "Creepy."

Alexandria rubbed her neck. "I wonder what they have in mind for the carrion ravens."

One of the mages approached. He was bald on the top, with fluffy hair around his somewhat-pointy ears. He wore the royal-blue-and-white-checkered robes. His deep, searching eyes seemed like they could see through the skin into the soul. Rubbing his hands together in a circular motion, he looked between Osgald and Alexandria. "We have several thousand hungry eyes that serve us now." He spoke with a mysterious inflection. "They will find Finster. We will find the savage as well." He looked right at Alexandria. "Our *circle* is bigger than all others now."

"Now what, sorcerer?" Osgald asked.

"Magus Unus." The magus looked onward to the other two sorcerers, who stood in their spots in a trancelike state. "Make camp. The time has come to wait."

Chapter 80

Shepherds herding a flock of sheep that grazed in the prairie grasses stood agape. The Black Tower, like a cloud, floated toward them. The sheep paid no mind to the hundred-foot-high black rock tower that floated thirty feet above them. The shepherds were split. Half ran away at full speed. Others dropped to their knees, bent over, and prayed. One goodly boy stood with his back straight, waving a hand, until an elder shepherd pulled him down. With knees quaking, the remaining shepherds fell under the shadow of the tower as it slowly passed above them.

Finster stood on the roof of the tower between the battlements, watching the shepherds, with his hands on the outer wall. Dizon, Rinny, Moth, and the horse were all present. Rinny stood between the tower's battlements, waving her hand at the boy.

Green veins rose like worms under Finster's skin, pulsating with a glowing light of their own. Through his fingers, he could feel every block in the tower as if it was a part of his body. Oblivious to the renewed stares of the braver shepherds, he frowned. "I must look hideous."

Beside him, Dizon said, "You are a handsome man regardless of the color of the blood in your veins. You need not think about it." She peeked over the edge of the tower. "Look at those men. Their eyes are as big as their sheep. They'll worship you like a king if you let them."

"I don't want to be king. I just want to get the kingdoms back in order," he said.

Rinny climbed up to the top of the square-shaped battlement and sat down facing Finster and her mother. Scrawny legs hanging over the ledge, she said, "Can you make the tower fly faster? It seems to be moving very slow."

"That's because it's heavy," Finster replied. "But if you would prefer to walk, that would be fine."

The tanned blond girl asked, "Can you make it spin, like you did me in the chair?"

"No," he said.

Rinny leaned forward. "But can you do it?"

"Child, go away. Lord Finster needs to concentrate," Dizon said.

Fearlessly, Rinny jumped from the top of one battlement to the other, with Moth watching from nearby. Rinny smiled at Moth as she did so, without a care that a stumble would send her plummeting more than one hundred feet to the ground.

The ravishing Dizon snaked her hands around Finster's waist and hugged him from behind. "You need to rest. How long do you think you can carry this tower? We've moved from day to night to day again."

"I have nothing better to do," he said as he touched heads with her. The more Finster used his power to probe the stones in the tower, the more he learned about it. Each block had been laid carefully and marked with a rune. The magic used was centuries forgotten but still maintained an ancient enchantment. Finster couldn't say for certain, but he believed that this journey was not the Black Tower's first journey through the air. He suspected it had flown before. "Have you ever had that strong feeling that you were doing something that you had done before?"

"You are talking about déjà vu. Did you not think that I knew what déjà vu was?" Dizon asked.

"Actually, I was asking you, as I forgot what to call it myself. I've never given it much thought before." Finster's weary eyes tracked through the clouds that stretched along the horizon. "This is familiar. Too familiar."

"Perhaps it is the blood of your ancestors that speaks," she said. Her hands started up underneath his robes. Finster stiffened. "Be still. I need to check your wound."

"Well, be gentle. Your hands are ice cold."

"My cold hands are soothing on your burning body, are they not?"

"Perhaps I'm touchy today," he said. "How does it look?"

"Aside from looking like you have been branded with a scarab, you appear whole." She pressed her finger along the ridges that the scarab in his back had made. "Does it move when I touch here?"

"Ow!" he said. A piercing bite started inside the meat between his shoulder blades. "Please, don't do that again."

"I'm sorry."

He let his robes down and took a seat on the wall in front of him.

Her gentle hand caressed his face. "Finster, please, set this tower down and rest."

He took her soft hands and kissed them. "I'm very certain that I won't be able to rest until this is over. And believe me when I say I want to rest." His eyes drifted to the land below them. Looking down on the ground at the small, shaken, and hapless people, he felt like a god. "But I don't want to give up the power. With the stone, I believe, I don't need any rest. Perhaps it will sustain me forever."

"Your body cannot sustain what courses through it. It is eating you alive. Do what you must do, and be done with it."

He looked away from her. Dizon's presence kept him in touch with reality. Without her, he might give in to the power of the Founder's Stone. Inside, he wrestled against its efforts to take full control of his body and mind. The magic inside the stone had a hungry ambition of its own. He'd imagined what would have happened if Ingrid captured the stone. With the rings of power amplified by the stone, she would have been able to level kingdoms with a thought. No, Finster could not risk the stone falling into the hands of a magic wielder who would give in to its ravenous powers. Or the rings, for that matter. For now, he would have to use that power to restore order to the Red Citadel and destroy the threat to the kingdoms.

Finster cast a look toward Moth. The brute was walking over the rooftop with Rinny on his shoulders. The savage picked up speed and rushed down the stairs that led to the fifth level. Rinny, bouncing on his shoulder, squealed.

Finster's shaking fingers balled up into a fist. "I need those rings."

"What?" Dizon asked.

"The rings. I need them. The savage has them." Finster couldn't help but scowl. "And the barbarian suffers nothing for it!"

"You don't know that," she said. "We've both witnessed the wounds he's suffered. That pain must be real."

"Not a peep from the savage. I don't think he feels anything." He clutched her by the shoulders. "Do you know what I would give to not feel anything for just a moment?" He was speaking of the fire inside his back. "Just to have my thirst quenched. The rings of power can grant me that. Talk to your daughter. See if she can get them for me."

Dizon recoiled. "You are hurting me."

Finster's fingers dug into her skin. He reeled her in so they were face-to-face. "You don't know what pain is, woman!"

Dizon twisted out of his grasp and slapped him hard in the face.

The entire tower trembled. The horse reared and whinnied.

Finster scowled at her. "You dare! You filthy whore!"

Dizon backed away. Without thought, Finster tipped the tower, sending her sprawling to the ground. She hit hard on her knees and elbows and groaned. Finster stormed at her. She cringed.

Then his hardening heart softened. He dropped to his knees. "Dizon! Dear Dizon, I am gravely sorry!"

Dizon pulled away from his extended hands.

Moth and Rinny raced from the steps up onto the roof. Rinny screamed, "Mother! Mother! What happened?" She glared at Finster. "What did you do?"

"I… I lost my temper." His heart sank the moment Dizon stood up and didn't give him a glance. She took her daughter's hand and led her down the steps. Finster found the sullen-eyed Moth looking down on him. The savage's eyes narrowed the slightest bit. Finster stood up and stared back at Moth. "I think it's high time we had a talk. And you aren't going to like it."

Moth turned his back. He walked toward the stairs.

Finster pulled stones from the floor, forming a wall in front of the savage. "You aren't going anywhere."

Chapter 81

Moth faced a wall of stone. He balled up his fists and pounded the granite.

"Will you stop doing that?" Finster asked. "It's a wall. You cannot just break it!"

Moth spun around. He had a wild look in his eyes like that of a caged animal. Glaring at Finster, he knitted his eyebrows together and started forward.

With a thought, Finster pulled more stones up from the roof on which they stood, forming a ten-by-ten roofless room that closed them both in together. Now it was Finster's turn to glare back. "Listen to me, Moth. You've saved me, and I've saved you. But now the time to communicate has come."

Moth dug his fingers between the stones. He started to climb.

Finster made the stone slimy, loosening Moth's strong hold. "Be still, savage! I'm no fool. I know that you understand me!"

The mute sneered at Finster for a moment.

"Ah," Finster said, raising his already-pointy eyebrow. "That was an acknowledgement. I know that you might not speak, but you definitely hear. I saw how you handled those wenches in the taverns with those apish arms draped over their supine figures. You know what they whispered in your ear. Now you will hear my whispers."

He pointed at Moth's hands, which were newly scraped up from hammering at the moving wall. "You know full well what those rings are doing to you. The question is, will you part with them or not?"

Moth's oversized hands opened and closed like the talons of a wild thing moments from tearing its prey to pieces. His lazy stare locked on Finster, passed through him, and scanned over the stone wall, which continued to shift and move. The barbarian squatted halfway. He suddenly thrust his shoulder into the wall and rammed into it over and over.

It was just like the time that Finster had been trapped in the dungeons beneath the Red Citadel. Moth reacted like a caged animal, fighting with ravenous madness to break himself out.

"You really don't care for close quarters, do you?" Finster asked. On that remark, he moved a block beneath his feet and lifted himself higher above his wall. From the aerial view, he continued to move the walls in Moth's way, trapping him everywhere he tried to turn. The wild man hit the wall harder and harder. Finster shouted down at him. "You aren't going anywhere until you learn to communicate better."

The blocks in the wall popped in and out and shifted up and down, moving like living things. Moth grabbed ahold of a two-foot-long block. He pulled it from the wall, lifted it overhead, and hurled it at Finster.

Finster stopped the block in midair then sent it back among the other blocks in the wall. "Listen to me, Moth. We need to discuss the rings of power. At some point, you will have to part with them. You've seen our enemies. You know they won't stop until they have what you have and what I have. It would be in the world's best interest if I had the rings, or at least some of them, until I can restore the world to order."

With his jaws clenched, Moth shook his head. He started hammering the blocks with his meaty fists. A series of loud cracks and pops followed his punches. The blocks exploded beneath the power of his fists. They disintegrated into dust.

"Oh my." Finster lifted himself higher in the air. With Moth twenty feet below him, he noticed the savage passing through the blocks into the flat rooftop's open space.

Moth locked his glowering stare on Finster.

The magus asked, "Are you going to listen or not?"

Moth bunched his legs underneath him and leapt at Finster. The savage cleared every foot, arms outstretched and fingers clutching.

With widening eyes, Finster quickly drifted out of reach.

Moth landed back on the ground and jumped at Finster again. The savage's second hop propelled him even higher.

Casually gliding through the air, Finster moved farther out of the way. Moth swam in the air the moment he started to descend. Finster half rolled his eyes. "If you could only see how ridiculous you look."

Moth's descent stopped ten feet from the roof of the tower. Somehow, he moved toward Finster again at an increasing rate of speed.

"Bloody rings! They aid you with telekinetic power." Finster lifted his arms. A wall of stones built itself in front of Moth. The savage plowed into it. The stones became water and burst. The savage glided right at Finster with fingers outstretched once more. They were no longer above the tower. Only the open ground remained beneath them. Finster continued his retreat. "Get back, you fool! You'll lose control and fall to your doom!"

Moth kept coming.

"So be it then." Finster let his stone pedestal lift him higher and higher. The Black Tower shrank beneath them. Dizon and Rinny emerged from the lower level. Aghast, they shouted up at the men drifting farther away from them. Moth continued his swimming in a bizarre aerial climb. Fueled by a burning aggravation, the distance closed between them. Moth's fingers charged up with brilliant light.

"Now what is happening?"

Strands of lightning erupted from Moth's fingertips. Coils of light spread all over the sky. The lightning passed through Finster's body. He shook like a struck sapling. The scarab clenched in his back. He teetered and then fell from his floating stone pedestal and plummeted toward the ground.

Chapter 82

WATCHING FROM THE ROOF, DIZON witnessed the angry explosion of lightning from Moth's hands. It lit the day. She shielded her eyes with her hands. The Black Tower quaked underneath her. Both she and Rinny fell to the ground. Worse yet, the tower began to spin. Keeping her eyes fixed on the sky-bound men, she saw Finster falling. His robes rippled around his body. She couldn't get a clear look at his face. The robes had enveloped his limp form. She ran for the wall. The tower tilted, creating an upward slant. She rolled backward into Rinny and tumbled into the stairwell. They didn't stop until they hit bottom. The Black Tower pitched back and forth. She locked her arms around her daughter and said, "Hang on to me. I think the tower is crashing!"

It was another one of those moments when time suddenly slowed down and life took on a new meaning. Thanks to the lightning that coursed through Finster's fragile body, the pain he'd been experiencing reached a whole new level. If it were not for that and the rustling of his whipping robes, he would have thought himself dead. The free-falling experience was enlightening. The problem was, it didn't last long. Fighting through the jarring pain in his extremities, he pulled the robes away from his face. He caught a glimpse of the Black Tower rushing right past him. He jerked his gaze toward the ground that rushed up to greet him.

Stop falling! Stop falling!

He stretched out his powers, reaching for anything his mind could latch onto. The ground closed in. Fifty feet. Forty feet. Thirty feet. Twenty feet.

Two blocks clamped onto the fluttering hem of his robes, stopping him in midair. His entire body jerked inside the fabric. His robes ripped. His halted body slipped out of the folds. He fell the last fifteen feet and hit the ground hard.

The jarring impact knocked the wind out of him. He lay facedown with a mouthful of grass. Fighting to catch his breath, he struggled to his side. A great shadow fell over of him. It was the Black Tower, dropping from the sky, right on top of him. He threw his hands outward, stopping the tower's foundation stones less than two feet from his chest. He crawled out from beneath it and gently set the entire tower down.

His torn robes landed beside him. Wearing only a pair of knee-length cotton trousers, he realized that he was half-naked. Catching his breath, he bent over, snatched up his robes, and draped them over his shoulders. He studied the sky, looking for Moth. The savage was nowhere to be seen. He used his detection spell to home in on the rings of power.

"There you are," he said to himself.

Moth, it seemed, had resumed his place on the top of the tower. So far as Finster could tell, the savage seemed content to stay put for the moment.

"I will have those rings, whether he agrees to it or not. Moth, today, we finish this!" He traipsed around the tower and noticed, several yards away, their horse lying dead on the ground. His thoughts raced to Dizon. *Oh no.*

The thought of her unfortunate death slapped his sensibilities back into him. He raced around the base of the tower, hoping not to see Dizon's broken body dashed against the hard ground. His frantic search didn't reveal any more corpses. Magically placing blocks underneath his feet again, he rose to the top level of the tower. There was no sign of Moth or the women. He raced down the stairs on his own two feet to the fifth level. His heart jumped at what he saw.

Sitting against the wall, Moth cradled Rinny in his big arms. Her hair was matted underneath a bloody bandage. Dizon was on her knees, holding her child's hands and sobbing.

Finster half stumbled forward on numb legs. He gripped his robes at the chest and muttered, "I'm so sorry."

Dizon gave him a sideways glance. Her face was wet with tears. In a shaky voice, she said, "You did this. Now my daughter isn't moving."

CHAPTER 83

"I DID IT?" FINSTER ASKED WITH a dejected look. "All I wanted to do was have a conversation with Moth. But the ignorant savage would have none of it. The brute attacked me. He is as much to blame as I am."

Dizon gave Finster a look that could kill.

Finster swallowed. He looked at the girl cradled in Moth's oversized arms. Rinny's chest rose and fell rapidly. "She's breathing."

Gripping her daughter's hand, Dizon said, "Her breath is raspy and shallow, and she is growing cold. This is my daughter. She is dying. And here we are, out in the middle of nowhere, with no means to save her." Dizon choked out a sob. She kissed her daughter's hand. "I don't want to lose my daughter. Not like this. Rinny, come back to me."

Finster wiped his watery eyes. Though he wasn't fond of Rinny, he was fond of Dizon. The woman, who had been nothing but good to him, hurt, and his own heart ached as well. Still, he was not going to take the entire blame for it. Moth had played a part in it. The barbarian had a mind of his own, and he could see concern in the sullen-eyed savage. He locked his stare on the tremendous man. "I think there is indeed a way that we can save her."

"What are you talking about, Finster?" Dizon asked.

Without taking his eyes off the savage, he said, "Moth can save her."

Moth's eyes slid over to Finster.

Dizon looked at Finster as if he was a madman. "What are you talking about? How can Moth save Rinny?"

"The same way he always saves himself," Finster replied. "By using the rings of power."

Dizon glanced at Moth's face and then at his fingers. She looked up into Moth's eyes. "Is this true? Moth, if you can save her, you must."

Stroking his chin, Finster said, "He can. The ring that regenerates the wielder does not stop a person from aging, but it can heal any wound. Its former wielder was Snard the Savant, a high magus of the ninth order. A lover of white gold, he was a very private magus, obsessed with dabbling in modern alchemy. How Ingrid managed to take the ring from him I'll never know. Perhaps the fool gave it to her in exchange for a kiss." He shook his head. "Such foolish men. Very selfish. Like I used to be."

Dizon ran her hands over Moth's hands. "I don't know if Finster's words are true, but you are fond of Rinny, and she is fond of you. Will you help her?"

Moth turned his hands over. He gave them a long look.

The rings embedded underneath the skin of Moth's fingers had slight differences in them. Bumps from the jewels in the rings rose underneath the skin in different patterns. Finster had seen all of the rings clearly on Ingrid's fingers. Each of them comprised a different combination of precious stones and metals in different patterns. The ring of power that regenerated had a line of wavy rubies that snaked along a ring of black iron. He pointed to Moth's left index finger. "If I had to guess, I would say that it was that one."

"How is he supposed to remove the ring?" Dizon asked.

"A good question," Finster said. "The only way I can think to do it is to cut the finger off. That is how we took out Ingrid in the end. It's the savage's choice, however."

Gently, Moth placed Rinny in Dizon's waiting arms. As he did so, he slid the dagger out of Dizon's belt. Kneeling, he planted his left hand on the ground and spread his fingers. He raised the dagger with his right hand and slashed downward. The blade cleanly cut his left index finger off at the bottom knuckle.

Dizon blanched.

Finster reached over and picked up the bloody finger. "You might want to look away. This is going to be gross." He squeezed the ring off of the bottom of the bone and into his waiting palm. Using his robes, he cleaned the fresh blood from the ring. It was gold with tiny pearls inlaid in the metal. With an arched eyebrow, Finster said, "It seems that I have erred. This is the protection ring once worn by—"

"I don't care!" Dizon said.

"Er… Moth, I believe you're going to have to cut off another finger," Finster said. The skin around Moth's fresh stump had already clotted and begun to regrow. Moth had a snarl on his face. "Don't look at me like that. It was an honest mistake. The rings have the same pattern of stones in them. Ah, try that one next." He pointed to Moth's right ring finger.

Glowering at Finster, Moth finally looked away and cut off his ring finger. Blood flowed freely from the new wound, dripping into the stones on the floor. His heavy stare landed on Finster again.

Finster squeezed the ring off of the finger and wiped it clean. The ring was black iron with a wavy line of rubies in it. He held it up. "This is the one." A strong part of him wished he'd had the savage chop off all the rings, but without the regenerating ring, his chances of getting them all increased dramatically. He handed Moth his finger. "I believe this is yours."

"Hurry, Finster," Dizon said. "My daughter is quaking in my arms."

The black ring could have fit three of Rinny's fingers inside it.

Finster slid the ring over her thumb. The ring slowly shrank to the size of her thumb. He shrugged. "We'll have to wait and see."

The rapid rise and fall of Rinny's chest started to steady. Her pale skin regained its rich sun-browned color. Dizon gasped when her daughter's eyes fluttered open. "It works," she said with elation. "It works."

"My head hurts," Rinny said, "and I'm thirsty. Why is Moth bleeding? Ew, and where is his finger?"

"Is my daughter whole again, Finster?" Dizon asked.

"I would give the ring time to fully repair the damage that has been done, but it seems to work quickly." He couldn't take his eyes off the black iron ring. His mouth watered. If it could heal her so quickly, what would it do for him? Could it take away his pain? Would its powers be amplified by the Founder's Stone? In the meantime, he held the gold pearl ring between his fingers. What magic powers would be revealed if he put it on? *I could have them all!*

Moth balled his right hand. Blood dripped from between his fingers as he watched Rinny bounce back to full life. There was a hint of gladness lurking in the wild man's eyes.

Just a foot away from having everything he wanted, Finster made an uncharacteristic decision. He handed the gold-and-pearl ring back to Moth. "I believe this is yours."

Moth plucked the ring out of Finster's fingers. He eyed it briefly then put it on Rinny's other thumb.

"Mother, is he proposing to me?" Rinny asked with a distraught look in her eyes. "I like him, but I told you, I'm not marrying him."

With tears of joy running down her cheeks, Dizon laughed. "No, I think he is only trying to protect you."

"Thank goodness." Rinny slipped out of her mother's arms. Dizon tried to reel her back in. "I'm fine, and my headache is already gone." She took the bandage from her head and started wrapping it around Moth's bleeding hand. "Did you cut your fingers off for me?"

Moth didn't say a word.

"Ew, that is really gross, but thank you."

Moth's huge hand palmed the girl's face.

"I'm going to be fine now. And I need you to be fine too." Rinny took the black ring from her thumb.

"No, child, wait," Finster warned.

Rinny placed the ring over Moth's left index finger. "This is yours, Moth. What you did for me, I repay."

Finster's heart sank. He wanted the ring for himself, but now he knew he would not get it. The savage had it again. The aching deep between his shoulder blades throbbed with new agony. He sighed. Rising to his feet with a groan, he said, "Well, everything seems to be in order. Dizon, I hope you will be able to forgive me. If not, I understand. But we can't continue to let moments like this happen. I can't speak for anyone else, but I think the time has come to see this all through."

Wiping her pretty face, Dizon said, "What are you talking about now?"

"I almost killed all of you, well, aside from the mute. I don't want to live like this. I have the stone. It has a purpose. It's time to make things right."

Dizon rose. "What are you proposing?"

"I'm going after King Rolem. I'm putting an end to this."

As he finished his last word, a pair of ugly black crows with a purple sheen on their wings and hooked beaks landed inside the spade-shaped portal window. Behind them, more of the birds flew by. A steady squawking came from the rooftop.

Finster made his way up the stairs with the rest of the group trailing him. Carrion ravens were lined up all over the roof ledges and battlements. All of their beady eyes turned to glare at Finster.

"They've found us."

Chapter 84

Alexandria sat in front of the campfire they had set up near the magi. Holger had roasted a rabbit on a stick. Osgald and Chet sat with them, chewing on hunks of hard meat and washing it down with water. The other knights and assassins were nearby, lingering by small tents and bed rolls, all on guard. All three magi remained within their circle. They sat quietly, and every hour or so, their gestures would shift the circle outward. They did so now, moving as one.

"Strange company that we have to keep," Osgald said as he looked on. "I prefer the way of steel compared to the dark and twisted ways of magic. They say no matter how pure the sorcerer may be, those seedy resources eventually corrupt them."

"All men are corrupt," Alexandra replied.

"Let's not leave out the women. After all, as I've been told, it was a woman that began all of this mess." Osgald's sword belt lay beside him. He pulled the blade from the sheath. The campfire's glow glinted off the finely crafted steel of the longsword. "This is the only woman that I trust."

Alexandria smirked. "You are no fool. I've never met a person that could be truly trusted. Everyone has a price."

"The River Knights cannot be bought," Osgald said as he ran a rag over his blade and eyed it with admiration. "We are faithful to the crown. To the mission. To the river. To the death. And if one is slack in his duties, his dishonor will undo him. To be a knight, you must be girded like this steel."

Licking his fingers, Holger said, "It's a very haughty statement."

"Oh," Osgald said, lifting a brow. "What do you mean by that?"

"Knights are born of a higher station. They keep their noses up and rear ends puckered. They aren't different from any other sort of man. They just have nicer armor."

Chet pulled a dagger from his belt. "I'll cut your insolent tongue out, cur! You know nothing of what you speak!"

Osgald stayed his knight companion with a firm hand to the shoulder. "Easy, brother. Our company has not seen us in action. He does not know what he's saying. We are knights, not tavern brawlers. Stick that dagger back in its rightful place. This is just conversation."

"Yes, put that blade away before you hurt yourself, River Knight," Holger added.

Chet jumped up, his cheeks reddened. He pulled his sword free of his sheath. "I'll not stand for that! Get on your feet, you filthy cur! You insult the knight, you insult the king. I'll show you what it is like to hurt from a blade."

Holger tossed a rabbit bone aside. "Are you challenging me, Sir Chet?" He laughed as he stood and wiped his fingers on his trousers. "Are you?"

Osgald gave Alexandria a serious look. "Your man needs a lesson in manners. I won't be stepping in to prevent his blood from being shed if he does not mind his tongue. My men have honor they will defend."

Alexandria stood. "My men take orders from me, but they are able to speak freely. I don't muzzle them like hounds."

"It sounds as if you don't approve of a knight's life either. A man forfeits his life to serve the crown with honor, and you would mock it?" Osgald asked.

"I have no issue with your duties. It was your man who pulled his sword. Not mine."

"Your retainer attacked the knighthood unprovoked as we sat here, working in good faith." Osgald's jaw clenched. "Let him suffer the consequences."

With a bored look, Holger glanced at Alexandria. She gave him a nod. He shrugged and drew his sword. His blade came smoothly out of the sheath. It was a rapier, double-edged, designed for thrusting and fencing. He sliced it back and forth and looked at Chet. "En garde?"

The group moved away from the campfire as the other knights gathered around. Chet's eyes narrowed on Holger. It was easy to see that he wanted to murder the impudent man who had insulted him. "This is not going to be a sparring match. It's a fight. You can yield, you can die, but it's too late to apologize."

"I don't have any intention of doing any of those things," Holger said with a crooked smile. "Let's have at it then, Sir Chet. Show me this honor that you're willing to give your life for."

Chet lunged at Holger. Making it look easy, Holger parried the heavier longsword and danced away. With a swipe of his light steel, he cut at Chet's eyes. The knight jerked his head out of the way. The combatants battled back and forth in a collision of blades. Chet chopped and thrust. Holger parried and countered with a smirk on his face. Chet had broken out in a heavy sweat ten swings into it. He wiped the sweat from his eyes.

Alexandria stood beside Osgald as they both intently watched the match. All of her assassins were proficient with almost any weapon, and many had mastered more than a few. Holger took full advantage of his lighter armor and moved cat quick, sliding away from Chet's hard swings, which would gore or mutilate a man. It was the best entertainment she'd enjoyed in days, including her romps with Osgald.

Steady as a bull, Chet chopped and thrust, unwavering in his efforts. Holger showed no signs of fatigue. His rapier cut quickly, slicing against the knight's armor. He poked a shot into the shoulder where the metal was thick. The thrust didn't penetrate. Chet unleashed a clumsy, decapitating blow that would have cut through a much lesser man's neck. Holger ducked. Chet overextended, leaving his gut exposed.

Holger took aim and thrust. Chet hopped away. Overextended, Holger looked up to see a victorious smile blossoming on Chet's face, followed by a flash of steel. Chet's sword took both of Holger's arms off at the elbows. His arms and rapier fell lifeless into the dirt. He stood, looking at the blood spurting from his elbows. Eyes the size of plates, he staggered back and fell. Bleeding out, he sat gaping at the atrocious wounds as his life's blood flowed out of his body.

Chet exchanged hearty handshakes with his fellow knights. All of them had broad smiles on their grizzled faces.

Osgald looked over to Alexandria. "Your companion was a fool. Chet is my finest swordsman. That's the reason he stays on my right hand. Heh-heh. Holger thought to toy with him, but it was the other way around. Everyone here knew it except for your companions and you. I'd teach your men to think twice before they question the fortitude of a River Knight again. It's not the armor and insignia that makes us. It's devotion to our duty and our training."

"He made the choice," she said coldly. "We all live and die by the choices we make."

"Yes, and Holger made a foolish one." Osgald patted her on the shoulder. "We'll help you bury him if you like."

"No, we'll handle it," she said.

Holger lay on the ground with his eyes wide open. As an assassin, he had been good, very good, but as a swordsman, he'd been thoroughly outmatched. His big, wide eyes told the story that he'd made a very foolish move and paid for it.

Her last two men kneeled beside her. Without giving them a look, she said, "Bury him in the grove. All of him."

The assassins picked up Holger's arms and sword and loaded them onto his body. They each grabbed a leg and dragged him away.

Alexandria joined Osgald by the campfire. Taking a seat, she said, "I'm surprised you didn't try to place a wager on it."

"Knights don't gamble. At least, not with our wages. We do what we do among ourselves as sport." He slid his sword back into his sheath. "So, did you just lose your best swordsman? That would be a hard thing for a bunch of sellswords."

"We'll manage. Besides, we have you."

"Yes," Osgald said as he stared into the flickering flames of the fire. "That you do… for now."

Chapter 85

Alexandria woke up at dawn. She lay on a blanket with her back to the still-burning coals of the campfire. She sat up, rubbing her eyes. Carrion ravens darted over her head and landed in the sorcerers' circle. The lanky robed men had moved out of their seated positions. They mumbled between themselves. Finally, Unus, the one in the blue-checkered robe, made his way toward the knights' camp. Alexandria turned around and nudged Osgald. He sat up immediately.

"We have company," she said to the knight.

Unus gave a nod. Smiling at them both, he said, "Good morning. We all wake to good tidings, as our efforts have paid off. The carrion ravens have found Finster and the savage called Moth."

Buckling on her sword belt and covering it with her cloak, Alexandria said, "Where?"

"As it turns out, he is not far from our position. He is moving west, back toward the Free River away from the lakes." Unus scratched the cottony crown of hair that ringed his head. "I see no reason why we won't be able to cut him off within a day of hard riding."

With a groan, Osgald got to his feet. "This armor becomes heavier every time I awaken. And it pins me to the ground like the dead when I sleep." He caught Alexandria's disapproving look. "But I love it for knights' sake. So, wizard, what is our course of action? Do we follow your ugly birds?"

"Precisely," Unus said. "My fellow mages and I are very eager to begin this journey. Please, have your knights and men make haste."

"What are they so excited about?" Alexandria asked. "What have you seen?"

"The very face of Finster. Isn't that enough?" Unus replied.

"It doesn't make any sense that he would be heading west. Why would he do that?" she asked.

"I agree. He'd be heading into the lion's teeth." Osgald strapped on his belt, put his fingers to his lips, and whistled. Knights awoke and began breaking down the camp. "How can we trust these birds of yours and your strange visions?"

"Did not King Mather have you accompany us for our bidding?" Unus asked.

"Aye. No need to rub it in my beard. I know my duties. I don't know how a bird would know who or what we are looking for," the knight said, walking away. "That dark insanity is not for me."

As Osgald helped the knights gather their belongings, Alexandria hung close to the mage. "If you have seen him, what should we expect? You are holding back. I don't think you should do that."

"Says the leader of the Circle." Unus sniggered. "You reek of magic to our fine-tuned senses, Alexandria. You might fool those knights that bulge with lust when they see you, but you can't fool us. The moment you used it in the Port, we knew who and what you were." He reached out and felt her cloak with his fingers. He closed his eyes and inhaled through his nostrils. "The Assassin's Shroud. A brilliant artifact of sorcery."

She jerked her cloak away. "You couldn't know that without someone telling you. By the river gods, King Rolem must chatter like a woman."

"Yes, but you are the one that shifted form to please the knight.

We caught that when you didn't think we were looking, but we were always looking for you. The king told us that he'd hired the Circle," Unus said. "Don't doubt the powers of the magi of the high orders. We can find magic when we know what to look for. Now we have Finster in our sights, and I believe it will be very, eh, entertaining."

"Rolem is such a fool," she said. "He has no patience."

"All kings are impatient. But to be clear, we have the same goal in mind. You can kill Finster, and we will recover the rings and the artifact. Don't fret that our destinies are now united. It should serve as a good thing. Still, I don't think that the knights will be very comfortable knowing that they are working with an assassin. They are honorable men."

She laughed. "He probably knows too."

Unus shrugged. "Well, we all have bigger problems to deal with now that the hunt for Finster is at an end."

"We'll see." She gave him a threatening look. "When the time comes, you stay out of my way, and I'll stay out of yours."

"Agreed."

Alexandria and her two men saddled up, and the entire group was quickly underway. Following birds that circled back from time to time, they moved southwest, the complete opposite direction from what she had expected. Things were not turning out as she'd hoped. The magi knew who she was, which bothered her. It wasn't because it needed to be a secret, but the fact that Rolem had not kept anything in true confidence was a sign of weakness. She'd become no more than a pawn on the king's chess table. She didn't like it. What other pieces were being played that she didn't know about?

Stay focused. Do what you were hired to do. Kill Finster.

Riding at a mix of gallops and trots, they didn't stop once until long past midday. Sitting on horseback as a group, knights, assassins, and sorcerers stared into the cloudy sky, searching for the birds that had led them. Every one had vanished. Even the wizards began scratching their heads.

Osgald was the first to speak to Unus. "Well, what happened to those wicked pigeons from hell? Hmm?"

All three sorcerers sat on the backs of their horses with their eyes cast upward toward a fixed point in the clouds. Unus was in the middle of the pack. Squinting, they talked in low voices among themselves. The one in the gold-checkered robes pointed upward. He had hairy arms and short-cropped, bushy black hair and thick eyebrows. The red-robed wizard was a smallish man, the least of the three, with thinning gray hair swiped over the top of his head.

Finally, Unus said, "We are here."

Alexandria and Osgald approached the sorcerers. "Yes, we are here. The question is, where are they?"

"You mean the birds or the ones that we chase?" Unus asked.

"Listen, Unus, I don't care for your sorcerous games. I see no birds and no men. Just dust, dirt, and clouds."

A carrion raven plummeted from the sky, hitting the ground hard near the knight's horse. Osgald jumped in his saddle. His horse and many others whinnied and stirred. "What madness is this?"

From high above, dead carrion ravens fell like rain from the clouds. Looking skyward, the knights covered their heads. Finally, the last of the birds hit the hard earth. A few floating feathers followed.

Chet jabbed a finger at the sky. "Osgald, look!"

Alexandria's chest tightened. Her heart raced. A black tower of stone descended from underneath the clouds. It was small at first but continued to grow. The massive structure drifted downward, right above them, forcing them all to spread out.

"By the kings, what in the world is that thing?" the marveling Osgald asked.

The tower hovered less than a dozen yards above them, leaving everyone's jaws hanging open. Alexandria managed to tear her eyes away and look at the sorcerers. The men gazed upon the column of stone with wide eyes that switched back and forth between wonder and fear. Then she heard Unus utter a phrase that chilled her bones. "Beware the black tower that flies."

Chapter 86

"LOOK AT THEM, SITTING ON their horses with their jaws practically touching their saddles." Finster stood on the top level of the tower, looking down at the knights and magi from between the battlements. Dizon, Rinny, and Moth stood beside him. "It's moments such at this that I live for. It makes the pain worthwhile, momentarily. Rinny, toss down another bird."

Rinny traipsed over the roof and grabbed the last dead bird that lay on the deck. Finster had killed them all with a shock spell he'd mastered years ago. Using the enchanted stones, rich in bits of ore, as a conductor, he'd sent a jolt through the rock. Fueled by the Founder's Stone, the shock was enough to kill them all. Finster's understanding of the tower's latent mystic powers grew in that moment. He watched Rinny race back and fling the bird downward at the sorcerers. It spun on the way down, missing the mark.

All eyes from below were peering up at them now. Rinny waved. Four knights with loaded crossbows took aim at the girl. Dizon pulled her daughter back from between the parapets. "Stay out of harm's way, and be still."

"But Finster—"

"Hush. Mind your mother."

Finster stepped up between the battlements and, in a loud voice, addressed the men below. "Who do we have down there, eh?" He scanned the men in the robes. He recognized the colors of magi of the higher orders. "My, has King Rolem dispatched more enchanters from the Violet Citadel? Have you not spoken to Satrap Chen, who tangled with me once? Oh, I suppose not, seeing as I killed him." He leaned forward. "Is that you, Unus the Uncanny? Why, I almost didn't recognize you from this stretch. And your jowls are sagging like a bloodhound's. Too much indulgence in sweet pastries, perhaps. No offense."

Unus shouted back, "It's been many years, Finster, you Rodent of Whispers. We only seek a parlay with you. King's orders, of course. Certainly, a servant of the Red Citadel understands."

"Ah, yes, you follow the orders of a king who had the magi of the Red Citadel wiped out. I can only imagine that my fate will be the same." Finster pointed to the knights. "I see you brought along some help."

"The River Knights of Rayland are duty bound to bring in the murderer of their king. That's you and the savage, Finster. You should come quietly and peacefully," Unus said.

"I thought that we were going to parlay."

"I think a polite conversation would be best. Perhaps the four of us can talk, magus to magus." Unus moved his hands toward the men on his left and right. "Richter represents the Violet Citadel's gold order, and Elam represents the high order of the red. We want harmony in the kingdom the same as you, I assure you."

"Hah! The only thing the den of wolves in the Violet Order wanted was to see the end of the Red Citadel." Finster wagged his fingers. "You are the dung heap of sages. I'm certain that you put your full support behind Rolem and Ingrid."

"I assure you, that is not true. We believe that Satrap Chen's efforts against you were misguided." Unus opened his palms in a friendly gesture. "It was an unfortunate thing."

Finster scratched his chin. "Unus, come up. We shall chat."

"I'll not come alone, animator. I fear the power that you have."

"You should," Finster remarked. "Fine, all of you come up, and bring some wine if you have some."

One at a time, starting with Unus, the sorcerers floated up out of their saddles. They sailed upward, floating on air, not stopping until they landed on the top of the Black Tower.

Finster created four throne-like seats from the stones of the battlements. He sat in one that faced the three men. Moth, Dizon, and Rinny stood to the side of him. "Please, have a seat."

Unus cast a nervous look to his clammy-faced companions and sat down. "You wield tremendous power, Finster. And this tower"—he scanned the area—"it flies on its own."

"It flies on my command."

The sorcerers shifted in their chairs. Unus wrung his hands as he spoke. "You command a great deal, Finster. And you do this with the Founder's Stone that you have mastered?"

"I do. It makes me omnipotent."

Richter of the golden robes, a middle-aged man, with a turned-up nose, scoffed. "No one is omnipotent." His caterpillar eyebrows wiggled when he spoke. "Such boasts are always full of folly. Look at you, Master of the Inanimate. Your veins pulse like worms. The skin on your bones is ashen. The power you wield has made a host of you." He stuck out his grip. "Trust us! For only we can see you through this dilemma."

"It's not a dilemma for me." Finster politely clasped his hands together. "I have all of the might I'll ever need. I have the might that will topple kingdoms. Now tell me, Unus, do you have an offer that I cannot refuse, or shall we just battle to the death?"

"Finster, no one came here for a fight. We came in the name of peace," Unus said.

"No, you came for the stone and the rings, the same way that

Ingrid and Rolem did. Don't take me for a fool. I'm a member of the high order, too, and none of us are beyond temptation, especially spineless wizards from the Violet Citadel like you."

Richter came up out of his chair with his hands glowing with fire. "You hurl insults like a fool! You will only bring about our imminent death and countless others too! There is enough blood on your hands, Secret Slayer! Do you want more?"

With a strong but withering voice, Elam of the red robes spoke out. "Richter, sit. We are guests in Finster's tower. We should show respect." The older man of the group wiped his thinning gray locks away from his forehead.

Richter sat. The glow in his hands cooled.

Elam looked on at Finster with dark, penetrating eyes. With a gentle wave, he said, "Finster, I want to hear what you have to say. After all, we have only heard one side of the story."

"And which side might that be?" Finster asked.

"Fine, then, two sides of the story. King Rolem's and King-Elect Mather's," Elam continued. "I want to know what you know."

Finster quickly fed them what had happened with Ingrid and all that she had revealed to him. Without giving away too many details, he walked them through the attack at King Alrick's dinner table. Catching them all up, he finished by saying, "It is King Rolem who started this war, not I. But I aim to finish it."

Elam nodded. "And when this war is over, what do you plan to do?"

"As a former Guardian of the Mystic Forge, I will distribute the Founder's Stone and rings of power for safe keeping. And I'll do what I must to restore the Red Citadel to full order."

"A wise plan, Secret Slayer," Elam said quietly. His eyes slid over to Moth. "But I'm afraid that we cannot let that happen."

Chapter 87

As soon as Unus and the other sorcerers cleared the top of the tower, Alexandria signaled her two men over. She stood on her horse's saddle. "Give me a boost."

Without a word, the two assassins stood on their saddles. In acrobatic maneuvers, one man climbed on top of the other assassin's shoulders. Then Alexandria climbed up both men, creating a pyramid high enough to reach the blocks that made up the tower.

"Astounding," Osgald said.

Alexandria's fingers found purchase in the narrow cracks between the rock joints. "Wait here." She climbed inside the bottom level of the tower using only her toes and fingers. Like a spider, she made her way to the inner wall. She moved on, hand over hand, foot over foot, taking a quick glance beneath her. Osgald and his knights gazed up at her. "I wouldn't wait around. The tower might come down and crush you."

The knights backed their horses away.

She made it to the bottom of the stairs that led up to the second level. Without looking back, she made the climb toward the top. If she was going to get another shot at Finster and this savage, this would be it. She couldn't have cared less about what the sorcerers were doing. She was going to kill Finster and the savage. All she needed was the perfect distraction. She had the feeling that the sorcerers would provide that soon enough. And if they didn't, she would.

She moved upward, level by level, noting that the tower was all but empty. It was notably bigger on the inside than it was on the outside. On the third level, she stopped and removed her sword belt and dagger. She understood more about Finster's powers now. He could control objects but not the flesh of the living—at least she hoped.

Before she left the kingdom of Mendes, she had made sure that her garb was made from only natural fabrics, without buttons or pins. And she wore no jewelry. She didn't think Finster could control all items. He'd proved he could manipulate metal, stone, and wood, but she hoped he didn't have such control over linen or the living. If her garb proved a problem, she would shed it.

She fished out a small vial made from glass that had a leather plug in the top and pulled the plug out. Wrapped around her forearms were dressings made from cloth. Inside those wraps were wooden needles like the ones that many savages used in their blow guns. She slid the long needles out, one by one, and dipped them into the jar. The inky-black poisoned ointment inside was the most potent in the land. It was made from a crimson berry found only in the higher altitudes of the Zorgaz Mountains. She had spent a mint to acquire it. Its touch would burn and paralyze. A stab of it into the flesh would mean instant death. No one ever survived it.

With nimble hands, she loaded the five long darts back underneath her cotton sleeves and wrapped them up tightly. She left just enough of the top of each needle peeking out so that she could pull it free. Patting herself down, she made sure that she didn't have a stitch of metal, a buckle, or a button on her. The wood of the needles was a risk, but they were so small that they should not be noticeable. Finally, she pulled the hood of her cloak over her head and instantly turned invisible. Heading up the next level of stairs, she said, "The Circle never fails."

Chapter 88

Finster tapped his fingertips together and addressed the sorcerers. "Unus, Elam, and Richter, respectfully, you aren't going to be able to stop me." He gave a nod to Moth. "Or him for that matter. If you try, I promise, it will bring you immediate peril."

"You gloat!" Richter said as his hands glowed with a mystic red fire from within. "We are not a group of underlings from the bottom of our order. We are the cream on the top. Founder's Stone or not, we will end you!"

"Is this a challenge, then? The three of you versus the one of me?" Finster asked. "And be careful before you answer, because I promise that I will not show mercy."

All together, Unus, Elam, and Richter rose from their chairs. Unus said, "We serve the kingdoms, Finster. And you are serving yourself. You should reconsider what you are doing."

"Pah! You three windbags have no intention of serving the kingdoms. You are serving Rolem and this Mather as well as yourselves." Finster stood. "What is the plan, insects? Will you take up residence in the Red Citadel and be the new advisors to the king? Will you control the Seven Kingdoms with the same parlor tricks that the Violet Citadel did, as I firmly recall? I know your methods and how you spread unrest and division among the fair cities. That is why the members of the Red Citadel beat you down. And now I will beat you down again!"

The three mages exchanged a quick series of glances. Nodding, Unus said, "We offer the challenge to you, Finster. You may fight or you may surrender, but we are obligated to use the full measures of our powers."

Finster turned to Dizon. "This shouldn't take long, but do move to a safe spot." He pointed to the stairs. "I'll holler when it's over. And if you hear screaming, it won't be me, it will be them." He looked up at Moth. "I'm not sure what you have in mind, but if you aren't going to help me—not that I need it—or protect the women, just make sure you aren't in my way."

"Do you fight alone, or do you fight with the savage?" Unus asked.

"I cannot speak for the mute, but I accept your challenge," Finster replied. He began feeding himself with the scarab's power. His green veins rose underneath his skin and brightened. The Black Tower quaked. The magi stumbled and caught their balance as the tower started to spin. "Do you want to fight me one at a time or all three at once?"

The sorcerers of the Violet Citadel spread out. All of their fingers glowed with red fire that lit up their finger bones. Richter aimed his hands at Finster. With a flick of his fingers, a bright bolt of energy shot out.

Using his control over the elements, Finster brought a stone up from the floor, blocking the attack. The rock burst into several large chunks. "Is that all you have, Richter? A little fire from your fingers? You're going to need a more potent attack than that." Using his telekinetic abilities, Finster launched a hunk of stone at Richter.

Richter flicked up a palm. A shield of energy with a red-pink hue formed an oval dome in front of him. The rock skipped away from the shield and smacked into the battlements. He fired another bolt of energy through the shield.

Finster lifted another wall of stones between them. The wall absorbed the fiery shot's jarring impact. It also blocked Finster's view of Richter. He scanned the rooftop for Unus and Elam. Elam stood where he had been. Finster sent a rock at the man. The rectangular block went right through him. Elam smiled at Finster.

Unus, standing to the left of Elam, smiled broadly. "Master of the Inanimate," he said to Finster. "We are more than prepared for this encounter. It's not too late to surrender."

"Surrender and die on mystic gallows? I don't think so!" Finster pulled ground up from underneath Unus's feet. The sorcerer stumbled and fell flat on his backside. Finster lifted a block from the ground and prepared to smash Unus in the face with it.

Out of the corner of his eye, he caught Elam running right at him at alarming speed. The older sorcerer's hands unleashed strands of spreading red fire. Finster lifted a row of blocks between them. The webbing of fire spread over the rocks and kept coming. Finster used the stones under his feet to lift himself out of harm's way. A bolt of power thrown by Richter caught him square in the shoulder. Finster's body quaked, and his hair stood on end. The taste of metal filled his mouth. "Shades!"

Finster gathered more stones from the battlements and formed a protective grid of moving stone around him. Below, Richter flung red balls of energy at him. At the same time, Unus had pushed himself to his feet and had multiplied into more than a score of mirror images of himself. The blue-checkered-robed sorcerers were everywhere now. To make matters worse, Elam floated up toward him like a creeping old coot. He snapped the strands of fire flowing from his hands like whips. All the while, Moth stood where he'd been standing the entire time.

"Will you do something, savage?" Finster yelled.

As Elam and Richter attacked with balls of energy and lashes of fire, Finster blocked their efforts with stone after stone. They knew what they were doing. All three of them used different offensive and defensive tactics to keep him thinking while they probed for him to expose his weakness. They'd gotten him with one shot already. How much longer until they slipped a more fatal one in? He moved stone after stone into the path of their attacks while steadily drifting away, twenty feet above the tower's rooftop.

I am all-powerful. I will not lose to these fools!

Realizing that he would need his full power of concentration, he lowered the tower to ground level. The tremendous building made a loud *whump* sound as its footers crushed back into the ground. He sped up the grid of blocks that began to orbit him like moons and planets. They caught the fires of Elam and Richter, keeping their efforts at bay. Finster tapped his finger on his chin.

They are testing me. Now it's time for me to test them.

The Founder's Stone served to magnify Finster's mystic abilities a hundredfold, but animating objects had its limitations. At the moment, all he had were hunks of stone to throw at people like some sort of Neanderthal. There was nothing cunning or crafty about it, especially given the multitude of intricacies that came from using sorcerous enchantments. To a degree, he felt a bit crude. His tactic to battle the men from the Violet Citadel was lacking, and it showed. His strength had become a glaring weakness.

Elam's tendrils extinguished. His ghostly form passed right through the asteroid field of stone. He came right at Finster, saying, "The time to surrender has passed." He extended his hand and spread out his fingers while placing his other hand over his chest. "The time has come to tear your heart apart."

An unseen hand reached inside Finster's chest and clamped down on his heart with a burning squeeze. Finster's back arched. He let out a loud gasp then screamed.

Chapter 89

THE TOWER'S SUDDEN DROP TO the ground made two horses buck and sent two knights out of their saddles. Osgald guided his horse over to the Black Tower and put his hand on the rock. He gave it a shove. Peering at the archway that led inside, he looked at Chet and drew his sword. "We are going up. River Knights, follow me!"

The train of knights, accompanied by the two assassins, rode into the bottom level of the tower. Osgald, with Chet right behind him, led the way, driving the horses up the stairs. The knights cast nervous glances over the broad space of the tower's inner sanctuary. One of them grabbed a burning torch from a bracket on the wall. Up they went, step by step, level by level.

On the third level, Osgald stopped, looked up the next stairway that hugged the curve of the wall, and listened. A small explosion, something like thunder, rumbled above. "The wizards are at war. Be wary." With expert horsemanship, he led his knights up the wide steps to the fourth level.

Dizon held Rinny tight in her arms. They had moved down to the fifth level and hid underneath the stairs that led up to the roof. Now all she could do was hope that Finster didn't turn the tower upside down. Her stomach dropped inside her belly the moment the tower hit the ground. Rinny let out a frightened squeak. "Hush," Dizon said, clamping her hand over her daughter's mouth.

The fine hairs on her arms rose like needles as she stared outward. The vision of the wall and quavering torch on the other side was slightly obscured. She squinted. Without seeing someone, she knew some presence was there. Unseen eyes had fallen upon her. The beat of her heart quickened. Her hand fell to her dagger. Then, as suddenly as the feeling had come upon her, it was gone like a smoke vapor taken away by the morning breeze.

"Mother, what is wrong?" Rinny asked. "You are squeezing me to death."

Scanning the room of arches, she eased her grip on her daughter. The clop-clop of horseshoes on stone caught her ears. She tensed. Pressing them both deeper underneath the steps, she said, "Be still. The knights are coming."

The River Knights noisily made their way up to the fifth level. Nervous hooves stomped the stone floor. Above, a steady cadence of explosions carried down the stairwell, echoing in the cavernous chamber below. Bright flashes of light came from above. A man with a low, commanding voice said, "First Rank, dismount."

Dizon, from her shaded position, took a peek. She saw half of the knights dismount while the others remained in their saddles. She was very familiar with the River Knights, each and every one a formidable man and very deadly with a sword. She'd seen Finster handle them with ease. She caught a glimpse of the River Knight bearing the commander's insignia. She knew him. It was Osgald the Bold.

On cats' feet, the knights started the climb up the stairs. Dizon slipped out from underneath the stairs. "Osgald, stop!"

Osgald's eyes brightened. A crooked smile formed on his lips. "Well, well, well, what a pleasant surprise."

The knights snaked behind Dizon and dragged Rinny all the way out from the alcove beneath the stairs. Rinny squealed. One of the knights popped her in the mouth with a hand half-covered in chainmail. The girl fell silent.

Halfway up the steps, Osgald's eyes filled with recognition. "Dizon, is that you?"

"Yes, Osgald. I'm honored that you remember me. If you value your life, I would warn you, don't go up there. You know full well that your armor is only a weapon that can be turned against you."

"Aye, yes, I know this Finster. That night you dined with King Alrick, Finster locked us up tight as a fencepost. But we must do what we must do," Osgald said. "My knights will keep you safe, Dizon. I suggest you stay close within their company."

"No, Osgald, you must listen to me. You know that Finster did not kill King Alrick. You were there the same as I. Where is your honor in a time like this? You serve the crown and not the slime wearing it."

"You should not insult the King of Rayland. It is a punishable offense, no matter where you speak it," he replied. "Men and women have been drawn and quartered for less."

With her arms held tight behind her back by one of the knights, she managed to fight her way a half step forward. She could see full well in Osgald's eyes that he knew he served a tainted purpose. "Don't be on the wrong side of this, Osgald the Bold. You should join Finster and liberate the kingdoms from the self-serving leeches who only want and never give. Now is your chance to truly make a difference. The only other outcome will be your death. All of your deaths."

The stalwart knights cast their hardened eyes on Osgald.

The River Knight commander lifted his chin. "Dizon, I appreciate the warning with all sincerity. Of all the women in the king's harem, you are one of the few that had any wits about them. But alas, I have my orders. I am Osgald the Bold, not Osgald the Spineless. I will not sit on my backside while the fate of a kingdom unfolds. What began as a search-and-seek mission has quickly become a battlefield. The River Knights are men of action. We fight. Farewell, Dizon." He lifted his hand and dropped it. "River Knights, ho."

Dizon's heart sank as the brave knights, on foot, snaked their way up the steps with steely looks in their eyes. They were good men, as good as they came, but still subject to political corruption, honor bound by duty that only served to shackle once-free and good men. She watched the last knight in the rank take a quick look back at his comrades, salute, and vanish at the top of the stairs.

Chapter 90

Sword clutched in hand, Moth sprang at the blue-checkered-robed sorcerer who came his way. The broadsword cleaved the sorcerer's body in half. The split face of Unus laughed out of both sides of his separating mouth as the shade of the sorcerer slowly dissipated.

More of the copies of Unus closed in on Moth in a mob. Their fingers stung like burning needles. Moth chopped into them and through them with mighty long-handed swings. One image of Unus the Uncanny would fade only to be replaced by another. They blanketed Moth, poking and prodding him with stingers in their fingers.

In a fury, Moth hacked with two hands as burning needles coursed through his limbs. He stabbed throats, hearts, and bellies, all to the sound of Unus laughing. With painful red welts popping up all over his half-naked frame, Moth hewed into the sea of multiplying men.

Ahead, he caught a glimpse of the sorcerer in gold-checkered robes. The sorcerer flung balls of mystic energy into the air. Great stone blocks tornadoed around Finster, shielding him from Richter's monumental efforts. Hunks of stone exploded in the sky. Bits of rocks and debris rained down.

Moth punched his way through the mill of bodies that had

stinging fingers. He needed something he could hit. Something that he could kill. He took aim at Richter, who hung behind a mystic shield dome. Hands over his head, with the enemies' fingers ripping into his abdomen, Moth chopped into the shield. The blade skittered off the glowing disk. Moth's sword bit into the ground. He cocked back his sword. A ball of energy smacked into his chest, sending him sprawling backward as if he'd been kicked by a horse.

Lying on the ground, he pushed up from his chest with a snarl on his face. Moth's chest had a black sear mark smack dab in the middle. His skin smoldered. The duplicates of the blue-and-white-robed mage laughed at him. They poked him repeatedly with their pain-delivering fingers. Moth made his way back to his feet. With spots in his eyes and the blood in his veins thickening like molasses, he slowly ambled forward. His sword swings became sluggish. The inside of his body burned. The sky filled with bright spots in a multitude of colored stars. They bubbled, wobbled, and faded only to appear again.

Moth staggered through the sea of sorcerers. He swiped at them with heavy, clumsy swings. His iron endurance began to cave against the sway of unseen forces pricking at his body. All he could do was swing at the growing, mad cackling of voices. He chopped on, thrusting his weight into them one by one. Finally, a man in armor waded through the strange flock with a sword of quivering, shiny steel in hand. Two more appeared right behind the first knight. They moved in as quickly as a brisk wind, stabbing Moth over and over again. The lights of the world went dim.

Osgald the Bold pulled his sword free of Moth's chest. Among the tapestry of strange blue-robed mages, his skin hadn't stopped crawling. Eerie dark forces were afoot. Unus's face was everywhere. The blue-toe savage lay on the ground with nasty black bleeding welts all over him. Now three gaping sword wounds had gashed the brute like a slaughtered pig. Osgald found a face of Unus and said, "What is going on here? Is the savage expired?"

All of the many images of Unus spoke as one. "I released powerful toxins from my fingers. The poison is spreading, turning the savage's mind into mud and blood into sand. Act quick. Cut off his hands and bring them to me. I will have those rings."

Osgald tipped his chin at Chet. His second-in-command knelt by Moth. Dagger in hand, he started sawing the savage's hand off at the wrist. Osgald glanced up at the field of stones soaring a dozen feet above his head. Through the flashing veil, he could see Finster, suspended in the sky, clutching his chest and gasping for air. Elam's ghostly form hovered in front of the magus with the fingers clutching and squeezing as if they were trying to crush a stone. "What of them? Is that situation under control?"

"It's been under control since the moment we came here," all forms of Unus said. "The fool never should have crossed the Violet Citadel. Now all the power will soon be ours."

Chapter 91

Elam the Red's ghostly form hovered just out of reach. The older sorcerer had a gloating look in his eyes. As if he had Finster's beating heart in the palm of his hand, he squeezed, turned, and twisted back and forth. With the snide look of a conqueror, he said, "Does that hurt, Master of the Inanimate? Hmm. Do you feel the sting of death, Guardian of the Mystic Forge?" His voice rose. "Will you plead for your life, Secret Slayer? I want to hear you beg!"

With sweat streaming down his face, Finster clutched his chest. Painful, blinding shards stung him from head to toe from the inside out. At the same time, the block he floated upon dipped downward. He crumpled to his knees on the rectangular hunk of rock and let out another gasp. Foamy spittle dribbled out over his lips and the corner of his mouth.

Laughing, Elam said, "What is the matter, Finster? Don't you have anything witty to say? Don't you want to mock the Violet Citadel and its inferior members? Hmm?" He extended his clutched fingers in front of Finster and squeezed tighter. Finster let out a pained howl. "Excuse me, what were you saying? I couldn't tell if it was an apology or a plea for your life."

"Neither," Finster moaned.

"Ah, still defiant. I like that about you. Even in the Violet Citadel, your words and deeds carried weight throughout our chambers. But I never imagined I would be the one to come in conflict with you. Still, I am honored. Since I am the second-highest magus of our order, your destruction will lead me to the top."

Slowly rolling his neck, Finster squinted one eye and looked upward at his attacker. Through sputtering lips, he said, "What an accomplishment to be the top beetle on the dung heap." He spit out foam. "And you dare call that a sorcerer's tower."

"I'm going to enjoy sharing the tale of your slaughter with my colleagues. We might even use your corpse as a decoration. Perhaps we'll turn you into a lich that guards our secret chambers." Elam flexed his hand. Finster groaned with every flex of his fingers. "We came prepared, Finster. Our plan was to nullify the effects of your amplified powers. And though we wanted to negotiate, all of us agreed that, in the end, to take the Founder's Stone, we'd have to kill you. The sooner the better. Goodbye, Finster." Elam put both hands together and squeezed them with all his might.

Body trembling, Finster started to stand. The rock he rode upon lifted him above Elam.

Doubt grew in the red-robed wizard's eyes. He clamped his hands together harder. "Die! Why won't you die?"

"Did you really think that you could take me with that cantrip that you call a spell? It is the pain that overloads the body and mind that kills. Unbearable, excruciating, chest-lancing pain that mortals would rather die than suffer." Finster pulled his arms back. His fists balled up at his sides. Showing his own gloating sneer, he added, "But there is something that you need to know, Elam. Pain and I are very close friends!"

Elam paled. He pushed his palms together, but the empty space between them grew wider as if a ball were expanding in his hands.

"What are you doing? This is not possible. I am a magus of the ninth order. None can survive my Heart Devastator."

Finster tossed his head back and laughed. Embracing his chronic pain, he used it to fuel his own anger and reached deep inside himself. The Master of the Inanimate's fingertips glowed like burning coals. Out of thin air, a cyclone of energy twisted around his body and filled a ball of energy inside his hand. The mystic powers he no longer practiced came back to him from the fuel of the Founder's Stone. Like the other sorcerers who attacked him, he brought forth that old energy. "Stand still, Elam," Finster said.

With growing concern on his face, Elam asked, "Why?"

"It's time for me to kill you."

Elam abandoned the efforts to crush Finster's heart in his hands and started swimming away in his ghostly form.

With magic hands, Finster caught Elam by the skirt of his checkered robes. He yanked the man backward and spun him around. With a thrust of his hand, he shoved the ball of fire into Elam's chest.

Elam's head rocked backward. "Guh!" Bright energy lit up the veins inside the man's body. Back arching, the red sorcerer's body solidified and floated toward the ground. He hit the ground on both feet and sank to his knees. Gasping for breath, he said with an agonized expression, "Mercy, Finster. Mercy."

Finster landed beside him. "You request mercy, and you shall have it. Look upward."

Elam lifted his eyes to the sky. Blocks of stone bigger than men hovered above him. "No, no, please."

Finster summoned two man-sized stones from out of nowhere. They smashed Elam between them like cymbals, pulverizing his bones and flesh. Blood oozed from between the rocks. "Crude but just as effective." He let out a long sigh. The images of Unus the Uncanny were clustered together with a group of knights on foot, who were bearing down on Finster with swords raised. With a wave of his hands, Finster took the sphere of stones from the sky in his mystic grasp and hurled them into the charging men.

The wave of blocks blasted the knights from their boots, crushing armor and breaking bone. The magi struck by the rocks dissipated into vapors. Finster flicked his fingers, watching the next wave of knights and wizards come right at him. He lifted more rocks with his mind. "Child's play."

Seeing rocks flying over the rooftop, the knights lifted their shields. With a loud bang, the group was knocked from their feet.

Casually, Finster said, "What am I doing? I don't need blocks. I'll use the knights' armor against them." Knight by knight, he took control of their metal-clad bodies and had them hack into the images of Unus, as well as striking at one another. With big white eyes, the knights unleashed fear-filled attacks against their allies as they shouted out prayers and pleas to one another.

Images of Unus fell underneath the power of sword and dagger, leaving only a few standing. Waving their hands, they started to run.

Finster sent four knights flying through the air like missiles. Their sword points gored the images of Unus. Two of the three faded. The lone remaining one bled to death. "Two down. Now where is the last moron from the Violet Citadel of dung hiding? Gah!" Finster felt a sharp needle bite down into his neck. He turned to see an image quaver before his eyes. It was a shapely, beautiful woman with the cold, expressionless face of a killer. New fire raced through his veins. "You!" He crumpled to the ground. "You're the assassin from Rayland."

She knelt beside him. "I am Alexandria, the High Executioner of the Circle." She offered a frozen smile. "We always get our man."

With his limbs seizing, his jaw locking, and dribble coating his lips, he said, "In the end, that bastard King Rolem wins."

Alexandria shrugged. "He's the king. Of course he does."

Chapter 92

Pinning Moth's arm down with his knee, Chet sawed into the savage's wrist with a dagger. "This barbarian's bones are like stone." As he cut, the skin bled, then quickly started to mend. "Curses! The skin sews itself. What bizarre madness is—*urk*!"

Moth punched the knight hard in the Adam's apple, sending him sprawling on the floor. Whatever dark force ailed him suddenly began to clear as a spring of cleansing energy washed throughout his body. The stinging welts all over his body faded from black to red and pink. Sword in hand, he jumped Chet and thrust downward, pinning the man through the heart of his armor to the stones.

Osgald and bleeding-out Unus exchanged a nervous glance. Above them, Finster, once dying, came back to life with a sorcerous glow about him.

Osgald shouted out a command. "River Knights! Rally!" He pointed his sword at the sorcerer and the savage. "Take after that sorcerer and take down that savage!" He led the charge toward Moth, while his third-in-command rushed over to aid Unus. Osgald, a master swordsman, stabbed his sword in behind Moth's exposed shoulder blades and drove it deep to the hilt. "Die, monster!"

Moth twisted his shoulders, ripping the sword free of Osgald's iron grip. He grabbed the River Knight commander by the arm. A jolt of lightning shot from Moth's fingers, lancing through Osgald's body and armor. Black marks spread out over the man's body. His skin seared against the hot steel. He started screaming.

A wave of knights plowed into Moth, shouting, "Save the commander!" They drove Moth down onto the deck. Daggers in hand, they stabbed and cut him.

With a sword still in his body, Moth wrestled against the stalwart brood with a tiger's ferocity. His big hands became hammers. He punched them off like a kick of a mule. The seasoned fighters spun away from his wild attack. Quickly, they clipped at Moth with their swords. Moth sprang clear over the heads of the row of knights in front of him. He landed on his big feet by the fallen form of Chet and yanked his sword free. With one sword buried in his chest and his broadsword dripping in his hand, he faced off against them.

The knights' eyes grew as big as saucers. The one in the middle of the three said, "It's not possible!" He pulled a shield in front of him. So did the others.

The raspy voice came from the throat of Osgald the Bold. His face was blackened and charred, and his hair was as crisp as fallen leaves. He said, "Cut his hands off and get the rings. Get the rings!" He went into a fit of coughing.

Moth pulled the other sword out of his chest. With both hands covered in blood and filled with steel, he charged.

The knights brought their own might into the collision. Putting their backs and iron-hard skill into every swing, they cut into the brawny savage.

Swinging both of his arms downward, Moth cut both arms off the centered knight at the same time. His broadsword sheared clean through the man's shield. He paid the price for it. A knight chopped his arm deep in the shoulder. Blood sprayed. Moth's shoulder hung slack. With his good arm, he gored the man in the belly, lifted him from his feet, and slung him off the end of his blade.

The last standing knight cut Moth open across the belly. "Die, barbarian!" The knight's eyes were filled with triumph as he looked at the gaping wound exposing Moth's entrails. But as quickly as he'd cut the barbarian open, the wound began to mend. "No," he said, shaking his head. The stalwart knight's steely spine fled him. He teetered a half step back. "Impossi—"

Moth split the man's head from the top of the skull down past his chin. The knight fell aside. Fixing his gaze on the wizards and knights who were scrambling toward a revived Finster, Moth started in that direction. A ball of red energy soared at his head. He ducked under it. Quick as a cat, he turned on his attacker. Another ball of energy caught him square in the chest.

"Die, you, you mindless brute!" It was the magus, Richter the Gold, flinging one golden-red ball of energy after the other at Moth. The fiery balls blasted into Moth's chest. He stormed at Richter as mystic flames engulfed Moth's burning flesh.

He hacked into the sorcerer's energy shield. The blades skipped harmlessly away. Moth flung them aside. He pounded on the shield with his glowing fists. The shield bowed against the weight of his blows. It chipped and cracked.

"Stop! Stop! What are you doing?" The exasperated Richter's face had become haggard. His confident expression turned into a growing frown. His shield flickered and buckled. "No, you must stop. You must stop!" His shoulders sagged. The last of his shield fizzled out. The flames inside his hands went dim. He cowered.

Without hesitation, Moth scooped the trembling magus up in his arms. He marched straight to the wall and threw him between the battlements. The exhausted magus hit the ground without uttering a scream.

Moth turned just in time to see flying knights gored and the last of the wizards fall. Far away, near the center of the roof, Finster lay on the ground. A woman on one knee gloated over the fallen wizard. Moth took in a deep snort of air, grabbed his broadsword, and ran right at her.

CHAPTER 93

"ALEXANDRIA IS A VERY PRETTY name," Finster said to the woman who looked down on him. "And you are a vision. It is no wonder that you are such a fine assassin. I never would have seen it coming." Deep inside, he knew he should be dead by now. The poison would have taken him if not for the scarab and the Founder's Stone. The powerful magic kept him together, but without him, it would die as well. His vision became cloudy, and he could barely see her face. "Alexandria. Such a pretty face and lovely name."

"Your death is boring me," she said with a cold smile. "Do you think you could make it quicker?" Her eyes drifted away from him.

Finster saw Moth approaching. In his weakened state, the big savage appeared as a shambling form. He coughed out a laugh. "You might have gotten me, but I don't think you'll get him."

"We'll see," she said.

Alexandria stood up. She had Finster right where she wanted him, but now she had to contend with Moth. The savage was the biggest, scariest man she'd ever seen. She slid two of her poisoned needles out of her sleeve. She moved away from Finster and squared off with the savage. "You might not speak, but I know that you hear. These needles have been dipped in the most potent poison in the world. The only cure is death." Her eyes drifted over Finster. He lay panting on the ground. "Ask your friend."

The sullen-eyed Moth gave her a deadpan stare.

A chill went down her spine to her toes. The savage had nearly crushed her before. This time, she wasn't going to take any chances. She pulled the hood of the Assassin's Shroud over her head and disappeared.

Moth's chin came forward as his eyes searched the area. From among the dead and the large chunks of fallen debris, the other two assassins emerged. With sharp longswords in hand, they flanked him.

Chapter 94

With his innards burning as if he were being filled with hot sand, Finster rolled to his side. Moth faced off with two assassins the moment that Alexandria vanished. Fighting with everything he had left in him, Finster tried to hang on. His fading vision became bright spotted and blurry. Through it all, the scarab still pulsated like a searing brand of iron in his back.

How can any one man be expected to endure such hellish pain? Of all men, why me?

Finster had been through hard times in life, but nothing had ever compared to this. Reason told him to give up. It was time to make his bed in the grave. But pride, anger, and envy kept him going. He wasn't going to let anyone get the best of him if he could help it. Still, the shroud of darkness continued to envelop him. He crawled, pitiful and shaky, like a wounded old man, as he walked a tightrope between life and death.

Moth chased the assassins across the rooftops. The agile killers sprang away from the giant man's massive swings. The assassins were clever, one darting in to attack Moth in the front while the other thrust deep into the savage's rippling back. Back and forth they went, striking at Moth like vipers in a pit. The unfettered savage came at them again and again. He unleashed terrific swings that knocked the swords out of his attackers' hands. One assassin drew a dagger from his belt and ran. Like a great cat chasing a mouse, Moth tracked the man's zigzag patterns. Cornering the assassin, he hewed the man down like a cornstalk in a field.

"It was inevitable," Finster said, spitting out saliva as he chuckled.

Moth chased the last assassin.

Finster caught a glimpse of another player in the field. Somehow, as he bordered between life and death, he saw in a different spectrum. He had heard that, in the dying moments of life, men saw the unseen world that held all life together. Now he had a glimpse for himself. Like a ghostly apparition, Alexandria closed in on Moth.

"You fool. It's a trap," Finster said, but his voice was barely a whisper. On hands and knees, he crawled onward, dragging his tattered robes over the rugged stones. He stopped, lifted an arm, and stretched out a hand. He concentrated on lifting the stones out from underneath Alexandria's feet. The entire length of his arm shook like a leaf. A stone shifted a few feet in front of him. He collapsed in a heap. It was all he could do to keep his head up and watch Alexandria close in for the kill. "No."

Springing side to side, Moth shrank the distance between himself and the last male assassin. The assassin raised his blade to parry. Moth brought down his broadsword with wroth force. The assassin's blade snapped. Moth's blade cut the man deep in the shoulder. Up and down his blade went, turning the assassin into meat on a butcher block.

Alexandria slipped in behind Moth and jammed two long poisoned needles into his back.

Moth spun around, unleashing a decapitating blow.

She ducked under the swing and backed away. She reappeared, backed away quickly, and took the hood from her head. "You will not survive the poison, blue-toe. None have. None will."

On wooden limbs, Moth gave chase. He swung his sword sluggishly.

Alexandria walked away from the lumbering man with the silkiness of an alley cat. There was victory in her steely eyes as she gave Finster a lasting look. She walked right at him with her shoulders back and chin raised high. She stood over him and said, "Now I am going to watch you both die."

Moth staggered toward her. His bare feet tripped over the stones. He collapsed hard on the ground with his sword falling free of his fingers. He lay flat on his chest, facing Finster.

"Hurts, doesn't it?" Finster asked his unlikely comrade. Moth convulsed. Finster was confident that the ring of regeneration would heal flesh, but poison was another matter. As for the other offensive powers of the rings, well, they were useless unless Moth knew how to wield them. "Bloody bones, I just want the pain to end." He peeked up at Alexandria. "The woman. The girl. Will you spare them?"

"I wasn't hired to kill them, but no, I won't spare them. They are loose ends," she said.

"You really know how to kick a man when he's down. It makes me angry." Finster looked at Moth. He could see the rings burgeoning underneath the thinning skin on the brute's fingers. He reached out to touch the savage's hand. "So close" was the last thing he said. The world became black. The sound of rushing water filled his ears, and there was nothing after that but Alexandria's fading laugh.

Chapter 95

"No! No!" Dizon screamed as she raced toward Finster.

Alexandria let the woman pass her by. She still had two poison needles left. They would be more than enough to kill the woman and child.

Dizon cradled Finster in her arms. She rocked back and forth with him. Tears ran down her cheeks. Sobbing, she asked Alexandria, "Why? Why? Why?"

"It's my job. Nothing personal," she replied.

Rinny kneeled over Moth. Her small fists pounded on his back. "Wake up, Moth! Wake up! Wake up and kill that witch!"

"Don't fret, little child. You will be joining them soon enough." Alexandria pulled the last two needles from her sleeve. "Now hold still. This will only hurt a bit."

Moth pushed himself up.

Alexandria's eyes bulged. She froze in her spot. "Impossible."

Moth put his hand with the regenerating ring over Finster's open hand. A great wind blasted forth out of their bodies. Alexandria sailed backward, not stopping until she hit the battlements, and crumpled to the ground. She opened her eyes, shook her head, and gasped.

Finster and Moth were both alive and well, both rising to their knees. A sphere of radiant emerald lines encircled them with the speed of humming birds. The woman and girl had crawled away, shielding their eyes. A mighty wind continued to tear at their hair and clothing, whistling like a howling banshee. Awestruck, Alexandria watched the bodies of Finster and Moth merge into one form. "No, this cannot be. I killed them," she said with an angry, trembling voice. "I killed them both!"

The swirling winds faded. The mystic light went dim. A towering man in tattered robes stood on the roof where the pair of scoundrels had once stood. Strapping and striking, standing like a demigod before his subjects, he had an emerald twinkle in his eyes. The seven rings that adorned his fingers shone with power. A knowing smile grew on his face. He tossed back his head and laughed.

Alexandria fled.

Chapter 96

Finster looked at his spread-out fingers. The rings of power shone brightly on his oversized digits. All of the precious metals and stones sparkled with a luster of their own. "I feel magnificent. All-powerful." He rolled his shoulders backward. "The pain. The pain is gone."

Dizon approached timidly, shrinking underneath his stare. "I hear you, Finster, but you are not you. You are both of you."

"I am he, and he is I," Finster said, looking at the strapping muscles that covered his arms. "I don't think that it is something either one of us wants to get used to. The savage wrestles within me like a caged animal. Or perhaps I wrestle with him, but at the moment, I feel delightful."

Looking up at the men that had become one, Rinny asked, "Moth, is that you?"

Finster patted her head. "I didn't do that. He did. Drat it." He let out a sigh. "Moth, you are making me look bad."

Taking Finster's arm, Dizon said, "Are you giddy?"

"Giddy with power, I'd say," he replied.

She squeezed his hand. "I am overjoyed, but how did this happen?"

"There are many mysteries that even I cannot answer. But this I know. The Founder's Stone had an intelligence all its own," Finster replied. "As I lay on the threshold of death and felt the hounds of hell nipping at my feet while the angels of heaven awaited, the savage's touch connected the rings to the stone. The Founder's Stone, hah, amplified their existing powers, and the poison that ran through our veins disintegrated. Hungry for more, the Founder's Stone brought one into another." He clenched his fist. "I feel elation, yet the Founder's Stone still hungers. It is a dangerous thing."

Tugging on his hand, Rinny said, "I want Moth back."

"Yes, well, believe me when I say, little gnat, that there is nothing more that the savage wants than to run the wilds again." Finster could see and feel every primitive thought Moth had. Memories were crossed and mixed. Moth had had a childhood, parents, splendid lands rich for the hunt. Moth was young. He'd seen countless horrors. They had been in the air he had breathed since birth. Like a hungry animal, a deep restless strength burned within the barbaric youth. His will was iron, tested by trials of fire. The Goth tribes battled over territory. Armies from the kingdoms chased and slew. Moth was a young man, separated, lost, enslaved. Within, there was no fear, only the calculating, cunning, wild-bred survivor. Little else did Moth show. He was fueled by the fight and the battle for survival. There was no quit inside him. He was stone cold and savage. Yet for his own stubborn reasons, he remained, because Finster had freed him and enslaved him at the same time.

"Interesting. Our savage friend is more than I'd come to expect. A crude honor is with him. Like a hound, he is loyal. It's the best loyalty there is." He shrugged. "I'm not sure if I'll be stuck with him or not. But first things first."

"What about the assassin? She needs to be finished, Finster," Dizon said. "We must go after her."

Finster cupped her face in his hand. "There is nothing you need to worry about anymore. She is running with her tail tucked between her legs. We'll catch up with her and the king in Mendes."

The handful of knights who had remained below with Dizon stood nearby, aiding their commander, Osgald.

"Get me on my feet," Osgald commanded. His knights lifted him to a standing position. His once-handsome face had red, swelling burns and blister marks all over. His beard was singed. He lifted a sword at Finster. "You are an enemy of the crown."

Finster faced Osgald. "And the crown is becoming an enemy of the kingdoms. Which one will you defend?"

"I've seen all of the madness that I care to see, er…" He tilted his head and stared at Finster. "Finster, I presume, if you swear that you are pledged to restore order, I pledge my sword to you and the Red Citadel."

"What about King Rolem's and King-Elect Mather's plans?"

"I'll make a statement to their conspiracy. It is on the record of many, including myself."

Dizon marched over to Osgald and slapped him. "You should be ashamed."

"I'll probably sway from the gallows for it," the shamed knight replied.

"True," Finster said. "Your words will hold little merit, I fear. But you and your men might have a future as citadel guardians." Finster used his powers of animation to strip metal from the fallen knights' armor. In a matter of seconds, like a master sculptor, he turned the metal from breastplates and chainmail into the shiny steel masks of citadel guardians, with rectangular slits and a dress of chainmail covering the back. He put them in the hands of the knights. "Try those on."

All five knights' new masks fit them perfectly. Each of them kneeled. "We pledge our swords to the Red Citadel," they chorused.

"Good," Finster said. The Black Tower lifted from the ground. "Now the time has come to bring order to our mad world."

Chapter 97

The kingdom of Mendes, rich in architecture, ran along the coastline of the Gallatan Sea. Much like the kingdom of Rayland, the castle, from a few miles' distance, overlooked the sea, just as the castle of Rayland overlooked the Free River. A multitude of galleons and brigantine ships filled the bay along with countless fishing boats. Along the coast were docks and boardwalks. Now, in an event that many would have thought was the Great Festival of the Sea, multitudes of people had gathered along the shoreline.

With the setting sun hanging above the clouds, the shine that normally whitened the alabaster blocks of the castle was blotted out in an eclipse of gray. On the fanciful patios of the castle stood the highest-ranking officials in all of Mendes, including King Rolem himself, the high guard that formed a protective wall around him, and a full host of mages from the Violet Citadel. Alexandria was among them, staring at the Black Tower that she'd departed from three days ago. Now it hung in the sky like a moon. The tower had taken its time, but it had caught up with her.

Everyone present on the king's porches and patios stood in silence, staring at the great Black Tower that waited one hundred feet above the waves of the sea. Strands of lightning had erupted from the flying tower's battlements the moment it arrived. Many of the citizens of Mendes murmured and panicked. They clawed at the castle's gates.

Thousands packed up and fled. But for the most part, the people craned their necks back as they crowded along the dock to stare at the tower.

Rolem plucked at his trimmed beard as he sat on his wooden throne. His foot tapped on the pedestal. "What is he waiting for? Hmmm? It's been hours and no word. No emissary. No sign of anyone or anything. How do you know that Finster guides this"—he rolled his hand and pointed skyward—"thing? Answer me, Alexandria. Is this a hoax?"

"It's not a hoax," she said. "He is in there, waiting for your surrender. Believe me."

The tower began to slowly spin in midair. Purple and red and white-hot lightning erupted from the top like lava from a volcano. Some citizens cheered, while others screamed. The faces of the mages from the Violet Citadel turned ashen. They grumbled among themselves.

"What are you chattering about? Tell me!" King Rolem slammed his fist on the arm of his chair. "Tell me!"

A man in his sixties with pasty skin and a vulturelike quality about him approached the king. He was Lucen, the Magus Supremeus of the Violet Citadel. He bowed to the king. "King Rolem, we are quite willing to take the offensive on your behalf. Clearly, this tower poses a threat. We would like to deal with it."

"Yes, you did so well keeping this matter under control before." Rolem rolled his eyes. "I hire the finest mages and assassins, and now I have this monstrosity on my very beach!" Eyes fixed on the tower, he sat up. "What is that? What is that? High guard, surround me."

The knights surrounded him. The other dignitaries moved backward.

A slab of gray stone floated from the Black Tower right toward the king's patio. It made a soft landing on the patio wall. It was more than ten feet tall and half as wide. Words that had been burned into the stone still glowed.

Alexandria and Lucen were the first to approach it. "It's a message," Alexandria said. Her eyes scanned the oversized writing. "From Finster."

"Get out of my way," Rolem said, pushing through his knights. He stepped up between the assassin and the wizard.

The slab on the patio read:

King Rolem,
Good evening. Confess to your conspiracy against the Seven Kingdoms. Confess to the murder of King Alrick. I have the witnesses. I have the proof. You are scum. You exercise poor taste in women. You are the sour grape of the vineyard. The spawn of rats. A lowly, undeserving king. Also, Alexandria, I know you are there. I see all. You, regardless, will be dead soon. King Rolem, once again, I state, surrender the crown with honor, or prepare to die.

Sincerely,
Finster the Grand

Aghast, King Rolem asked, "Is this a joke? Is this a jest? Take this abomination off my castle. High guard, rid my eyes of this lying monstrosity!" He stomped the ground. "Immediately!"

The high guard knights moved across the patio to the slab. They tried to push it over the ledge. It would not move.

"Fetch a hammer," one of the high guards said. "We shall smash it to pieces."

As the high guard knights railed against the slab, more slabs descended from the tower to the beaches and the streets.

King Rolem kicked the patio wall. His handsome face turned red as a beet. "Of all the insolent behavior! To mock me! The king! Lucen!" He pointed at the tower. "Execute that lunatic sorcerer!"

Chapter 98

On the rooftop of the tower, Finster marked up another huge slab of stone with a glowing finger that carved out and seared its surface. He'd been at it since they'd moved out of the Fringe, writing in detail all that had happened in regards to King Rolem's conspiracy. Casually writing with a deft hand, he said, "How many is that so far, Dizon, twenty?"

"Twenty-one," she replied. She and Rinny were standing at his side, examining his work. "But I don't think these words will do any good. Men like King Rolem only respond to force."

Finster finished writing. Admiring his handiwork, he said, "Twenty-one should do it. It's a number of good fortune." With a wave of his hand, he sent the slab up into the air on a course to the streets of Mendes, where the citizens waited. "I don't disagree with you at all, my love, but as a sworn peacekeeper of the kingdoms, I am obligated to inform the people of the truth so that they can understand what is about to happen and why." He approached the tower wall and looked out over the battlements. He was joined by Dizon, Rinny, and the new Citadel Guardians. "They need a warning too."

"Just make it quick, Finster," Dizon said. "Kill the king, and be done with it. The people will side with you."

"No, my eager maiden. It is imperative that what is about to transpire is on the record. Give it time, and we'll see how King Rolem and the likes of King-Elect Mather respond."

Finster was referring to the kingdom of Rayland. On their way to Mendes, Finster had left the same slabs throughout that city and on the castle porches and added Osgald the Bold's endorsement.

Placing his hands on the wall, he leaned out toward the city. King Roland's armies, numbering in the thousands, had gathered along the beaches and docks. The colorful banners of Mendes waved among the ranks. Right below them, the war ships on the sea readied themselves for battle. "It would be sad if I had to kill all of them. The kingdom will need them."

"What must be done must be done," Osgald said from behind his metal mask. "War is war."

"Aye, thousands against a few." Finster shook his head. Physically he felt invincible. He could lift a horse with his mighty frame. The pain from the scarab was gone. He had all of the rings of power under his command. It was everything he had wanted. But inside him, another war was being waged. The Founder's Stone, fed by the power of the rings, wrestled against his own will. At the same time, Moth wanted freedom. The savage's great will wrestled against Finster's. "Still, we must hope for a peaceful resolution if my words are going to hold salt with the other kingdoms. My name must be cleared for the Red Citadel to find its station among the kingdoms again."

"You are too noble." Dizon took his hand in hers and squeezed it. "It is you that should be king, not these other fools. Take them all down, and start over again while you can."

"I don't want to be king. The people can sort that out among themselves. I prefer to stay in the background and keep a close eye on them." As they watched the people of Mendes react to the stones he'd sent into the streets, Finster sat on the wall and leaned against the battlements. He felt the rings on his fingers. They were everything he had desired. He could throw lightning, disintegrate flesh, and make fire, water, and ice on command. The telekinetic powers allowed him to fly. At the same time, he could summon forth shields of protection and regenerate.

Nothing in the world could stop him. Nothing in the world could have stopped Ingrid and Rolem, yet somehow, he had. Still, at his strongest, he'd almost died several times. With the powers in hand, he'd become a magnet for his own destruction. He twisted the black iron ring around his index finger. It took away his pain, destroyed the poison within, but there was still a chronic nagging in his back from the scarab. The Founder's Stone and Moth gnawed at his mind. Before long, he knew, one would destroy the other. He was not that strong.

"I need a drink."

"No," Dizon said. "That is the last thing you need. You will finish this task first."

He sighed. Night came. He waited for a message from King Rolem. None came. Instead, the shoreline remained quiet. The army of Mendes stood by campfires and carried torches. The people in the streets watched the Black Tower with fascination. There was little activity on the king's patios either. Everything was at a standstill.

Osgald approached. From behind his metal mask, he said, "It's going to be a long night. It always is on the eve before a battle."

"You don't think that Rolem will give, do you?" Finster replied.

"I've served three kings and met with many more. I've never known any of them to admit to being wrong." Osgald looked out over the sea to the armies that waited below. "They are scheming."

"Kings are excellent schemers. Especially this one."

"I have much respect for your efforts, Finster." Osgald patted his sword pommel. "But Dizon is right. There is only one way out of this. It will bring casualties. King Rolem will sacrifice every citizen to save himself."

"I know. And I will risk myself to save the kingdom. In the end, it is the right thing to do." Staring into the star-filled tapestry in the sky, Finster said, "I have enough blood on my hands from serving kings such as him. I was young. The crown was an excuse to do evil. Guilt drove me another way. I found myself in the thick of it once again but with new perspective. Someone in the fallen world must stand for what is right. It has to be the Red Citadel. We must lead the kings with wisdom."

"Men will always be men. Kingdoms rise, and kingdoms fall. The only thing that matters is that good men do what they can." Osgald put a hand on Finster's shoulder. "Fight the good fight until the bitter end. Protect the ones you can."

"Aye." Finster turned his attention to Dizon and Rinny. They traipsed over the rooftop, holding hands and yawning.

From the stairwell that led onto the rooftop, slimy tentacles snaked out of the dark opening. Like whips, they snared Dizon and Rinny by the ankles and yanked them into the tower's bowels. Rinny's screams echoed back.

Chapter 99

Lucen, the Magus Supremeus of the Violet Citadel, along with a score of his mages, journeyed from the shore to the king's war galleons on a rowboat. Inside the hull of the warship, they linked arms. There, they chanted a chorus of twisting words that carried over the ship's deck, souring the otherwise durable sailors' stomachs.

When the sorcerers finished their incantation, they slunk up to the ship's deck and looked over the bow. Fifty yards away, the Black Tower hovered dozens of yards above the water. The shining moon brought a glimmer to the mineral-rich stones of the slowly spinning cylinder, glinting now and again like tiny bits of firelight. Below the tower, the water jumped. A round surge started in a circle, rolling toward the galleon, causing it to pitch and rock.

The white eyes of the sailors and soldiers could be clearly seen. They pointed at the spot in the water that had started to gurgle and create sea foam. The spot began to spread.

The captain of the galleon, a slender sailor with muttonchops and a heavy stare, stepped in behind Lucen. "What is amiss? My hairs are dancing on my neck."

Lucen's sharp, vulturelike features cracked a smile. "Captain, in all of your sea adventures, have you ever encountered Tubulkaan?"

"The sea god? I dare not say the name." The captain's Adam's apple rolled. His face beaded with new sweat. "But once I believe I saw him. My eyes would not close for sleep. The sea god took a brigantine down into the belly of the sea and feasted on all of the sailors. Tell me you have not awakened him." He cast a nervous look at his men. "Tell me you jest."

"Tubulkaan does not sleep. He is fully awakened… now," Lucen said with a chuckle.

Like a great fountain, a geyser of water burst out of the sea. The marveling sailors gasped. The geyser surged upward to the bottom of the tower. From the top of the water, black-purple tentacles wriggled out. The writhing things stretched upward, and like the slimy limbs of an octopus, they latched onto the tower. Pulling upward, a bulging creature with a huge, misshapen body as large as a gray whale's climbed inside the tower. Its body was long and covered with tentacles and spikes like sea urchins. The hulking sea monster vanished into the tower. The geyser collapsed into the water, making waves that quickly became a part of the sea.

"Tubulkaan, the sea god, has successfully been summoned," Lucen said with a winning expression. His fellow mages shared thin smiles. "As old as the sea, as merciless as the waves crashing against the rocks, nothing can stop him from devouring his prey. Isn't that right, Captain?"

"The sea god is as immortal as the sea itself." The captain sucked his teeth. "It's like trying to kill waves with a sword. Nothing can stop him. Nothing." He took out a handkerchief and dabbed his forehead. "We should row away. Far, far away, back toward the beach."

"The sea god has been summoned. I think he would be offended if his audience abandoned his efforts. Stay put, Captain. Stay put, and watch the show."

The captain backed away from the magus. He gathered the sailors and soldiers, and they started praying.

Chapter 100

Rinny's cry sent a jolt through Finster. The black tentacles that had taken the girl and Dizon were spreading out onto the rooftop in a wave. Propelled by a will that was not his own but rather Moth's, the combined man ran straight into the heart of danger. Sword in hand, they hacked through the thick, bulbous tentacles. The sword cut clean through the appendages, but the monster didn't flinch.

What is this ghastly thing?

The sorcerers of the Violet Citadel had made their move. They'd summoned an abomination from the deep water. It had slipped inside the tower, unnoticed, ready to feed on everything that moved.

One of the new Citadel Guardians let out a scream. Tentacles encircled the man's entire body. His metal chest plate bowed inward. Bone crunched. The tentacles reeled the man into the hulking monster that waited below.

Meanwhile, Moth hacked into the flesh-hungry sea monster with berserk fury. Sharing his body with Finster, he fought his way down the steps. Rinny still screamed, her voice carrying through the darkness like a nighthawk of terror. Moth surged forward. Finster's will wasn't strong enough to tear control away. Instead, he let Moth control the body. He focused his mind on the power of the rings and tore the rooftop away. The rocks dropped into the sea. Waiting below, filling the chamber, was the bulging, jellylike horror spawned in the waters of hell. The monstrosity had many eyes around a cave-hole of a mouth filled with many rows of shark-like teeth. There was great intelligence in those hungry, fearless eyes. Its jaw opened and closed. It drew Dizon and Rinny, both kicking and screaming, toward it.

"No!" Finster managed to scream. Somehow, as Moth chopped a path through the mound of flesh toward the woman and girl, Finster commanded fire from his fingers. Strands of lightning erupted out of the savage's free left hand, smiting the sea god. The semi-gelatinous body of the sea god quavered. Its tentacles straightened, and it flung Dizon and Rinny over the wall of the tower. Finster watched in horror as the women disappeared. "Noooo!"

On command, Finster summoned the powers from the telekinetic ring made from silver and adorned in garnet gems. The small stones flared. He envisioned himself catching the women who were plummeting toward their deaths. Suddenly, dozens of tentacles burst out of the sea monster's mouth, engulfing Finster's new body head to toe and yanking them down to the awaiting maw.

The Black Tower dropped straight down into the sea with a titanic splash. Lucen stood with his fellow mages, mouth wide open with joy. The sailors and soldiers let out a wild cheer. They flung their caps into the air. The boat rocked to and fro as the tower sank like a stone. It came to a stop with the very top of the battlement jutting up out of the water like teeth.

Unable to contain his elation, Lucen said, "Hah!" He shook his fist. "Take that, Finster, you lowly crud from the Red Citadel!"

A jovial cry erupted from the shoreline and carried over the crashing sound of new waves. The brass horns of victory blared throughout the ranks of the waiting soldiers.

Lucen shook hands with his fellow mages. They were all very quick to congratulate each other. He looked to the captain of the galleon. "Captain, ready the rowboat. Take us to shore. I'm certain King Rolem is eager to congratulate us on our victory."

The captain nodded. "Aye. We'll row with godly speed, mighty wizard."

Alexandria stood beside King Rolem, looking out over the patio. The king's strong hand gripped hers like a vise. It tightened the moment the Black Tower dropped out of the sky and plunged into the seawater.

"Yes!" The king pumped his fist. "Yes!" He grabbed her face with both hands and kissed her. "We did it! It is done! That foul wizard is finally sunk."

"I wouldn't rest without seeing his washed-up corpse," she said.

"Yes, yes, I'm sure the water will wash him up." King Rolem broke away from her. He faced his constituents. "Wine! The finest wine for everyone. This travesty is over! We need to have a hearty salute to our mysterious colleagues from the Violet Citadel!"

"Hear, hear!" someone said.

"Hear, hear!" added another.

Eyes fixed on the water, Alexandria felt something gnawing at her gut. The longer there was no sign of Finster the better. No man could hold his breath forever. She watched. She counted. The savage and the sorcerer had slipped free of death's icy grip more than once. *Be gone, Finster. Be gone.*

Moth controlled the physical portion of the body he shared with Finster. Inside the bowels of the monster that had swallowed them whole, the reckless savage unleashed all his fury with the sword. Flesh came off the sea monster in hunks. It didn't matter. It replenished itself almost as fast as it lost. At the same time, thousands of sharp teeth lining the monster's throat swallowed their body deep into its black, watery bowels. The jagged teeth rent flesh on the way down. Only the regenerating ring kept them together.

Summoning forth the power that he controlled in the rings, Finster released everything that he could think of. Fire. Lightning. Disintegration. The mystic onslaught tore through the bestial, water-bloated hulk with wroth force that would wipe out an army. The monster shook, but its devouring efforts never slackened. Ancient, evil, and hungry, the sea monster took everything that Finster had. To Finster, fed by his own growing anger at the deaths of Dizon and Rinny, he realized that time was running out. Using the onyx and copper ring of disintegration, he tore a hole through the monster's flesh. Moth still swung like a madman.

"Fool!" Finster screamed inwardly to his counterpart. "Swim out!"

The savage had none of it. He was enraged as a wounded and wild thing, hell-bent on avenging the women.

The gap that Finster had made in the monster's body started to close. Seawater filled it. Now, fully submerged, they would drown. There was nothing Finster could do about that. Yet fed by his rage and Moth's, combined with the hungry powers of the Founder's Stone, they fought on. He tried to pushed them out of the body with telekinesis. He used lightning to carve a new path out. The monster held them fast with jagged teeth and spines sticking to their flesh.

Finster choked on salty water. He dispersed all of the energy at his disposal, lighting the sea god up with the glow of a jellyfish. *Everything has a weakness, sea god or not.* He had learned that long ago. *Find its heart, and kill it!* He concentrated, listening for the beat of a heart or something else within the vile beast.

That was when the primitive instincts of Moth kicked in. The savage's keen senses picked up on the steady, distinct *thump-thump* of a heart beating inside the monster's body.

Moth swam deeper down the flesh-rending throat of the beast. Finster pushed with telekinetic power. All the while, their shredded body began suffocating. Time running out, with tremendous effort, they pushed onward, foot after foot, toward the growing sound of the heart. Using the rings for light, they came upon a mass of muscles as big as a man. Moth plunged his sword deep into the thumping heart. Finster channeled all of his power through the savage's sword arm. The blade pierced deep.

The sea monster made an unearthly underwater squeal.

As one, Finster and Moth went elbow deep into the muscle of the monster. Finster discharged all of the rings' unified energy with their final breath. Tubulkaan's heart exploded. The world went black.

Chapter 101

At Castle Mendes, it didn't take long for the celebration of Finster's demise to blossom into full swing. It had barely been an hour since the Black Tower had sunk in the Gallatan Sea's bay. With no sign of Finster surfacing in the water or on land, King Rolem led the revelry. Now, joined by Lucen and the rest of the brood from the Violet Citadel, along with the king's high guard and the highest-ranking dignitaries, they sang and toasted in sheer revelry.

Alexandria remained close to the pack, listening in on their conversations, and King Rolem and Lucen conspired to somehow retrieve the Founder's Stone and the rings. Their faces wore impish expressions filled with greed. King Rolem had also dispatched his soldiers, with sledgehammers, to break down the slabs that Finster had dropped all over the city. It wouldn't be long before King Rolem would be in full control once again.

Moving toward the balcony's edge, she stared out, fastening her eyes on the top battlements of the sunken Black Tower. Her jaw muscles clenched. There was emptiness inside her. In the end, she wasn't the one to take credit for killing Finster. Instead, that honor would go to someone else. Despite all of her great efforts, she had failed. In all truth, she hoped that Finster and the savage had survived the monster. Then she would get a shot at them one more time. But that ship of opportunity had passed. The honor went to the savage and mighty sea god Lucen identified as Tubulkaan. She brushed the hair out of her eyes and moved back toward the party, just missing the monstrous dead husk of the sea god that emerged on the surface in the bay.

Waving her over, King Rolem said, "Alexandria, come, come!" His smile was as broad as a rainbow. He handed her a goblet of wine. "You have yet to have a toast with me. And just so you know, I plan to give both you and Lucen credit for your role in this."

"The Circle would prefer your discretion in the matter," she said. "What is known between the three of us will suffice."

Lucen showed her a razor-thin smile. "I see the Circle and the Violet Citadel assuming many more charges together, High Executioner. It will be my honor."

King Rolem hefted his glass. "To victory. New conquests. Bolder alliances."

Alexandria and Lucen responded in unison. "Hear, hear!" All as one, they drank.

As they finished the toast, water dripped down from above them like rain. King Rolem held his hand out. "Why, it's rainy, yet I don't recall seeing any clouds." He looked up. His face turned ashen, and he dropped his goblet. It shattered on the patio.

Alexandria's blood froze the moment she cast her glance skyward. Finster stood in the air, dripping wet, in tattered and disheveled robes that covered a now-formidable body. His eyes were burning emeralds. An angry visage held everyone below agape. Many gasped and cowered.

He spoke in a thunderous voice. "I should have listened to her. I should have killed you at the very beginning. Like a fool, I showed a killer mercy. Never, I say, again."

Stammering, King Rolem replied in his own loud and cracking voice, "It is you that committed murder, killing my innocent Ingrid and countless more, monster." He looked at Lucen. "I thought he was finished. Stop him."

Lucen's brood gathered in the half circle. They aimed their fingers at Finster.

The king's high guards' spears were ripped out of their fingers. They shot across the patio, goring the exposed bodies of the sorcerers en masse. Each spear struck true through a heart, killing them instantly. The dignitaries fled in full panic. Many jumped the patio walls and dove over the decks.

Finster continued to talk as the air picked up and swirled. The deck chairs and tables lifted, forming a vortex around him. At the same time, it trapped the king, Alexandria, and many others on the deck. "You killed my dear Dizon. Her child. The King of Rayland. And the queen." His hot stare landed on Alexandria. "Your time has come to pay for that."

Alexandria tried to pull the hood of the Assassin's Shroud over her head. It was ripped right off her body and sucked into the swirling vortex. She and Rolem were lifted off their feet and into the air. The panic-stricken king swam in midair, somehow making his way toward her. They locked arms as they floated up in front of Finster.

Finster glowered at them like an angry god. He reached out with both of his naked hands and gripped them by their wrists. Drawing them in with a white-hot stare, he said, "As of this day, you both will cease to exist."

In a final move, Alexandria drew a poisoned dagger with her free hand and buried it in Finster's chest. The sorcerer-savage didn't so much as flinch. Her stabbing hand began to disintegrate. In agony, she looked right at King Rolem, whose handsome face cracked. He let out a final cry before his mouth crumbled away. His body and clothing turned quickly to ash. One moment, she was the greatest assassin in the world, and in the next moment, she was dust drifting out to sea.

The Founder's Stone and scarab pushed Finster and Moth's anger to the limits. Enraged by the deaths of Dizon and Rinny, they toppled every soldier like dominoes. Galleons and brigantines were capsized at sea. Castle Mendes shook and trembled. The walls and foundations cracked. Finster and Moth were both caught up in a maelstrom of violence. They were becoming something else, two beings, now merging with the hungering Founder's Stone. Finster wanted it to stop for the world's own good, but driven by his older, darker ambition, the Founder's Stone took on a new life. He and Moth would forever be a part of that now, and the world would be doomed.

As they cruised the air around the city, casting bolts of light from their fingers, he or Moth caught the sound of screaming voices within the storm. He looked down on the abandoned shoreline. Three people stood by a small skiff on the beach. Two of them were waving their arms and calling up to them.

"Dizon! Rinny!" Finster shouted. The sight of the mother and daughter calmed Moth's raging spirit, cutting the thirst from the Founder's Stone. Without hesitation, they landed. Dizon and Rinny, who were accompanied by Osgald, threw their arms around Finster. "You live! You live! I thought the sea had taken you."

"No," Dizon said, kissing his face. "Your invisible hand caught us at the last moment, softening our landing."

Clutching her hands, he said, "Rolem is no more. The assassin too."

"Good," she replied. "But what about you and Moth?" Dizon looked over his body, which was bursting with glowing green veins. "You are not well."

"No, we are not. That's why I must return to the Red Citadel."

Chapter 102

For the time being, Finster had control. He was back inside the granite walls of the Red Citadel, where he'd spent endless hours scouring the library tomes in search of a way out of his dilemma. He needed to separate himself from Moth, the scarab, and the Founder's Stone. But it was the Founder's Stone that had pulled them all together, and it did not want to let them be free.

In the days since they had arrived at the Red Citadel, some good had come of Finster's brave efforts. The citizens of the kingdom of Rayland, prompted by the great slabs—now called the Slabs of Truth—had overthrown King Mather and hanged him from the gallows. The citizens of Mendes and its new leadership reacted very much in the same manner and were holding a council on how to handle a kingdom without a king while they all weighed in on Finster's case.

The news of the Black Tower carried up the coast along with Finster's deeds and sea-god-slaying efforts. Times, if possible, were good. Meanwhile, the Red Citadel, no longer bereft of leadership, had become a hive of new activity. Many magi of the Red Citadel had returned to aid Finster in his cause. And with the Violet Citadel fallen wayward, many of its dozens of men and women were eager to follow Finster's lead as well.

Still, none could rid Finster, or Moth for that matter, of his curse. Now, in the company of Dizon and several magi robed in scarlet, Finster stood in front of a slab door made from solid stone. He looked down at his trembling fingers, at the rings of power that had grafted themselves on top of the skin. It was a sickly sight, not the radiant adornment that he'd once longed for. He glanced at Dizon. The woman's light, pretty eyes were filled with worry. She was cleaned up now, honey-blond hair tied back in one braid behind her head. Her robes were a pale-pink cotton. She kissed his hand while still holding it in hers.

Finster took a deep breath. He stood before the doorway to the Mystic Forge. The rune-covered slab concealed a twenty-foot opening. Long ago, when Finster had been a young sage, he'd stood guard at the Mystic Forge for months. It hadn't been standard sentry duty, made for soldiers, but a situation in which the forge chose its guardian by revelation. The Magus Supremeus of the Red Citadel revealed that honor to Finster. Finster stood week after week, eating and sleeping little, on chronically aching feet. Nothing ever came of it except one thing: he knew how to open and close the great doorway.

With quick lips, he muttered an incantation and pressed the arcane runes in a particular order. The slab groaned as it scraped upward along the framework, revealing a kaleidoscope of scintillating light within.

Dizon, Rinny, and the present company of Osgald, the new leader of the Citadel Guardians, and several more sorcerers in scarlet shielded their eyes. The Mystic Forge was a fountain of energy in which magic items were enchanted and shaped. Water flowed into two separate wells at the top and bottom of the chamber, allowing its spectacular energy to ebb and flow upward and downward like two intersecting rivers.

Finster pulled his hands from Dizon's firm grip and gave her a kiss on the cheek. Tears ran down her tanned cheeks.

"Be strong." He stepped inside. The slab came right down behind him, sealing him inside. With the fiery illumination warming his face, he stepped closer to the searing mystic waters. He didn't see any choice in what he was about to do. He couldn't live with the Founder's Stone and scarab inside him. He could do without the savage trying to tear himself free as well. The question was, would Moth go along with what he was about to do? Jumping into the fountain, no doubt, would kill them both, but it would end the curse too. There was no other way if they were going to keep others safe, and that was what Finster was sworn to do.

"Give your life for others, and the others' flower beds will bloom," he said quietly. He tried to step forward. His limbs seized up. He started to sweat. "Moth, we have to do this together. The stone won't let me budge. I need your strength matched with mine. It's now or never, or we are lost forever." He raised his voice. "Do you understand?"

Suddenly, Finster's legs bent at the knees. Coiled to spring, he heard Moth's voice growl inside his head. Together, they burst out of the Founder's Stone's chains and launched themselves into the forge's fires.

Dizon paced back and forth for hours. She heard nothing on the other side of the slab, and all of her tear ducts were dried. Rinny was in the same situation. Osgald tried to offer them comfort, but the knight found few soothing words to say. The host of magi didn't have any answers either. Only Finster had the ability to open and close the door, though many of them tried. Finally, Dizon said to Rinny, "Let's get something to eat."

Rinny had sat down in front of the door. She wouldn't budge, but her tummy made a loud rumble.

Dizon reached down to pick her up. The slab started to lift. With bright light washing over her, she squinted. A huge man washed in colorful light emerged from the glimmering chamber. It was Moth, returned whole, with a shine about his features. The sullen-eyed savage was followed by a gangly man, lither in frame, whose new scarlet robes seemed to be holding him together. The door closed behind him. He leaned back against the slab, shaking like a leaf.

"Finster!" Dizon wrapped the man up in her arms.

He returned a weak hug. "I pray I never have to go through that again." Separating himself from her, he opened his hand. A scarab lay in his grip. He crushed it into dust. "And to think I invented the cursed thing. Shame on me."

Still holding him tightly, Dizon asked, "You are whole?"

Nodding, he replied, "The Mystic Forge, with unseen powers one will never fully comprehend, showed mercy on me." His gaze drifted to Moth. "Both of us it seems. Now the Founder's Stone feeds its fires. It's a fitting home for it, I believe. Perhaps that is where it was forged to begin with."

"What of the rings?" she asked.

He showed her the black iron and ruby regeneration ring on his ring finger. "I'm keeping this one, maybe another." He patted his robe pocket, which jingled, and smiled. "As the Magus Supremeus of the tenth order—and I don't think any will dispute it—I'll find worthy men and women to be the bearers of them now."

Rinny hugged Moth's leg. "Don't leave me, Moth. You can't leave me."

The bare-chested and bald Moth peeled her away and took a knee. Laying a hand on her head, he stroked her forehead with his thumb. Moth dusted the tears from her eyes, wiped them on his cheeks, hugged her, and stood. He gave Finster a long and lasting gaze, shook his head, and started walking away.

Finster, Dizon, and company followed Moth out of the citadel to where the road led back into the rolling green hills. Moth never looked back once. He walked at a slow and easy pace, long, powerful arms gently swinging, appearing now and again between the humps along the road.

Sniffling, Rinny asked, "Do you think we'll ever see him again?"

"After this last encounter, I'd hope not," Finster replied. As he watched Moth disappear once and for all, he wondered, had the savage saved him, or had he saved the savage? "But for some reason, I don't think this is the first or last kingdom that he has helped save."

Holding onto her mother's leg, Rinny asked, "We don't even know what his real name is, do we?"

"I don't think he knows what his name is either, but I think Moth will do," Finster replied. He put his arm over Dizon's shoulder. "I don't know about you, but my tongue longs for a flagon of wine. After all, how often can a man celebrate saving a kingdom if not two?"

From the Author

Thanks for reading The Red Citadel and the Sorcerer's Power. I hope you enjoyed reading it as much as I enjoyed writing it. As for further adventures for Moth and Finster, I don't know, but please let me know how you feel about it by contacting me anytime.

Please leave a review. They are a huge help to me!

*I'd love it if you would subscribe to my
mailing list: www.craighalloran.com.

* Look me up on Bookbub.com and please
follow! Craig Halloran at Bookbub

*On Facebook, you can find me at The
Darkslayer Report or Craig Halloran.

*Twitter, twitter, twitter. I am there, too:
www.twitter.com/CraigHalloran.

*And of course, you can always email me
at craig@thedarkslayer.com

Other Books and Author Info

Craig Halloran resides with his family outside his hometown of Charleston, West Virginia. When he isn't entertaining mankind, he is seeking adventure, working out, or watching sports. To learn more about him, go to: www.thedarkslayer.com.

Check out all of my great stories…

Free Books

The Darkslayer: Brutal Beginnings
Nath Dragon – Quest for the Thunderstone

The Odyssey of Nath Dragon Series

(New Series)
(Prequel to Chronicles of Dragon)

Exiled
Enslaved
Deadly
Hunted

The Chronicles of Dragon Series 1 (10 Books)

The Hero, the Sword and the Dragons (Book 1)
Dragon Bones and Tombstones (Book 2)
Terror at the Temple (Book 3)
Clutch of the Cleric (Book 4)
Hunt for the Hero (Book 5)
Siege at the Settlements (Book 6)
Strife in the Sky (Book 7)
Fight and the Fury (Book 8)

War in the Winds (Book 9)
Finale (Book 10)
Boxset 1-5
Boxset 6-10
Collector's Edition 1-10

Tail of the Dragon, The Chronicles of Dragon, Series 2 (10 book series)

Tail of the Dragon #1
Claws of the Dragon #2
Battle of the Dragon #3
Eyes of the Dragon #4
Flight of the Dragon #5
Trial of the Dragon #6
Judgement of the Dragon #7
Wrath of the Dragon #8
Power of the Dragon #9
Hour of the Dragon #10
Boxset 1-5
Boxset 6-10
Collector's Edition 1-10

The Darkslayer Series 1 – 6 books

Wrath of the Royals (Book 1)
Blades in the Night (Book 2)
Underling Revenge (Book 3)
Danger and the Druid (Book 4)
Outrage in the Outlands (Book 5)
Chaos at the Castle (Book 6)
Boxset 1-3
Boxset 4-6
Omnibus 1-6

The Darkslayer: Bish and Bone, Series 2 (10 Book series)

Bish and Bone (Book 1)
Black Blood (Book 2)
Red Death (Book 3)

Lethal Liaisons (Book 4)
Torment and Terror (Book 5)
Brigands and Badlands (Book 6)
War in the Wasteland (Book 7)
Slaughter in the Streets (Book 8)
Hunt of the Beast (Book 9)
The Battle for Bone (Book 10)
Boxset 1-5
Boxset 6-10
Bish and Bone Omnibus (Books 1-10)

Clash Of Heroes: Nath Dragon meets The Darkslayer mini series

Book 1
Book 2
Book 3

The Gamma Earth Cycle

Escape from the Dominion
Flight from the Dominion
Prison of the Dominion

The Supernatural Bounty Hunter Files (10 book series)

Smoke Rising: Book 1
I Smell Smoke: Book 2
Where There's Smoke: Book 3
Smoke on the Water: Book 4
Smoke and Mirrors: Book 5
Up in Smoke: Book 6
Smoke Signals: Book 7
Holy Smoke: Book 8
Smoke Happens: Book 9
Smoke Out: Book 10
Boxset 1-5
Boxset 6-10
Collector's Edition 1-10

Zombie Impact Series

Zombie Day Care: Book 1
Zombie Rehab: Book 2
Zombie Warfare: Book 3
Boxset: Books 1-3

The Red Citadel and the Sorcerer's Power original shorts

The Sorcerer's Curse – Sword & Sorcery Novella
The Sorcerer's Power
The Sorcerer's Command
The Sorcerer's Trick
The Sorcerer's War

Other Works & Novellas

It's not him, It's them (Jerk of All Trades) 1 book - Drama
Gorgon Thunder-Bot Incinerator of Worlds (1 book, childrens)

www.ingramcontent.com/pod-product-compliance
Lightning Source LLC
Chambersburg PA
CBHW030350310726
48979CB00001B/253

* 9 7 8 1 9 4 6 2 1 8 5 0 6 *